LETTERS TO BARBARA

A NOVEL BY GLENN MEETER

William B. Eerdmans Publishing Company
Grand Rapids, Michigan

For Marlene

Copyright © 1981 by Wm. B. Eerdmans Publishing Co.
255 Jefferson Ave. S.E., Grand Rapids, Mich. 49503
All rights reserved

Printed in the United States of America

Library of Congress Cataloging in Publication Data

Meeter, Glenn.
Letters to Barbara.
I. Title.
PS3563.E334L4   813'.54   81-15235
ISBN 0-8028-3557-0   AACR2

CONTENTS

It is a new America,
To be spiritualized by each new American.

—JEAN TOOMER

GRANDMOTHER'S HOUSE

ON a Sunday in April Elizabeth and I and Barbara, our oldest daughter, drive down to Orangetown to visit my grandmother, who is ninety-three years old.

From the city near the Wisconsin border where we live it is only a two-hour trip, by the tollway skirting Chicago, and we should visit Grandmother more often than we do. Our last visit was on New Year's Day (I remember listening to the Rose Bowl game in the car on the way back), and before that I can't remember. Possibly her birthday in September.

"When is your next monthly visit?" Grandma will say when we see her. Also when we leave and at intervals during our visit; she is an old woman who appreciates the value of guilt in human affairs.

The three of us in the car, representing the third and fourth generation of the Vanden Vaarten family, live nearer to Grandma than any of her children except for Aunt Gert, her unmarried daughter who lives with her in the old house. Orangetown is our hometown, Elizabeth's and mine. Our high school friends have moved away or have grown distant from us without having moved. Elizabeth's mother, widowed, lives with a sister in Paterson, New Jersey. My own parents moved away two years ago. From their retirement home, an aluminum trailer, they send us boxes of Florida grapefruit or Wisconsin cherries, depending on the season, and they stop at our house twice a year on their way north or south. We have no one to visit in Orangetown except Grandma and Aunt Gert. Our trips are limited to holidays and other special occasions which force us to ask, "Who knows how long Grandma will be with us?"—a question we first asked fifteen years ago, when my grandfather died.

In the summer Barbara Sue, who is eighteen (her second name is my grandmother's) will be leaving for Europe, a participant in an exchange program. She will live with a family in Denmark and she will be gone for twelve months. The thought amazes us more than it does her. For her, Europe is a place to get away: on the application's request for preferred location she wrote, "Anywhere." She is the first of either of our families in five generations to set foot on another continent. The first since my grandmother's grandmother left the Netherlands in the 1860's and sailed to the center of North America in a Great Lakes steamer (where Grandma's mother was born) and got off at Chicago.

"She'll give you a lot of advice," Elizabeth warns, while I pay an Illinois toll. "Just smile and accept it"—for Barbara has been showing signs of developing a mind of her own.

"Don't emphasize time or distance," I add. "She hates departures. Or anything that reminds her of aging. Or death."

At Grandma's ninetieth birthday celebration I had been on a fishing trip and came wearing a beard. We celebrated at a country club where one of my Michigan uncles had a membership. Of the twenty-three participants I was the only grandchild and the only one wearing a beard. Not for Grandma was the tact of Aunt Gert, who explained that men with weak chins wear beards, or of my mother, who pointed out that beards carry germs. "It looks terrible," Grandma said. "It makes you look a hundred years old." I congratulated her on ninety years of happy life. "Where is your ear trumpet, old fellow?" she said. "Do I speak loud enough for you?" To the waiter who cut her splendid cake she pointed out how ancient her grandson looked with his beard. To my uncle, the host, who toasted her ninety years of good health, she complained that she felt better at sixteen, insisting also that if he would take the trouble to look up the baptismal records in the First True Reformed Church of Roseland, in Chicago, he would find that she was eighty-eight or at most eighty-nine.

"Be sure to eat," Elizabeth says. "Take a small portion first and ask for seconds and thirds. She always worried because you were so peaked and frail."

Barbara laughs—she is on a diet, she has been warned that the

Danes eat five meals a day. Elizabeth does not laugh. She has heard from Grandma concerning both our daughters, as my mother before her heard about her three sons, that they were peaked and frail and needed a tonic; that they needed more meat, more sunshine, more fresh air; that they had worms. (Once this turned out to be true.) One Christmas when I was eighteen I stood on my head for sixty seconds on Grandma's porch in the snow to insure a ruddy glow on my cheeks when I went inside, and my mother spent that Christmas explaining why my two brothers looked so peaked and pale in comparison to me.

I pay the last toll. "Don't mention Linda," Elizabeth says. "Let me tell her about Linda."

Our second daughter, a year younger than Barbara—Linda Sue is her full name—is staying at home today. She is saving money for college (she thinks her specialty will be the dance) and she has a job serving hamburgers at a fast-food drive-in that requires her to work this afternoon even though it is Sunday.

Grandma's religious faith is what it has been for ninety-three years, the faith of the True Reformed Church. As a conservative Christian she takes pride in never having forgiven me for joining a liberal or, as she would put it, American church. Fortunately for us, our apostasy has been counter-balanced by that of Aunt Gert, who has lately taken up strange ideas concerning prayer, miracles, and faith-healing, which she gets from tracts sent to her by a certain preacher on the radio. "There's such a lot of that going around now-adays," Grandma complained during our New Year's visit, as if faith-healing were a contagious disease. "They talk so pious about the Holy Spirit it just makes me sick!" She knows that theological conversation may bring upon her a challenge from Aunt Gert to say whether she is Saved or not; being Saved is one of three areas, the others being sex and old age, in which Grandma prefers reticence and modesty.

In matters of practical religion like sabbath observance, however, her frankness is unencumbered. It will not do to say that Linda is sick; on New Year's Day she really was sick, and Elizabeth cannot face the inquisition which two illnesses on two successive visits would bring down upon her motherhood. Nor can I argue, as I used to with my father, who rather enjoyed doctrinal equivocations, that since this job involves food (that is to say, drive-in hamburgers) it should fall under the category of *necessary* Sabbath work. Grandma knows nothing of rational argument; with St. Augustine her only commandment is Love the Lord and do what you like—though her version runs Love the Lord and do what *I* like. St. Augustine, I remember, lived only to age seventy-six.

Elizabeth plans to stress the fact that Linda is saving for her college education, a phrase that will be received with respect for my Grandfather Arie's sake—though for herself Grandma would wish for all women (and probably all men, excluding ministers and doctors) to remain untainted by higher education. Nevertheless, better to be educated than to burn with desire, like Aunt Gert with her tracts and strange ideas.

We will not point out that Linda intends her college education to involve the study of the dance, for this surely, despite all Biblical references to various rhythmical ways of praising the Lord, would bring Grandma's gray hairs in sorrow to the grave.

Blue hairs, rather, for since the time that Grandfather died Grandma has used a strong rinse.

I turn off the tollway and onto Ridge Street, and we drive past a clutter of used-car lots and fast-food shops to grandmother's house. An imposing white colonial, it could be one of those houses that, as a nostalgic Midwestern writer once put it, are "still called through decades by a family's name." My grandfather built it not long after the First War, and people of True Reformed persuasion may still call the house by my family's name, owing to my grandfather's former importance in the Church. But the True Reformed who once made up half of Orangetown's eight thousand souls now represent less than a sixth of its thirty thousand. Even they, if they look at the house at all, probably think of it now as the house across from the drive-in bank.

I make the left turn across two lanes of traffic, the bank flashing messages at us from its marquee, and we are there. Grandma welcomes us in the foyer, Aunt Gert calls hello from the kitchen.

"Who cut your hair?" Grandma says to me, ignoring my beardlessness. She compliments Elizabeth's figure: "You've put on weight!"

From Elizabeth and me she accepts a peck on the cheek. From Barbara a hug, gingerly given; Grandma is not steady on her feet. Also, Barbara is too old. Grandma was once a great, smothering hugger—would be still, if she had the chance—but only for pre-school-aged children. "Oh I could eat you up!" she used to say to our girls,

x

hugging them. I remember her saying it to me when I was four or five years old, just about the time when the story of Little Red Riding Hood, which I received for Christmas that year, had to be put in the drawer under my socks so that the pictures wouldn't frighten me.

We enter the living room—there is the fireplace where the Christmas tree used to stand!—and when Grandma is seated we give her the news. Linda's absence. Barbara's impending trip. The disappointment of the first is buried, for the moment, beneath the shock of the second.

"Denmark? Denmark! They eat horse-meat there, don't they? And have a lot of crazy ideas!"

"Well—do you mean Kierkegaard?" Barbara speaks as one who first heard Kierkegaard's name this past week.

"Just think," I say, "she'll be the first of our family to set foot in Europe since your grandmother left."

"Left? Why of course she left! Good-bye and good riddance! You didn't see her going back again, did you? You think she wanted to eat horse-meat all her life? Who wants to go backward? Those old people knew what they were doing!"

Like her own grandmother, Grandma focuses on the present. "You'll let them take advantage of you," she tells Barbara. I assume she means Danish young men, but she means the Danish housewife. "Cheap help, that's what they're after. Cheap help! Don't you do all the work!"

"I'll take care of myself," Barbara says.

"That's what you say, but will you do it? You're too soft, you let people walk all over you, just like your mother!"

I mistakenly advance language-learning as a justification for travel. But who, she replies, who, knowing English, would want another language? Don't I remember how my grandfather worked to make English the official language of the Church? (I do not remember; it is of the legends before my time.) Hasn't she herself forgotten all the Dutch picked up from her parents, except for those indispensables having to do with laundry, morals, food, and children's illnesses?

I remember having the children's illnesses twice, once in my mother's English and again in my grandmother's Dutch.

"That's true," I say. "I always thought 'peaked' was one of those Dutch words."

xi

"What? Peaked! Why of course it is! How would you say it in English? See, you can't say it in English, there's no word for it!"

From this philological discussion Aunt Gert, broad-faced and freckled, smiling apologetically, still sandy-haired at almost sixty years of age, calls us into the dining room. The table, though without extra boards, is set as festively as it was on the old holidays. Then we would open a window to let out the heat or to hear the birds; now we are protected from the traffic by air conditioning and permanent storm windows. Across the street where I used to see someone else's holiday going forward (the Hardemas and all their children, later the Brantleys with their large dogs and small cars), I see the time and temperature flashing alternately. Also what must disturb my grandfather, if the heavenly souls can be disturbed: an advertisement for the state lottery.

I am the only male present. "Adrian will ask a blessing," Aunt Gert says.

Phrases from my father and grandfather rise to my lips out of the chair on which I am sitting.

"Amen," Aunt Gert echoes, loudly and pentecostally.

"Ya, so *vroom*," Grandma rebukes her daughter. "Very pious," she says to me across the table. "And you let your daughter work on Sunday."

Aunt Gert covers for us. "Be happy in the present moment," she says. "Sufficient unto the day, after all. Think of what we have to be thankful for! Here we are, gathered together as a family, young and old alike—"

Grandma has had difficulty getting her legs under the table. Even her joke ("Good thing I'm not a cow, I'd have to do this four times") could not hide her chagrin. "Old!" she interrupts. "Who's old? I don't see any rocking chairs here. I don't see any canes. You speak for yourself!"

Aunt Gert disposed of, Grandma begins filling Barbara's plate with food and her head with advice. Never speak to strange men. Never sit with idle hands. Never go upstairs or downstairs with empty hands. Remember that the morning hours are golden—a proverb which sounds better in the old language, I force her to admit; but for this she takes a sudden vengeance.

"And don't get any crazy ideas," she says. "Your father went away from home one summer. That's when he got mixed up with that colored girl."

I blush. Elizabeth looks at her plate. Aunt Gert laughs wickedly, delighted that the heat is off her.

"Why Mother! What a thing to say! You make it sound as if—"

"What? What? Why of course he was! He went away one summer and got a lot of crazy ideas and got mixed up with that colored girl. No as ifs, ands, or buts about it."

Grandma's large blue eyes flash over me, a faded gray-blue like her hair. Spacy with cataracts and far-sightedness, they still have the roguishness that attracted Grandfather Arie at their legendary meeting over the Carom board when she was eighteen, the year of the Boxer Rebellion.

"Your father was smitten, that's all there was to it. He was just smitten for a while, and then he came to his senses and married your mother. She was the girl they named you after, did you know that, Barbara?"

No one picks up the gauntlet. Aunt Gert laughs the laugh of a parent at a naughty child.

"I always thought I was named after my mother's Aunt Barbara," Barbara says.

"What? Why, of course, it was after that colored girl. The one he got mixed up with when he went away for a summer. So don't you get any crazy ideas."

And always put your key in the same place, she tells her great-granddaughter. Then you'll know where it is. And hang your clothes up facing the same way, so you can dress in the dark. The dark before sunrise, that is, when you are planning the meals for the day. And always leave your room tidy, because the way you leave it is the way you'll find it. And don't let anybody walk all over you.

"I won't," Barbara says.

When the meal is over, the dishes finally done, it is time for Grandma's nap. We know this from the fact that she urges us all, several times, to go upstairs and lie down. We insist it is time for us to go. Barbara wants to hug Grandma good-bye. Being hugged Grandma says, "When are you coming for your next monthly visit?"

In the haven of our car, a nuclear family once more, we drive by the Orangetown landmarks on our way to the tollway. On previous trips Barbara has not allowed these to interrupt her perusal of fairy tales, horse stories, romances ancient and modern. Now her eyes are opened. Improbable as it may seem, her existence has been determined by that of her parents, the existence of her parents by that of their own, and by the things outside this window. The high school where Elizabeth and I met, the church where we were married, great-grandpa's onion-set warehouse (now a pre-fab cabinet factory), the old house where I grew up and the newer one surrounded by apartments, which my father built during his attempt to enter the construction business—all these things she will bear with her, willy-nilly, across the Atlantic and wherever she goes.

"Tell me about the scandal Grandpa John and Grandpa Gerrit were involved in."

Her bluntness seems a ghost of the house we have just left—except that Grandma, fearless in bringing up my past, would not have mentioned this episode in the life of her son, the reason, as she knows, that he has not been elected either elder or deacon in the twenty years since, not even (so far) in Wisconsin and Florida.

Barbara's face in the mirror looks nervous but determined.

"Didn't it all happen at the same time as . . . ? You know. What Grandma was talking about."

The blond ponytail, the skin without makeup, the straightforward gaze, troubled now by a V-shaped frown above the nose, remind me heart-swoopingly of her mother two decades ago. It was the summer that Elizabeth's father, Barbara's Grandpa John, died.

"It's a long story, Barb"—her high school nickname—"and I don't know that I would call it a scandal, exactly—"

"There was no scandal," Elizabeth says, meaning, I take it, that nothing was made public. "There never was anything like a scandal. Be careful with your words, for goodness' sake."

We drive west, then north, in the April twilight, through the April traffic on the tollway. Barbara finds her way back to the subject my grandmother brought up. Her name. Barbara Sue. Did we really name her after two people—one black, one white? One old, one young? Pagan and Christian? American and European?

"Well, I would have called them both Christian. Certainly both American."

"That's totally beside the point," Elizabeth says. "That has nothing to do with it. You were named after two relatives."

After a while, Barbara, from the back seat, says, "I'm going to keep a diary next year when I'm abroad. You two should have done that when you were young. Then Linda and I could read it now."

"Yes, maybe we should have done that."

"I'll want to know about all this stuff eventually. Linda ought to know too."

"Yes," I agree.

"But not tonight," Elizabeth says. "I'm too tired after this visit to think straight."

We stop at a tollgate and I throw thirty cents into the machine. Satisfied, the State gives us the green light.

Elizabeth turns on the radio and finds some orchestral music on the state university station. We drive north and then west again, out into the country toward home, and I wonder whether Barbara will ask for the popular-music program on which she can hear the top forty tunes.

Her face reappears in the mirror, her two hands resting on the back of our seat.

"Can't we get some news?" she says finally. "I'm trying to get ready for this summer. They'll want me to be able to talk intelligently about everything going on in my country."

CHAPTER ONE

SUNDAY

WHEN I was a teenager my mother was slow, small, round—"petite" at five foot two but with an appealing tendency to roundness—and thoughtful, otherworldly, absentminded, her eyes so circular and blue they sometimes seemed vacant, like the sky. My father, fourteen inches taller than she, was skinny everywhere except around the middle, where his posture threatened a potbelly; his thin hands and angular chin and nose and green eyes behind his glasses were forever on the move, and when his mouth wasn't busy talking, eating, smoking, or coughing, he was probably asleep.

He was an extrovert and a day person. She was an introvert and a night person.

On Sunday mornings he woke us with the smell of his cigarette and the sound of his cough and the choked clearing of his throat as he buttoned his collar and knotted the mandatory tie. "We're going to be late," he would announce into the bedroom where Gordon and I still lay bunked. "We're going to be late," we would hear him say into his own dark bedroom. "We're going to be late"—this into Paul's room at the end of the hall; at which point my mother from somewhere near the edge of her bed would murmur sleepily, "I know it. I know it."

While we dressed he would get himself out of the way by going downstairs to smoke another cigarette in the kitchen, this one with a cup of coffee. At eight-thirty he would call up the stairs: "It's eight forty-five." Groans from my mother; wagers between Gordon and me as to whether it was really only eight-fifteen, half an hour being the outside limit of this well-known bluff of his, except on the October Sundays when we returned to Standard Time—then he would try to secure a full hour by pretending he didn't know. We would hear him, after his breakfast, clattering his dishes in the sink as if it really were eight forty-five or even nine o'clock, and when we came down for breakfast he would go to sit in the car, smoking and winding his watch. Sometimes he came up the back porch steps and spoke to us through the screen door. "We're going to be late."

"Well, we're not going without our orange juice."

My mother in her robe—up till now she had been busy finding us the clean socks she had brought in from the line on Saturday night and the Sunday shirts she had ironed after supper—would be revolving sliced oranges against the sombrero-shaped juicer. Since vitamin C could not be stored in the body we had to have orange juice every day. Since she had to squeeze the oranges first and since, as she often said, she needed a glass of orange juice herself before she could wake up, we sometimes drank it on our way out the door.

"Well, we're going to be late," my father would say, but mildly, because he hadn't yet had his own and did not intend to. Once she brought him some to the car and they argued over whether or not he would drink it while the nine-thirty church hour drew closer and closer.

Once the four males had had their breakfast she could make herself ready, a long process behind closed doors—bedroom, bathroom, bedroom—from which she emerged, finally, looking as if she had "just stepped out of a bandbox." That was my aunt's and grandmother's phrase for it—always with the implication, I thought, whenever I heard them say it, that a bandbox was a touch too worldly a place to spend quite so much time in on Sunday morning.

Entering the car was a multi-stage process. Half-in, half-out, she would explain that a wide skirt would have allowed her to enter the car more quickly—this while my father, who had already sounded the horn during her dressing, ground his teeth and tapped his watch crystal—but she didn't have any wide skirts, a short woman had to learn that she couldn't wear a wide skirt, not unless she was willing to look positively dumpy. Oh, they were all right for a hot day, she would grant you that, but for church. . . . My father being busy racing the engine and preparing to let out the clutch with a snap, it was generally Gordon or I who held the door for her, trying to please one parent with our courtesy and the other with our haste; when she was in you had to jump fast for the rear door, because before it even slammed we would be backing out the driveway for the short, fierce ride to church.

"Gerrit"—her body bouncing like a child's on the seat as we hit the railroad tracks, taking the "country" route for the sake of speed, presumably, though I suspected the real reason was so that my father could ram us over these tracks in payment for our sins—"Gerrit, aren't we breaking the speed limit?"

Having gained 192nd Street, he speedshifted past the empty on-ion fields and Bok's Grove, swerving around those slow pagan driv-ers—probably from Calumet or Calumet Heights—who were only out for the ride. Luckily, there were few of these in our town.

"We're late, Cora. We're late!"

"It doesn't seem right, driving like this on a Sunday. 'How good and pleasant is the sight, when brethren make it their delight—' "

"We're late! Can't you see that? We're late!"

" '— to dwell in blest accord.' *Accord*, Gerrit."

On our last turn into Ridge Street he would plunge through the stop sign in second gear, my mother's right hand clutching the door handle, her left the pillbox hat on her head.

"Gerrit, you drive like a Jehu! Do you remember how he died, Adrian? Anyway, I'm sure he didn't die a peaceable death. You have to consider the example you're setting for your sons, Gerrit. Adrian has his license and it won't be long before Gordon—"

"We're late! We're late! We're late!"

At last we could see the red brick church, square-built and high-shouldered, one round blue window segmented like a grapefruit high above the still-open doors. We would hit the parking lot in a shower of gravel and then walk into church at the very last minute (give or take a minute either way) behind the ambiguously smiling usher, right down to the very front row, living examples of the foolish virgins who hadn't trimmed their lamps, exhibiting our dilatoriness, our narrowly-missed Sabbath-breaking and shortcoming and sin to the entire con-gregation and especially to my father's parents. My grandparents cast long shadows of financial astuteness, domestic diligence, and moral uprightness everywhere over my parents' life, but nowhere more than in church. Down to the front row, the last open seats, and if infants were being baptized, as they were once a month in our fertile con-gregation, it would mean folding chairs in the aisle for all of us, the last refuge of the Sabbath scapegrace. The church clock, a round-faced

3

black-and-white electric, hung above us on the eastern wall. It always seemed to me as much a liturgical object as the pulpit and its Bible up front, and the communion table with its collection plates, and the three large chairs (representing the Trinity, I used to think), only one of which was ever occupied, though I remember having dreams in which I or some other shadowy figure would be sitting in the second or third chair. "There they are," my grandmother would be saying to my grandfather in their pew just under the clock. Now she could relax; Gerrit and his family had made it once again. "Doesn't Cora look like she just stepped out of a bandbox!"

After church it would be my mother who was first in the car; she had the dinner to think about. Meanwhile my father talked and talked, moving from one dwindling group of friends to another. One by one my brothers and I came back to wait with her, and still my father talked: sometimes sports (which meant baseball), sometimes politics (which meant Republican), sometimes gossip, mainly business—it didn't matter, it was all fellowship. Christian fellowship was one of his favorite concepts. Sometimes in moments of exasperated daring my mother honked the horn at him. When he came he would be still talking over his shoulder, still talking across the roof of the car as he fished the key out of his pocket. At last we would leave the church parking lot as we had arrived—behind everyone else.

"That guy is hard to break away from," he would say.

We would drive slowly home, past the new county airport or the new homes being built up toward Calumet or a new foundation he had laid or some other marks of progress.

"Gerrit, how can I get dinner ready with you dawdling—"

"This will only take a minute." And a half-hour or forty-five minutes later, depending on whether or not we found someone to talk with, we would arrive back home.

And then the mid-Sabbath. We three boys are on the living room floor, reading the funnies or playing checkers or doing whatever the current state of our Sabbatarian controversy allows—for keeping the Sabbath Day holy is serious business: it involves distinctions between necessary and unnecessary and "neutral" work (until I read Calvin I thought the neutral category was my invention, and my brothers and I pushed it hard), between Sabbath-breaking and contributing to Sabbath-breaking, and between sacred and profane and "neutral" amusements. Can we deliver papers on Sunday? Of course not; but can we

4

buy a paper on Sunday? No; but can we read the paper on Sunday if we buy it on Saturday night? Can we read it if we know for a fact, because somebody who knows somebody who works at the *Tribune* told us so himself, that the Sunday edition is printed on Saturday? Otherwise, don't we have to give up reading the Monday paper—because actually it is printed on Sunday? Can we play baseball? Can we play catch? If not in the front yard, in the back? Can we play inside games where the only weaker brethren we could tempt would be ourselves? Can we play games with dice? Games with cards? Can we *watch* games—the Cubs, the Sox? Can we watch the amateur games in Bok's Grove, where no money changes hands? Can we watch games for free—this question came later, with the television set—except of course for the advertising? Can we listen to games, then, on the radio? If we can't listen to ball games, don't we have to give up music also? News? Jack Benny?

It was hard to be a good True Reformed father in those days when every morning brought forth a new invention, every invention a new temptation. My father steered us through these shoals with the aid of two principles that served him as chart and compass: one he used in advancing (You've got to draw the line somewhere) and the other in retreating (No system is perfect). He used them, too, in settling the theological questions we brought up in connection with mealtime Bible reading—my father was ahead of his time in allowing such questioning—such as why Pharaoh's innocent horses as well as his evil men had to perish in the Red Sea while the Israelites, our spiritual ancestors, passed through the midst of the sea on dry ground.

These principles gave him a great deal of flexibility. My father liked Jack Benny—one could even say he *needed* Jack Benny during that time when he was trying to make it as an independent construction operator after years of working for someone else. He answered the Jack Benny question by saying that since you had to draw the line somewhere, he would draw it at six o'clock, at the moment when Jack's theme song and the Lucky Strike commercial came on the air; the Israelites, after all, had run their Sabbaths from sundown to sundown, and if you averaged out the time of sundown over a whole year you would find that six o'clock came as close to the average as any. This meant that between the time my mother finished the ironing on Saturday night—*her* Sabbaths ran from midnight to midnight—and the time of Jack Benny's arrival, we had a short Sunday; but as

5

for that, and for the fact that immediately after Jack Benny we would turn the radio off and drive to the evening worship service as if the Sabbath had never ended at all—well, no system is perfect; and, anyway, except in the summers we had the second service in the afternoon.

Once I inadvertently caught him listening to a baseball game on Sunday. I was ten years old, it was the Series of '45, the Cubs and the Tigers, with Newhouser and Pafko and Cavaretta and Hack, and Bert Wilson at the microphone. It is a scene I recall even now with a certain awe, as if in walking into his bedroom I had found him bent furtively over something more primal than a radio, like one of Noah's children discovering Noah's nakedness—or as if, like Jacob's son Reuben, I had found myself lusting after my father's concubine, since it seemed clear that Sunday baseball had been his secret mistress all along. The shock in my own face was mirrored for a moment in his. Then, cool-headed as ever, without even bothering to turn off the bedside Philco, he explained that while a game was only a game, a World Series was more of a world event (especially when it involved Chicago)—and thus one could listen to it with a clear conscience on the Sabbath, just as, for example, we had listened to the announcement of the beginning of World War II on Sunday, December 7, 1941!

The three of us, then, are on the living room floor reading the funnies or playing checkers. My mother is in the kitchen scrubbing the potatoes, peeling the potatoes, polishing, it seems, the potatoes. My father is at the desk, too small for his six-four frame, doing something connected with the construction business, something he will defend, in case anybody asks, as necessary work. He is paying bills. I see him spearing the paid bill on a spindle, then folding the letter and envelope and throwaway advertising, if any, and tearing the pile into halves, and quarters, and eighths, like a strongman dealing with a telephone book. To save space in the wastebasket, he says, though I sense also a discharge of violence, violence that might have struck elsewhere if not lightning-rodded away. In college, when I heard the statement (from a teacher who was refuting it) that the God of the Old Testament was a "dirty bully," I thought of my father tearing up these piles of letters, envelopes, and brochures, paper sinners in the hands of an angry God. There is wrath and righteousness in his movements, as well as human frustration. He is a man of action and life is full of obstacles. Rip, rip, rip, and freed from another debt!

In the summer he frees his own body the same way, beginning

6

with the tie hung over the back of the chair, then the white shirt, then the shoes and socks, then, retreating upstairs, the trousers, so that he ends in B.V.D. shirt and a pair of cut-off yellow pajamas that serve him as Bermuda shorts. Thus ripping and stripping—and chain-smoking, the living room is full of the smoke of Marvels or Chesterfields—he works himself into a state of unencumbered simplicity in which he can rewrap the checkbook and accounts in their wide rubber bands and replace them atop the china closet next to his wallet and keys and the leatherbound Bible and, with a cup of coffee, relax. But not for long. He must check the basement for dampness, the backyard for moles; he must stalk through the house pulling down the yellow shades and turning off all lamps, muttering as he does so, "Light makes heat." He must get the exhaust fan from upstairs and experiment with it, blowing in, blowing out, blowing along the floor; the devils of thermal pollution are everywhere on the holy ground of our Sabbath.

Meanwhile my mother is rubbing and scrubbing the potatoes, slicing and dicing the potatoes. She sings something slow and stately and beautiful. Remember not, O God, the sins of long ago. Or, He shall keep His flock like a shepherd. She has a lovely contralto voice. "If you could sing something fast once in a while, like 'Yankee Doodle,' maybe the potatoes would get done," my father calls from the desk. Now that we are home and dinner preparations are under way, she has lost her sense of urgency, he has regained his. He wants a nap and Jack Benny before the evening service.

Suddenly she appears in the archway between living and dining rooms, a glistening potato in her hand, her light blue housedress matching her eyes. Her forehead is damp with kitchen steam. Something has reminded her of a comment she wanted to make on the sermon. Sermons for her do not end with the sound of the pastor's voice or the departure from the church parking lot; rather, they begin their true life then by waving slowly back and forth within her mind, like flowers on a tropical seafloor. Mary and Martha sermons are among her favorites, the conflict expressed in those two sisters exists within herself, she admits it, but. . . . Something distracts her: my father's smoke. Gerrit, don't you know what you're doing to your health? The body is the temple of the Holy Spirit, remember, and that includes the lungs. And think what an example you're setting for your sons! The potato waves like a slow fan in the smoke. My father, though tempted to answer by lighting another, decides instead to give

7

her a good example by getting on with his work. How can the dummy send another bill, he exclaims, he hasn't cashed last month's check!—hurling the thrice-torn bill with violence into the basket. My mother turns toward her sons. What did I come in here for? Oh yes, the sermon. It is all very well for the minister to say that Mary had the better part—quoting Jesus, of course, so he seems on safe ground there—but wouldn't we all be in a pretty fix if it weren't for the Marthas of the world who actually do all the work? "Cumbered with much serving" is certainly a lovely phrase when you think about it, it could be applied to Jesus himself, for instance. . . . Until at last my father shuts the checkbook with a snap and says, Cora? Are we going to be late?

Sometime after two o'clock, perhaps, we sit down to dinner, my mother in her blue dress, my father in his B.V.D.'s and cut-off yellow pajamas. Everything is rich and heavy and good, and when we rise from the table my father checks his watch, shakes his head, decides to try for a nap anyway "or at least lie down." My mother may join him or, more likely, catch up on her reading. My brothers and I do the dishes behind a closed kitchen door according to what I assume is an unspoken agreement (though with our mother you can never tell) that we will do girls' work if she will not come in and observe that we have the Cubs' game on very low. All is Sabbath peace. But in a short time my father will awake, and the race for the evening service will begin.

True, some of our Sundays began with a cheerful breakfast, high-lighted by coffee cake from Grandmother Susanna and concluded with the reading of a Psalm—Psalm 100 or some other five-verser, maybe, but still a Psalm. Sundays were memorable for shining waxed linoleum and clean shirts and sheets; for perfect tulips in vases on the polished table and piano-top; for serious conversation with perhaps Bach instead of baseball in the background (though that had to wait until we got the "hi-fi," the year of my graduation from high school), so that "Jesu, Joy of Man's Desiring" or the Toccata and Fugue in D Minor need not contribute to the Sabbath-breaking of any disc jockey, sacred or secular. Once we even fulfilled a lifelong ideal of my father's by *walking* to church together. This was on a vacation trip to Michigan, and I remember single-filing down the highway for a quarter of a mile, my mother with short legs and short skirt in the rear, my father well in the lead and complaining vigorously of the heat, but keeping to the ideal, a Sabbath witness to all who passed by.

I remember learning with surprise from Huck and Tom, friends of my boyhood and spokesmen for another denomination in another country, that Sundays were mournful and lonesome. How could that be when so many bodies pressed for space under the clock on the high eastern wall, so many voices competed in song for Heaven's ear; when there were so many hands to be shaken or avoided, the pressure of so many eyes?

I came to puberty at exactly the time, or so it seemed to me, when America's salesmen discovered the mass media and the mass media discovered sex. But all through the sense-stunned fifties and sixties no image remained to me as movingly sensual as that of the young mother I remembered seeing in church with a pre-schooler squirming at each side, a younger sibling at nurse under a placid blanket or diaper, her easy fingers busy with their hair, their necks, their noses, her lips seen moving against their ears, her crossed ankle swinging with the beat of her heart and ticking away the three major points of the sermon. Once after church (my mother waiting in the car, my father still talking), an old man confided to me as we watched some of these young mothers driving off with their crew-cut husbands, "You know, they'll go home now, and they'll have a nice dinner, and they'll put the kids to bed for a nap, and then they'll take their pleasure." He was about fifty-five (old to me then), and he had had six children of his own and then a heart attack. He sounded wistful.

Sparkling, orderly Sundays, richly sensual Sundays—with so many Sundays to remember it must be for personal reasons that I choose as typical the ones that I do. Perhaps the reason is that, trying to remember my last summer home, I think of the Sunday in August when Johnny Van Dyken died. A Sunday marked by extremes of sorrow and violence and—I do not want to forget—exultation; and yet it was also typical. My mother, as usual, celebrated. With perhaps an unexamined serenity she insisted on celebration no matter what duties pressed, no matter whose timetable said she was late. My father, who ordinarily smoked and fretted and paid his bills on Sunday no matter what celebration was going forward, spent that day doing something he would be sorry for, something he must have described

9

to himself as necessary work. Unfortunately—though at the time I thought I had freed myself from Orangetown's Sabbaths—it turned out to be typical for me as well. I was hiding a Sabbath secret from my father, just as he was hiding one from me.

Or so it seems to me as I sit at my own desk on a Sunday afternoon and try to remember how it was during my last summer home.

CHAPTER TWO

AT HEBRON

THAT was the summer I "went away," as my grandmother puts it— the summer after my college graduation when I went to work for the Calumet, Indiana, Recreation Department.

Calumet was a city just across the state line and to the north of Orangetown, part of the belt of industrial towns along Lake Michigan's southern shore. I had seen a newspaper article on Calumet's playgrounds the summer before, when as usual during vacations I was shingling roofs and wheelbarrowing cement six days a week for my father and attending church twice on Sundays. I cut out the part of the article which pictured a slender black girl seated tailor-fashion on the grass, the capstone of a ring of seated children, her fingers fanned out toward them in graceful invitation. No two of the children had complexions the same shade—some were darker than the girl in the center, some lighter—but each wore a smile that echoed her own, the haloed focus of the black-and-white picture. The caption read, "Barbara Robinson finds that *all* children love to sing."

My own debut as a singer had been as a first-grade soloist in church. I stood beside the pulpit and sang, staring (as I had been told to do) at the round blue windows high above the heads of the congregation: "You cannot hide from God, His eye is fixed on you! You cannot hide from God!"

I kept the article on my desk all through my senior year as a pre-seminary student at Hebron True Reformed College and Seminary in Hebron, Iowa; and in the spring I added to it a letter from Mr. Harmon, Calumet's Recreation Director, accepting my application for the position of playground leader—"pending, of course, our inter-

11

view." The letter said that play-leading experience had proved invaluable in teaching and "other leadership careers."

In the same folder with the clipping and Harmon's letter was a sample Law School Admission Test; an application form from the Harvard Graduate School; an unfilled entry blank for the St. Louis Cardinals Open Tryout to be held in Des Moines; and a picture of Henry Aaron loafing under a fly ball in the new Milwaukee County Stadium. Baseball was the only career in my file that I had definitely ruled out—but on the strength of batting .300 as a substitute third baseman for the Hebron Templars in my junior year I had allowed myself dreams of taking Eddie Matthews' place as Aaron's faithful white companion, and I kept the picture for sentimental reasons. There were also pamphlets from the Foreign Service Examination and Graduate Record Examination people and, at long last, in April, a letter from Vanderbilt University offering a graduate fellowship for Prospective Teachers of the Humanities. The stipend, I noticed, was $300 less than that provided for Prospective Teachers of the Sciences, but I was in no position to quibble. Shelved along with my "career file" were a paperback copy of Schweitzer's *Out of My Life and Thought*; Barzun's *Teacher in America*, from the school library; Harriet Wildervank's *Home Missions White Unto the Harvest*, from my Aunt Gert; and the Modern Library *Scarlet Letter*, in which I had underlined Hawthorne's description of Dimmesdale, the neurasthenic Puritan minister, as one whose mind "impelled itself powerfully down the track of a creed."

My doubts about the power of my own mind, and about the narrowness of the track down which I had been impelling it, had come to focus more and more on one class in particular; and so when the fellowship offer arrived in April I arranged for an interview with my instructor in New Testament Greek.

We met in his cubicle in the basement of the administration building. On his desk books were piled in great towers, smokestack fashion, and among them, covered with cigarette ash, lay pages of his own manuscript—in German, as nearly as I could tell from my seat in the chair he had with apparent reluctance pulled up for me. He was a slight, pale young man, still in his twenties, with long black hair and thick glasses. His family had emigrated from the Netherlands to Canada; he himself emigrated four years later after taking a degree at the Free University of Amsterdam—going not to his parents' dairy farm in Ontario but to Hebron Seminary in Iowa. After finishing his seminary work he was staying on a year or two before entering the True Reformed ministry in order to practice his English and teach Greek to Hebron's undergraduates. He had been nicknamed "Mr. Van Wetback" by some of my classmates, a usage I avoided as unworthy and also, perhaps, because I admired our instructor's intellect and was more conscious than the others that he was a possible role-model for myself.

Somehow, I told him, I'm dissatisfied with the work I've been doing in the course.

He looked at me through his thick lenses. The system of "withdrawal" privileges at American colleges, the kind of counseling that seemed to go with it, the attention that was beginning to be paid to students' "interests"—all were no doubt foreign to him; probably he wondered why he should be bothered with the matter.

"I think you have been doing very well in the class," he said. He pronounced it, "I sink you haf been doing fairy vell." He added, after a moment, "In comparison with some of the others."

I had entered the pre-seminary program four years before after writing the required essay on the Christian doctrine most meaningful to me, choosing as my topic the Catechism question and answer, "What is your only comfort in life and death?—That I am not my own but belong to my faithful Lord and Savior Jesus Christ." In recognizing that I belonged to Christ I felt I was giving myself to the largest, most universal service I knew. But the college and the town of Hebron seemed the opposite of large and universal. Here, for example, were the headquarters of dozens of organizations unknown to the larger world, organizations such as TRY (True Reformed Youth, an anti-Scouting youth group) and CLASP (Christian Labor Association in States and Provinces, an anti-AFL-CIO labor union). CLASP was affiliated with Christian Labor for Orangetown Shops and Enterprises, or CLOSE, of which my father was a member back home. Each of these groups had its own newsletter or journal—TROT for teachers, TRUMP for musicians; I was familiar with the conservative quarterly TRUTH (True Reformed United in Truth against Heterodoxy) and the liberal monthly TRUST (True Reformed Union of Scholars and Teachers), between which two poles most of the Hebron faculty could be found ranged on a narrow grid.

My parents had met at Hebron. My mother, a Wisconsin farm

girl, was working here as a store clerk and saving to enter the freshman class of 1931—which she never did, choosing to marry instead;
but she kept her copies of Jowett's edition of Plato and Vedder's
translation of Bronkema, the True Reformed theologian, both of which
she had read all the way through in anticipation. My father visited
Hebron as often as he could while making his rounds as salesman for
the Ramshorst Pickling Company of Orangetown. Later he liked to
portray himself as a kind of Jude the Obscure hovering in intellectual
yearning outside the college's walls, but it was my mother and not he
who had read Plato and Bronkema. I imagine he came simply because
Hebron was a good place to meet girls, serving the True Reformed
of North America in the same way that the patriarchs had been served
by the community wells of the Promised Land, where Jacob had found
his Rachel and Rebecca her Isaac.

In fact, my four years here had increasingly given me a feeling of
centripetal motion, not the centrifugal one I longed for. I had begun
to envy Elizabeth, my high school "steady," who was in training at a
Chicago nursing school; her situation seemed at once more secular
and more spiritual.

"Somehow the course isn't what I expected," I told my instructor.
"I mean as a preparation for the ministry. It seems overly—overly
grammatical, perhaps."

He observed me a moment, smoking his cigarette. Then he
plunged among the towers of books and, coming up with a Hebron
College catalog, read from the course description: ". . . in which the
significance of lexical and syntactical detail for the interpretation of
the text is everywhere emphasized."

"Yes?" he said.

"Perhaps my expectations were wrong. Perhaps because it's the
New Testament I expected something different. More content, perhaps. Less emphasis on form. Isn't it a matter of emphasis? 'For the
letter killeth, but the spirit giveth life'?"

He raised an eyebrow above the smudged frame of his glasses. I
was afraid I had been too bold, but he seemed to be smiling. He
stubbed out his cigarette and leaned toward me.

"You quote St. Paul to me in the English?"

My cheeks grew warm. "I'm sorry. I don't know the Greek as I
should."

14

"*Littera enim occidit, Spiritus autem vivificat?* This is the point you are making? But why in English?"

His Latin, too, had a foreign accent, the *v*'s of "vivificat" unvoiced.

"I'm sorry," I said, "I don't speak Latin. I mean I can read it, but I don't think in Latin. I'm afraid I think only in English."

"And sometimes the English of King James! Don't be ashamed, it is a world language after all! But why use language?"

"I don't understand," I said.

"You say we have a class in language only? And you wish to deal not with language only? You wish the content? The essence? The substance? *Das Ding an sich?*"

"Well, yes."

"You wish for the Spirit? The living Word?" ("Spdeet," he pronounced it. "The living wart.")

"Yes," I said.

"Then why do you not tell me this in the spirit? Why do you not tell me this in the living word?"

"I don't understand."

"But I think you understand me! Why do you tell me with human words? Why do you tell me with language?"

"I suppose because language is all I have."

"Ah! Because language is all you have! But is not Christ the living Word?"

"Yes," I said.

"And do you not have Christ?"

I felt an opening here for something more personal and perhaps more useful than we had yet managed, but I did not know how to take advantage of it.

"Not—not as a means of communication," I said.

"But you know Him? You have knowledge of Him?"

"Yes."

"But how do you know this living Word?"

"Out of the Scriptures."

"Out of these words?" From the top of one of the towers of books he pulled a Testament. It was the Merk New Testament in Greek and Latin (*Novum Testamentum Graece et Latine*), with preface and apparatus in Latin, published in Rome, the seventh edition. He laid it on the desk next to his glass ashtray.

"These Greek words?"

"Well, yes. Basically."

"And this is all we have of Him? These Greek words?"

"No," I said. "We have more."

"Ah, you think we have more! And what more do we have?"

"We have the Church."

"Ah! The Church! And we as Christians (vee ass Chdistens) are the Church! And how do we as Christians maintain the Church? And by what marks do we as Christians know her?"

"By preaching," I said.

"Ah, yes, preaching! By what preaching?"

"By preaching the Word."

"These words?"

"Yes."

"Greek words?"

"Yes. Basically."

"Basically yes, to be sure! And by something else do we recognize her?"

"By the preaching of the Word and the administration of the sacraments."

"Ah, sacraments! And the sacraments, where are the sacraments ordained?"

"In the Word. In the gospels and the epistles."

"Gospels and epistles, very good! In the Word! Greek words?"

"Yes."

"And the Church herself, where is she ordained?"

"In the Word."

"In the word? What word?"

"In the Greek words in the Testament you have on your desk."

"And this is all? Is there something else (sumsing else), else than these Greek words by which we know Him?"

"There is the Spirit."

"Ah, the Spirit! Many spirits! And we as Christians, how do we as Christians try the spirits, to know that they be of God?"

"By reference to the Word."

"These words?"

"Yes. These words in Greek."

"So. These words in Greek. But there is yet something else, else than these Greek words, by which we know Him?"

"There is the example of others."

16

"Yes, the example of others. The saints, the heroes of faith. And from where do you learn the saints, the heroes of faith?"

"I mean the example of other people in general," I said. "I believe in common grace as well as special grace."

"Even so, all the better! Holy Socrates, pray for us!—to put Erasmus's words into English. In people in general you see the example of the living Word. In me, for example. In me you see the Word once again become flesh?"

What went through my mind then can best be explained in this way: it was not a good time for the True Reformed ministry. A hundred years ago a pastor named Van Horne had brought many bands of immigrants, schismatics from the state church of the Netherlands (which had separated from *them*, they would have said), across the Atlantic, down the Great Lakes, and across the prairies to Iowa. He had laid out the streets of the town of Hebron, established its government and its churches and its schools, and planted the oak trees which still stood in the town park. In the center of this grove stood a large boulder into which was set a bronze plaque commemorating the first sermon he had preached in the state. He founded Hebron College and Seminary in 1876 and served as its first president. He was the mayor of the town and district representative to the state capital at Iowa City as well as minister of the Center Street Church. The last heirs of his tradition of worldly learning and broad leadership, like my own minister back in Orangetown, Pastor Boom, were aging—or deceased. A younger generation who had served as chaplains in the Second War or in Korea, or in foreign missions or city ghettos, or in industry or politics, was still to come. Meanwhile the dominant generation were those whom my father in an unguarded moment once called "stiffheads," men who had survived the doctrinal and factional clashes in the twenties and whose major qualifications were a narrow experience and rigid views—a harsh judgment, perhaps, but I was a pre-seminary student then and, like my father, something of a stiffhead myself, and this is how I saw the examples before me.

On the other hand there was my instructor in Greek, four or five years older than I. He seemed older than that. He possessed seven or eight languages, finding it normal and natural to discuss Aristotle in Greek, Aquinas in Latin, Calvin in French, Luther in German, and Bronkema in either Frisian or Dutch. He spoke English with a stronger accent than I had ever heard in Orangetown, an accent thickened, in his case, by a sinus or adenoid condition. The body in his scheme of values ranked low. He had acne and poor teeth and wore double-breasted suits. He seemed to take no nourishment except coffee and cigarettes. He had no recreation but chess and the piano—now and then in the evenings the piano in the student lounge would pour forth Chopin, Beethoven, Tchaikovsky into the surprised air, and we would know that it was Mr. Van Wetback or one of his immigrant friends. (He must have known something of soccer; once at a seminarians' picnic he caused a sensation by trying to play volleyball with his feet.) He had never set his hand to the plow, or to the screwdriver or lawnmower, or even to the steering wheel of a car. He was the family scholar and represented a tribe of relatives who were proud to pay his way through the university and seminary with manual labor of their own.

I, however, was patriotically monolingual, as we had all been trained to be since the liberals of the twenties had won their battle to make English the dominant language of church and school—their lone victory, not counting the use of the Christmas tree (which would have happened anyway), or the adoption of Sunday school (supported by liberals because it was American, and by conservatives because it added another hour's activity to the day of rest). I knew that one justified the intellectual life by being well-rounded, by participating in many "activities," and by earning callouses in the real world. I sang in the choir, I played third base, I swam and did the long jump, I participated in the Literary Club and, hesitantly, in the Philosophers' Circle, which was dominated by Greek-speaking immigrants; and in the summers I hammered nails and poured cement for my father.

I was an American, and Mr. Van Wetback (as I now to my chagrin began to think of him) was not; and nothing could be done about that.

"Yes," I said finally. "You are such an example to me."

"I am glad to hear you say so!"

He smiled, a weak, tentative smile, and I saw that the conversation had been a test for him as much as for me, and that he wished we had been able to speak more personally and openly. He needed acceptance, as we called it. Instead of giving him that I had managed to challenge him on the only ground where he stood firm—his instructorship.

18

"And by what means do you know me, or anyone else, to be such an example?"

"By reference to the Scriptures, the Testament you hold in your hand."

He stood up. I stood up with him and we shook hands. He was perspiring.

"Do you see at what I am driving? It is hard too much to emphasize the importance of the word!"

"I agree," I said.

"Of course do not misunderstand me! Historically speaking your point is well taken, the Spirit produces the Church, the Church produces the Word, that is all perfectly correct!"

"Well, thank you," I said. "I'm sorry I took up so much of your time."

He shrugged and smiled briefly. When I left to walk home through the April evening, trying to think of myself as a Prospective Teacher of the Humanities, he was lighting another cigarette and turning back to his manuscript.

CHAPTER THREE

AT CITY HALL

I arrived at Calumet's City Hall wearing the wool jacket and knitted tie I had taken along from school to make a good impression during my interview. But I hadn't counted on the heat. It was a warm May Saturday, and after climbing the two flights of marble stairs—the elevators seemed not to be working on Saturdays—I paused to catch my breath. The Park Department and Sanitary Disposal offices were dark behind their frosted-glass doors, but between them ("halfway between Parks and Garbage," according to the departmental joke I heard later) the Recreation Department office was open, the lights on. I wiped my forehead with a handkerchief, and when my heartbeat slowed I went in.

The outer office was a long L-shaped room. Behind a counter there were rows of green wooden chests, some with lids and some without, that seemed struggling to contain basketballs, softballs, scissors, shears, coping saws, bats, bases, volleyballs, jacks, sandpaper, crepe paper, tacks, brads, nails, checkerboards, ping-pong paddles, horseshoes, beanbags, rubber rings, paste, hammers, glue. Piled among the crates were overturned wooden benches and tables and sawhorses, all in Park Department green, some with fresh paint and some with broken boards. Atop these piles lay ping-pong and volleyball nets as if to dry. In front of the counter, leaning against it, were three people about my age: playground leaders, I assumed, since they looked at home where they were and one of them—the dark, slender one— had a T-shirt with "Calumet Rec. Dept." stenciled on it. He talked excitedly, waving his arms.

"Kid, that's marvelous! You see what pull means in this department?"

21

His voice was high and conspiratorial; dark whiskers showed through his shave. The other male, a husky redhead, gripped a softball bat and kept taking short golf-iron swings with it toward his feet. He wore Bermuda shorts and a T-shirt: "Michigan State Spartans" stretched across his chest in two green rows. The short blond girl between them wore a wrinkled cotton skirt and, like the others, canvas shoes. "But God," she was saying in a loud whisper, "can you imagine what that park would be like in fifteen minutes if she didn't—I mean if she wasn't—I mean, God!"

"God," the redhead agreed. He shook his head, chipping another practice shot past his bent knees.

I edged past the three play-leaders toward a gray-haired woman who sat behind a desk at the end of the counter—Mrs. Nikkerson, the playground handicrafts teacher, I learned later; but at the moment she contributed to my feeling of being overdressed. She wore a gray smock decorated with a tissue-paper flower and around her neck a lanyard with a silver whistle. She had a way of smiling toward me and frowning at her typewriter at the same time that made her seem both cheerful and worried.

"You must be Mr. Adrian, ah. . . ." On the folder on her desk I recognized the two capital *V*'s. Behind me the eager whispering suddenly ceased, and I felt perspiration slide down my ribs.

"Vanden Vaarten. I'm here for my interview with Mr. Harmon."

"Oh, yes. Now, let's first fill out your staff card, shall we?"

She was a slow and hesitant typist, and as she read questions from the card in her machine I had to recite the answers and then spell them out. My name. My grade school, my high school, my college. My religious "preference." As I repeated the words "True" and "Reformed" and "Christian" for the fourth time it was a relief to hear the conversation resume behind me. The three voices were kept low, apparently so that Mrs. Nikkerson could not hear, but I caught what sounded like "tough park" repeated several times and, repeated more than anything else, the word "God." "God, Red, you wouldn't want it, I wouldn't want it, I mean after all, my God!" For the blond girl it was a two-syllable complaint: "*Gah*-ud, that's *terrible*!" "Gah," the red-head would say, or "Guh," like a word for excrement, and I could picture the bat swinging down toward his feet. For the dark-whiskered young man it was a diminutive prefix, an expression of tenderness or endearment, as in "Oh God kid I know," or "God Red that's too much." Despite all I had been taught to feel about the breaking of the third commandment—hatred for the sin, pity for the sinner, sorrow for the adulteration of our mother tongue—I found in my heart at that moment only a kind of envy for the ease of their profanity, and a feeling that of the three I liked the dark-haired one the best.

"Are you a citizen?"

"A citizen?" In my confusion I was about to produce my wallet and draft-registration card.

"I mean of Indiana," Mrs. Nikkerson said.

"Oh, no. I live in Illinois."

"It's for the state income tax," she said. "You can be glad if you're not."

While she filed my staff card I waited on a metal folding chair. I wanted to take off my jacket but didn't want to be taking it off at the moment Mr. Harmon called. The other three had their backs toward me, their heads together confidentially. Remember Fourth of July last year? God yes, but do you remember the Circus? And the party? The party we had after Olympic Day! Remember when Schultzie and Sue and Mason and Hermie and Josie and the kids from St. Cat's and that little kid from Purdue, what was his name—my God, do you remember that?

My own memories of Calumet were of Christmas shopping trips when I was a boy. Coming from the south and west you had to pass City Hall in order to get to the stores downtown, and Gordon and I would watch for its gray, vaguely Roman bulk like sailors trying to sight the Cape. Each office window would be decorated with a wreath and candle, and a string of colored lights marked the piazza railing. The tall blue spruce in the square was spiraled with paper chains and popcorn balls made by schoolchildren, and lit with bulbs turned on by Calumet's mayor in the same way that the President turned on the lights of the national tree in Washington. Behind the decorated spruce, during the shopping season, stood a wooden cottage or office trimmed with cardboard icicles and candy canes, where if you stood in a long line you could get to see Santa Claus—though for us he was a pagan figure and as much off-limits as Sunday work. But the Christmas when I was six, with the connivance of an aunt from Michigan who was worldly and taught in the public schools of Muskegon, I got to stand in line outside Santa's office on the City Hall lawn, the Jackie Robinson of my sect, and finally to tell Santa what I wanted and what a

23

good boy I had been, while my mother waited doubtfully outside in the snow. In later years she took Paul and Gordon to see Santa herself—"Adrian got to go," she told my father; in fact Santa took the same road into our Christmas as the Sunday papers into our Sabbath.

Another memory: Thanksgiving in a fancy Calumet restaurant when I was nine or ten, Paul still a baby. My father, perhaps to compensate for our daring in celebrating away from home, made his thanks-giving louder and longer than usual, and as he prayed on and on I became conscious of a changed quality in the clatter around us and opened my eyes. Beyond the centerpiece of Indian corn, chrysanthemums, and pipe-cleaner Pilgrims I saw a tall man in a dark suit, faceless behind a camera. A flashbulb went off, then another. I closed my eyes, and when at last the "Amen" was said the man and his camera were gone. I never saw him again, nor did I see the picture I was sure would appear in the Trib or some other paper, showing all the family bowed in thanks except me with my scared eyes open and Paul in his high chair waving a peppermint-striped swizzle stick. Except for the flaring fireballs I saw whenever I blinked he could have been a projection of my own mind.

"Kid! You're new this year, right?"

I stood up. The dark-whiskered playground leader had come suddenly toward me and was shaking my hand with both of his. "Listen, I'm Sammy and this is Debbie and this is Red. Say hi, you guys, this is—what was your name again? This is Adrian, you guys! I'm Sammy, this is Debbie, this is Red. Don't you just hate introductions? Hey, I hope you like it! Listen"—Sammy's face came toward my ear and his voice dropped. "Whatever you do, don't let them stick you with a tough park. What was your name again? Anyway, Adrian, I hope you'll have a great time here. I know you will, we all do!"

The door to the inner office opened and Sammy and the others turned to welcome the tall Oriental girl who came out. She wore a smock like the secretary's but without the paper flower. "Jeannie! Did you make it? My God, that's marvelous, what park did you get? Really? Kid, it'll be like old times, we'll all be together again!"

Jeannie too wore canvas shoes and, like the others, no socks on her bare brown calves. I heard the four of them laughing behind me, and as the secretary showed me to the inner office I felt I was moving forward on feet that were bound, in their Sunday leather, like the feet of the Chinese women I had heard about in stories of the missionaries.

Mr. Harmon was a white-haired man in his early fifties, taller than I and broad-shouldered, with a large hand and a powerful handshake. His voice, jovial and insistent, reminded me of my father's, but it had a formal dignity about it that was new to me. Later I learned that he had been brought up in Texas and had gone to school there, selling shoes to put himself through, and had been a track-and-field athlete and a Rhodes scholar before coming to Calumet in the thirties to found and direct its Recreation Department. He removed my jacket and hung it on an empty coatrack. He wore a short-sleeved shirt that at first I mistook for a basketball referee's, but as the interview went on its blue and white stripes together with Harmon's white hair and ruddy complexion, and his habit of leaning forward with two fingers pointed at me, steeple fashion, merged in my mind with the figure of Uncle Sam in recruitment posters down on the first floor.

The playground system in Calumet began during the Depression, Harmon said, as a program of stay-at-home vacations for the poor and unemployed, a program to keep people off the streets—"though that was never my idea of their primary purpose." Over the years the playgrounds had begun to assume their more important and more exciting functions, until now they were primarily places of recreation—re-creation, Harmon stressed—and education. "The very first contact of many of our youngsters, Adrian, with their community and government, the first chance to find a place in some kind of community in which they can develop a sense of responsibility and discipline and usefulness and dignity. . . ."

Harmon's office was not the plush, air-conditioned suite my father imagined when he spoke of tax-eaters and bureaucrats, chiding Gordon and me at the same time for working as if, like WPA men, we were "afraid to kill the job." The temperature was as tropic as any I had faced while heaving slabs of shingles up a roof. The rug (parkboard green like the chests outside) was threadbare, the furniture Spartan. Plain board shelves carried a few books and a dusty row of athletic trophies and team photos. There was a plaque from the Franklin Street Mother's Club honoring Harmon for "promoting brotherhood." Under his glass desktop I could see the Declaration of Independence clipped from an insurance ad: "When in the course of human events" at the top, the Hartford stag logo at the bottom, and, in between, the phrase "the pursuit of happiness," which I had quoted (disapprovingly) in a term paper on Carlyle and John Stuart Mill earlier that year. Taped to Harmon's gray filing cabinet was a glossy photo of a girl who was singing, or so I imagined—her eyes were closed, her arms were outstretched, and a microphone rose toward her wide smile. Her face and her round, thin arms were dark, and though she wore a white gown—not dungarees, as in the newspaper clipping—I was sure it was Barbara Robinson from the brilliance of the smile and her air of abandonment in the audience, the moment, the song.

"Now, Adrian." Harmon opened the manilla folder which Mrs. Nikkerson had put on his desk. "You have prepared for the ministry, have you not?"

"Yes, sir, I have. But I'm graduating with a degree in Humanities."

"And these are all parochial schools you've attended? Grade school? High school? College?"

"Well, yes, sir." There was a distinction we made between our schools, which were run by a board of laymen, and other religious schools which were run by the Church, and thus properly "parochial," but I decided not to go into it.

"And you have had to study Latin? And Greek?"

"Yes, sir, although my major, as I say—"

"And you have worked for your father during the summer months? In the construction business, full time, every summer?"

"Yes, sir. I was able to get in some sports in high school and college, though . . . ."

My mind raced along my file ahead of Harmon's eyes, and I wondered whether he would give me a plus for weighing 165 and standing 6'1" or for having younger brothers and reporting that I liked children but hadn't had much experience with them.

"What do you think, Adrian"—he asked this suddenly, with an air of catching me off guard—"about the Supreme Court's decision?"

Any reference to "the Court's decision" then meant the 1954 decision on racial integration in public schools. I answered that I was totally in favor of it. I was pleased to be able at last to declare allegiance to the public and the people so often mentioned in Harmon's history of the Calumet playgrounds—though when I remembered the Court's opinion that "separate" schools were inherently unequal, I wondered whether I should have qualified my answer.

After that, as Harmon began asking specific questions about the playgrounds, I felt my chances sinking. Before my father got into the construction business I had re-created myself like other Orangetown boys and girls: by cutting asparagus and weeding onions and picking tomatoes. What I knew about the playgrounds I had learned since receiving Harmon's letter—by driving past several of them on my way to the interview.

"Do you happen to know anything about Hoover Street?" Harmon asked finally, leaning back in his chair, and I suddenly remembered that there was a place in Calumet called Island Park, not far from downtown, where the city held its annual fireworks display. Orangetowners sometimes visited there on the Fourth of July to escape the tamer celebration in Bok's Grove, where sack races were held and cotton candy eaten to raise money for the local schools. In order to get there from the south you took a street called Hoover Street through the Negro section of town.

"I believe Hoover Street is on the south side," I said.

"That's it!" Harmon leaned forward, smiling, his steepled forefingers aiming at me. "That's exactly right, Adrian. You are exactly right, and I'm glad you know something about the area. That is the playground where I think you can help us most. I think you can do a great deal of good for our program and learn a good deal yourself for whatever career you choose. Now. How does that idea strike you?"

"I would like that very much," I said. My relief was so great I did not notice for a moment that Harmon went on talking as though he had me to convince. He was confident that he could get Barbara Robinson back for another summer. She was an experienced leader— she had had a year on Hoover Street—and she would be a great help to me. The playground supervisor, Mr. Nikkles, whom I would meet at the June orientation, would also be a great help. He was sure that between these two and the rest of the playground staff I would get all the help I needed in order to do a first-rate job. We were standing now, Harmon's voice jovial and congratulatory; he was shaking my hand, and I realized that the interview was over. When he asked whether I had any questions, I could only think to ask where, exactly, Hoover Street Playground was.

"Sixteenth and Hoover," Harmon said. "There is a traffic light there, so you won't be able to miss it. And is there anything else?"

I asked whether the photograph on his filing cabinet was of Barbara Robinson.

"It is indeed, Adrian. I believe that must be the Anthem she's singing; it was at the beginning of last year's Playground Circus. The Star-Spangled Banner. In addition to her other talents she has a very fine voice. She's an absolutely first-rate person, and I'm sure you'll get along very well together. As I say, I'm confident we'll get her back."

With his right arm around my shoulders, his left hand presenting me my jacket—why don't you just carry this, he said—he brought me to the outer office. I was disappointed to see that Sammy, Jeannie, Debbie, and Red, my four colleagues, had already left. He introduced me to Mrs. Nikkerson as the new boys' leader at Hoover Street.

"Congratulations," she said, smiling at me and frowning toward her typewriter. "We have just one more form for you to fill out and sign. Be sure to do it accurately. It allows the City to pay you."

I leaned over the counter, writing carefully. The space for the signature had a small X inked in next to it, and above that was a statement which I read once, and then again more slowly, about the city's liability being limited to those accidents which occurred in the line of duty. As I signed the form, something in Mrs. Nikkerson's air of waiting, or perhaps Harmon's joviality, made me think of Sammy's words of advice.

"Is Hoover Street what they call a 'tough park'?" I asked.

Mr. Harmon, who had been standing behind the counter, came around to the front of it, laughing agreeably. His two hands gripped my shoulders.

"That's exactly why we want you for the job," he said.

CHAPTER FOUR

ORANGETOWN

DURING the two-week interval between the end of school and the beginning of the playground season, I moved my things from Hebron back home—or rather to the new house which my father had finished that spring. It was a brick "ranch-style" (as I had to learn to call it) in an open marshy area south of the Grand Trunk tracks, with parquet floors and central air-conditioning—a necessity, my father admitted, since it stood on treeless land and had no attic and its flat, dark roof absorbed the sun—and with conscious audacity he was planning to ask thirty thousand dollars for it.

My mother vacuumed the new drapes and carpets every day and kept the thermopane windows spic-and-span because anyone who drove by was a potential customer. The front yard had a For Sale sign before it had a lawn. We didn't finish spreading the piles of black dirt until late in the summer, and the big "V" of my father's new logo, doing double duty for "Vanden" and "Vaarten," pointed downward into bare brown clay. Entering the back door you saw a rectangular metal sign that said "Doors and windows are all-aluminum," and entering in the front you saw "This house is heated electrically" instead of the sampler that met your eye in the old house on Indiana Street, "Work, For The Night Is Coming," which had been stitched (during daylight hours, I always hoped) by my grandmother's mother.

My mother loved the new house but was afraid to get used to it. Sitting in the living room with my *Calumet Playground Manual* I would see her go into the kitchen in the dark and then hear the garbage disposal go on, and then off, and then the overhead fan, on and off, before she finally hit the switch for the light above the sink. On the new "built-in" stove she consistently turned on the back burner instead of the front, the left instead of the right, sometimes lighting all four burners before getting the one she wanted. She had spent a good fifteen years in the other house, and I suppose she kept the old neural connections the way an immigrant unconsciously keeps his lips, tongue, and teeth ready for a return to the old language, or the way she kept her Plato and Bronkema with her over the years; they had become a part of the self.

The house had three bedrooms, none of them for me. Paul's old bed had been sold, and he was sleeping on my bunk, above which he had hung model Spitfires and Messerschmidts and P-48's as if in remembrance of the dreams I used to have while sleeping there. The other bunk was in Gordon's room, which was full of his orange and blue OTRCHS sweaters and jackets, and pictures of his girl friends, and dumbbells for his biceps. It was planned that I, for the summer, should sleep on the old sofa in the basement. The old gas refrigerator was down there—generally filled with six-packs of beer, as I recall, for my father smoked and drank more that summer—and the ping-pong table which Gordon and I had put together out of oak boards. After the season started I would sometimes have breakfast or lunch alone at the ping-pong table under its spotlight, sitting on boxes of my old books (Huck and Tom and Penrod and Mowgli the Jungle Boy), which were awaiting the sale of the house or my departure, whichever came first. And I would read one of the biographies, Washington or Lincoln or George Washington Carver (the "boy with the green thumb"), which my mother used to read with me in the old house after Gordon went to bed.

It was through a loan arranged by Elizabeth's father, Johnny Van Dyken, who was the town mayor and a director of the Savings and Loan, that my father was able to build the new house. Johnny was a good friend of my father's; they often talked of going fishing in Wisconsin together—in the fall they hunted rabbits and pheasants, though my mother refused to cook rabbit, which reminded her too much of a baby, she said—and that spring they bought a boat and outboard motor together. When I drove home from school and saw the boat in the garage, slanting forward on its trailer like a ship ready for christening, I thought I had the wrong house. "When will you use it?" I asked him, knowing that he worked six days a week and ceased on the seventh only because he was commanded to do so—and the same commandment forbade him to use the boat on Sunday.

He would only grin, enjoying the moral problems brought on by wealth. Maybe he would ask the minister to go for a ride, he would say, nudging me in the ribs; "Then we'll all be in the same *boat*."

He and my brothers spent hours in the evenings "breaking in the motor," which was clamped to a barrel of water in the garage. After the playground season began I would come home at nine or even ten and they would be pouring gas and oil into it from the red flex-necked can; the garage and the driveway would be full of smoke. "Start her up again—start her on Start, don't be a dumbhead! Use less choke this time. Pauly, you want to lose a hand? Don't force it, don't *force it*"—my father's voice, although *forcing* things was a bad habit of his own, as he had had to admit most recently just the summer before, when it cost us a burned-out clutch on the Jeep.

I would go inside and find my mother scrubbing the new stove and sink, putting linens away in the new closet, dusting the new living room. "Think about where you're putting your feet! I just got this place cleaned up." I would go to the basement and read Myrdal's *An American Dilemma* and Arna Bontemps and J. Saunders Redding and the other books I had brought home from the Calumet library, sitting on the old sofa and reading by the ping-pong table spotlight, and perhaps not seeing the others at all unless my father came down to get another beer.

If I felt left out it was my own fault, for my father had made it plain that I could be his partner if I wanted to. During the pre-playground period, after a day of hauling cement or laying tile together, we would stand in the backyard next to the piles of dirt still unspread, the smell of the north wind from Gary mingling with that of his can of beer and burning cigarette, and he would point southeast along the railroad track. "We've already bought the land"—"we," I took it, meaning him and the bank— "and now I'll put a couple more houses on it, *or*," as if I had objected, "maybe a house and a couple of apartments. You see what I mean?"

I asked whether the presence of the railroad tracks wouldn't lower the value of residential property. No, no, no, he said, I had it all wrong; of course the land was cheaper to *buy*, but once a house was built the railroad became an advantage. It provided a built-in view. It preserved a certain amount of open space for the homeowner, like a lake or a park. Trains were becoming a quaint, old-fashioned means of transportation; in a few years' time to have a railway in your backyard would be as much a prestige factor as having a stable or a fleet of sailboats was now. "City people love trains, Adrian." Hearing him talk like this, transforming the oilcars and coal-gondolas that rumbled by four times a day into something out of *The Little Engine That Could*, and his property into the prestigious Semaphore Estates and Grand Trunk manor houses of the future, I found myself wishing for more than one reason that he had remained a salesman and left the building of houses to others.

"What about Barnema?" I asked. Old man Barnema, the owner of the tarpaper-brick farmhouse just across the tracks, had known the advantages of railroad-side living all his life. Thrice widowed, he had fourteen children, most of whom, with their families, drove over after church every Sunday morning. During these visits Barnema's full driveway and the shoulder along 192nd Street looked like part of a used-car lot, and we could smell the aroma of percolating coffee at my father's house. One corner of Barnema's yard was marked off from the heavy clay of his fields by a windmill, the other by a carved wooden duck, both arms flying in the wind; between these there was a porcelain hen and baby chicks, a live goat, a rabbit hutch, three white geese, a German shepherd, and many cats. When his family came over on Sundays, Barnema's yard looked like the children's section at the zoo.

"That's a good point," my father said. "He's old, some day he'll sell. The two farms next to him too. We can expand east. All that land will go residential, clear up to the supermarket. Those onion fields are already drained."

Beyond the three farms we could see the searchlight at Harvey's Supermarket, new that year, and another mark of the town's progress. Beyond that were the dark oaks of Bok's Grove; beyond that, invisible, the church and Pastor Boom's parsonage; and to the northeast the glowing lights of Calumet and Hammond, Whiting and Gary. How he enjoyed looking eastward, planning his future! "Look, I've got to carry more money around with me now than I used to make in a week"—showing me the inside of his wallet.

These talks left me uneasy, though not enough to change my mind. I remembered an incident from my high school years when the new expressway went through and the telephone service was consolidated. There had been some trouble then—some street signs knocked over, some telephone directories stolen and burned—when Church

Road became 192nd, Van Groningen 189th, and so on. At the time I had been too preoccupied with getting away from Orangetown to pay much attention. But now the memory of that wild and futile gesture, which had been applauded by at least some of the teachers as, I suppose, the last flourishing of a flag, made me aware that progress once started is not always conveniently stopped.

Now that I was looking forward once again to leaving my hometown—at the same time resenting my father's attempts to sell the home and change the town—I should have recognized that his joy in seeing Orangetown "move" until it joined the wider "area" was not much different from mine at the prospect of joining Barbara Robinson and the humanities. But I kept my distance. I must have felt his notion of progress was less spiritual than mine. In any case, he offered a share of his dream, I refused, and the rest of the summer we kept ourselves apart. Staring eastward past the piles of unspread dirt, gesturing toward Barnema's house first with the beer can, then the smoking cigarette, he dreamed aloud as persuasively as he could while I edged away toward basement and bunk and books, my real life. No, no; sorry; my plans are all set. He could carry on without me, I thought, just as he had during the four years I was away at college, worrying about Greek and baseball, and Shakespeare and sin and love.

One night during that two-week interval, Elizabeth's last night at home before leaving for the Michigan sanitorium where she would begin her first job, we went together to the Calumet Skyway Drive-in to say good-bye.

Although movie-going was one of the worldly amusements prohibited by the fathers of our church, going to the Skyway had become a kind of tradition for us. During my sophomore year at college and Elizabeth's first year as a nursing student we went there in order to return each other's class rings, a ceremony we undertook so that we would each be free to date other people and find our own independent futures. Somehow, though, the ceremony needed renewing. In high school I had gotten through my adolescence by playing the role of skinny wiseguy, all elbows, knees, and mouth; Elizabeth Van Dyken then seemed to me serene and poised, self-consciously solid and stately in figure but with a beautiful shy smile that made her seem suddenly, appealingly frail. In college, when I entered my serious stage as a preseminarian, the memory of her face—neat blond hair framing a complexion that had never known or needed makeup, at a time when the standard look was a bright slash of red across the mouth—used to tantalize me with a hint of something exotic and worldly. Perhaps my image ebbed and flowed in the same way in her mind. Whatever the reason, the pattern of our relationship during the last three years had been two semesters of dating others followed by a summer of dating each other, often at the Calumet Skyway, where we renewed our vows not to go steady with more passion and tenderness than we felt with any of those we were renouncing each other for.

If there was a reason for choosing the drive-in theatre for this annual ceremony, other than the movies themselves (*The Country Girl, Roman Holiday, The African Queen*), it might have been the fact that Hollywood had been certified worldly by our spiritual leaders, and it was exactly The World that we planned to confront and conquer in our own futures, together or separately. We discussed freedom and responsibility at the movies as earnestly as an earlier generation debated Prohibition while drinking. Perhaps we felt something of a deflowering taking place in this quasi-rebellious act, and thus a commitment running counter to our vows of renunciation—though in fact Hollywood had taken my own virginity some years earlier, on a trip to Chicago with the same Michigan aunt who had introduced me to Santa Claus (thus earning the nickname "Aunt Pandaria" for her role in my life), when after a quick tour of the Museum of Science and Industry I was exposed to The World in the form of *I Remember Mama*, starring Irene Dunne and Barbara Bel Geddes.

This time, however, we were saying good-bye at the beginning, not the end of the summer, and we were both leaving home, so we thought, for good. Perhaps that contributed to our confused emotions that night. It was a clear, cloudless evening, and as we topped the brief swells where the expressway rose over Chicago and Lake and Calumet and State Line Avenues we had a view of the grain elevators looming behind us in Calumet Harbor, the cloudy fires of Gary thickening the horizon ahead. To the north foundries were banging and yard-engines rammed trains together behind piles of coal and scrap, and millions of people lived by loyalties unknown to us and unimaginable, except as they appeared on billboards along the way; to the south slumbered flat farms and leafy villages raised out of the wetlands years ago by True Reformed pioneers too late or weary to go with

Pastor Van Horne all the way to the good land of Iowa—people who trusted their distance from the City and, later, the expressway with its double fences, to keep their towns unspotted. There among those steeple-and-water-tower towns (five steeples for every tower) we had grown up together, but as separate as a year's difference in age could make us, discovering each other belatedly in the "mixed" junior-senior classes (Chemistry and Physics, alternate years, Mr. Radius) by the accident of alphabetical proximity that later seemed providential. There lay our childhood and youth. Like the senior girls who had cried when Miss Kooy read "Fern Hill" on the last May day of their high school careers, Elizabeth was wiping her cheek even before the late darkness descended and the movie (*The Story of Ruth*) came on, and seeing her take her handkerchief from her purse I felt the premonitory lump in the throat which is the male's substitute for tears.

We skipped our usual debate on moral choice vs. moral compulsion that night. Nor do I recall that we repeated our vow not to think of each other as the only one, not to feel *obligated* to write. Perhaps by now it had come to seem unnecessary or even comic. We took consolation from the postponement of our own moral choice until later—Michigan was not so very far away, and I would be home all summer—and after that we were content to sit close together thinking our own thoughts.

On the screen outside our windshield we saw being dramatized the famous words of loyalty that came through our car windows along with the shrieks and giggles and slamming of doors that made us feel already adult: Whither thou goest I will go; thy people shall be my people, thy God my God. We recognized the story, but the portrayal of Ruth as a Moabite love-goddess before her transformation into a God-fearing Israelite farmer's wife was new to us, as was her meeting with Boaz on the threshing-floor under what seemed rather pagan circumstances. The stars, slowly circling above the Skyway until south became north and north south, echoed our disorientation as we watched. Who was to be Elizabeth's Boaz, where would I find my Ruth? And—a question that might have occurred to Ruth herself, when sick for home she stood in tears amid the alien corn—in which direction lay The World, and where were the people of God?

All in all, however, it was not an unhappy occasion. Like the graduating seniors of my high school class, we were not really sad; we were young, our lives were before us, we were shaking the dust of the past from our feet and starting clean, a fresh new start away from home, and with wholesome nostalgic memories to boot. We left the theatre before the last lights came on, and when we said good-bye again on Elizabeth's front porch we were smiling, not crying. A fresh wind was blowing out of the west, where a first-quarter moon had just gone down, and spring peepers peeped in every ditch. I drove home to my basement bed, somehow feeling—just as Ruth must have felt, I thought—that what we were doing was right.

I met my parents' new neighbor, old man Barnema, for the first time that summer on the Saturday before the playground season began. It was also my last meeting with Johnny Van Dyken. It was in the morning, and my father and I had been stapling rolls of insulation into the attic of a new house he had started. Paul, who was only thirteen, was being given Saturdays off (something I didn't recall happening when I was thirteen), and Gordon was home to help my mother with the shopping at Harvey's, since she didn't drive. My father habitually worked in bursts of furious labor, during which it was hard for anyone to keep up with him, let alone someone with as many chromosomes from my mother as I had been given; he paused frequently, however, for rest and for fellowship with whoever came along. Ordinarily I preferred to contribute my share by working ahead while he stopped to chat with the plumber or the mailman or drove off to Dommer's Diner for midmorning coffee; but on this Saturday the sun on the other side of the roof was baking hot, the job dusty and breathless, and I went with him in the pickup and felt that the chill along my arms from Dommer's noisy air conditioner had been earned.

Dommer's on a workday morning—which meant every morning but Sunday, when of course it was closed—was a kind of men's club for the town, just as in the afternoons at three-thirty every day it became a club for teens. On Saturday morning farmers who were in town for fuel or machinery parts met in three- and four-man clots along the curving counter. Retired farmers came in to talk about weather and prices, and on every day but Saturday, when he visited the sick, my grandfather as a retired onion-set man would join them in their booth in front of the plate-glass window. (His retirement routine included a walk to the bank, a walk to the post office, and a walk to the diner—though my grandmother used to wonder that he preferred Dommer's coffee to hers.) West Ridge merchants, sometimes joined by some of the men from downtown (where the old Orange Restaurant had been taken over by a Greek from Calumet Heights), liked to sit in front of the window where they could keep an eye on the flow of traffic; the pop man, the laundry man, the bread-and-pie man grouped together near the cash register where they could settle accounts with George Dommer when he came by to ring up a customer.

My father liked to meet Johnny Van Dyken at the diner, and that meant taking two or three tables in the middle, since Johnny, along with being mayor and a director of the bank and member of the Area Development Committee, was something of a humorist—his humor had a sober, melancholy hue, I always thought—and he generally drew a crowd. Today he was with Lamberts the electrician and Jake, a short, stocky milkman for Swets Dairy and a firm backer of CLOSE—as a boy I would hear him shout in his high-pitched voice to another milkman, through the open full-length doors of their trucks, while icy water dripped, hissing, on the pavement: "Hey, Dick, remember we don't have no truck with the Teamsters, ha-ha-ha!"—and a house painter named Pete and the body man at Vroom's Ford Agency, and some others I don't recall.

Johnny Van Dyken was a good-looking man, his dark, curly hair showing a touch of gray; unlike Elizabeth, who cared more about neatness than style, he liked new clothes and was, as my father said, a "sharp dresser." That day he wore on his lapel a red-white-and-blue button that said "Business Is Good." He was the only one with a lapel to wear it on, but some of the others had buttons pinned to their coveralls or uniforms. "One of Johnny's ideas," someone explained. "Helps pump a little blood around town." They were all laughing, happy and self-congratulatory, and when my father asked for a button I remember Johnny taking his off to give to him and saying, "We don't need these any more, Gerrit. Business really *is* good." He sounded slightly nervous and worried, unlike the others, I thought—or perhaps I think so now, in retrospect.

Business Is Good was the theme of the conversation, along with the new supermarket and how Johnny deserved credit for bringing it to town. Perhaps as a compliment to me (and, by implication, Elizabeth) someone mentioned how hard it was to get his kids to think about college, because they had no sense of sacrifice and thought only

about working for the buck and didn't realize that without a degree
you wouldn't get far in this world. And some darker notes: the possible effects of outsiders' moving in among us, though the group
conceded that if they were attracted by our clean streets and honest
tradesmen and work-free Sundays they should be welcomed; "Let 'em
drop their paycheck in the collection once instead of the tavern," as
Jake put it. My father began to take a ribbing about the price he had
put on his house, with Johnny curtly defending him, and at this point
I noticed old man Barnema sitting alone at the counter—thin, white-
haired, deeply tanned—and I took my cup over to join him.

It was hard for me to think of him as lonely. Two dozen of his
descendants had been in his yard on the previous Sunday, and my
mother told me that each of his daughters and daughters-in-law had
him over for dinner twice a month, leaving him (according to my
calculations) with only one or two days to taste his own cooking.
Today, though, I had seen him trying to begin a conversation about
the fields' having too much moisture, or perhaps it was that they
needed more moisture—first with the farmers, then the retired farmers, then, as a last resort, with the delivery men; and now he sat
between two empty stools staring at his cup.

"Hello, neighbor." I thought I would ask him about Bobby, one
of the fourteen Barnemas who was a classmate of mine and whom I
had lost track of since high school.

He looked up, his eyes wide and startled.

"Adrian," I said. "Gerrit's boy. The new house across the tracks?"

"Oh? Ooh, hello." There was no recognition in his face but his
voice was high and eager. "Did you know George has a new baby?"

I did not, but I assumed old man Barnema was trying to place me.
"George was older; when he was in eighth grade I was only—"

"Lois has a new baby too. She lives north of Chicago now."

"That's nice. I think Lois was a year ahead of me."

Old man Barnema took a sip of cold coffee and smiled as if this
were the best of chats. "Did you know Joe was getting out of the
army in the fall?"

"No, I didn't know that. Joe was the youngest, wasn't he?"

"Unless they ship him overseas. They might do that. Were you
ever in the army?"

I shook my head.

38

"You must be Bobby's age. Bobby has to move, you know. Houston, Texas."

"Oh?"

"Him and the whole family."

"Bobby has a family? I didn't know he was married!"

"He works for the gas company. They gave him a big raise, he couldn't pass it up."

"Congratulations," I said. I tried to imagine Bobby Barnema, with whom I had thrown snowballs in the winter and played marbles in the spring, tossing his children into the air in Houston, Texas. I drank the rest of my coffee feeling as if I were late for something.

"That's no place to bring up a family," Barnema said. "None of our people out there."

"That's too bad."

"None of our churches. None of our schools."

"Yes, well—"

"How's that?"

"I say, that's too bad."

"I won't see them again. Maybe not even Christmas."

My father had paid his bill and was heading for the door. I tried to end in a major key. "It's a good thing Bobby isn't the only one," I said, edging away.

"That's right, Bobby isn't the only one. Elaine's husband wants to go to California. And George. Pearly's husband has to move, he doesn't know where yet. Did I tell you they might ship Joe overseas?"

"I think I'd better go, Mr. Barnema. I have to help my father."

"Your father?"

"Gerrit. The builder."

"Oh, Gerrit." He smiled and then his face clouded. "Aren't you the one who moved away?"

"No, I haven't moved. I've been at school."

"Did I tell you where Bobby's moving?"

"Yes. Good-bye, Mr. Barnema."

"Houston, Texas. That's over nine hundred miles, did you know that?"

I nodded, putting down a dime on the counter. "Good-bye. Maybe I'll see you sometime this summer."

My father had the motor running in the pickup, ready to go. "I thought I'd better get started," he said. "He's tough to break away from once he gets started talking."

Looking back at the diner I recognized, among the shadowy figures of the other customers, our new neighbor and Elizabeth's father, one white-haired and the other dark, waving good-bye to us through the plate-glass window as we drove away.

CHAPTER FIVE

HOOVER STREET

HOOVER Street! O Hoover (pronounced Hoo-vah, short for Hoover and Sixteenth Streets Playground), loveliest playground of them all! Not so large and rustic as Island Park between the two rivers, not new like Marquette-Joliet with its roofed patio and a cement floor so smooth you could slide on it, no, nor so well-equipped as the asphalted schoolyards with their basketball hoops and cyclone fences; yet in my memory it stands spacious and well-furnished and forever green, green as its grass and dandelions, the brightest spot on the map in our meeting room in the basement of City Hall. A tidy two-acre farm of which I was bailiff and warden: in the southeast corner the equipment shed and sandbox and kiddy toys; in the northwest the eight-by-eight foot backstop (largely ceremonial until with hammer and staples I closed the running hole along the bottom); down the right-field line a row of tall elms, down the left a gravel alley where the big kids parked their cars in the evenings and I lit fires for marshmallow and wiener roasts; on the south the swings and slides along Sixteenth Street, and on the east the lilacs and spirea along Hoover Street running back to the shed and headquarters.

What seems hard, now, to believe, I know was true: we were fenced in on two sides only, a low wire fence meant to protect children from traffic. On the west we looked toward a dead-end right-of-way and vacant lot owned by the valve works; on the north to the backyards of houses along the alley, where people sat on their porches of an evening and watched us play ball. I remember on one porch an old man, brown and bald, always wearing a blue shirt and red suspenders, and on another a large white woman who must have been the mother of the two children about six or seven years old, both spastic, who lurched and hobbled across the wet grass early in the mornings to sit on the bottom of the slide or hang on the monkey bars before the other children arrived. These people never seemed afraid that we would smash a window-screen or flowerpot with a stray line drive or vandalize their property while chasing it down—and though we chased many a foul ball down the alley I do not recall that we ever entered a backyard, fenced or unfenced, without courtesy and care, or that we were ever met with hostility.

Perhaps I have repressed or forgotten some incidents. Perhaps the people living in those houses were renters only and could afford to be relaxed about breakage they would not have to pay for. Perhaps the owners lived far away and were holding the property in hopes of selling for a good price when the Hoover Throughway came to pass—as it eventually did about ten years later. Now you can ride right over the top of the old Hoover Street Playground on six broad lanes north and south between I-80 and the Chicago Tollway; the only recognizable landmark is the valve works next to the Sixteenth Street off-ramp. Even so, I think of those benign watchers on the back porches as typical of the esprit of the neighborhood and the park that summer. If this be romantic nostalgia, I indulge it without apology. O sylvan Hoover, how often, in the space of twenty summers and winters, has my spirit turned to thee!

On the first day of Get-Acquainted Week (that is on Wednesday; Monday and Tuesday were for staff orientation), I parked my '48 Chevy under the elms and, after a moment's hesitation, left it unlocked. It was raining. Not a child was in sight, but my fingers were clumsy handling the new key ring at my belt and my heartbeat made the silver whistle tremble on my chest. Unlike the other leaders, who came to their playgrounds two by two on this rainy morning, male and female, like animals entering the ark, I had to face Hoover Street alone. Barbara was still at UCLA, Harmon had told me. From the other leaders I heard the reasons: west coast schools had a later semester than others; she was making up some work she still had to turn in in order to graduate; there was some difficulty about transferring to another school in the East. The stories differed, but their message was the same: first, Barbara was so important to the playground and the Department that they would let her arrive late; and, second, I would have to face Hoover Street for the first three days without her.

I see that I have borrowed the trick of oral outlining used so often during orientation by Curt Nikkles, the playground supervisor: "A, stationary equipment; B, issued equipment; C, non-returnable equipment. . . ." Fresh out of college, I suspected then that oral outlining betrayed a deep-seated fear of confusion. It was the kind of camouflage that appeared whenever any of my courses in history, literature, or philosophy approached the twentieth century—in other words, whenever information overwhelmed knowledge. Like the other oral outliners I had known, Nikkles made generous use of mimeographed handouts, masses of unsynthesized data in reams of purple and white. Ten weeks of programming, sixteen playgrounds and thirty-two leaders, thousands of children and truckloads of equipment together generated a nearly infinite number of possibilities for joyous combination, but also for collision, confrontation, and theft. (D, disappearing equipment, was Nikkles' humorous addition to the catalog.) Nikkles' job was to mediate between these millions of possible events on the one hand and Harmon's lofty principles of recreation on the other. About forty years old, with crew-cut hair (like myself and a third of the other male leaders), he was square-built and raspy-voiced; and although he bore the harrassments of his middle-administrative position with as good a grace as could be expected—it is not always easy to be detached and humorous about having to clean up the debris left by others—I tended to view him during orientation with the wary eyes of a recruit looking at a top sergeant.

I seemed to be the only rookie. While I jotted notes to myself and underlined in the Manual and the Handbook and tried to commit Nikkles' collected works to memory, the others, all of them veterans or at least the friends of veterans, leaned backward in their metal chairs in the basement of City Hall and gabbed contentedly, dressed in crinolines and cottons as if for a picnic. My left hand, not busy with the pencil, seemed constantly in the air. When was it, again, that the johns were best kept locked? What, exactly, was the difference between high-organized and low-organized games? About handcrafts, did you say we should forbid the carving of guns and knives or just discourage it? After such sessions, those leaders who could still tolerate the sound of my voice would take me aside and advise me to

43

rely on my "playground sense" and on Barbara—neither of which was available to me, however, on opening day.

And yet, come to think of it, it was the very sympathy of these veterans, it was their tongue-clucking over the unwisdom and the un*fair*ness of sending a greenhorn to a "tough park," it was the head-shaking allusions to Hoover's children "getting cut" or "pulling a knife," it was their sorrowful admonitory references to a chap named— I can't recall, but it was a long, polysyllabic name, a name from non-Anglo-Saxon Europe, a white boy's name—who got "run off" from Hoover Street the year before, or in one version "broke down" in August, so that Barbara had to finish alone—it was their sympathy, so-called, that was worse than all my ignorance.

Not only had I never played on a Calumet playground, I had not yet seen a black person face-to-face except for the Nigerian missionary who had been trained by our denomination to run a hospital somewhere between Kano and Kaduno, and who showed films at Hebron and talked about "the bush" and elephantiasis and sleeping sickness in an accent (I thought) like that of David Niven in *The Moon Is Blue*, which I had sneaked off to Dubuque to see. Compensatingly, I was almost as innocent of prejudice as I was of knowledge. My father mingled, at least on its lower levels, in the world of commerce, and the commercial world's categories, including ethnic ones, came easily to his lips—except that my mother, whose commerce was in the world of books and whose categories were the official ones of the democratic State and the all-embracing Church, exerted a dampening effect. Once, during the war, my father told us he had seen in the bakery two Jamaicans who had gone to the end of the line when a white woman entered; they "really knew their place." This he said with genuine pleasure in his voice, pleased, no doubt, at the modesty shown by the black foreigners but even more at the liberalism he was able to display by admiring it before my mother. I think he genuinely intended to please and surprise her. Instead he was surprised when she let him have it with both barrels, sacred and secular, St. Paul and the Gettysburg Address. As a result of her influence he was, in fact, one of the more liberal members of his race, class, time, and place— at least when my mother was around. He was the first father on our block, I remember, to admit before the second Joe Louis–Max

Schmeling fight that he would be pulling for "the American" rather than "the Kraut."

Just before my Hoover Street summer, I think it was, the young Henry Aaron made the sports pages as a result of his innocence when warned about the famous pitchers he would soon have to meet. "How will you do against Don Newcombe, Henry?" "Who *he?*" was Aaron's reply. In like manner I, when facing on opening day the various bogeymen of popular culture thrown up to me by my well-meaning new colleagues, would have preferred to think "Who he?" and preserve my innocence as long as possible. One of the sympathizers, after all (it was Red, Red Buchler), had asked me whether my hometown was the place where the farmers were required to beat the roosters off their hens on Sunday—a remark which, while it did not exactly shatter the truth of the Hoover Street rumors, did suggest that whatever truth they had belonged to the level of myth and not of fact.

And then to think of the terror and determination I wasted! For not a single one of the innuendoes of my veteran sympathizers had more than a grain of truth. Was it I who had to call the police because a suspected child-molester had appeared for the third straight day, and then watch two men in blue drag him to the squad car with perhaps more blows to the sad, shabby coat covering his midsection than were absolutely necessary? No; it was Sammy at Island Park, gentle, friendly Sammy, who was *so* concerned when he heard about my assignment. "Kid, they have knives *that big!*" Did I have to spend my lunch hour locked inside my own equipment shed, and by my own Junior Leaders, until my colleague of the opposite sex arrived with his key? Never; but Debbie Doll did, and it happened at respectable West Side. "Hoover Street!" she had commiserated. "My God, Adrian, those kids are cute when they're little, but when they get big—God!" Did I have to break a finger like my friend Red Buchler, whose neck perhaps was as red as his hair, because I was using it against the jaw of a loudmouth who started a fight over a baseball bat (luckily for the City, after playground hours)? Job's comforters, hypocrites, whited sepulchres—look at the beam in your own eye!

True, there was the "former Golden Glover" who came by one night and offered to "teach me how to box." Against Barbara's urging

I let him, and there could have been trouble (he was psyching himself from hard-edged friendliness into meanness), except that as I backed around the jungle gym and fended him off with long, tentative jabs Barbara laughed him into playing ping-pong instead. There was the character in shoes without laces and shirt with no buttons, his head looking strangely crushed on the right side, an evil-looking fellow of about forty, with bloodshot eyes and badly stained teeth, who motioned me to the drinking fountain and said, "I want me a *wuh*-man, you know where I can get me a *wuh*-man?" This was during Barbara's supper break, the playground empty except for twelve-year-old Verella, lithe-limbed Verella, our sprinter, who was swinging on the swings not ten yards away. He had a knife in his closed fist. It was a pocket knife, a boy-scout knife, and it was closed—the closest I came all summer to the famous long knives of Hoover Street, and I didn't get to see the blade. "Not here," I said firmly, and then, as he took a long drink of water, "*not here*"; and he walked slowly away down Sixteenth Street, spitting between his teeth. I did notify the police, after that, from the phone at the liquor store on the corner, and we never saw him again—nor the police, except once or twice in the evening flashing the spotlight from their car against the brick wall of the valve works.

What I remember better are certain poignancies, moments that threw their own sudden spotlight on the separations between me and my "kids," as we called our clients, customers, and charges. "You *know* niggahs ain't got no chance," I heard a sixteen-year-old boy tell another one evening as they leaned against a parked car waiting to bat— whether about a job, a driver's license, or a parking ticket I didn't know; what struck me was his embarrassed confusion when he realized I had overheard, as if he had been caught at something secret and suspect. "You the best," a ten-year-old girl told me during one of our Doll Contests, a smiling and friendly joke referring to the "Doll with the Bluest Eyes" category. Most of our dolls did have blue eyes, as well as yellow hair and pink, rubbery skin, but she was pointing out that I was the only person who did. During the Baby Brother and Sister Contest, Nikkles had told us—there were ribbons for fattest, tallest, most freckles, and so on—we could "paint on" some freckles! Unnecessary, I thought, as red hair and freckles did appear now and then on our playground, though the hair was more tightly woven and the freckles sparser than elsewhere. It turned out that other playgrounds used paint too, producing red, green, and blue freckles just for the fun of it; but I remember my shock when hearing this suggestion at a staff meeting, and Barbara's loud laughter as she nudged me.

I was color-conscious at the time because of the free Friday-night travelogs the Department sent out (boys' leaders took these late-night events alone)—ancient, misbegotten armchair-vacationer films whose implied audience combined wealth and insensitivity and unenlightened hedonism in measures unheard of at Hoover Street or, I hoped, anywhere. The Department had gotten them for nothing, and they were worth it. "Our ship approaches Haiti, magic Haiti still throbbing with the savage beat of voodoo drums, as the smiling waiter serves native delicacies at our poolside table. . . ."

As our ship approached Haiti the blue-eyed waiter responsible for dishing up this American delicacy was feeling paler than usual and expecting to be attacked by local voodooists from their child-sized benches on the grass. He was wondering whether to pull the plug of the extension cord that snaked back into the socket in the girls' john, and if he smiled his smiles were part of a shuffling Uncle Adrian routine invented on the spot as his best disclaimer of responsibility; or perhaps he hoped that Henri Christophe would rise gigantic and black from his royal Haitian grave and swallow both ship and travelers, to end the film in a burst of cinematic justice while incidentally taking its humble, unwilling purveyor off the hook.

"Shut up laughing, them's your *peoples*, Jake." It is a family idiom with us now, Elizabeth reciting it to me as I read an angry letter in one of the *TRUTH* magazines her mother still sends us from New Jersey, or I to her as she peruses *Time* or as we watch the evening news. The originator was Wesley, Hoover's fourteen-year-old checker champ, who was reprimanding Jake, one of our most reliable volley-ballists, during some of the same kind of clumsily cute footage dealing with the feather-topped Zulu, the elephant-destroying pygmy, and the plate-lipped, copper-necked, earlobe-stretching women of the Ubangi. I tried to make it clear to Nikkles that what I objected to was not the subject but the handling, the perspective of the alien, the dilettante, the gawking rube at a freak show, which these films forced upon us. Our third and last trip gave us rose-cheeked Heidi, her goats and cheese and jerkin, and the piously papist, happily brawling tipplers of the Emerald Isle, and hairy Swedes flagellating themselves with twigs before plunging naked into the snow (pleasantly for me, no tulips, windmills, or wooden shoes); and so I considered that my protest had been, after a fashion, effective.

There was drama and tension enough at Hoover Street, but less from the spilled blood of my colleagues' imaginations than the small change of everyday life. If I ask why our days on the playground, Barbara's and mine, are so bright and halcyon in the memory, and were so full of pleasure, all things considered, I can give only part of the credit to her experience and my innocence. Some of it surely belongs to the spirit of the age, or rather the period or day—that brief lull between the Court's decision and the later-appearing black rage and white backlash that whipsawed the country about the time my own children entered the public schools. And to the place: racial feeling in Calumet was safety-valved off to the South; compared to Arkansas and Alabama we thought we looked good. Barbara had been a shining star at Washington High, which was ten percent "non-white" then, including my colleagues Jeannie Lo and Larry Marquez Peinado. The three Wright brothers—Julius, Theodore, and Woodrow—who turned up at the playground now and then on off-hours from their jobs at the supermarket and swimming pool, had established a dynastic lock on the positions of left halfback and Student Council president. And the cream of black Calumet took at least a passing interest in Hoover Street (unlike the cream of other neighborhoods, who summered in Colorado or Canada or Maine) because we were, after all, *the* black playground, and we were so not by official ordinance or non-negotiable grass-roots demand; it was a happy accident of the free choice of hundreds of freely-choosing northern American citizens.

That was our faith—perhaps it was our illusion; but believing in our freedom to go elsewhere made us work a little harder, my playground and I, to be nice to each other. When I closed the playground in the near-dark of eight o'clock and asked for bat, bases, and ball I generally got them with no trouble—in contrast to poor broken-fingered Red Buchler. "Hey, man, give the man the ball, can't you see he be closing up the park?" We protected each other. I was from Orangetown, they from Hoover Street; we protected each other from ghettodom, certifying the presence of the larger American world, and so we got along.

On the morning of opening day raindrops splashed in puddles

under the swings and slides and beat upon the shingles of the equipment shed, an old cement-block building about the size of a one-car garage, with a ten-inch transom running around the top of the four walls, and toilets at either end which were entered, when they were unlocked, from outside. No children were there or were likely to come, but to ease my nervousness I got out construction paper and crayons and made signs for the bulletin board. Adrian 10-12, 1-6, 7-8; Barbara 9-11, 12-5, 6-7. BARBARA BACK MONDAY. I unplugged the floor drain and swept water off the floor—rain blew in a fine spray through the transom—and with the small nails we had been issued strengthened some of the wobbly-legged tables as best I could. I made another sign: NO SITTING ON TABLES. All the items in both boys' and girls' boxes were accounted for, and the rest of the equipment stacked haphazardly against the wall seemed in fair condition except for the ping-pong table, a fiberboard rectangle which we had to carry outside to the patio and lay across two sawhorses; it looked as if it had been used to post messages. I got out the handcraft sandpaper and sanded the roughest holes smooth.

Curt Nikkles came by, startling me by opening the door without announcement and ducking quickly inside. He told me I could come down to City Hall basement in the afternoon and cut out candles for the late-season Lantern Parade—our standard procedure on rainy days—or, since it was opening day, stay and wait for the weather to clear. I showed him the ping-pong table's surface. "It looks like somebody stuck pins in it."

He took a quick look, stretching his neck-cords above the collar of his short-sleeved shirt. "Do you really think the kids would do a thing like *that*?" Presumably Harmon had once said something to this effect. Nikkles enjoyed portraying himself and the staff as suffering together at the front while the higher brass kept their heads in the clouds (or, alternatively, in the sand) somewhere behind the lines. He made a note on his clipboard, and after telling me to park closer to the building, and to lock my car next time, he left.

When I arrived home for lunch my father and brothers were there waiting for the rain to stop; they had run out of inside work. Paul, who had been whining all morning, so my father said, and had backed the Jeep into a ditch and dropped a roll of insulation in the mud, was asking to take the boat out, rain or no rain. "We only get *off* on rainy days," he said, and my father said, "Why don't you just go along with Adrian? Then you can play with the niggers."

Probably it was the word "play" that he meant to carry the sting in the sentence; he seemed increasingly conscious, that summer, that there were large groups of people, including union members, government workers, professional ballplayers, Negroes, and me, who did not work as hard as he did. But it was the racial term that caught my mother's ear, a breach of the decorum of her kitchen as much as a black heel-mark on the tile. The room seemed suddenly small for the five of us, my tennis shoes jostling work-boots under the table and our wet clothes steaming in each other's nostrils along with the smoke from my father's cigarette. Moving distractedly between table and counter with plates of bread and ham and cheese, sometimes pausing in transit, the sandwiches tantalizingly out of our reach, my mother lectured my father on his failure to set a good example, chewing him out with all the painstaking thoroughness with which she would fold the laundry or make a Sunday dinner. His vile language. His temper. His driving habits. His smoking and drinking, which were ruining his lungs and his belly respectively, and taking his youth and his health and even his looks, proving it was true that something rotten in the soul like bigotry would find its expression in the body. My father hunched silently within his damp flannel shirt, puffing his Chesterfield and sipping his Edelweiss. It was as if he had goaded her on purpose out of some twisted need for punishment, or to provide her a release for frustrations he knew he had caused; I felt as if I were watching an act of vice between consenting adults.

"I've got to get back," I said. No one hindered me. Grabbing a sandwich and an apple I headed back to my playground, whose children, according to Harmon, came all too often from broken homes, where there was only one parent to furnish the love and stability a child needed; and on the way I tried to remember the Handbook's Twenty Rules.

The Twenty Rules, like the Ten Commandments read each Lord's Day in Orangetown, were a summary of years of moral experience and, also like the Commandments, were stated mainly in the negative. You are not a buddy. You are not a doctor, cop, parent, janitor, spectator. . . . Of all the rules my favorite was "You are not a loud-speaker." The principle was that we were to talk directly, person to person, with any offender and not make a public issue or confronta-

50

tion out of the fact that he was, let us say, walking up, instead of sliding down, the slide. It was the only rule, I felt, that I could have been sure of following if left to my own inclinations.

After the ten prohibited roles—only relatively prohibited, for under certain emergency conditions we might have to play janitor, doctor, or cop—came six Aristotelian excess-defect rules (don't be inflexible, but don't be too soft; don't keep an activity going too long, but don't stop it too soon); and then, at the end, four miscellaneous rules which had to be important because their asymmetrical ruggedness and abruptness echoed life's own urgency, and because they dealt with property and "discipline," which as I saw it were Nikkles', if not Harmon's, major concerns:

- Stay out of the equipment room.
- Equipment is in use or out of use—never abused.
- Do not award prizes.
- Keep your hands off the children.

The rain was still falling as I arrived, though not heavily, and the playground was still empty; but the lights in the equipment shed were burning. I saw them through the transom as I turned the corner and again as I got out of the car—locking it this time, as Nikkles had told me. Two sixty-watt bulbs incandescent inside their wire muzzles. I was positive I had turned them off. Also that I had fastened the padlock, which as I cautiously approached I saw hanging open by its metal forefinger from the latch. I was not to be a policeman. Should I summon those who were? Call the cops on the very first day? From inside came scuffling sounds and what I hoped was a childish giggle. I opened the door and stepped inside.

Thunk!

A feathered dart smacked into a tabletop. It was the ping-pong table I had sanded that morning, now standing vertically against the wall. Three more darts bristled from its surface, and on the opposite side of the room, standing on a green handcraft table, a skinny but wide-shouldered boy held another one, ready to fire. His eyes were so wide and frightened that for a second I thought I was going to get it right in the chest.

"You'd better give that to me."

He did it, climbing down off the table with a readiness that surprised me as much as the firmness of my own voice, and I turned to

51

face his friend. This was a bigger boy, round and chunky as the first was linear. His attitude was as truculent as he could make it—the pink of his underlip showing, his butt and right elbow moving as if he wanted to throw a punch, or a spear, but overdoing it just enough, I thought, to let me call his bluff.

"You, too," I said. I had to take a step toward him before he would give up his dart. Not wanting to push my luck, I took the other darts out of the table myself.

"Do you boys realize you're defacing public property?"

There was no answer—except, inside my head, the mocking echo of my father's voice saying of *course* it was public property that got defaced, everybody's business was nobody's business!

When I turned around they looked cowed and frightened enough that I thought I could transform them from outlaws into allies. The bigger boy had a long, curved forehead, his hair beginning so far back that it could have been a set of fleecy ear-laps tied up for the summer; with this extra length his face was extremely mobile and expressive, and just now as he peered at me with his head cocked first to one side and then the other, as if to take me in with both sides of his brain, I imagined twitching muscles inside his skin labeled bemusement, belligerence, contrition, and fear. The smaller boy's face was as lean as his body; nothing moved but his round dark eyes.

"I'm Adrian," I said. "The leader." I paused to let that sink in. "What's your name?"

The little one spoke immediately. "Frankie." He had a shy, husky voice. His bare torso was shaped like a captial T, the skin soft and grainy like shoe polish.

"Where's your shirt, Frankie?" The equipment shed was chilly and damp. He pointed to a white shirt hanging from the knob of the handcraft cabinet, too small for its adult hanger; it was as if he had been doing the ironing.

"His mother whip him if he get dirty," the big one jeered. His own shirt, grubby red-and-white rings ascending his round torso, proved he was above such fears. I took advantage of his entry into the conversation by asking his name.

His lower lip came out, his head cocked to the right. "You spose to be the park teacher?" he said. "Where Barbara?"

I unlocked the cabinet, careful of Frankie's shirt, and took out the signs I had made. "She'll be back Monday," I said, adding, for authenticity, "She's still at UCLA."

"You got a whistle?"

I took it out of my pocket and hung it around my neck. "I have keys, too." I indicated the ring clipped to my belt, smiling with what I hoped was friendly irony, but he only stiffened his lower lip. "Now can you tell me your name?"

"You give me my darts, man, I tell you my name. They's *my* public property."

"Suppose you tell me how you got into the building."

Since the padlock had been open I knew he must have a key. I could easily switch the padlock with another from one of the equipment boxes or cabinets, or, assuming he had a whole set of keys, get a new set of locks from the Department. But what I wanted to do was establish enough trust so that he would give up the key on his own. Frankie seemed eager to tell, his eyes going from me to the floor and back, his lips working silently; but his friend held up a fist. "We don't answer no questions."

"All right."

I let him watch as I locked his darts in the cabinet. At the same time I got out the Department's official-looking registration sheets for the Olympic Day contests the next week. I pulled a bench up to a handcraft table and sat down, pencil in hand.

"Do you remember Olympic Day last year? You probably went down to Island Park and ran races. Sprints? Broad jump? High jump?"

The big one allowed his face to relax. "Man, I won me three ribbons!"

"You too fat." Frankie laughed huskily. "You didn't win nothing."

"You can both be on the team this year," I said. "I'll need your ages and your names in order to register you."

"You put me down," the big one said. "Write me down, go on, man."

"I'll need your name and age in order—"

"Name Willie B. Weaver, anybody tell you that! Can anybody on the playground tell you that, man! You ask did anybody win three ribbons, they tell you Willie B. Weaver."

"Old Beaver," Frankie said, chuckling. He seemed relieved to have it out in the open.

I wrote it down, asking Willie for the spelling in order to confirm my small victory. Now he was jivy and theatrical, full of spread-eagle declamation as he spelled out the W and E and all the rest like a cheerleader—give it a A, man, now put down a V—as if he had never had anything to hide and had always been proud to have his name published and would soon be making public disclosure of all his financial activities. All summer long he was capable of flip-flops like these, moving from irony and tragedy into festive comedy at the slightest hint; the trick (which Barbara knew, but I never completely mastered) was to drop the right hint. Whereas Frankie was steadily serious and therefore more obviously vulnerable, and it was his vulnerability, I suppose, that made me favor him.

Willie was ten. Frankie was seven, and his last name was Bumpus. (There was a family named Bogus on Hoover Street, and a girl whose first name, Barbara said, was Petulia. "Ah, some funny names on this playground!" I made her blush—visibly, through the dark of her skin—by asking whether she included my own. Easy to laugh, Barbara, when on life's name-tags you wear the name of Robinson!)

While the rain gradually slowed and stopped we sat together at the table—we could open the door, now, for light; there were no windows—and organized Olympic Day. The two of them pondered and dictated names and ages, and I wrote them down.

"Jimms. Put down old Jimms, man, he *good*."

"Last name or first?"

"First name, put down Jimms."

"You mean Jimmy? James? What's his last name?"

"*Jimms*."

I wrote down "Jimms."

"You say he can run?"

"Man, can't nobody not run!"

We filled two or three columns with names like Junior, Brother, New Shoes, Motley, and Sweets. I didn't consider my penciled list official, but I had them busy, I thought, and committed. "Fleet" was another name I heard. "Old Fleet, he got a scholarship," Frankie said, mouthing the word carefully. Since Willie claimed he was eighteen and therefore too old I suspected that this was Lee Roy Williams, a young man I had met during orientation, a freshman and a sprinter at Indiana. A graduate of Washington High, he was in training this summer for the real Olympics—he hoped—and because of his training schedule was working for Parks instead of Recreation. "We only work from seven to three, not dawn to dusk like you guys. And we're on union scale." I wondered whether he was telling me he could have had my job if he had wanted it, but he didn't want it. "Good luck," he said when he learned I was to be at Hoover Street; but unlike my sympathetic colleagues he offered (or at least I took it as an offer) to "be around if you run into trouble." I put him down as a possibility for assistant coach.

Then we organized the week, beginning with a scavenger hunt scheduled for that night in order to produce orange crates, old toothbrushes, coffee cans and so on (non-returnable, non-issued equipment) for our handcraft periods. The rain had gone now, and although the ground was wet we could manage a high-organized game like a scavenger hunt. I urged them to bring everyone they could.

"Prizes?" they both said. It was in the imperative for Willie, though Frankie made it a question. I felt my way toward flexibility in the rule against prizes.

"We'll make some."

We spent another hour in the equipment room cutting out cardboard stars with coping saws (no wood until the scavenger hunt) and construction-paper ribbons with scissors. Everyone would get a prize. We set up the ping-pong table then, and I had the two of them sandpaper the fresh holes they had made. Willie began with enthusiasm, any new tool or activity finding its instant place in his repertory as a stage property or piece of business; but as we finished I could see that the transition from creative to restitutional work, and therefore penal work, bothered him.

"You fitten to be a tough park teacher?"

He had entered his downward phase, his lower lip out, the Santa Claus cheeks dragging sullenly, his color not ebony but gray.

The word "fitten," as I later learned it on the playground, meant "fixing" (though I never learned why it should), as in the sentence, "Is the park fitten to close?" Not knowing that then, I replied that I *was* fitting to be tough, if I had to be. That went over in silence.

"What about last year's boys' leader? Was he a tough leader?"

"Willie run that cat crazy." Frankie chuckled, and Willie, though not to be shaken out of his role, had to smirk a little at the memory.

After the sandpapering I had them make some more signs for Get-Acquainted Week—Willie working steadily and silently—and when it was time for my supper break I took a calculated risk. I held up two shiny badges which were the size, shape, and color of a silver dollar. Made of heavy paper covered with a metallic paint, they were embossed with Calumet's emblem, a feather-fringed pipe of peace. "You boys have helped me organize our program. You've shown some responsibility, now, for the playground equipment. How would you like to be my Junior Leaders for the week?"

Instantly Willie was his festive self. When he had pinned the badge on his shirt he ran through half-a-dozen impressions of authority figures from the senatorial wheeler-dealer to the hotel doorman, deep-throated gargles of satisfaction, such as might have emanated from the adult double chins of an alderman on the take, alternating with childlike "whoo-ee's" as he pranced around the shed, his round butt wagging like a puppy's. "Whoo'eee! Willie B. Weavah heah, and I'se fitten to be tough. You sah, kindly step around to the rear and ah will have de john do' open in a jiffy, just cross my palm with silver, now you talking. No sah, not silver, you hear a voice say silver? You better listen again, that not the Lord talking, that *you*—Lord wants folding money! Whoo-ee! Step on back to the back of the bus, ladies and children up front, yes ma'am, his highness and his ladyship gone be with you directly. You sah, what you got to say for yourself? Why you be defacing your public property like that, man? That's right, man, all we want is the facts. . . ."

Frankie held his badge in his hand, frowning toward it as if oppressed by its weight. "I'm showing this to my mother," he said. Since his shirt was still on the hanger I thought he would put it through a belt-loop on his jeans; instead he pinned it in his hair.

I got ready to close, putting the outside padlock on the boys' chest and keeping its lock for the outside door.

"Hey, man," Willie said. "You giving me my darts? This is your Junior Leader talking, man. I scrubbed and scraped on that table. I made all them signs and cut out all them prizes—"

"The name is Adrian, Willie."

"Right, man. Aryan. I scrubbed and scraped for you, man. You giving me—"

"You've done good work, Willie, and I'm trusting you with the badge. If you trust me enough to tell me how you got into the building, I'll give you the darts."

He was tempted; but other temptations were greater. "You too tough for me, man." He gave me a sweeping bow.

Frankie, as I bent down to hand him his shirt, whispered, "He be telling you sometime."

"I know it, Frankie."

Outside in the fresh air, the leaves dripped silver as the evening sun of June slanted across the valve works. The two boys headed home by way of their shortcut through the spirea bushes to the Hoover Street sidewalk, and Frankie asked me to help him over the fence. I swung him up to the pipe running across the top between the metal posts; from there he jumped nimbly down. The weight of his light, wiry body gave me a rush of brotherly affection that was something new to me. Gordon had always been too close to my own age, too much the rival, to inspire it, and Paul was too flinty and hard-edged. He was more like Willie, who climbed the fence himself.

"Don't forget the scavenger hunt," I called after them. The sun glinted off the silver badge in Frankie's hair. Willie strutted ahead like a drum major.

"We won't. Bye, Aryan."

"So long, man."

The great baseball pitcher of the Negro leagues who late in life was brought to the majors, Satchell Paige, once remarked that you should never look back over your shoulder, because "something might be gaining on you." In the front seat of my car before going home for supper I opened the Handbook, ignoring Paige's advice. The four miscellaneous rules were as I remembered them. I was feeling euphorically that I had made an excellent start on the playground, considering how the afternoon had begun, and nothing in the Handbook could discourage me. Obviously there would be exceptions to every rule—for rainy days, for example, and for prizes you made yourself. All in all I thought I had followed the spirit of the Department's program very well.

Still it was a fact that my Junior Leaders and I, in less than a single day, had broken all four rules.

CHAPTER SIX

OLYMPIC DAY

ON Mondays the boys' and girls' leaders closed the playgrounds together at five, because of the staff meetings held in the evenings after supper, and opened them together at ten in the morning.

When I got to work on Monday morning, half an hour earlier than I had to be there, the lights were on in the equipment room. The volleyball net was up, with a sag in its middle, and two of the beanbags were flying over it. The volleyball, neither in use nor out of use, waited on the ball diamond for someone to come along and kick it. The kickball was bouncing on the sidewalk for two girls trying to play jacks with it, so close to the street, I thought, that had the ball rolled forward across the parkway I might have hit them as I parked my car. The small rubber ball for jacks was flying into center field followed by an eight-year-old named Sonny, followed by Sonny's brother, the two of them wheeling softball bats like polo sticks, their legs galloping like horses.

No children skipped toward my car as they had last week, bouncing on their toes and singing, "Is the park fitten to open? Hey, everybody, Adrian fitten to open the park!" Why should they? I was neither fitting nor fixing to open the park; the park was already open. My only greeting came from Verella, who stood among the swings rattling the chains of the baby seat twice around the supporting bar in order to raise it to her own pre-teen height; her brother, aged four or five, was testing the rubber of his new tennis shoes by mountaineering up the face of the slide. To make the climb challenging he had dusted the slide with sand. I could trace his steps across the cindery packed dirt by a thirty-yard thread of beach that led to the sandbox. On the wooden sandbox seats, keeping out the smaller children who should have been there (instead of in the equipment shed, where I could hear ping-pong balls ricocheting off the walls and floor), sat Verella's lanky friends, my volleyball team. They were laughing and talking, and sifting through their casual fingers (and, in one case, toes) the sugar-sand which, according to all playground lore and logic, would soon be flung with adolescent abandon into somebody's eyes.

Consequently the guideline: no one over ten in the sandbox.

It was the first day of Olympic Week and the day of Barbara's return. I had stayed late at the playground on Friday night, after my travelog trip to Haiti and the Caribbean, cleaning, organizing, and arranging the new padlocks which Nikkles had issued me. The playground was ready. I had wanted to be ready as well, on top of things and waiting at the door, when Barbara arrived.

I got Verella to lower the baby-swing and put her brother into it—"before he kills himself, please?"—and sent her after the jack-players at the curb. Having band-aided the nearest symptoms I headed for the equipment shed and what I assumed was the center of the disease, Willie B. Weaver and the new set of keys he had miraculously made over the weekend. On the north side of the shed, in the shade, two of the handcraft tables had been set out. On one of them, Boys' Handcraft was in progress, six-shooters and daggers being cut from my scavenger-hunt crates (also from the table, to judge from the sound of the coping-saw blades). On the other sat a new girl, her knees in blue jeans drawn up to her chin, her feet and seat in a neat three-pointed landing on the green boards, her slender back in red blouse hiding the bulletin-board sign that read NO SITTING ON TABLES.

"Ahhh!"—her long-drawn-out laugh, with the *recitativo* and *glissando* of a singer in it, and then a wide, charming smile. "You must be Adrian! I'm so glad to meet you, Mr. Harmon has told me all about you!"

The ringlets around her face were more profuse than I had imagined from the picture in Harmon's office, her skin more half-tone brown that I had expected after the deeper black of Frankie and Willie. The horn-rimmed glasses perched schoolmarm fashion on the end of her nose had not appeared in the picture. It was her thinness, her air of alighting rather than sitting on the table, that let me recognize her. I wondered how she had recognized me. Perhaps Harmon had told her I would be red-faced, irritable, and sweaty.

60

"I hope I'm not late"—my first words to my co-worker Barbara, who had a year's seniority on me and outranked me by ten cents an hour on the Department's pay scale. "I wanted to be here early, I thought I was, but then I saw the lights. . . ."

Her left hand, fingers tilted downward, was outstretched. I took it, uncertain whether a handshake was expected or, perhaps, a kiss offered on bended knee, and with the slightest forward pull she was on her feet.

"And how have you been finding the playground in your very first year, a bit of a drag, no? Ahhh! I must say you have things highly organized in my absence, highly organized. Mr. Nikkles will be very proud."

She was so much in motion, her head tilted, her smile moving in and out of laughter, her hands moving, individual fingers stroking the air as if to sculpt Nikkles out of it before our eyes, that I imagined she had not been sitting on the table at all, only in butterfly transit across its surface. I said something about Willie, my voice gruff and low, a forty-five RPM dropped to long-playing speed. When I saw the lights I was worried, Willie had somehow gotten in on opening day, I had locked his darts in the cabinet but I made him a Junior Leader. I hoped that would be all right, he had done a good job, I wanted him to give me the extra key himself but for the weekend I thought we had better have a new set of locks, I guessed Harmon had told her about that?

"Ah, Willie!" she said. "Willie and his darts! I do believe you've got them in a very good place. How he does love to terrorize people with those darts of his—oh yes, I've been wondering when I'd see good old Willie and his darts!"

"Well, but what do you think, is it a good idea for me to work on him this way? I really needed him last week, but do you think I ought to make something of it that he broke in on the very first day?"

She was still laughing, as she had been from the first mention of Willie's name. Her hand slapping her knee, she addressed this pantomime of cracking up to Melody, a six-year-old who was trying to tell us that she wanted to play in the sandbox. "Willie, Willie," and she bent toward Melody as if the two of them were chuckling over his escapades, as if Willie himself were hanging his head and chuckling with them over his humorously recalled sins. "Willie, Willie, what make you so bad, Willie, why you want to do me that way with them bad, bad darts of yours?"—and Melody smiled, her lips moving with Barbara's and her head shaking too in mock disapproval: ah Willie, Willie!

"So you think I ought to keep his darts locked up in the closet? Or"—my voice rising with my sense of being outside the play going forward—"should I tell him I'm going to take them to Nikkles? Or maybe to his parents? I'd really like to know what you think!"

She straightened up. "Ah, what I think! Oh, yes, what I think, hmm—what I think is, you going to be an old man by August!"

It was my decision, after all; I was the boys' leader. Rebuked, I mentioned that I'd like to go over my plans with her, I had our Olympic Day teams lined up, practices scheduled. . . . I indicated my manilla folder, wrapped in rubber bands and stained by my sweaty palms.

"You get along and play." She made scooting gestures with her hands, and Melody, confused but willing, started toward the sandbox. Included in these motions of Barbara's, I thought, was the desire that the sandbox should be cleared so that Melody could get along and play in it, and that the volleyball, kickball, jacks ball and beanbags should be rotated back into their proper places so that the teenage volleyballists could clear out of the sandbox. A whole world of harmony and order seemed to issue from those gestures, and I found myself entering as willingly as Melody into their spirit. I blew my whistle, I ran to centerfield, right field, home plate, issuing orders and making rearrangements. I appointed *ad hoc* leaders to carry messages. I hustled into the equipment shed and enticed the ping-pong players to the handcraft table, where I promised they could cut out a gun or a knife—"just this once," I apologized to Barbara in passing, "since they've already taken apart the crate; but I think we'd better keep them out of the shed. . . ."

Barbara was telling stories with the volleyball players while they waited for the ball to arrive and the practice to start. When I had everything ready, and the ping-pong table outside, in case anyone wanted to play a proper game, and the shed door closed and locked, I laid out my plans for Olympic Week. "You really do have everything down there," Barbara said. "Mm-*hmm*." Then she went to play volleyball. They needed her, Wes and Jake and Verella and the others, in order to make the sides even. I sat at the table and erased what I had written for the first morning, and in its place wrote Boys' Hand-crafts, Teen Volleyball Practice, and Low-Organized Games.

The last category was one I thought I would be using more of in the future.

"How they do love that volleyball!" Barbara called to me from the volleyball court. The ball flew splendidly though the net sagged. "It's our only *mixed* game. Ahhh!"

As Olympic Week went on I realized that playground "teams" were bound to be unstable, the team members coming and going as the free spirit of summer moved them; they were not locked into a pattern of bell-bordered academic hours like high schools teams. All the more reason, I thought, to keep a schedule. Let the little athletes know that if they showed up at three for a two-o'clock practice, they had missed practice!

However, Barbara's approach was more fluid than this. When a game was in progress, even a relay race, she would be invited to enter it. Invited, she often joined. Any game she entered, even a game she watched, was likely to turn into a skit, a dance, a song. For example, a volleyball song entitled "Hey You Girl Get Back," which I learned on the first day of Olympic Week:

> Hey you girl get back
> Roberta gonna spike the ball!
> Hey you girl get back oh yeah
> Roberta gonna spike the ball!

I knew the phrase "poetry in motion," but I had never seen motion so regularly turned into poetry. Even without Barbara my athletes had a tendency to exploit the rhythmic possibilities of every utterance, every wayward movement of ball or hand or foot, and thus turn a game into something else: a form of art, not a contest. These art forms, these "happenings," modulated easily into other events—hand-craft sessions, for example. How we loved to make tissue-paper flow-ers, and paper-ring necklaces, and leather bracelets, and swagger sticks, and Olympic "laurel wreaths," singing as we did so, around the table, and playing a low-organized game! We had the happiest teams in town, I knew, and the best dressed, even the boys not scorning to thrust a tissue carnation into the meshes of their fine-spun hair. But when were we going to practice?

63

While Barbara was the center of activities like these, I wandered around the edges encouraging minor sports like checkers and horse-shoes, and keeping the equipment either in use or out of use, and worrying about the keys she let her Junior Leaders use, and in general feeling more like Barbara's aide than her colleague.

There was also the matter of rules and guidelines. For Barbara, being the center of activity often meant sitting tailor-fashion (princess-fashion, Buddha-fashion) in the center of a playground table. When I mentioned this habit of hers—you like to sit on tables, don't you?—she said, Adrian, I'm so light I couldn't hurt a table, unlike some people I am not a person of gravity!

Ah, hah-hah.

Once when I sat on a playground bench—that was where we were supposed to sit, on benches made for people four feet tall—waiting for her to come back from her supper break so I could take mine, she came up behind me and put her hands over my eyes.

"Frankie Bumpus," I said.

"Guess again."

"Willie Beaver."

"You're getting colder."

"Kim Novak?" I finally asked, and she said, "Ahh! It's me!" and let me go. I meant the actress's name as a rebuke. I had decided that she did not, as I did, take the playground seriously, but was only passing through on her way to something more grand.

At staff meeting Nikkles warned us that this year Olympic Day was going to be different. Last year's games had provoked controversy because certain playgrounds had used athletes who were A, over age, B, not properly registered, and C, not in regular attendance at the playground in question. The playground or playgrounds in question remained anonymous, but last year's winner, Barbara told me, was Hoover Street.

"By a very narrow margin." This I learned from the leader of the North Side Barons, Red Buchler, who gave me the message with the kind of head-shaking insinuation of malpractice that I used to see in my parents on election nights, as they waited up late for the downstate returns that, as they admitted later, never had a chance, anyway, of matching the Democratic hordes mustered in Cook County. It was Buchler's Barons, the year before, who had come in second.

64

But this year was to be different. Each entrant was to have a certificate of age, signed by the child and countersigned by the leader. Each entrant was to wear an emblem of his playground with his or her name written on it, and fastened by two pins (provided by the City) to shirt or blouse. Each entrant was to have a form signed by a parent giving permission to participate, and another form allowing the City to provide such emergency medical attention as might be et cetera, et cetera. Also a sack lunch, provided by parent or parents, with entrant's name written clearly upon it. Each entrant was to furnish a schedule of the events in which he had been entered, properly made out and signed by the child and the leader and turned in *in advance*. And so on.

Was this demand for bureaucratic exactitude and "functional literacy" an example of covert racism? I had no real reason to suspect it. For me the paperwork was simply another hurdle I had to surmount in order to be a good leader, no less logical than many of the others. Barbara seemed to accept it as a not-unexpected outgrowth of Nikkles' nature, already familiar to her. "Looks like another one of our blue-thumb nights," she whispered when he trundled out his volumes of paper. She loved to use me, the rookie, as straight man for these theatricalities, which were meant to be audible, and were, to Nikkles and the whole staff. "Wait till we get to the Nature Hike, Adrian. He will make us certify what terms they use to refer to—pardon me— the elimination of bodily wastes. Ahhh!" Nikkles seemed to enjoy her mimicry and mockery, feeling, perhaps, as so many playground children did at any kind of attention from her, that it authenticated him as a character.

If I suspected any aspect of the new regimen as unfair, I would have suspected the emblems. Those "emblems of the playground to which each individual entrant is attached," said emblems to be attached in turn, by two pins, to each individual entrant—what hours and hours of practice they took from me! And yet, contrariwise, what hours of pleasure they afforded! I favored the Hoover Street Stars— or, better, triangles or squares, anything easy to cut out of wood, paper, or cloth and get us into uniform and our show on the road. Instead, we toyed with fuzzy-maned lions and flimsy gazelles (at which I balked, Barbara's notion being to cut them from tin cans); then Bears and Cubs and Sox made their appearance, and, by association, Wolves, and then Panthers (from the Pulaski Panthers of Pulaski Junior High), and even "Valves" (from the valve works), and many more, until in the middle of Olympic Week Barbara and her committees finally produced from a storehouse of Oriental imagery unknown to me the Royal Dragon. I made a special trip to the city supply room in my car to get the precise shade of purple for it. The long, serrated dorsal fin was hard to cut out of tagboard, but we did it; I can still see Barbara during the last days of Olympic Week surrounded by pots of paste and pleated piles of purple, cutting out with our scissors-wielding athletes what looked like long-nosed kangaroos, the Royal Dragons of Hoover.

I began asking myself why I should care so much, and whether it was right to care at all, about an Olympic Day victory. In the late afternoons the "big boys," as we called them, would arrive at the park, those who worked the night shift and played ball in the evenings after sleeping during the day. They were young men, rather than boys, impressively muscled, beards darkening their faces like a second skin. Their games easily absorbed my Olympians either as spectators, or, for the older and luckier ones, as players. I let them be absorbed. When the playground was busy, happy, and creative, who was I to object? Weren't my schedules and practices, even victory itself, all designed to produce happiness, busyness, and creativity? Wasn't I confusing means and ends?

The "big boys" themselves seemed to think so. A closely-fought contest is interrupted by the arrival of a new player. "That man don't get no rap!" an outfield poet sings out. Then his infielders join him, then the pitcher and catcher, and then the spectators (dark girls in white shorts among them, sitting on the hoods of parked cars, wearing Barbara's flowers in their hair), and then even the team at bat, all of them chanting together. Oh, oh, oh, that man don't get no rap! Uh, uh, uh, that man don't get no rap! That man don't get no rap (clap, clap)! That man don't get no rap!

On this evening my assistant coach Lee Roy Williams rode up on his English bike (or "skinny-tire," as all three-speeds were called then) and stood next to me, watching. After a moment he spat, a thick glob of white.

"Are they even keeping score?"

"I believe they're going to start over. Jake just got here and they were having a discussion about whether he should bat."

"Discussion." He spat again, or perhaps used one of the words for the elimination of bodily wastes, a word which when he said it was like an expectoration. It was the only word he pronounced in what I took to be the Southern fashion.

"Looks like you're letting your playground get out of hand."

There was an edge of rivalry between Lee Roy and me. Earlier we had held a race of our own, a fifty-yard dash, in order to inspire our mock-Olympians by letting them watch the work of a potentially real one. Lee Roy's right leg was heavily taped, protection for a thigh muscle he had often pulled. He was short and stocky whereas I was long and lean, and it occurred to me that once he stopped accelerating I might possibly pull up on him. . . . What a feather in my cap! Lee Roy never stopped accelerating, however; he accelerated the whole fifty yards, beating me by ten or fifteen. Though my loyalists, led by Frankie and Willie, claimed that I had "done good," considering that I was not an athlete, while Lee Roy had a scholarship, I felt the natural shame of a loser; and Lee Roy complained that he had had to limp most of the way, beating me as it were on one leg, and by implication blaming me for re-injuring the other.

The fact was, I thought, that as an assistant coach Lee Roy was pretty much a failure. Most of our athletes leaped their longest, jumped their highest, and ran their swiftest (as measured by Lee Roy's own stopwatch) on their very first time out. Lee Roy's coaching, which tended toward the negative and sarcastic, produced greater effort but not measurably greater results. "Plumbers" was a term he used a lot. I supposed it originated in Big Ten locker rooms and implied that one carried lead pipe in one's pockets. I didn't like the term (perhaps out of residual identification with my father and the building trades), and the children didn't seem to care for it, either. It might have motivated men, but our boys and girls were intimidated by it, like Frankie, or, like Willie, turned off. In Lee Roy's absence Willie would strut around the playground, dragging his right leg like Captain Ahab on the quarterdeck and shouting, "Hey, you plumbahs! You plumbahs releasing the baton too soon! Do it again and get it right, you plumbahs!"

Once I heard Barbara say to no one in particular, from the center of a crowd of paper-cutters, "Ah, that Lee Roy, he tries so hard but he just doesn't have it"—a remark I treasured up and pondered within my heart.

And yet, when Lee Roy swung his taped leg off his English bike at four o'clock, after putting in a full day for the Park Department plus a double workout on the high school track—"a few miles easy, to warm up, then a few hundreds, maybe some two-twenties, plus quarter-miles in the afternoon to get my strength up"—when he came with his dour black face wearing opaque motorcycle-cop glasses, a V-shaped frown like a scar between his eyes, an upside-down sailor hat like a pith helmet on his head, wearing his Indiana sweatshirt and shorts and with them the aura of his scholarship, I was as intimidated as Frankie.

"We schedule sprinters for four o'clock?"

"Well—I got the chalk marks all laid out, see there? Some of the kids thought it was kind of hot, they wanted to sit in the shade and help Barbara make cobras, and then some of the bigger kids came to play ball and—"

"Cobras?"

"For the playground emblem. Hoover Street Cobras."

Spit. "Cobras." Spit. "What's all this trash in the sandbox? This supposed to be our jumping pit!"

"You know these wooden forts, they make them out of popsicle sticks? Barbara had them collecting popsicle sticks all morning, so I let them go ahead and use the sandbox. . . ."

The woman thou gavest me, she gave the children the popsicle sticks, and I let them destroy our practice. I knew it wouldn't work for me any more than it had for Adam. I was the boys' leader, after all, and I was letting my playground get out of hand.

That evening when the ball game broke up, during Barbara's supper break, I gave my team members a speech. To get their attention I had all the equipment brought in and locked in the shed, and then we sat in a circle on the grass. Lee Roy stood outside the circle, his arms folded across his chest, listening. I spoke of winners and losers. At first I had thought Hoover Street was a playground of winners, but now I wasn't sure. Winners were like game fish, like the trout that swam deep in the big lake north of Gary, in the clean blue water far north of Chicago. Losers were like carp, like the carp in the sluggish brown river that wound around Island Park. They ate the crud and garbage of the whole city! And how could you tell winners from losers, game fish from garbage fish? You could tell because winners were tough, they would swim in cold water, they swam upstream against the current—but losers only drifted!

The idea came from a *Tribune* article on the depradations of the parasitic sea lamprey among the trout of Lake Michigan. The fact that I knew the game fish were dying, even as I spoke, while the carp of the world went from strength to strength, may have accounted for the stridency I heard in my voice.

"That should get the little plumbers off their butts," Lee Roy said when I finished. He called for a practice on the spot, Frankie and Willie and the others leaping effortfully into the sandbox, which they first emptied of its popsicle towns; cursing their luck and the sand which stuck to their sweaty skin, they lined up to leap again. And that evening, after supper, some of them brought me their signatures from home.

"Ahh, you'll make us a preacher!" Barbara said to me the next morning. Someone had told her about the speech. The reference to preaching startled me and raised a blush, something that always made her laugh.

"Look at Adrian, Verella! Roberta, look! Look at Adrian blush!"

"I didn't want you to hear about that," I said. "I said some things I didn't mean."

"Don't blush, Adrian—you the preacher of the playground! You changed them little tadpoles into sharks!"

So we drifted and swam toward Olympic Day, Barbara handling uniforms, Lee Roy doing coaching, and I providing administrative support regarding team scheduling and parental signatures. I even collected some signatures myself, going without supper those last two nights and visiting the homes of negligent or forgetful athletes during my break. On these visits I learned to come without the playground folder, which gave me too much the look of an insurance salesman, perhaps, or free-lance photographer. What defensive postures I aroused, at first, with my businesslike charge up the front porch, as if I had come about a stolen beanbag or cracked window, or another F in spelling! "It's about your son Teddy, what we need is. . . ." Better to avoid the term "playground leader," I found, or even the more familiar "park teacher," in favor of appearing as Teddy's coach, down at Hoover.

I learned to take my time, speaking as slowly and as Southern as I could, making everything a friendly visit about one of those absurd administrative details under which we all had to labor day by day, and leaving, after fifteen or twenty minutes of conversation among the

sprouting hollyhocks and sunflowers in the front yard, with another
set of signed forms, and the promise of lunch and bus fare for another
athlete. It was mostly fathers whose signatures I got, contrary to Harmon's broken-home theory of playground sociology; perhaps the single mothers were the ones who sent in signatures without a special
visit. One father reversed himself when asked for his signature, saying
that he was actually Teddy's uncle, as it happened, but he would see
to it that Teddy's mother sent the forms in the very next day. Which
she did. But mostly they were fathers, gentle-spoken bus drivers,
mailmen, and, a somewhat brusker group, factory workers, whose
easiness (though I was interrupting their mealtime) made me ashamed
of my haste. Once I was invited to stay for supper—an offer I declined
with regret, for though I didn't know hush puppies from chitlings or
black-eyed peas, the aroma of whatever it was frying in deep fat had
in my nostrils the fragrance of all pre-Orangetown America, from the
Civil War two-and-a-half centuries back into the beginning. I felt I
had been invited to a banquet of my country's history, to sit down
before one of those watch fires of a hundred circling camps which I
had sung about but never seen.

As for Barbara: while Lee Roy coached and scolded, and I nagged
and administered, she kept alive the spirit of pleasure in it all—though
by the morning of Olympic Day itself she too looked grim. At the
bus stop where our boys' and girls' teams lined up after an early
breakfast, complaining of "chilly bumps" on their skin and looking
like National Guardsmen on bivouac, I thought, with stenciled lunch
sacks instead of duffel bags, she sent back our ten-year-old ring-tosser,
Elvirah, to get her emblem and her forms. "You better run," Barbara
told her without a smile; and a short time later, as Elvirah's chubby
legs churned toward us, racing the bus, she called uncharacteristically,
"Girl, can't you run any better than that?"

Out of almost thirty team members taking the early bus, Elvirah
was the only one who forgot something. Looking at their pinched,
cold faces I couldn't take much pleasure in the fact.

My assignment at Island Park was to run the long jump, which
was held in an isolated area down near the river (which was brown
and muddy and full of carp, as I had predicted). I was kept busy lining
up the children, checking off their names and measuring their dis-
tances, and raking the sand smooth again for another jump. Whenever

I ran across a Hoover Street athlete I tried to undo some of the damage I thought I had done. Relax, I told them in my Southern tones. Relax, Frankie, it's only a game after all, and you did the best you could—though in an absolute sense Frankie's best jump was half a foot longer, made during the first day of practice. He took third place in the Midget Division with a leap just over five feet, and he was in tears because he thought the yellow ribbon made him a loser. Poor Frankie, giving Willie his white shirt to hold while he tried to force his thin legs into a thrust that would take him out of reach of the dirty water forever! Willie took third in his division, the Intermediates, and I had to break up a fight between him and another boy who Willie claimed was pushing him in line. Relax, Willie, you'll do just fine! Relax, I told Homer Proudfoot, who became champion of the Juniors. Relax, I said to Bettye Lou White, who took the blue ribbon for Senior Girls. Relax, winning isn't everything!

I did take the time, however, to check the final score before going back. I finished late. Like the pole vault in the real Olympics, our long jump, with each of its many entrants measured individually, was the last event to report, and when I turned in my results at the scorer's table Barbara and most of the children had already gone. I went over the tallies on the big chalkboard roped to two trees outside Sammy's equipment shed, checking them twice, my heart beating faster each time. Could it be? Could it really be? I checked again with Nikkles, who as the apex of the mountain of certification he had brought into being was feeling harrassed at the end of the day and answered me rather peremptorily, as if he thought I was questioning his arithmetic. He was still at the scorer's table, sitting behind a row of Island Park's igneous and sedimentary rocks being used as paperweights, and writing up the meet's results for the weekend paper. The chalkboard tallies were correct, he assured me. *Correct*. I turned and ran to catch the bus going south—and then, catching sight of some of Hoover Street's children at the bus stop, I slowed my pace as best I could, achieving a modified sort of hop-skip-and-jump, in order to prolong the moment and let them read the story in my face before I told them the news.

The bus was crowded with home-going workers, stolid men carrying barn-shaped lunch boxes and the jackets they had worn that morning, with glossy I.D.'s pinned on them, and working housewives looking forward to starting supper when they got home. The half-dozen Hoover athletes and myself scattered among these weary strap-hangers like fragments of bubbling happiness. Above the diesel's hum and roar, and the hiss of doors opening and closing, I heard whispers, then giggles, and then from the rear—from Willie B. Weaver—a low, deep voice singing. "Oh Mrs. Jones?" And then from a half-dozen seats, as if in a secret code, came the sound of fingers tapping: a-tap-tap-tap! And from my fingers too, on the bar above my head. I knew the song, I had heard it tapped out on the tops of tables and the bottoms of overturned coffee cans during a score of what I thought were wasted practices.

"May I come in?" A-tap-tap-tap!

"Oh Mrs. Jones may I come in. . . ?" A-tap-tap-tap-*tap*!

And then a tide of laughter from all over the bus, and even a few smiles from the ranks of silent commuters, those less fortunate than we.

"Bye, Adrian!" The children shouted happily as they left the Six-teenth Street bus stop for home, and I for my car. But before I drove away I opened the equipment shed and wrote in big letters on the bulletin board, using four sheets of construction paper, to be ready for Monday morning:

HOOVER WINS!
Them: 74
Us: 168
C O N G R A T U L A T I O N S !

That night there was an Olympic Day party for all the leaders—an annual event, so Barbara told me, ever since Sammy had begun playground work three years earlier. It was to be held at his parents' home, or rather their summer home, on Lake Michigan. A map show-ing the way into the private dunelands east of Gary was one of the items Nikkles passed out at staff meeting on Monday.

I hadn't planned on going. Of the three leaders I met at my interview I had liked Sammy best because he was the friendliest. I was a stranger then, and he took me in. During orientation and staff meeting, however, he kept on taking me in, sympathizing with me and introducing me and clucking over me so insistently that I avoided him, afraid that in his presence I would remain an unhatched neophyte forever. "But what would you do if they *did* pull a knife? Oh, kid, I'd be so scared! Listen to me talk, I'm such a dummy, aren't I, Loretta? I'll make poor Adrian a nervous wreck. Look, do you two know each other—Adrian, Loretta, Loretta, Adrian? Loretta, tell him not to listen to a thing I say!"

"A little dancing, a lot of drinking"—that was Barbara's answer when I asked her what the parties were like. I was beyond my twenty-first birthday, but at Hebron College in those days drinking was as much discouraged by the State (Iowa being "dry" then) as dancing was by the Church. You could smuggle a thermosful of martinis into an Iowa restaurant, or a bottle of red wine in a brown bag, and drink them from a coffee cup or a water tumbler; in the same way you could smuggle a square dance into the college (and, on one memorable occasion, even a rhumba) by calling it a musical game. I suspected that the training of my colleagues in both areas had been more thorough.

But on Friday night, when I had posted the Olympic Day results, I was not in a mood to put an end to the day. Such a victory deserved to be celebrated before Monday. Barbara would be going to the party—the shrug with which she answered that question had been affirmative, if not enthusiastic—and it occured to me that we would both be guests of honor. I could talk about our famous victory with more ease than I could drink or dance. In fact, I wanted to talk about it. There was a kind of biblical extravagance in the margin of our win—the Philistines routed by Gideon's handful, the five thousand fed with baskets and baskets to spare—and like the doubters and nay-sayers in those stories I didn't know what to make of it all. Clearly there was a meaning, but what was it? A blessing so whoppingly out of proportion could be taken as a reprimand, and since double-checking Nikkles' scoreboard I had felt alternately triumphant and embarrassed.

When I got home I showered quickly in the basement and changed into clean wash-pants and a sport shirt. "Come just as you are!" Sammy had said.

"A *party!*" my mother said. She didn't like surprises. I stood in the kitchen, my crew cut still damp, and tried to explain it to her. She kept her back to me, working away at stove and sink.

"You mean you aren't going to eat with us again? I thought you

73

didn't have to go back to work for once. Because of that Mount Olympus business, you said."

"I'm sorry. I didn't think I was going to go at first, but the playground won such a big victory today—"

"But I made this special stew for you!"

"I'm sorry, Mother. Don't worry, I'll get something to eat at the party."

"Oh, sure. Now they make you go to a party. Last week they made you show movies. Next thing you know they'll have you working on Sundays."

"Nobody's making me go—it's only a kind of celebration! Because our playground won!"

"You mean a victory dance, for goodness' sake? Surely they won't allow any drinking—how would they expect you to keep order?"

"No, no, it's only a party one of the leaders is giving—"

"I shouldn't think the colored people would like it either, to have an outsider there."

"It's not at the playground, it's at somebody's *house*, and I'm sure they're very nice people—"

" 'In all things practical we can be as united as the hand, but in all things social we can be as separate as the fingers.' Don't forget one of their own people said that. Just remember that and maybe you won't get so carried away with this job of yours. Gerrit, Adrian says he can't eat with us, they're making him go to a party! He says he'll eat at the party, but how can he get any meat in his stomach?—they can't serve meat at a public playground on a Friday night!"

My father had come in and was taking off his muddy boots on newspapers spread in the entry, his tall form, bent over, filling the narrow space.

"I've been trying to tell her," I said, "it's only a private party. A staff member is giving it. I'm going because Barbara and I are the guests of honor, because Hoover Street won the Olympics today."

I could hear Gordon and Paul in the garage yanking at the starter-rope on the motor.

"It's not getting any gas."

"It's got to be getting gas."

"Well, it's *not* getting any gas."

"Let him go," my father said, working at his second boot. "After a hard day on the playground a man needs a little rest and recreation."

"Right," I said. I headed for the entry, on my way out—but not until my mother made me wait for a ham sandwich. I stood on the newspapers next to my father's boots while he went down to the basement; I heard the refrigerator opening, a beer can popping, the shower going on. My mother muttered to herself as she sliced the ham and bread and spread the mustard. *Washington, Washington. . . . Carver?* When she handed me the sandwich, the waxed paper neatly folded in triangles at the back, she had what she wanted. "It was Booker T. Washington." She planted the sandwich firmly in my hands. "You'd better see what he has to say on the subject. And let your boss read him too."

By the time I found my way back through Calumet and then past Hammond and Gary into the dune country, the sunset was gone. In the dusk I recognized the entrance to the duneland residences by the iron gate across the road; it had the kind of vertical spikes that could have worn a pirate's severed head, or a trespasser's—though on either side there was no fence, only sand and the reedy grasses of the dunes. A uniformed attendant, an elderly black man, sat on a folding chair near the gate, reading a paperback book by flashlight. As he came to my window I saw that it was Richard Wright's *The Outsider*. Hoover Street's victory had made us both insiders, I wanted to whisper to him; but looking into his lean, stern face I could only repeat the words I had been given at staff meeting. "I'm going to Sammy's party."

"Yes, *sir*!" he said, straightening up with a broad, white grin. "Lots of folks going to Sammy's party tonight. You all have a good time, hear?"

The lane led into the hills past mailboxes and walkways and drifts of sand. I followed it until I came to a line of cars parked along the shoulder, their right wheels in sand and clumps of beach grass like the cars in automobile advertisements. Mostly from the finless forties and earlier fifties, they did not match their location. A log stairway wound upward to the top of the hill, each of the three landings lit by a gas coach-lamp surrounded by gnats and midges trying to get in. Lights were on in the game room (as Sammy had called it); the windows were round, and they made the house look like a ship sailing into the night. Music was playing, and as the music died you could hear, behind laughter and the clatter of glasses, the wash of waves on the beach. I couldn't see the water, which lay behind another ridge, down another stairway, but I could smell it and hear it. The lights of Chicago glowed in the northwest. I mounted the stairs, my heart beating as nervously as on the day of my interview with Harmon, and I imagined Elizabeth on the eastern side of the lake, walking on the beach in front of the sanitorium, perhaps, and far to the north, in the dark water, the fighting lake trout and parasitic lamprey eels.

"Adrian! So glad you could come!"

Sammy, in a wine-dark jacket and a bow tie, hailed me from behind a row of tall, unfamiliar bottles at the bar. The bottles had been in use, according to the playground rule, and the party, from my brief glance at it, seemed on its way to becoming what a later generation would call a "gross-out." Jeannie, the Chinese girl, was dancing with a glass in one hand and a cigarette in the other. She wore an orange muu-muu, a tentlike dress that together with her shining hair and the smoke from her cigarette made me think of wigwams. I saw Red, Debbie, and others I knew—all of them drinking, some dancing. Red had a glass in one hand and a paper cup in the other and stood in front of Jeannie as she danced, telling her about the short man and his girlfriend, the werewolf and his girlfriend, the vampire and his girlfriend—the kind of brutal one-liners that achieved their effect by coming at you one after the other while Red, aggressively deadpan, dared you to flinch. Jeannie was giggling, tears sliding from the corner of first one eye and then the other as she tilted her head, and she was using one of the words for the elimination of bodily wastes. "Isn't that the shits! Isn't that the shits!"

I stepped inside carefully; the door had a slop-sill, like those in the captured German submarine at the Museum of Science and Industry. The game room was dim and smoky, but I could make out the vertical blue of a navigation map of Lake Michigan on the opposite wall, and behind me, as I closed the door, a print of an ore-boat in distress. Superior Never Gives Up Her Dead. Outside there was a swimming pool and a patio or "deck." Through the open door and the porthole windows I could see more play-leaders—Barbara not among them—and a tall, thin woman wearing white, with half-lens glasses on a chain around her neck, whom I took to be Sammy's mother.

"Adrian, you guys were spectacular, how did you ever *do* it!"

I made my way toward Sammy. The topmost arc of a ship's wheel rose from the front of the bar and I grasped two of the spokes, feeling like a captain.

"Well, for one thing we must have had an awful lot of luck, but beyond that—"

He put his hand on my arm. "Kid, I'm sorry, but what were you drinking?"

"I'll have a beer, Sammy."

Sammy tapped a keg and handed me a foamer. Under the keg on the floor a row of white towels sopped up spillage. "Don't worry about the floor, Adrian, just drink your beer. It's my party."

"Right." I tried to focus my thoughts as I drank. "Besides luck I think the biggest factor was the emotional one. I suppose it's like any kind of mass movement. You reach a certain place where there's a kind of tidal wave effect, you just can't be stopped."

Sammy's eyes and mouth formed O's, his hands meeting at his nose as if in prayer. "Don't mention that word in this house, you'll scare my mother to death! She thinks we were crazy to buy the place anyway, with beaches caving in all around the lake."

"Really?" I pictured a blue wave moving from the top of the map and gathering strength until it crashed into our game room at the bottom. "I didn't know they had them on the lake—have you ever seen one?"

His hand was on my arm again. "Sorry to interrupt, Adrian, but this is important. Have you seen Barbara?"

"No, I was just going to ask you—"

"Kid, I know she came with Red and Jeannie and those guys, I just talked to her. She must be in the w.c. Listen, Adrian, where did you say you were from again?"

"Illinois."

"That's just what I told her! Barbara was trying to tell me it was somewhere else, wait till I see her!" He went over to the record player, shouting, clapping his hands and, to boos from our colleagues, blowing a playground whistle he took from his jacket pocket. He hoisted the curved lid—the record player was built like a sea chest—and stopped the music. "Listen, everybody! Adrian is here now—do all you guys know Adrian by now, he's at Hoover Street with Barbara?—and because of their big, *big* victory we're going to play their school songs. Come on, you guys, give them a big hand!"

Most hands in the room were busy with cups and glasses, and in the silence after brief applause, while Sammy squinted along the record to find the right groove, I heard his mother say, "If she won't sing for us maybe *he* will, Sammy." Then the needle was placed, the lid came down, and my school song came out of the game room's PA system: "We're Loyal to You, Illinois," by the Fighting Illini Marching Band and Chorus.

It took me a moment to realize that Sammy had supplied me with a new identity, and while I finished my beer and poured another I pondered the ethics of the situation. On the one hand I was not actively deceiving anyone; I was only drinking my beer and enjoying the party. On the other hand I doubted whether Sammy had the Hebron Hymn on his record. And, if it was my school song that Sammy's mother was planning to ask me to sing, "We're Loyal to You, Illinois" was much more rousing.

"Dance?" Jeannie asked. She swayed before me and I swayed with her, the two of us swaying in rough relation to the beat of my school song. "Our team is our fame-protecta, on boys, for we expecta, vict'ry, from you, Illinois!"

"How do you like working with Barbara?"

"It's great—I just hope she enjoys it as much. Did you see how our kids did today? They seemed to reach an emotional peak at just the right time, it was almost a qualitative change that you could sense. All of a sudden everything was going right."

I could see her almond eyes, squinting through smoke, begin to glaze over as Sammy's large round ones had done.

"How do you like working with Red?" I asked.

"Oh, he's a riot. He really is. He really has a sense of humor."

Her voice was light and wispy, like the delicate flower I persisted in imagining her as, even though she stood five-ten in the white socks that appeared and disappeared under the rim of the muu-muu.

"You're more the serious type, though, aren't you," she said.

"Oh, I don't know, I like to have fun—"

"You guys must have really worked hard for Olympic Day. To win by so much."

"I don't think we worked so hard. Actually, I don't know why we did so well. It's a mystery, one of those things you just can't explain."

"Red says you over-recruited."

"Over-recruited?" I stopped dancing. "What in the world does he mean by that? How can you recruit on a playground?"

"I wouldn't take it too seriously. You know how he is—"

"I know, he has a sense of humor. Where is he now, at the AAU? Filing a complaint?"

"I think he went to the john. You know what he said? He said he has little kidneys for such a big guy!"

"Well, he has a big sense of humor for such little kidneys."

"I wouldn't take it too seriously, Adrian."

"I won't."

"He probably meant it as a compliment. You guys really did a good job."

When I went back to the beer keg Barbara was sitting on a stool in front of the bar. I had last seen her early that morning, and her appearance startled me. She wore a white suit, high heels, pearl earrings, and no glasses. She was smoking a cigarette and not smiling.

"Congratulations!" I said. "You've heard about our famous victory?"

She nodded. "Frankie got the score for our bus. He was really tickled."

"So was Willie," I said. "Everyone seemed to be thrilled."

She nodded, looking out at the game room through her smoke.

"I understand even Red was tickled about it," I said.

"I know. I rode up here with him."

"You did? What did he say?"

"I wouldn't worry about what he says, Adrian."

"I'm not worried. I just wonder what he said."

"He said we were piling up the score."

"What! How can he say that? I didn't even know what the score *was* until the end!"

"I didn't either."

"Listen, everybody!" Sammy was at the record player again. "This is Barbara's school song in honor of Hoover Street's big victory today, so everybody listen!"

Another band played another march. "Do you want to dance?" I said, to show her I wasn't worrying. She laughed, her first laugh of the evening, but it wasn't directed at me.

"Ah, he did the same thing last year! That's not my school song, that's 'Conquest'! That's USC, our big rival!"

"You want me to tell him about it? He probably only skipped a groove on the record."

"No, what's the difference. We went over it last year anyway."

I drank my beer and she smoked her cigarette while we listened to her school song. She seemed definitely to be brooding about something.

"Well, the title is certainly appropriate," I said.

"It certainly is." Her eyes without their glasses were amber in the dim light.

"You're all dressed up," I said. "Sammy said come as you are. I thought you'd be wearing a purple dragon."

A small smile. "He said that last year too."

"Was last year's party rougher than this?"

"Wait and see," she said.

"I didn't know you smoked. I thought you had to be in training for dancing and singing."

With her forearm braced across her chest she pointed the cigarette at me, like one of her own slim fingers less richly colored. "It's to fend people off with," she said.

"Barbara, is something wrong? Is it something I said? Or—Red?"

She shook her head. "Don't mind me, Adrian, it's just one of my moods. You enjoy the party—you deserve it."

"Well, so do you."

Sammy came by to congratulate us both. "I told you Adrian was from Illinois," he said, shaking Barbara's hand. "What were you doing, pulling my leg or something? Kid, how nice your contacts look, no kidding, they make your eyes look gold!"

He asked me if I knew someone named Kermit Wellwether.

"Wellwether? No, I don't believe—"

"You must have heard of him—everybody at Illinois knows Kermit!"

It was my moment to confess. I thought of my school song: Hebron, Hebron, banners waving high; follow the truth, on truth alone rely. . . .

"Illinois is a big school," Barbara said. "It's a large, secular university, Sammy."

"Well, I know, but kid! A music major? A tall, thin guy? He played trombone at half time in front of the whole stadium!"

"I never got to any of the games," I said truthfully.

"Adrian had to study pretty hard. Just hitting those books, right, Adrian?"

"Kid, I guess you did! What was your major?"

80

"Animal husbandry," Barbara said.

"Wait a minute, are you guys kidding me? I knew Barbara was a kidder, Adrian, but I thought you were the serious type."

"I'm really looking forward to Pet Week," I said.

"Listen to this, Loretta—gee, Loretta, how nice your hair looks!—listen, tell me if these guys are trying to pull my leg. Nobody majors in animal husbandry!"

"I knew someone at Wisconsin who majored in that," Loretta said. "I went out with him once, he was a real nice kid. Kind of serious minded, but nice. Or was it plants? I can't remember, there was somebody in plant pathology, I think it was. . . ."

As they drifted away I felt Barbara's hand on my arm. "You live south of town, don't you, Adrian?"

"Yes. In, uh, Illinois."

"Could you give me a ride home, if you're planning to go soon?"

"A ride? Yes, sure. Of course."

"If you want to stay longer—"

"No, no, I'll be glad to. There's only one more person I want to see."

While she went to talk with Sammy's mother (fending a little, I thought, with her cigarette), I went out to the swimming pool to say my good-byes to Red Buchler. He was a football player, I had learned, and he must have done some weight lifting as well. He was showing a group of boys' leaders how to "press" the human body to arm's length. He had Schultz, the rather solidly built leader from West Side, above his head when I came out, his right hand on Schultz's chest, his left between Schultz's clamped thighs, his own freckled triceps bulging. The other leaders cheered.

When he dropped Schultz's feet to the ground I told him I was sorry if he thought we had deliberately tried to humiliate anybody. "That's not true," I said. "We weren't trying anything like that. We didn't even *know* the score."

He surprised me with a large handshake. His face was still perspiring from the elevation of Schultz. "Not your fault," he said. "Not your fault."

I withdrew my hand. "I don't think we have to apologize," I said. "We were trying to win, sure. But any time you win that big there has to be more than individual human effort involved. There's a kind of enthusiasm that develops that's bigger than any one person. What

81

I mean is, it sort of takes over, it's like a great natural force, like a tidal wave. I don't really know how to describe it—"

"Yeah, yeah," he said. "Don't give me any of that mystical crap. I'm a zo major. I know better than that. Running is no mystery to me, it's physiology, that's all it is. Your kids have got more striated muscle, that's all. Plus a little different bone structure, a little different arrangement of the tendons." He made a muscular movement of his head and neck—presumably looking for Barbara, since he put his face close to mine and lowered his voice. "You ever take a look at their feet, for Christ's sake? Huh? Did you?"

"Not really," I said. "Not with the eyes of a zo major."

"Well, do it sometime. I'll tell you one thing, though, you take something where guts is involved—football, for instance—and there you've got a different story. You can recruit them and train them and give them all the pads and helmets you want and it's never going to do a bit of good, you're never going to pile up the score on us in football, no sir—there the shoe is going to be on the other foot because football is a game of guts, and in football guts will tell."

In the years of football-watching I've done after that summer on the playground, I've often thought about Red Buchler's striated-muscle speech and wondered whether he's retained all his theories. Back then, however, I knew that I was not an expert in either zoology or football, while Red, apparently, was an expert in both.

"I guess you've got nothing to worry about, if that's true," I said, and walked away with what dignity I could, trying to clear the anger from my face before saying good-bye to Sammy's mother.

I found her near the record player in the game room—"looking for some oldies," she said. "That means the thirties, I'm afraid. I suppose at your age 'an oldy' means a song from last summer."

Sammy must have gotten his height from her. She was as tall as I, or taller, and very straight and thin, with a bright scarf and a high collar worn around her neck. Her eyes were a wide, almost startled, dark blue, and her mouth, also round, seemed pleasantly on the edge of a smile, as if she were happily, secretly amused at everything around her. Perhaps the accident of having a beautiful face perched at that height had given her an ironic outlook denied to the tall and plain or the pretty and short.

I thanked her for having the party at her house and told her that Barbara and I were sorry, but we had to leave.

"I don't suppose this has anything to do with my threatening to ask you to sing," she said. "No, of course not. I understand Barbara has a sore throat—she seemed to be taking a cigarette for it. What's your story?"

"Well," I said, "she does have to get back home, and her house is right on the way for me. I live south of town."

"But tell me," she said suddenly, and her eyes were candid and interested. "Sammy has worked for the City for three years now. I'm curious about how they assign people to these playgrounds. You're not a colored person, I take it?"

"No," I said. It was a straightforward question and deserved a straight answer. But I was piqued by her use, like my mother's, of the word "colored," a word which was out of fashion in my generation—we didn't like to think of Americans as if they were piles of laundry—and it made one of the thoughts I was unable to express while listening to Red Buchler spring to my lips now. Sammy's mother looked like someone who would understand a pun.

"I do have colored blood, though," I said.

I saw her eyes flit across my face, checking for an abundance of striated muscle, perhaps, or other giveaway signs. Then they widened delightedly, and I knew I had stumbled into a leg-pulling contest with someone who enjoyed the game and would give as good as she got.

"Oh-ho-*ho*, so that's the way you want it! Well, Master Adrian, I won't ask you to tell me the color of your blood. Since you're blushing so hard you save me the trouble. But don't think I'm going to let you off easy. I may have you sing for us yet. There *is* a fellow with blue eyes, you know, who leads a singing group—Sammy," she called out to the crowd on the deck, "who was that fellow who sings all the Negro spirituals? Help me find the record, will you? I want brother Adrian to sing for us."

We were interrupted by the sound of someone entering the swimming pool, followed by cheers and a cry of "Man overboard!" Red had been "pressing" his co-worker, Jeannie—despite her giggles he had gotten her over his head five times—and as a climax to his act had allowed her to drop into the water, where she stood at a depth of four feet like a shiny-haired lily, her muu-muu floating in a circle around her. Some of the others were attempting the same. Schultz, for one, had Debbie stalled halfway up his chest, her skirt flapping around his shoulder, his knees wobbling, while my colleagues called out "Watch it, don't drop her!" or else "Drop her!"

"Oh dear, I hope Sammy doesn't get the notion to try that," his mother said.

I excused myself and went out on the deck. Red had Barbara by the wrist; *her* he could press ten times, he was saying, and she was laughing, Ahh, Red, no, her high heels skidding on the wet tiles.

I found myself, although without a plan in my head, putting a hand on Red's burly shoulder like a policeman. He turned to me with Barbara's wrist still in his grip. I offered to lift him above my head. "Five times," I added recklessly, and he dropped Barbara's arm.

"*You*? You're on, buddy."

Instantly he assumed the position: on his back on the wet deck, legs crossed, ankles taut, his hands ready to clamp my hand to his chest, where small hairs poked through the weave of his jersey. "I'm down to two-oh-five for the summer, but even so you'll never make it. Look, I'll even take my shoes off." He kicked off his loafers. His feet in their fuzzy socks looked heavy, as did his legs in their tan wash-pants. "You'll find out it's a lot harder than I make it look when I do it. A person isn't the same as a barbell. Come on, you can use your legs, anything you want. I'm waiting."

"How am I supposed to get a grip? There's so much striated muscle everywhere."

"Your problem, buddy."

"Follow the wisdom of the blood, Adrian," I heard Sammy's mother call from the game-room door. My blood-wisdom whispered that it would be sweet to let myself be washed by a tidal wave of anger and adrenalin and perform the miracle of raising Buchler above my head, and still more sweet to drop him into the pool. But another wisdom told me I had never trained for this event and that the victory was won without it.

"You're right," I said. "I'd never make it." I allowed myself the pleasure of standing briefly over his prone body before turning and heading back to the game room. "I give up," I called back over his protests. "I don't want to pile up the score!"

Sammy's mother shook hands with Barbara and me at the door. She advised Barbara that she really should have accepted a dip in the pool; after a cigarette it was the best thing for a sore throat. "I don't care what color your blood is, Adrian," she said to me, "you two look real cute together."

As we left, stepping carefully over the slop-sill, we heard more bodies splashing. Then we were outside on the sandy stairway, with the sound of the waves coming from behind us in the dark. We went down the stairs, winding past the series of coach-lamps, and the music of a Negro spiritual followed us down the hill. "Sometimes I feel discouraged, and think my work's in vain. . . ."

I let Barbara in through my door, the passenger side too sandy for her high heels, and we drove back down the dark lane. The attendant with his flashlight was gone, the gate wide open to let us out. I found the road home easily. The only sound under the flying, moon-lit clouds was the roar of our motor. Barbara was quiet and subdued, arms and legs folded within her white suit on the far side of the seat. It was strange, I thought, how much she seemed in a party-going mood on the playground, and how little at a party. I began humming to myself, the many songs of the day going through my head to the tune of the racing engine, and I heard her chuckle.

"What's the matter, wasn't I doing it right?" It was a song I had heard Willie B. Weaver sing on the playground, usually during long-jump practice. "Going down to the river"—deep-voiced, eyes rolling as he loped down the runway—"gonna jump overboard and drown. . . ." Lee Roy, waiting at the sandbox with his tape measure, would spit.

"I realize I'm not a professional singer, but I didn't think I was that bad."

"Ahh, don't be sensitive, Adrian. You put me in mind of Willie, that's all."

"I guess I am over-sensitive. Seems like everybody was scoffing at our victory."

"I'm not scoffing," she said. "I'm proud of it."

After a while she said, "You didn't really graduate from Illinois, did you? Harmon told me it was a little school in Iowa."

"Yes. I was pre-seminary for a while but I graduated with a degree in humanities. It seemed like a lot to explain, so I let Sammy play the Illinois song."

"I know what you mean," she said. "Were you glad I covered up for you?"

"I can't thank you enough. I was afraid I'd have to sing the Hebron Hymn."

"Ahh! You repaid me a thousand times with your gallant rescue—I thought I would be baptized for sure!"

It was good to hear her laugh again. We drove through Calumet's dark streets, past the neon-lighted bars with drunks in shirt-sleeves sitting at the curb, past teenagers peeling rubber at the stoplights. I got her to teach me the right tune to "Going Down to the River," and when we reached her house we were both singing. Her house was much like others I had visited during the week, a slender two-story, frame and stucco, with three dark cedars screening the front porch from the yard.

"You didn't really have a sore throat," I said. It pleased me that we had risked to each other things we had trusted to no one else at the party.

"You're a genius, Adrian."

She smiled, and the look she gave me then—her smile like a light turned on above the white suit, her fingers soft on my forearm—was so suddenly warm and personal that I felt dizzy, as if I had raised Red Buchler to arm's length and spun him like a propeller. She got out of the car and smiled at me again through the open window. "I do thank you," she said. She was an actress and a singer and had many voices and moods; now I heard a kind of Southern formality. "I thank you very kindly for the ride." She clicked away rapidly on high heels up the front steps of her porch. The door, with its glass oval covered by a curtain, opened and closed; then the porch light went out. I drove home humming Willie B. Weaver's tune.

CHAPTER SEVEN

IN THE SUPERMARKET

DURING the week after Olympic Day I had a dream—so often repeated and meditated upon that it came to represent, like a postcard or snapshot or home movie, that time at the end of June when I was becoming "smitten," as my grandmother puts it, with Barbara.

If I was in fact falling in love, I was slow to realize it. Elizabeth and I had recently repeated our intention to go out with "others," and I might have been expected to notice that Barbara fit this category. But consciously I had in mind nothing that could lead to a "mixed marriage"—I hadn't imagined, in other words, that "others" could include people outside the True Reformed (or, possibly, Michigan Reformed) communions. As for miscegenation, it was a word I looked up for the first time that week; set in my pocket dictionary between "miscast" and "miscellaneous," it made a lurid first impression. It went without saying that a prohibition of mixed marriage would also, *ipso facto* and *a fortiori*, prohibit that.

Mixed marriage, after all, meant what Samson had done with Delilah. It meant what Joseph had refused to do with Potiphar's wife—or at least I had gotten the impression in some Sunday school class or other that Joseph's virtue lay not so much in what he didn't do as in who he didn't do it with. Nor did I imagine that the Philistines or Egyptians had a color different from that of the Chosen in the stories (that is, different from my own). I suppose I did imagine them as having dark hair—in fact I probably imagined both Samson's and Potiphar's wives as looking something like my Aunt Pandaria from Michigan: tall, regal, worldly, with high heels and trembling, hooped earrings. But the essence of their foreignness, what made them forbidden, was not looks or language but worship of something other than the True.

To prevent mixed marriage, Abraham had sent to his kinsman in a far country to obtain Rebecca for Isaac. To prevent mixed marriage, Rebecca had sent Jacob on the same trip to obtain Leah and Rachel, and in modern times Dominie Van Horne, in order to prevent mixed marriage, had established True Reformed Christian schools and Hebron College. Prophets and ministers had warned against mixed marriage. Tribes and kings and kingdoms had suffered from mixed marriage. Waves of conquering unbelievers had swept across Israel to punish mixed marriage. Divorce statistics proclaimed the evils of mixed marriage. A four-thousand-year investment of divine attention to this problem kept me, at first, from seeing that falling in love with Barbara was even a possibility.

It was during discussions surrounding the Supreme Court's 1954 decision that I first heard the question designed to make the unthinkable thinkable: would I want my sister to marry one? I had no sister, and as for my brothers, I ordinarily didn't care what they did as long as I could do it as well, or better, or before they did. The Negroes I knew—Mays, Banks, Minoso—were stars, and like other stars belonged to heaven, where there is no marrying or giving in marriage. Besides, since they were ballplayers who played on Sunday, my theoretical sister would have rejected their proposals out of hand. As for the Nigerian whose hospital our denomination supported, he was forty at least, and one pictured him asking for a girl's hand only in order to check for signs of leprosy or kwashiorkor. Granted, of course, he must once have been younger, even of marriageable age. Supposing, then—this was how the question appeared at Hebron College— supposing this twenty-year-old Nigerian Christian pre-med were asking for your sister's hand, and supposing he spoke English as it was meant to be spoken and not like David Niven: whom would you rather have her marry, a black believer or a white unbeliever?

Thus was the challenge posed by the liberals among us, of whom I am sure I was one; and when the die-hards maintained that one could convert an unbeliever—a Catholic, say—to the truth, while one could never change a black skin into a white one, our disgust was less for their racism than for their stubborn inability to think abstractly and accurately, as we could.

Only when I went to Hoover Street that summer did I actually begin to think what once had been unthinkable. The bride of Solomon sang, "I am black but comely, O ye daughters of Jerusalem." So might our Verella have sung, lovely long-limbed Verella, twelve years old, gliding on the swing of an early morning while I water down the sandbox (what a job for Adam in Paradise—watering down the sandbox in the morning!) and push the little two-wheeled chalk-lime machine along the right- and left-field foul lines. Swing, swing, dark and comely. Swing low, sweet chariot. So that was what the Song of Solomon meant—so that was what *Othello* was about! *Would you let your daughter* was not just a literary question, people might have practical reasons for asking it!

It is not only Verella who is black and comely, I note—perhaps to reassure Verella's parents in case they have overheard my thoughts— but also Lucetta, and Wesley's sister Rosellyn, and also the volleyball player named Sugar, and the older girls (more judiciously, some of these girls) who sit on the older boys' cars with flowers in their hair at the ball games in the dusk. Dark and comely. And if my theoretical sister were four years younger than Paul she might find eight-year-old Sonny, playing now in the watered sandox, to be dark—or rather, brown and comely; Sonny seems to find himself so, suggesting always by his approach to life that he is Mr. Cuteness in the flesh.

"Am I dark? Am I dark?" says Wesley to his sister and the other girls one night at the ball game, scanning his bare chest and arms with the gaze of a chef at take-out time—and what I see, besides the parody of Whitey at the beach, and the grace with which he carries off his racial self-definition, is the quality of his darkness: he is darker than some and lighter than others. And what did that fact mean, along with such things as the red hair and freckles I had seen before on the playground and now saw again, suddenly, with a diachronic eye? Only that what could be thought could also be done—*had* in fact been done, done very often indeed, as my researches after-hours in section E185 of the Calumet Public Library (Anthropology, Ethnology) increasingly confirmed. So often that even where forbidden by law (as in the land of our sister Reformed Church of South Africa) a special new category, intermediate to black and white, had to be set up by the Church's secular arm to account for the result! So often that even in Europe and its colonies, my amazed eyes read, and since the time of Othello, black ancestors had been supplied for such Northerners as Beethoven, Dumas, and Mann, as well as white ones for Ralph Bunche and Roy Campanella.

Among the writers I read that week was W. E. B. DuBois, who in his autobiography described the country of my own ancestors as "an engaging mud puddle, situated at the confluence of the French, German, and English languages." But what of the possibility, I wondered, for other than linquistic confluence in that land where the commerce of river and ocean met, where the silt of all Europe met the flotsam of the seas? Germans, French, and English had been there; also Spaniards, Moroccans, Jews, Arabs, Poles, Vikings, Romans, Indonesians, and Negroes from the Caribbean. Were those Dutch traders whose eyes first fell upon the fresh green breast of the New World, according to *The Great Gatsby*, interested in fresh green bosoms only? Had those Dutch slavers—the first to bring Africans to American coasts—eyes for nothing but profit and loss in their cargoes? Was bowling the only recreation of Henry Hudson's crew among the doe-eyed Indian maidens of the Catskills?

The answer was before my mind's eye: right in front of me, in Senior English, the tight blonde curls of Glenda Lieveding, so tight and curly that she could carry a pencil there, and sometimes did. I had several times plucked it out, golder than the pale coils of her hair, without thinking of the human geography that had placed it there for me to borrow. To the left of me a Mediterranean eye; here an olive cheek, and there an abundance of striated muscle. In my own family—the darkness of some aunts, the noses of some uncles! And in my own face in the mirror: something Hamitic in the upper jaw, something Semitic in the curve of nostril, something somewhere that might have caught Sammy's mother's eye and now caught mine.

In *Joseph and His Brothers* I read how Tamar, foreign-born daughter-in-law to Judah, son of Israel, twice insisted on her right to bear children by her dead husband's brothers, and finally bore a child by Judah himself—so fiercely intent was she that her blood should flow down the main channel of history. There was a new thought: the holiness of miscegenation, and the truth that how and where one "fell" in love might influence the destiny of nations, even nations yet unborn.

It was thoughts like these that circled my blue-eyed, brush-cut head as I watered and chalked in the mornings while Barbara sang and clapped hands with our dark children in the shade, and as I drove home from work to sleep and dream in the evenings—at first back to Orangetown, then later to the Calumet YMCA, where, in the first week of July, I moved my things.

It was about this time that my mother made the remark—and although she denies it now, I can picture it so clearly I have absolutely no doubt she made it—late at night, me with my odd hours lying before the TV watching Steve Allen; my mother with her night-person perfectionism folding clothes at the dining room table, the rheostat turned up full so she can see her work, each bundle so neat that we should have tied a ribbon around it instead of ripping inside as we did for a clean shirt or handkerchief; and my father and brothers, to complete the Oedipal picture, tucked into their beds awaiting the sunrise and its labor: "If you want to bring my gray hairs in sorrow to the grave, Adrian, you will marry a Negro girl."

She was using the King James version, I noticed later while brooding on her statement. Quoting what the patriarch Jacob said when told of the death of his son Joseph. Joseph, however, was not dead; he was safe and prosperous in Egypt, and married to an Egyptian wife (possibly a quite-dark Egyptian wife, as section E185 of the library would indicate), and had two half-Egyptian sons named Ephraim and Manasseh (Gen. 27:12-15)—and Jacob was overjoyed to see him, as no doubt Rachel would have been too, had she been alive!

Out of context the remark sounds uncharitable, and perhaps that is why she now denies making it. (Or is it that it sounds trite and inartistic? Those bundles of folded laundry were the work of an artist, one who should have had less perishable material to work with than clothes, and food, and children.)

In context it was different. Only someone who had actually thought about miscegenation, after all, could have made such a remark. *My mother had considered it*—so ran one of my earliest reactions—*therefore it was, clearly, a real option.*

Besides, she feared above all things that state of affairs known as having too much hay on your fork, too many irons in the fire, or more bitten off than you could chew. Now she was considering a new job, her first outside of mothering since my father carried her away from Hebron. It was the selling of plastic kitchenware at "parties" given in the hostess's home. The job might bring in some money, but the primary object was to bring prospective buyers into the new house. Old man Barnema, our neighbor, had recently made a surprise decision: going a step further than the father of the prodigal son, who had merely waited at home for his wayward child, Barnema was selling out and intending to visit his far-flung colonies, beginning with my former classmate, Bobby, and his wife and family down in Houston. My father, it turned out, was not the only one who coveted Barnema's acres. It was rumored that Harvey's Supermarket had designs on the three farms between itself and the railroad tracks, in order to build a shopping center and thereby better serve the South Calumet Area. While the rumor obviously called for a speedy decision, my father could not afford to take on a second piece of property without having realized anything from the first.

No doubt there were second thoughts in Orangetown about the enthusiastic welcome given the supermarket when it first arrived to "pump a little blood around."

Into this vortex of economic pressures I thrust my decision to move away from home. A long argument with my father finally ended when, after the ten o'clock news, he went to bed. His basic mistake, as he now saw it, was in letting me have my own car three years ago. True, I paid for gas, maintenance, title, insurance, and license; but the $300 initial cost had been borne by the family treasury (to which, however—as I pointed out—I had contributed more than $300 worth of summer sweat). The coming of the car marked the time when, in my father's somewhat mixed metaphor, I got a swelled head and became too big for my britches. That led to my uppity, unilateral acceptance of the Vanderbilt fellowship instead of going on to Hebron Seminary as the family in its consensual wisdom had once agreed (though the Seminary without a fellowship would have cost much more, I pointed out). And that led, the final straw, to the crass arrangement of my working for wages instead of for my father—and at a playground! for the government!—and paying my own family, as if I were a stranger and a hireling, fifteen dollars a week for room and board, a sum which was dirt cheap—even if I was sleeping in the basement—if you considered what I ate, as I would soon enough find out when I started paying the Y fifteen a week for room alone. Oh yes, a very logical progression of steps, he had to admit, once he had made that first fundamental error of letting me have my own car.

Having thus earned for me a couple of retributive glances from my brothers—not for my role in changing our primitive family communism into capitalist individualism, but because I had dashed their hopes of also having wheels of their own—he led them away to bed and left it to my mother and me to finalize the arrangements.

"And who do you think will be doing your laundry?" Miffed, she folds with meticulous care a T-shirt which I immediately seize and roll up, Navy fashion, after the style of my bachelor uncle, her brother, a ne'er-do-well who never settled down or amounted to anything after getting out of the service, and shove it into my gym bag.

"I'll do it myself. You won't have to worry about a thing. They have these machines at the Y—"

"Oh, sure, you'll do it yourself. You'll mix white and colored, that's what you'll do. That's what Gerrit did when I was in the hospital with Paul, just threw everything in together—"

"I'll do it right, I promise. Anyway, I'll be doing it myself all next year. It'll be too far to send it home. Barbara always does her own laundry. She never sent it from UCLA, the postage alone would be more expensive—"

"I suppose whatever Barbara does you have to—what are you doing with that undershirt? Don't you know 'wrinkles in the face mean character'—goodness knows I ought to know about that—'but wrinkles in the clothes mean. . .'? What would that be?—Lack of character, I suppose, lack of every kind of. . . ." She rummages in the bag, finding the shirts I have stowed there, and brings them out. "For goodness' sake, be faithful in the little things and the big ones will. . . . Haven't I taught you that, at least?"

She puts the reassembled T-shirts into the bag, and I follow them with six pairs of white sweat socks. She readjusts the pile I have taken them from.

"What about your food? With those odd hours of yours you'll be skipping breakfast. Don't you know the body can't store vitamin C?"

"There's a good cafeteria there, cheap, and plenty of restaurants where the leaders always go after—"

"Leaders? What leaders?"

"Play-leaders, I mean. Workers, my fellow workers—Barbara, for example, and Red, and Schultz—"

"Just who's doing the leading, that's what I'd like to know. You or this Barbara."

"Anyway, when you figure the cost of driving home from work, the maintenance on the car, the wear and tear, the depreciation. . . .

Plus you have to figure my time is valuable, not to mention yours. You won't have to make an extra meal when I come home late."

Now my Sunday shirts, two of them, starched and ironed, laid carefully over the table instead of hanging from the door lintel as they would have been in the old house; she will not make the least scratch that the mythical prospective buyer might see. She buttons up the collars.

"Oh, yes, I'm glad to see my time is so valuable all of a sudden. What about weekends? Surely you'll come home weekends?"

"Well, of course I'll be glad to help out on Saturdays, if Dad ever needs me." I produce two hangers for the shirts. "On Sundays I'll be kind of busy. We have to prepare these staff reports and plans for the whole week to be ready for Monday's staff meeting. That takes time. Anyway, I'll want to be cutting down on all these trips so next year I can come home sometime on vacations. After all, there are just so many miles left in the car—"

"And where will you go to church?" she asks, turning toward me with the two shirts, one white and one colored, shoulder to shoulder in her hands. And then, her blue eyes wide and blazing with a prophet's vision: "Don't tell me you'll be going to *her* church? If you want to bring my gray hairs in sorrow to the grave, Adrian, if you want to do the one thing which will bring my gray hairs in sorrow to the grave. . . ."

Which indicates the importance that *going to somebody's church* had for us, as a ritual act measuring seriousness of intention in courtship. And also my mother's real gift for prophecy—since it turned out that Barbara not only had a church but a father who was its pastor; though I was perfectly sincere at the time in saying that nothing was further from my thought, I didn't even know whether Barbara went to any kind of church or not.

Then there was the moral context. Pastor Boom was doing a sermon-series on Elijah and Baal in which Elijah's modern-day enemies included not just the secular world but its allies within and among us—our permissiveness, our growing tolerance for TV and Hollywood, our general tendency to find ourselves at ease in Zion and to relax our watchfulness on her walls. No doubt as my mother looked forward to my grandparents' biweekly visit she was prepared to see all her best acts of charity questioned: her defense of the Jamaicans' right to a place in our bakery line, her tenderness for offbeat types in the church, for latecomers, for "oncers," even (long ago when I was in grade school) for the adulterous couple who had to stand up publicly in church to confess their sin—all this she was prepared to see thrown up to her if I should bring her gray hairs in sorrow to the grave. So this, Cora, is the result of your wool-gathering tolerance—your son runs off to marry an American girl, in an American church, and a darky to boot!

No one would blame my father's conventional pragmatism—though he had helped bring in the supermarket that was now threatening, as we heard, to stay open on Sundays, besides forcing Swets Dairy and Ramshorst Pickles and Swart Bakery to meet the Chicago competition of Meadowmaid and Mother Bowers and Countryfresh. No, they would blame her and her tolerance. It was Gerrit, after all, who used to mock the black fishermen we would see along Stony Island Road on our infrequent trips to Chicago, dragging their lines in what is now Calumet Harbor: "Look at that! Anything to fool away the time! *They* know there's no fish in there!" While it was Cora who would respond with her Mary/Martha defense, that is, the superiority of the contemplative life; or the American pluralist defense (it takes all kinds)—or even, warming to the subject, an attack in the name of good parenting: "Can't you see they have nowhere else to fish? Maybe if some of us spent more time fishing with our sons we would be better fathers. Maybe we wouldn't smoke so much, either."

It was she, not Gerrit, who would have to do penance for her permissiveness. I would have ruined her defense of liberal principles by showing that I took them seriously.

The dream occurred after one of Harvey's Super Saturdays. (It was several years later, after Pastor Boom's retirement, that they became Super Sundays.) Super Saturday was when Harvey's ran its Lucky Shopper contest. If you were in the store then you got a Shopper's Certificate, a white ticket with gilt edging, from a girl wearing a tall hat and short skirt, and as you passed the meat counter you put it into a wire cage, or barrel, making sure to keep the stub. Later the barrel would be whirled around like a cement mixer on its cradle, and the girl in tall hat and short skirt would pull out the lucky ticket. She would hand it to a dapper young man in black, who had been pinning orchids on ladies as they arrived; he, from a platform laid across sacks of charcoal and softener-salt and peat moss, would announce the lucky number. If it matched the one on your stub, you were the Lucky Shopper. You would have five minutes to fill your cart with everything you wanted from Harvey's thousands of items; and all of that, plus whatever you already had in your cart, would be yours absolutely free.

I suppose I was there that day to provide an extra ticket for the contest, as well as to drive my mother to and from the store. (My mother did not drive; when we lived in the old house she would have walked down to Groen's IGA and had one of us carry the groceries home later, or she might have them delivered. Once the supermarket opened she ordinarily went with my father on Friday nights. In some ways he missed the pickle business, and it was a kind of recreation for him to keep up with the latest marketing techniques.) There were hundreds of cars there, and Orangetown's two policemen were directing the overflow from the Illinois side onto the grass of Bok's Grove, and from the Indiana side into the True Reformed Church parking lot.

The supermarket, like an airplane hangar or a fieldhouse, had no pillars supporting its roof; from the parking lot it looked like a giant glass bow about to aim a shot at the sky. Through advertisements on the glass we could see marshmallow-shaped lights suspended from the ceiling, pyramids of canned goods rising to meet them. Next to the store was a shallow pool with a pipe jetting rhythmic bursts of water in its center. There were coins visible on the bottom, though no sign indicated this was a wishing pool. Beyond the pool you passed through the "air door," made solely of swirling air, and you were inside, where, at least on this June day, it was fifteen degrees cooler.

Of the hundreds of shoppers inside Harvey's, the only one I recognized was a boy Paul's age called "Hoogie." He was the youngest of the nine or ten children of the Hoogenwerfs, a True Reformed family recently arrived from the old country and therefore almost by definition one of the "poor" of our church. He was thinner than Paul, and he wore his faded sweatshirt (possibly from a deacons' collection) with the hood up against the air conditioning. Because I was Paul's brother, I suppose—we had met a Sunday or two before—he attached himself to me, and as we went from aisle to aisle I was his guide.

Except for a cold tour through its frame and foundation during the previous Christmas vacation, when my father proudly pointed out where the checkout girls would stand, and where the frozen foods would go, this was my first visit to Harvey's. My previous grocery shopping had been limited to picking up a few bags at the IGA. Although Groen had introduced the cart system, his aisles were still dark and crowded, and you had a sense of foraging; if you took long enough old Groen himself would appear from behind the meat counter, wiping his hands on his apron and asking, "What is it I'm hiding from you?" At Harvey's I felt I was hiding from what I didn't want: towers of jam, pyramids of candy, bins of ice cream and troughs of canned ham, wicker funnels pouring out fruits and nuts, and ten-foot paper palm trees, fertilized by the gods, bearing bananas, pineapples, coconuts, even monkeys.

My grandmother loved to go there. "Oh, oh, oh, it's more fun than a picnic! Just to see that lovely red cabbage—it looks so fresh, Cora! Everything is so *tempting*." She would quote my grandfather's aphorism about a well-turned-out meal—"the looks is half"—and my grandfather would just grin, his usual sobriety lightened by pleasure in her pleasure, even though *temptation* was something he prayed regularly to be delivered from, and did it with such a weight of dignity at the table that your flesh would creep at the very word. (In the same way when you left their house his last words, "Be good!" were always immediately transvalued by my grandmother's: "But have a good time!")

I could see how she would like the store. It had something of the same air of material well-being and abundance one exerienced on stepping into her own kitchen on a holiday or on a Sunday afternoon. Music sounded from the walls (I remember the Pilgrims' Chorus from *Tannhäuser*), and we smelled not merely wet, waxed wood with traces of spilled soy and vanilla, as at the IGA, but bakery goods baking, delicatessen meats turning over live flames, coffee urns bubbling. Costumed figures welcomed us: Aunt Jemima with her pancakes, a Swiss Maid with triangles of cheese, a cow walking on its hind legs offering chocolate milk, a Calumet Giant, from the Little League, with a bucket of autographed baseballs. On behalf of a product whose name I couldn't catch, a farmer in straw hat and coveralls was filling free balloons with helium. The paper sacks at the checkout stands said "Harvey's Holiday" in red-and-white peppermint stripes. All that was missing was my grandfather at the door greeting us with his high-pitched "Hi, hi, hi!" and a glass of once-a-year wine to symbolize holiday revelry. There was a white-haired gentleman wearing baggy pants and wooden shoes who slipped me a tiny red bottle of "Western Michigan's finest wine," but this, he cautioned, could not be opened in the store.

No doubt to Hoogie, who had been in America less than six months, this was stranger than it was to me. He would put an item into his cart, waver, ask me "How much?", then put it back again. "Too dear." This was a phrase he repeated with increasing force as we turned each new corner and passed the salespeople pressing their samples upon us. Although my appetite was whetted by now, I could not have tasted a new potato-chip dip in front of Hoogie any more than I could have in front of Gandhi. In the hood around his thin-nosed, dark-eyed face, in the hand-me-down belt with three extra holes punched in, there was something monastic that impeded me. When at last the dapper young man took the microphone and announced that the moment of the Lucky Shopper was at hand, Hoogie and I stood together in a corner of the store between stacks of motor oil and cases of cola drinks, and the bottoms of our carts were hardly covered.

Harvey's furnished the setting for my dream, and Pastor Boom's recent anti-Baal sermons help account for my playing the role of Elijah the prophet. It was Hoogie's misadventure as the Lucky Shopper that must have triggered in my subconscious the unpleasant notion that I had to slaughter him, as well as others, at the brook Kishon, as Elijah slew the four-hundred-fifty priests of Baal and four hundred priestesses of Asherah.

In real life it was unpleasant enough. The moment the dapper young man finished reading out the lucky number, Hoogie, whose number was at least two digits higher, as I recall, took off with a shout down the aisle. He had the kind of urgency that compels belief. For a second there was no sound except for Hoogie's breathing and the thump of one eccentric cart wheel. Then came shouts of encouragement: "Steaks, kid! Go for the steaks!" I did not have much time to think. Two scenarios in particular plunged through my mind, one in which Hoogie was lionized, everyone's favorite-son candidate for Lucky Shopper, and another in which he was pursued by stockboys bearing knives for trimming lettuce, while the manager called out range and bearing through the PA system. There seemed nothing to do but run after him, catch him by the collar of his sweatshirt, and then, explaining things as best I could while he looked up at me with intense, hopeless eyes, deliver him to his mother and father, whom I found near the manager's glassed-in office. The glances I got from the other shoppers as we marched along—my right hand comfortingly, I hoped, at the back of Hoogie's neck, my left hand gesturing—were not entirely understanding; there was even some booing, and since then I've always pitied those officials at a ball game who have to escort a lost dog or unruly fan from the playing field.

The manager was a stocky, energetic man in a white shirt who wanted to make things right. For some reason he and Mr. Hoogenwerf, in their discussion of what to do with Hoogie's small cartful of groceries—augmented now by one six-pack of cola—both turned to me as translator and/or arbitrator. Manager: "Tell him Harvey's regrets this very much, and we want him to have these groceries absolutely free with compliments of the store." Me, reluctantly, to Mr. Hoogenwerf, whose balding face is fiery above his double-breasted pin-striped suit: "He says you should keep all this for free." Mr. Hoogenwerf to me: "You say I pay," indicating by the direction of his scowl that he thinks Hoogie has tried to run off with the shiny cart; no doubt Hoogie, like his friend Paul, is in love with vehicles of all kinds. Me, shrugging, to manager: "He says he will—"

But the manager, a person of action, is already packing the stuff into two peppermint-striped sacks. Nodding affirmatively, he gives them to Mrs. Hoogenwerf. She is as pale as her husband is red, but she hugs the sacks, nodding with the manager, her eyes fastened on his. The manager grasps Mr. Hoogenwerf's hand and shakes it, still nodding and smiling, and Mr. Hoogenwerf, puzzled, says "Wonderful," meaning either "Thank you" or, as I translate it silently to myself, "The supermarket is very strange."

In real life it is over then. The Lucky Shopper is a large, stately woman from Calumet, a Mrs. Stanback or Staubach or Stanhope, who has come prepared with a list; and as she moves efficiently through the packed aisles and the dapper young man broadcasts ("Now she selects Harvey's three-pound coffee special, flavor bred in the bean. Next her attention is claimed by—no, she chooses the German chocolate cake, fresh from our own bakery, with a little over four minutes of shopping time remaining"), my mother and I pay for our groceries and bundle them into my car and drive back home. My mother, preoccupied with her pre-Sabbath Saturday work, pays no attention to Hoogie's misadventure, except to point out that I needn't have been so rough.

But in my dream I can still feel Hoogie's hard, wiry nape under my fingers. We are running together past the checkout slots and through the air door out to the brook Kishon, which flows between white stones and ornamental cedars to the pool whose fountain spurts like an artery. Harvey's customers are running, too—the dapper young man and the girl in short skirts in the lead—out to where their cars wait in long herringbones on the parking lot. "Don't let one escape!" I shout, and the young man and the girl are brought back by the angry crowd, and I feel their napes under my hands, the young man's as slick as my own when my brush cut needs a shampoo, the girl's soft and startlingly round under her hair, without the bump at the base of the medulla oblongata that, according to high-school lore, is as sure a sign of the masculine as its absence is of the feminine.

The three necks bow before me. Can I do it, actually destroy even a Nazi or filthy idolater? And if so, how: by the sword, which their bowed heads seem to ask, or the easier way—by water, which seems expedient, the brook being hard by. . . ? But instead I am diving toward the pool of stones which is as deep and wide as the pool at Sammy's mother's house in the dunes, and arched with the streamers that Barbara and I used to decorate the playground in that hot week before the Fourth when we brought out the sprinkler and let the children leap through its silver galaxies. As I dive the three sacrifices dive with me: Hoogie emerges as Frankie, the badge glinting in his hair as drops shower from his still-dry wool; the girl in short skirts is Barbara, dark limbs and trunk chastely veiled in water to the shoulders, her head and two hands above the surface thrown back as if to give me a set-up in a game of volleyball. The dapper young man remains struggling and bubbling on the far side of the net that puts Barbara and Frankie and me on the same team. Though his head shows indistinctly, now as Willie Beaver's, now as Red Buchler's or Lee Roy's, it is always on the other side of the net, the same white-topped volleyball net that I wrap up every evening at eight o'clock, and over which I am about to make a terrific volleyball spike, Frankie to Barbara to me.

There the dream always ended, at that perfect volleyball moment. I never asked, in my musing replays on the way to Hoover Street in the mornings, how it all came out; I knew that whoever was down there in the foaming deep never came up again, nor did the ball I spiked, but sank with the whole opposite side of the net to the bottom.

What I did ask, on some of those mornings after I had moved to the Y, and drove to work from the north instead of the south, with the sun on my left instead of right, was another question: what color was I in the dream? Was I dark like the others, or was I white like Hoogie and the girl in short skirts before their immersion? Nothing gave me a clue; I could get no replayed image of my own limbs or face or hair, no mirrored glimpse of my skin—only that I was happily reflected in the faces of the others. Perhaps dreams come from so far inside that one can see only out. Finally I concluded, as I parked off Hoover Street and welcomed Frankie running toward me in the heat ("Aryan, we fitten to turn on the water?"), that it was a question for the waking world only, and did not apply to dreams.

CHAPTER EIGHT

INDEPENDENCE DAY

"NUMBER one," Nikkles told us during staff meeting for Doll Buggy Week, "watch out for anyone who wants stuff for his kid sister. First you see the sister and the doll buggy; *then* you give out the crepe paper. First you see sister and her buggy in the parade; *then* you give out the Cracker Jack. One year we had a playground where every trike and buggy was decorated in red. I'm not kidding! Mrs. Nikkerson can tell you—am I right, Hildy? Every vehicle in the parade, nothing but red. Somebody ran off with the blue and white. Okay. Obviously it must have been an adult, because we all know the kids wouldn't do anything like that.

"Okay, that's not the point. One year we lost a case of Cracker Jacks. Two? *Two?* All right, two, all I know is I'm running around at seven o'clock on the weekend of the Fourth trying to find a case of Cracker Jacks. I'm lucky to find *one.* You want to see some angry parents? You try telling them at the end of the parade their kid doesn't get a Cracker Jack. 'I'm sorry, Mr. and Mrs. Taxpayer. Somebody swiped a case.' You think they care about your problems? With little Susy screaming her lungs out? 'What is this, Mack, I'm a taxpayer too, huh?' Am I right, Debbie? Huh? Schultz?

"Okay. You know how to count. You know your playground. Some of these kids got more brothers and sisters than a dog's got hairs. *Sure* they want crepe paper. Let them come and get it. Make them decorate the vehicle in front of you. Otherwise you come to the parade—and where are they? They're sitting at home watching the television, that's where they are. With six rolls of crepe paper shoved under a table leg somewhere. Waiting for brother to haul in the Cracker Jacks. So, number two, you want to be sure and plan a program for the older kids. Something to take their minds off the giveaways. Otherwise. . . ."

On Hoover Street those who had outgrown trikes and buggies coasted all week long on the achievements of Olympic Day. They were so eager for dramatic replays that on Friday, when Nikkles brought our Cracker Jack in his own car, they were still running and jumping.

"Looks like your kids are really gung-ho," Nikkles said.

I told him they had been practicing harder this week than last. I did not add my suspicion as to the cause: Lee Roy, working time-and-a-half overtime for the Park Department in this week before the Fourth, never showed up to watch.

Willie B. Weaver, who had the true sixth sense for movement in the City's dispensaries that Nikkles feared, was on hand for both deliveries, tri-colored truckload on Tuesday and caramel-flavored carful on Friday. "Here it comes, everybody! Stand back! Whoo-eee! Turn them papers loose, man, let the old Beaver do all that hauling and sweating, this public property we talking about here"—but for all his talk, and despite all the stomach-patting and eye-rolling he gave Nikkles as the two of us hoisted the Cracker Jack into the shed, we had nothing but peace and good will on the playground. When the sun grew too hot for Olympic-Day reruns we brought out hose and sprinkler, for those who had swimsuits, and let the others sit around the tables where Barbara and I had placed them, near the swings on the shady southwest side, and help the little ones create their decorations for the parade.

Barbara's decorating teams differed from mine: on my weekly plan I simply listed those most likely to be present, while she, more elaborately, tried to assign responsibility to the "creative ones," as she called them. In practice it made little difference; wherever Barbara was became the center of playground activity, and children from the outlying districts of ball diamond, horseshoe pit, or sandbox gathered around to help with the vehicles or just to watch and listen. "Why don't we put a tad more twistiness in this streamer, don't you agree, little sister? The, ah, goals and history of the, ah, Department would seem to indicate"—and as her throaty mimicry moved from Harmon to Nikkles and into various voices on the playground, deep and shrill, the older children crowded around, grinning, to see who would be singled out and recognized. "Number one, more twistiness, and number two, it would seem to be of the utmost importance that we make use of the entire color spectrum down here on the lower left wheel. Kimosabe? That right, you plumbers? Ahh! Old Adrian worried we running out of red, *n'est-ce pas*, Adrian? Look at that, Frankie, I do believe he is turning red himself. Ooh, lookah here, look at Sugar's ruffles! Show us how you make all them pretty ruffles, Sugar!"

Around us the grass and leaves were busy with birds calling and whistling; robins hopped two-footed through the sprinkler, and starlings swooped bits of patriotic crepe paper to their nests. At night when I locked up after softball and volleyball, the older boys' cars roaring off along Sixteenth Street, the sun winked out of unexpected northwest openings in the trees, and when it sank the fireflies floated upward in the twilight, dimly pulsing: *light . . . light*. In the neighborhood, people sat on their porches after supper, or else inside with the windows open, behind unread newspapers, the women wearing light-colored dresses, the undershirts of the men gleaming in the dusk like vests of armor. It seemed enough just to sit and watch the evening progress.

On Friday night Barbara and I gathered the children on the sidewalk behind the equipment shed and led them and their wheeled toys—blooming red, white, and blue—across Hoover Street, first to the east, then back again going west. When we returned, Willie B. Weaver—one of that age group whose dangerous bicycles, Nikkles had warned, were likely if we were not careful, to careen in and out among our tots and toddlers and create havoc in the parade—was there to help me break open the cardboard cases and distribute the goods, his own guffaws and cries of delight adding to the delight of the children; and if he skimmed something for himself off the top I did not see it.

The Doll Buggy Parade was a favorite with picture-takers. When Barbara bent down to help the three and four-wheeled vehicles across curbs and other danger spots, flashbulbs popped around her on the street corners, and the dark porches rang with calls of greeting. She was at the head of the parade, photogenic in her contact lenses, patriotic in red shirt, blue dungarees, white socks, and bright smile. I brought up the rear, and my audience was sparse, my success more modest. But when we reached the playground a father in a moustache and sportcoat, a light meter swinging like a medallion around his neck, asked me to kneel and face the sunset between his son and daughter, their vehicles on either side, their hands, sticky with Cracker Jack, on my shoulders; and in two clicks of the shutter I was part of their history.

That weekend was my first at the YMCA. In the dark of Sunday morning when a series of trucks rumbled by, one after the other, three stories below my open window, I woke up and lay on my back listening, imagining until I fell asleep again that they brought strawberries from Michigan, early watermelon up from the South, and condensed in their cargoes all the sweetness of the summer.

I slept late on Sunday. At eleven o'clock, feeling pagan, unshaved, and free, I went out and bought a Sunday *Tribune* and spread it over the bed and small chair and table in my monastic cell, with a dozen powdered doughnuts and a quart of milk, and read it from cover to cover and listened to ball games on the radio all afternoon into the evening, and read my books from the library. On Monday, the holiday, I worked down at Island Park in the morning. The City ran sack races and other games then, and gave away more Cracker Jack; Nikkles had asked for volunteers from among "those who will be in town," and I counted myself, now, in town.

The afternoon was open. I worked a bit on my correspondence with Nashville, Tennessee, concerning the fall semester, and then decided on an impulse to go to the beach. It was a hot, bright day, and my family's annual picnic in Bok's Grove would not begin until evening. I put my trunks on under my jeans and borrowed a red-striped towel from the Y. Hoover Street was on my way, and driving past the playground—just to take a look at it, with its swings hot and silent in the sun—I met Barbara getting off the Hoover Street bus.

She had worked at the concession stand all morning, she said. Debbie had come to replace her after lunch.

"But what are you doing here?" She put her head and both elbows inside the passenger-seat window, her chin comically supported by the back of one curved wrist. "Are you aware that the, ah, goals of the Department do not include paying you time and a half on Independence Day?"

"I moved to the Y," I said. "To be closer to my work."

"Ah! Your work!"

"Actually I was just on my way—"

"Ah, yes!" she said. "We know how you love your work!"—and

riding on the easy wave of her laughter I invited her to go along with me to the beach.

Her eyes flicked to my rolled-up towel, and for a second she reminded me of Willie on opening day when he asked to see my whistle.

"Where's your suit?"

"Underneath." I patted my denims.

To my surprise she was in the car agreeing to go along. She seemed in a holiday mood, telling me all about how Harmon had entered the peanut race that morning, "his old white-headed self chugging along, looking so fine—wearing a *tie*!"

Nothing was stirring at her house but the curtains behind the three front windows, opened to the day. After a few minutes she returned, patting the rear of her Bermuda shorts.

"Mine too," she said. "That accounts for my unusual, ah, bulk."

" 'You thin, Barbara, but—' " I quoted a gesture originated by fourteen-year-old Wesley, whom Barbara had been reassuring one night because he said he was too skinny. *She* didn't mind being thin, she said, and Wesley with his skinny, expressive hands shaped an hourglass in the air, and we all laughed. "You thin, but, you know—"

"Drive the car, man," she said.

We rode to the beach with music. First from station WLS, while Barbara's lively fingers played the dashboard and my Hebron class ring clacked rhythmically, I hoped, against the steering wheel. When the ads came on she turned off the radio and led me, playground style, in a series of rounds: "Scotland's Burning," "Tommy Tinker," "Frère Jacques." Besides the deep, full soloist's voice that I heard later, when she sang at the Playground Circus, she had another voice that was easy to harmonize with, a clear, pure tone that rang against my baritone like a bell.

"Look at him! I requisition someone who can sing and look what Harmon sends me! Let's see you try this, you think you're so good."

It was a dialect song, Scots, about a man who catches his death of cold while courting Mary Jane on a mountainside without his hat. It had lugubrious words and a rousing melody in two parts, male and female, sung madrigal style. She did both parts with me until I learned it, and then we sang it through again and again, eight verses, all the way to the sand at the edge of the parking lot. People along the way, black and white, smiled at us through the open windows of their cars and from the warm sidewalks—first puzzled, then happy—as people are supposed to smile in the opposite season when carolers go by.

"You're really good!" And then, to cover the insult of her surprise: "We're really good together!"

"Where did you learn that?" I asked. When she shrugged—"church camps, you know"—I said "Oh," as if I understood.

Through the reeds and over the ridgy sand I tried, and partly succeeded, to walk as lightly as Barbara did on her dancer's toes, finding the strips of sand between couples who oiled each other's backs and nuzzled greasily, like seals on blankets. The difference in our skins was not greater than that of some of the couples we passed: my forearms darker than the pale ones, Barbara's darker than the tanned. We stepped delicately among sandy families and their lunches and lotions, guiding each other with the rolled towels that linked us like a relay baton. There were Negro couples sunning themselves, and a Negro family busy in the sand; I glimpsed brown, beige, tan, and pale white like the sand that shaded orange underneath as we kicked it. It squeaked under our feet as we ran. We ran beyond the farthest blankets, and where the beach was slender and gravelly we dropped our clothes, traveling light—Barbara, remembering, came back to tuck her contacts into a cylinder in her shirt pocket—and headed for the water.

"I can't swim well," she said—though her suit, a shiny black one-piece that looked brand-new and must have been bought in California, sported on its left hip a tiny pink-and-white red-capped swimmer with perfect form. Her own limbs above and below the suit's black outline tapered from light to dark.

"I'll teach you how to float."

The water was warm at first, then cold underneath. The deeper we went the more cold there was. She held my hand with both of hers and I pulled her along on her back, her white cap making a wake against the waves. We went out beyond the line of the farthest bathers to where, as my head bobbed, I could just feel the sand under my numb toes. I held her under her back and taught her how to float. Her arms were rigid, her spine arched. The sloping shelf of her buttocks tightened as the swells rolled by, head to foot.

"Breathe easier. Relax."

She opened her eyes and rolled them at me. "Just be glad I'm breathing."

When I stopped holding her, her legs sank and I felt the cold from her kicking feet. I turned her around, holding her waist, and taught her how to tread water by moving her arms back and forth horizontally, fingers closed. Her waist was taut and small beneath the wet, stretched elastic: a singer's.

"You're so light I could hold you up with only *one*—"

"Don't try," she said.

In the glitter of sun and waves her smile, with the halo of her rubber cap, made a single radiance. She felt better with her head up and her eyes open, but her fingers still clawed at the water. When her kicking slowed I pulled her back to a sandbar and felt her relax as her feet touched.

"You could have saved my life by teaching me that. If I'm ever on the *Titanic*."

"That's true. You'll have to teach me another song."

We practiced treading water and then floated some more, letting the waves take us in. She was not as lively in the water. We splashed each other and played king of the sandbar, but mostly we just floated, our fingers sometimes touching, sometimes our feet touching sand. We watched four-motored planes roaring over us on their way to or from O'Hare. Underwater we heard the buzzing, like metallic insects, of outboard motors; lifting our heads we could hear the calls and cries of humans on the shore. Behind us was the littered edge of Gary, East Chicago, Whiting. Off to the northwest under smoke and clouds we could see the buildings of Chicago. The dunes rose dimly to the east, and ahead of us stretched the long blue lake.

When Barbara grew chilly we went to the shore and lay down in the sun on our towels. She lay on her stomach and I on my back, warm and lazy, watching the big clouds pile up over the shore to the west.

"We can teach that song to the kids for the Playground Circus," I said. "Now that I know it so well."

She murmured as if asleep. "That's in August," she said finally. It seemed a long way off.

The piling clouds turned blue-black along the bottom, silver gray above that. "There'll be a storm," I said, watching. The sun went behind them and Barbara sat up, shivering. But when the wind shifted and the first fat drops came down she laughed and took my hand for one last run to the lake. We stood knee-deep in the water which splashed silver bullets around us and watched the rain wash people off the beach and turn the pale sand brown.

"You're shivering!"

Even her hand in mine shivered, and her lips looked purple. We ran back to our clothes and for the moment had the beach to ourselves. Our clothes were wet. I shook out the towels, which had lain beneath, and wrapped both of them around Barbara's shoulders. Her shoulders were wide and thin, like Frankie's, the gentle half-spheres of muscle covered with goose pimples.

"I'm all right," she said. Her eyes without their contact lenses had an unfocused softness that made me feel responsible. We struggled back over the wet sand to my car, carrying our clothes, the slim green reeds at our feet bending like the tips of fishing rods in the wind. I turned the heater on and shut the windows.

"You okay?"

"I'm okay."

We drove back through the smoky rain in silence, except for the beat of the wipers flicking water from the windshield and the blast of the heater drying us off. The headlights of other cars passed us like swimming fish. Barbara sat with her eyes closed, her brown knees under her chin, her arms around the towel around her knees. Gradually her teeth stopped chattering and the skin on her arms lost their—what did the playground children call them?—chilly bumps.

"I'm warm now," she said.

When we got to the expressway I turned the heater off, and as we reached Calumet the shower dribbled away and stopped. The sun was shining again. I opened my window, and Barbara found her contact lenses and put them in.

"You-all having a celebration?" she asked. The "all," I guessed, meant my family.

"Maybe they'll have a picnic in the evening. My father probably worked today, if it didn't rain there." Orangetown seemed far enough away to have missed the shower. "He builds houses," I added.

"Uh-huh," she said.

"How about you?"

She shook her head. "Monday is always my daddy's quiet day," she said, letting me hear the South in her voice. "He's a preacher, you know."

"Ah," I said.

Hoover Street's pavement was dry, with only a puddle here and there in the gutter to show that it had rained. When we reached Barbara's house the three front windows, one large and two small, were still open as they had been when we left.

"Looks like it hasn't rained at all, here."

"Sure did where we were," Barbara said. She rolled her wet things inside her towel. "I'm going to feel strange, running up the front steps dressed in a bathing suit."

She did it nimbly and easily, her lean legs unselfconscious in sockless tennis shoes, carrying the bundle of damp clothes under her arm as if it were a purse and I a cabbie who had dropped her off after a day of shopping. At the screen door she gave me a triumphant grin.

It hadn't rained here more than a few drops, I judged as I drove back downtown. Here and there I saw dirt streaks on the hoods of parked cars, but their windows were all open. When I got back to the Y, I pulled on my shirt to enter the building; and as I passed the phone booths and busy ping-pong tables in the lobby, the damp strips of cloth along my shoulders reminded me of the storm that had passed over us where we were at the beach and left me, I felt, with something new to think about.

At my family's picnic that evening there would have been no more than six or seven people, unless a Michigan uncle decided to come down; but on an ordinary Fourth, late as I was, I would have found them with no trouble. This year, however, Bok's Grove was for the first time the site of a beauty contest (Miss South Calumet Area) and fireworks display, and both the church and supermarket parking lots, flanking the Grove, were filled. I had to park downtown and walk. The brightly-lit outline of a Ferris wheel showed above the Grove's darkening oaks, and under the trees hung the lights of a row of tents where men with "ADC" stenciled on their Nehru-style caps operated concessions and games. A toy train for the children, pulled by a real steam engine, circled the tents on a roadbed of sand. In the grass of the lower area a platform had been set up and a speaker talked into a microphone, his voice alternately timid and strident as I worked my way through the sunburned, sweaty crowd, passing in and out of range of the loudspeaker set in the trees: "Her shopping cart . . . half the world's radios . . . six million miles of wire . . . over half of its telephones. . . ."

In this hullabaloo I missed my familiar landmarks—the pony ride, ice-cream tent, and OTRCHS alumni band that were usually brought out by the School Society fund-raisers; and in the dusty crowds around the tents or the quietly waiting folk on blankets and folding chairs I saw no sign of my parents or, in fact, of any Orangetown reunion. Perhaps my father had convinced the others to picnic in the new backyard, from which they would be able to see the fireworks above our piles of unspread black dirt. I started down 192nd Street on foot, but when I had climbed the railroad grade just beyond Barnema's house I could see that they were gone—there was only the pickup in the driveway, and the boat under canvas, and a yard light to discourage burglars.

"The berries are all gone," I heard someone say.

Old man Barnema, who had apparently been watching from behind his screen door, came toward me across his lawn, kicking up fireflies as he moved. His silver hair gleamed in the twilight, and the eyes in his lean, tanned face looked as round and innocently surprised as when I had spoken to him in Dommer's Diner.

"We'll have beans tomorrow, though," he said.

There were two signs in the lawn, one in black paint on cardboard, PICK YOUR OWN BEANS, and the other the FOR SALE sign of a realtor I didn't know.

"I didn't come for that," I said. "I'm your neighbor."

"Oh?"

"Gerrit's son," I said, pointing. "Your neighbor. Over there across the tracks? I went to school with Bobby."

I meant to ask him where my parents had gone, but once he understood who I was he began a confused speech about some kind of "trouble" Bobby was in down in Houston, apparently financial trouble, and then about the fact that, as he put it, "the colored is a human being too. The colored has a soul like you and me. You better tell your father that!" I wondered whether Bobby had run off with one of the migrant girls with whom he used to work in his father's fields—and then, a thought that struck harder, whether Barnema was rehashing a defense of me that he might have made earlier that very day, perhaps to my father in the diner. Who knows who might have spotted my Chevy at the beach?

"I don't mean a Catholic," Barnema said. "You take fellow with one of those what do you call them on his dashboard—"

"Saints," I said.

"— he put that idol in his car of his own free will. Isn't that right?"

"Well, I suppose that's one way of—"

"How's that?"

"Right."

"But you can't blame him for how he's born! Can you? For his skin? Is that his fault?"

"I guess not."

"How?"

"That's an interesting distinction, Mr. Barnema—"

"You're absolutely right! Absolutely! You better tell your pa that! You tell Gerrit that for me!"

In the deepening dark the speaker was concluding, his voice coming to us past the quiet supermarket: "drives her family . . . millions and millions . . . three times the size of our Area!" There were scattered cheers which broadened suddenly into shouts when the first loud rocket went off.

"Now they're starting up the contest." Barnema came closer and lowered his voice. "You see? In my day we had to cover up their legs. Even the infants. Any more, they make their rubber pants with ruffles on them. To show them off, you see? Changing times! You better tell your pa that! Changing times!"

"Well," I said. "I appreciate your interest."

I left him to interpret that as best he could and headed back along 192nd's double row of parked cars and then downtown to where I had left mine. I wondered whether Barnema's "pick your own" salesmanship would be more successful than my mother's kitchenware parties—and then, as I thought in that way of the sale of the two houses together, it occurred to me what Barnema might have been saying he had done to my father. *The colored has a soul too. Not of course to those who worship idols of their own free will, but to a colored man and a Protestant. . . .* And then I thought again, this time hoping it was the truth, that he or one of his family might have spotted me and Barbara at the beach.

I could have gone on looking for my family in the Grove, or at my grandparents', but it seemed a little late for that. I unlocked my car and drove out of town toward Calumet.

The three weeks after the Fourth were—though not necessarily in this order—Crafts, Games, and Hobbies Weeks. I remember pushing wire through tissue paper to make flowers, twisting rubber bands around the paddles of wooden boats, collecting bottle caps for the wheels of racing cars, clamping together the glued pieces of tie racks, trivets, napkin holders, and wren houses. Each day we carried the green tables out under the elms on the west side border; the leaves dropped tiny, sticky specks of sap in our hair, as they did on the roof of my car, and the sunny hours were full of the smell of sawdust and turpentine. If in the mornings while watering the sandbox I felt like the first Adam, in the afternoons I felt like the second: hammering, sawing, sanding, nailing, gluing, painting, shellacking.

In the evenings, after softball or volleyball, we sometimes roasted wieners over the embers of our saved-up scraps—I remember Barbara's deep, bright laugh in the firelight—and, if we could collect enough nickels, we had a watermelon party. Thirty slices at a nickel each equaled a twenty-pound watermelon. I would drive a mile north, to the old Harvey's Market there, and ask the manager for a special rate; once I got it, and once, I recall, I paid the difference. I sliced, using the knife Barbara brought from home in a paper sack—*that* was the longest Hoover-Street knife of the season, though at the time I thought only of how guileless our playground was, eating watermelon and singing songs around the fading embers while travelers along Hoover Street gazed at us through the bushes. Barbara and our Junior Leaders for the week distributed the sweet, dripping triangles; and afterward the children helped me wrap up the rinds in newspaper and took turns hosing down the tables and quenching the fire.

One evening during the first week after the Fourth, Lee Roy came back. His right thigh was still bandaged—he wore track shorts and his Indiana sweatshirt—but when he played softball it seemed to me he was running hard. At his urging I went out to home plate to call balls and strikes, leaving Barbara with the low-organized games at the equipment shed. He played his center-field position with dash and flair. "Watch this smoker: frozen rope to third, Jake—ye *gods*, what kind of effort is that! Give me a real third baseman and you'll never take that kind of liberty with my arm, I'll tell you that."

Center field was the position nearest the equipment shed, and just before seven, when Barbara began putting away the smaller pieces before going home, I saw him talking to her between innings, pushing the overturned sailor hat back up on his head with both hands, his torso bobbing in what seemed to me an exaggerated show of joviality. I excused myself from umpiring, and as I came to the shed to help carry in the ping-pong table—standard procedure at seven o'clock, so that neither of us would have to handle it alone—I heard Barbara say, "Ahh, no, Lee Roy. Thanks, but you know we have to work so late on Friday with the Craft Show and everything. . . ." I stopped soon enough, I thought, so that Lee Roy should have seen my long evening shadow or heard the clearing of my throat; but he kept on.

"Maybe we can, you know, go somewhere afterward?"

I heard one of the older boys behind me yell, "Hey, Fleet, you playing ball or just going to fool around?"

Barbara took an end of the ping-pong table and laughed in my direction. "Come on, Adrian, I've got all this heavy stuff to do." As I took the other end she added, "You *know* you too young for me, Lee Roy!"—but her friendly laughter didn't soften the look I glimpsed on his face as we wrestled the table inside.

"Oh, yeah," he said, and with a crisp jerk, one hand fore and the other aft, snapped the sailor hat back over his eyes. "See y'all around, then," he said—the second Southern pronunciation I'd heard him use—and walked away, dragging his right leg a little.

I was not eager to resume umpiring while Lee Roy played, but when Barbara left and I came out of the shed for my last hour he and his three-speed bike were gone. The older boys invited me to play in his place.

I spent that weekend in my room, and sometimes in the muggy park across the street, where sidewalks crisscrossed at a gazebo near the Civil War memorial, and read the New Testament. It was a recent translation in paperback which I had bought as an aid for my class in Greek. It was laid out like a novel: lines of print running the width of the page, verse numbers in tiny type in the margins, chapters subsumed under larger headings like "Journeys and Encounters." It was too free a translation to be helpful for the kind of analysis we did in Van Wetback's class, but now I read it like a novel, reading through most of Saturday while I ate cheese sandwiches prepared with my pocketknife, and while I listened to ball games with the sound turned off during the advertising; I finished the five books of stories late Sunday morning and in the afternoon skimmed through the letters, winding up Ephesians while Philadelphia was beating the Cubs for the second straight time.

Despite all the passages that had flashed by me about letting the dead bury their dead, setting brother against brother, and giving up father and mother for the sake of the kingdom of God, when I finished reading I felt close to my family. Close, but also, remembering the evening of the Fourth, anxious. Whatever Barnema had been talking about seemed to involve me and my family—or was it, possibly, nothing at all? I waited until nine o'clock that night, when I judged they would be home from church, and then went down to the pay phone in the lobby and called.

"Where've you been?" my father said as soon as I'd said hello.

"Fine," I said. "How are you all?"

Before I could rephrase my answer he was talking off-mike. "How should I know what he wants? I just picked up the phone. *You* want to talk to him?" There was more noise, muffled.

"She doesn't want to talk to you," he told me. "She's all in a dither about one of her parties coming up"—there was a background of protest, my mother's contralto rising to soprano, and I could picture my father leaning both elbows on the kitchen table and covering his left ear as he over-rode her—"so she says she'll let me do the talking. I don't know if she will or not but that's what she says. What seems to be the problem?" He amended it: "How are you?"

"Okay," I said. Things seemed tense at home; my own palms were sweating. "I tried to get to the picnic on the Fourth, but—"

"You didn't go to the Grove, did you? That place was a madhouse. We were in Dad's backyard all night. Tried to take the boat out—Pauly's been after me and after me—but it rained real hard there for a while and I said, 'For Pete's sake, Pauly, you want to take it out for the first time in the rain, with your allergies and everything?' He's been kind of weepy lately, especially in the morning. Cora thinks he's got allergies. My theory is he doesn't get enough sleep. Gordon's out tomcatting somewhere in the car. I was telling Johnny this morning at church—no, wait a minute, it was tonight—at least that's one way to get the car washed once in a while. You hear anything from Elizabeth?"

116

"Just a postcard that came when I was at home. She says she likes her work—"

"Well, there's no reason for me to butt in, that's your business. Johnny's just a real good friend, that's all. I don't know what I'd do without him. I don't know, seems like Gordon can stay out till all hours night after night and still be healthy as a horse, but every time somebody sneezes Pauly catches cold. He needs more sleep, like me—I'm ready to turn in right now except I want to hear what the weather's going to do."

There was more muffled noise; I assumed he was telling Paul to get to bed.

"Says she's got too much to do to talk on the phone," he said, coming back. "But I notice she keeps getting her oar in. She wants to know what are you doing on weekends besides not coming home?"

"Well, I've been doing a lot of reading. Like today I read practically the whole New Testament." I paused, but he didn't react. "Saturdays I mostly do the laundry, get a haircut, buy fresh fruit and stuff at the market, take care of the car. . . ."

"Does his laundry," I heard him tell my mother. "Sleeps in on Sunday and reads the Bible."

"You don't call that Christian fellowship, do you?" he said to me. "Isn't that kind of *afgescheiden*? All by yourself with your nose in a book?"

"Well, maybe." I resisted an urge to say that I had to draw the line somewhere. "Speaking of fellowship: have you by any chance seen Barnema lately?"

"Who? Him? Why, what about him?"

"I just remembered he was supposed to be thinking about moving. I wondered if you happened to run into him. At the diner or anyplace."

"Listen, is that a pay phone? I hear somebody playing table tennis—sounds like you and Gordon in the old house when you built that thing. You must be out in the lobby. Yeah, I've got some things to say about—on that subject, but not over the phone. Anyway, it doesn't pay to scream before you're hurt. Or even if you are. Don't tell everything you're thinking, my dad always says."

He was silent a moment, and the cops-and-robbers atmosphere generated by his last remark struck me as foreboding. On the other hand, there seemed no dramatically bad news to report.

"You got anything else?" he said finally. "I don't want to break away, but I want to see if it's going to rain tomorrow."

"Well, just that I hope you're all okay, and if you need me to work on a Saturday—"

"No, look. You're a grown man, you've got your own life to lead and I've got mine. If you don't want to get involved in building and contracting I can't say I blame you. You're in the mud in this business in more ways than one. Everything is always in a state of flux, you're not in control of your life. I know I've done the best I could to give you and the boys a start in life, and I guess that's all anybody can ask. Maybe I'll have to ask a return favor someday, but not now. You just go ahead and get ready for your school—I know that's no picnic, either. I couldn't sit with my nose in a book all day to save my neck. Well, look, I know you're paying for the call. . . ."

He had sounded so emotional during this speech, and I was so relieved at having been given, as it seemed, an honorable discharge, that I found myself saying, "Well, thanks for everything." I added, after a moment, "Say hello to everybody for me."

"Okay," he said. "You do the same." Before I could ask what he meant, he hung up.

One morning during the next week I asked Barbara—casually, just before she left for lunch—what church her father was pastor of. "Methodist Holiness," she said. "You ever hear of it?"

"No, I don't believe—"

"It's just a small denomination." There was a note of concession in her voice that seemed to excuse both the church, for being small, and me, for not having heard of it.

"Well," I said, "there are a lot of small denominations."

"My daddy always says, 'God must love the small churches or He wouldn't have made so many'!"

That night in the yellow pages of the Calumet telephone directory I found the name of her church. Methodist Holiness. Sixteenth and Pine. The Rev. John C. Robinson, Jr., Pastor. *Meeting at 11:00 AM.* The time of the service was of interest to me. Years later, when interracial "sit-ins" were being held in some of the nation's churches, I was surprised to hear someone refer to eleven o'clock on Sunday morning as "the most segregated hour in American life." I had always thought of that honor as belonging to nine-thirty, which was the hour when True Reformed congregations met after shaving at seven, break-fasting at eight, and arriving in the parking lot at nine so as to get a good place. It was the rest of America, I thought, who met together (in time if not in space) at the ecumenical and integrated hour of eleven.

I asked her one evening how she had happened to choose singing and dancing as a career. Like most people our age who were graduating from college she must have had experience with that question, I thought, and might have evolved a formula for it. But she hesitated, and when she spoke it was with the same combination of brusqueness and timidity I had sensed when she spoke of her father's church.

"It was more or less in honor of my mother. She died when I was two. In childbirth—he would have been my baby brother."

It was the time when the playgrounds were emptiest, the "dead time," as play-leaders called it, between four-thirty and seven, when our supper breaks were scheduled, first Barbara's and then mine. We had begun using these hours for conversations of our own—that is, on non-playground matters—which we couldn't carry on when the children were there. I would bring a sack of sandwiches and fruit and stay on during my break. Barbara, after going home to fix her father's supper, would sometimes come back before six. She would find me sitting on a bench near the equipment shed, overseeing a child or two in the sandbox, another on the swings. "Guess who?" she'd say from behind, her fingers bandaging my eyes.

"Willie Beaver. Your hands are sticky."

I would take out my paper sack and we would sit on the bench and talk, leaning against the warm bricks of the shed while the sunlight turned yellow and faded, until the children came back for the evening schedule of events.

"She would have been a good singer. She was a Baptist, but she was a good dancer too. My daddy always said so. She had a scholarship to the New England Conservatory when they got married."

From her clipped, determined way of speaking I felt that she must have thought often about her mother's death.

"Did your father make her give it up?"

"Ahh! My daddy? He wanted her to have a career! He can come up with a theological argument for anything at all. You ought to meet him sometime, Adrian."

In another conversation we had discussed the question of infant baptism. I had won her respect as a theologian, or at least as a casuist, by my easy recital of the True Reformed arguments in the affirmative—the proof texts in which so and so was baptized "together with his whole house," the analogies with circumcision and the crossing of the Red Sea, and so on—although I was beginning to find these arguments specious myself. I was glad to hear that the Methodist Holiness people supported baptism of adults—"not necessarily by immersion, though," as Barbara said; "sprinkling is okay."

"They warned her not to have any children after me, but"—her laugh was subdued—"she went ahead and did. She had high blood pressure and a clot developed."

"I'm sorry," I said.

"Daddy wanted her to go ahead, but she gave it up for him. Said she could be a singer or a preacher's wife but not both. Ended up neither one."

To take the edge of sorrow off our talk I said that I would like to meet her father sometime.

"Oh, yeah!" she said, her eyes widening with delight. "He'd love to argue with you!"

I drove by the corner of Sixteenth and Pine at a little after eleven o'clock that Sunday morning and stopped for a moment to take a look at the Methodist Holiness Church. It was a white frame building, grimy with years of soot, like most of those in the neighborhood, and looked like a large house except that it had its front door at a corner, with a small bell tower above it, and the three windows on each side were opaquely colored, mostly in sections of faded green and brown. The lower panes had been opened, and through the window screens I could see the dark shapes of the congregation inside. The church looked crowded.

Judging by the scant number of cars on the street (there was no parking lot), the ratio of churchgoers to vehicles must have been two or three times greater than it was in Orangetown, where my estimates were about four to one in the morning and two to one at night, when the smaller children stayed home and some of the teens drove cars of their own. Here at last was the church of my father's ideal Sundays— whole families must have walked together to worship, a pedestrian parade of Christianity coming along the wavy, up-and-down sidewalks of Sixteenth and Pine, wearing navy and white polka-dots and wide-brimmed summer hats, some of them carrying Testaments, the men in dark, narrow ties carrying suitcoats over their arms, their white shirts flashing in and out of the shade of the elms whose roots humped the sidewalk. The squat, square-built shape of the church suggested that sometime, maybe fifty years ago, before the Second War and maybe the First, it could have been walked to by a different, more Truly Reformed kind of congregation, one that believed in baptizing infants instead of adults—except, of course, that in that case they would not have walked, since they would have been farmers driving in from the country; there would have been hitching posts instead of elms, and the sidewalks would have been boards or mud.

One of the double doors in front was opened, and a bald, high-domed gentleman whom I took to be an usher looked out at me curiously. I drove up to the stop sign, and as I slowly turned the corner I could hear the singing from inside:

> Hallelujah, praise God!
> For the battle is done!
> For the vict'ry is won!

The singing had a large, adult gravity that was different from the singing on the playground—there was more masculine depth in it, and more aged vibrato, than in the treble-piped sounds around our handcraft bonfires, and the sound of many hands clapping was solid and mature. It made me feel that this was where the playground, grown up, met on Sundays.

As for my own schedule: the playground with its ten-hour days kept me busy during the week. After closing at eight I would hurry to the downtown library, arriving at this sister institution in time to check out a few books before my fellow public servants started dimming the lights; these and a newspaper would see me into the wee hours, or whenever the Y's third floor cooled down to sleeping temperature. In the mornings I slept late, late enough to make my ten o'clock opening hour seem normal and natural and, finally, early. On Monday nights we had staff meeting until nine, and then Barbara and I would go out for something to eat with the other leaders—Sammy was always there, Debbie and Jeannie sometimes, Red seldom—and I would give Barbara a ride home, which saved her from having to wait for the bus.

But as the weeks became fuller, the weekends loomed longer and emptier. I needed no more than one haircut in a fortnight. The wax job I had put on the Chevy the day before visiting Barbara's church would protect it from falling leaves and the insults of birds heading south and even from snow (if they had snow in Nashville) before it would have to be replaced. The New Testament was good for one weekend but not for every one. On Friday night I had considered checking out a two-testament Bible and reading backward from Matthew, but the book was so heavy in my hand, and Genesis so many pages distant, that I put it back on the shelf. I began to see the point of the value my father set on fellowship. By All-Star break the Cubs and Sox were already out of the pennant races; and all the reading I did in section E185 during the week made it seem anti-recreational on Saturday and Sunday. After coming back from my ride past the church—the Y was waking up now, both ping-pong tables in steady operation—I spread the *Tribune*'s entertainment section over my bed. While I ate some pears out of a can and drank the sticky juice I looked for something I could ask Barbara to go to with me, in order to shorten the weekend. Or, conversely, to lengthen the week.

On Monday night, as we drove home from staff meeting and pizza, I asked Barbara whether she would like to see a Bergman film with me on Saturday. Her answer took longer than I had expected. Not that I expected an automatic yes—as I hastily reminded myself— but I had, after all, given the matter some thought, and had judged that the phrase "Bergman film" would prove not unattractive to someone who had spent her college years in the movie capital of the nation (in contrast to a Hebronite like me, who had just learned to separate Ingmar, the filmmaker, from Ingrid, the actress—and her, in turn, from Garbo, whose famous desire to be left alone I had been achieving the last few Saturdays and Sundays). She might have other plans, of course. It might possibly be that she would consider me, if not too young, like poor Lee Roy, for whom I was already anticipating some retroactive sympathy, then perhaps too . . . too much something else. Okay to spend time with on the playground, when you were being paid for it, but not on the weekend.

We stopped in front of her house, and my face grew warm as I realized that what I had asked for was a "date." The spontaneous trip to the beach could be considered an outing, a ride home after pizza and beer and staff meeting might be called a professional courtesy (or an occupational hazard)—but this was apparently different, this was to be a *date*. "So I asked her for a date!" I imagined myself saying to Nikkles or Harmon when confronted with some hitherto-suppressed Handbook rule against "dating" one's co-leader. "One little date, so what?"

"What time would we be likely to go?" she asked finally. Serious. Cautious. Had I asked her to go to Mars? I remembered that there was an afternoon as well as an evening showing. Her father, being a preacher, would want her in early.

"We could go in the afternoon. . . ." But would a "holiness" preacher, whose service began at eleven, be likely to be a Sabbatarian? Wouldn't it seem I had offered the matinee out of cheapness? "Or we could go in the evening. I really don't care, it's all the same—"

She was already smiling her consent. "Why, I think that would be just fine," she said, and I detected the same formal tone I had heard the previous Monday night, when she had thanked me "very kindly" for the ride. She got out, and her bright square smile shone in my window-frame. "We can discuss the details tomorrow. Okay?"

There were more than one day's worth of details. On Tuesday, before she went home for lunch, we settled when I would pick her up, what time the film began and ended, when we would be likely to return. On Wednesday, while we carried tables outside, then inside, then outside again, as the gray clouds turned their showers on and off: "You going to wear a jacket—on Saturday?" Thursday we spent an eight-hour workman's day in the basement of City Hall while the rains poured outside, cutting long candles into short ones and carving out wicks for them, for later use in the Lantern Parade. "Why don't I pack us a lunch to carry along?" she said when I drove her home afterward. "On Saturday, I mean."

I began to see in all this a worry about how we were to appear in public—about how we were to be legitimatized as a couple. We were legitimate while at work, apparently, or when thrown together haphazardly on the National Birthday, when all kinds of excessive statements on freedom were tolerated, along with the popping of otherwise dangerous and illegal firecrackers. But as for a day which was neither fish nor fowl, workday nor holiday—

Did she prefer afternoon to evening because there were fewer implications of courtship—or, not to put too fine a point on it, of the exchange of genetic material, which even the twinned nightcrawlers in the dewy playground grass accomplished by night and not by day?

Did she wish me to wear a tweedy jacket, uniform of the collegiate foreign-film lover whose "date" just happened to be a foreign-film lover of visibly divergent ethnic background? And the lunch. Chicago was of the Big Leagues. Any restaurant would gladly serve Nellie Fox and Minnie Minoso if they clickety-clacked in together wearing their baseball spikes, or Andy Pafko and Ernie Banks—though I wasn't sure what would happen were Ernie to come in with Andy's wife, or Andy with Ernie's. Did Barbara imply that I belonged to the bush leagues, Dommer's Diner and other such places, where Andy went inside to eat while Ernie chomped a drumstick on the sidewalk?

Or did I get good marks for deciding to appear by daylight rather than hiding in the dark? Did she want to save me money? Was she allergic to restaurant food?

I decided to take no thought for Saturday, what we should eat or drink, or wherewithal we should be clothed, but simply play everything by ear. I said I would wear a jacket if it looked like rain. If not, not. Period. Don't bother about the lunch, I told her. If we get hungry we'll stop at a restaurant. If we don't, we won't. Period. End of discussion.

"Ah, you just let me fix us something to carry," she said. "You must be tired of eating in them restaurants all the time."

Her coy lapse into Willie B. Weaver's grammar did not hide the fact that she was insisting. Nor did her concern about my digestion. Should I insist in return? My car would not break down far from home—look at that wax job, Barbara? I would not deliberately run out of gas on a dark, lonely road in front of a moon-haunted, spider-webbed castle and starve her into submission to my wicked will if she had no lunch along?

It seemed pointless, finally, to argue. I shrugged and said okay, and it seemed that that was the right answer. After a week of planning we were ready for our date.

Saturday was sunny but humid, the sky clear blue above but raggedly gray around the edges, and I threw my zippered poplin jacket, with "Hebron Templars" in Gothic script over the heart, into the back seat, to wear over my cotton shirt and "dress" wash-pants in case it should rain.

Barbara waited on her porch in a bright red shirt and stylish blue Bermudas. Also the horn-rimmed glasses I hadn't seen since Olympic

Week. She carried a sweater and a brown paper bag. I had braced myself for a meeting with her father—perhaps he would be clipping dead peony stalks in the yard, or in the doorway saying good-bye— but both porch and yard were empty. I imagined him working on his sermon for tomorrow. Meditating. Praying. Fasting? I had never seen a "holiness" preacher at work, but I could not picture him simply banging away at a typewriter, as I had once seen Pastor Boom doing, or finding his inspiration in clouds of cigarette smoke like my instructor of Greek at Hebron.

"That's a good-looking lunch," I said.

She set it down between us on the front seat, her glasses slipping down her nose as she did so. "Just cold chicken. Don't expect any miracles."

We headed down Hoover Street to the expressway. The dark bars with pink neon signs, the gray frame houses settling toward each other like an old man's teeth, the house with the PALMS READ sign, the two-pump gas station, the signs for Alaga Syrup. I hadn't been this way in three weeks.

"Why not?" I said. "Who knows what may happen?"

"You referring to my lunch? Or the movie?"

"Well, you made the lunch, and Bergman the movie, so. . . ."

"I hear it's supposed to be sad."

"The lunch?"

She seemed in no mood for fooling. "It's supposed to be gloomy, I heard. All that death and suffering."

"Is that why you wore the glasses? Because tears will wash out your contact lenses?"

"Ah, you! I didn't mean it was the soap-opera kind of sad!"

She was trying to find some music on the radio, but there were no messages but commercial ones. "Don't you like these old glasses of mine? I can't wear my contacts in the smog. Big city air," she added, waving at the traffic and its layers of exhaust.

"I know," I said. "Even country boys know that"—although for a moment, forgetting about her Los Angeles education, I had thought "smog" was another of the playground words I was slowly mastering. Like Frankie's puzzled "Say *what?*" or Willie's use of "blouse" as a transitive verb: *I'll blouse your eye, I'll blouse you upside the head*—even, with exaggerated gestures, *I'll blouse you upside the ruby-duby*. "I always thought you wore the glasses for comic effect."

125

"Yeah?" I caught a glimpse of her face, the thick, flat curls around her head like the hair of a Greek statue, her delicate dark neck reflecting the red of her shirt. She pushed her frames up the bridge of her nose.

"You know, like when you talk to Willie. 'What make you so *bay-ud.*' "

She laughed, but not deeply. "You must be feeling mean today, Adrian."

"I'm sorry," I said. "Maybe it's the big city air. Why don't we sing something?"

In a low, husky voice she began the song I'd heard on the playground before Olympic Day. "Going down to the river, gonna jump overboard and drown/Because the one I love—" She stopped. "Ah, it's too early in the day for blues."

"No, keep going, I wanted to learn that one!"

She shook her head. "Anyway, it's bathos, not blues. Why don't you sing us something."

We had turned north on the expressway and were heading away from Orangetown deeper into the smog, soap opera, tragedy, bathos, and blues of Chicago. I hadn't realized there were so many forms of sadness. Off to our left was High Prairie, the last True Reformed town before the big city. High Prairie's largest church, Grace True Reformed, was a traditional powerhouse in the summer softball league I used to play in. I began the song that had furnished Grace Church's nickname, tuning my voice to the whine of tires over the Little Calumet bridge: "Ama-zi-ing Grace—"

Barbara was laughing, slapping her knee.

"What's the matter?"

"Ahh!" She could hardly talk. "We always used to do that one with a long *e*. You know, 'A-mee-zing Grace'? Ahh!" She took off her glasses and wiped her eye with a hanky out of her shirt pocket. "You know why?"

"No, I can't say I do."

"It was after the AME Zion Church. The AMEZ's, you know? The ones that split off from the AME's?"

It was all Greek to me—in fact, it was like hearing Sammy and Debbie discussing fraternities and sororities at a pizza party. I closed my eyes and help came to me from the Calumet Public Library.

126

"You mean the ones that split off from the African Methodist Evangelicals?"

"Right, right! Only you mean Episcopal."

"Oh, yes."

"That was before the war. 'Befoah de woah,' you know, the Civil War—"

"Right."

"— and then *after* the war, it was the CME's that separated. Mainly from the white Methodists. You know, in the South."

"So that would be what—Colored Methodist Episcopal?"

She did the comic schoolmarm, signaling approval over the tops of her glasses. "You go to the head of the class, Adrian."

"Well, I knew it wouldn't be 'Cracker.' "

"Ah, yeah. Then when the sharecroppers and all moved up to the North, my grandaddy, John C. Robinson, Sr., came up to northern Indiana with them. That was around the First World War. He's the one that started the Methodist Holiness."

"So that's why you used to sing 'Ameezing Grace.' "

"That's right. That was down in Indianapolis, me and my cousins—"

"Sort of in mockery of the AME's, and the CME's, and the AMEZ's? Because they acted like they had a monopoly on salvation?"

"Right again! We were just kids, of course—"

"And the Methodist Holiness Church your grandfather started— that would be a Pentecostal church?"

"You a genius, Adrian."

I thought of the "jokes" I used to hear as a child, jokes aimed at our liberal brethren up in Michigan. (Irate minister to small girl selling kittens: "Yesterday you told me these were Michigan Reformed kittens—today you tell me they're True Reformed! How do you explain this?" Small girl: "Today their eyes are opened, sir.") I didn't have to ask Barbara why her grandfather had dropped the "African" and "Colored" designations from the name of his new denomination; *Pentecost* implied all nations, tongues, and races.

"Look there!" Barbara said.

We were passing Lake Calumet Harbor. Before the expressway came through, the fishermen used to line the bank along Doty Avenue and annoy my father, as we drove by, with their apparent lack of guilt at being away from work. Gordon and I, on these trips, would close our eyes and guess where we were by the consecutive smells that finally overlapped and mingled somewhere around 111th Street: first the paint factory, whose sign—a green globe being coated like a taffy apple ("Sherwin-Williams Covers The Earth")—confirmed the smell; then a marshy compound of mud and dead fish and reeds and water; then the garbage dump, where men wearing bandannas around their noses were bulldozing the city's refuse into a new shoreline and eventually, so it was said, a park. The paint factory's sign was still here, badly corroded, and farther north the bulldozers still leveled garbage, but the harbor project and expressway had encroached on the lake's edge, making deep places shallow and shallow ones deep, and now the fishermen were gone and the marsh was dry.

She was pointing to a shack or house—its boards still showed paint, but its windowpanes were gone and the roof sagged—on the west side of the expressway.

"My daddy used to take me there! An old man used to live there, all by himself. He sold bait. I remember this! I haven't been here for years!"

"Shall we explore it?" I said.

"Can we?"

"Why not?"

"Do we have time?"

"We're not being paid by the hour. We can do anything we want."

We had some trouble with the off-ramps, but we finally found a two-lane dirt road heading south of 113th Street that wound through the cattails toward the bait-seller's house.

"There it is!"

The road stopped at a steep pile of rocks that was a railroad embankment. Over the top of it we could see, about fifty yards away, the house, its cement-block foundation lying on a kind of spongy knoll surrounded by green water and weeds. The rail spur that had cut the bait-seller off from the lake had backed up the water around his house.

"There used to be some kind of dock here," she said. "We'd go over and my daddy would buy us a bucket of minnow bait and the old man would give me a soda."

"It looks like an island now." The rushes were thick and green; the cattails looked as if from the level of the water they would stand almost as high as Barbara's head.

128

"Ah, look, there's a boat!"

We climbed down the embankment to the beige-gray snout she had seen leaning out of the rushes. It was made of metal and was very heavy; it looked to have been made of pieces of furnace sheeting riveted together. Half in the water, upside down, it was too awkward to pull up the embankment, but when we heaved it over it floated, about twelve feet long, with a half-foot of water in the stern. I found a drain plug in the back and unscrewed it, and then we hauled it up on the rocks.

"Look at that, it's dry!" She was jumping up and down on her toes, applauding softly, and I could see her as a ten-year-old out fishing with her father in her bright red shirt and horn-rimmed glasses, grinning, her dark hair in pigtails with blue or white ribbons.

Where the boat had lain there was a single oar lying half in the water—wooden, but not yet rotted through.

"Ah, look at him, he's found us a paddle."

"An oar," I said.

"Didn't I say you were a genius? You ever have a boat, Adrian?"

"No. My father just bought one, though. Trouble is you need two of these."

"You could pole it over," she said, going through the boatman's motions.

I cracked the rotted part of the oar on a rock, and there was enough left to pole with if I stayed sitting. The bottom was only two feet down, near the rocks, but soft and mucky; there was another bottom a foot below that. Barbara sat in front, parting the rushes and using them to tug us along.

"Look how brave she is," she said, "now she knows how to tread water."

Almost to the island, we found the old man's mailbox hovering like a rusty loaf on its post above the water. Barbara tugged it open and looked inside: empty.

"At least he came back one time for his mail."

"He never got any mail," I said. "He didn't want any."

I imagined that he was secretly glad of the water and the railroad that had made his house an island; he had moved into town to look for work but left his boat to come back.

When we got to the island we spoke softly, though we had both slipped and wet our feet and ankles coming up the slippery slope.

The only sounds—aside from the roar of the highway a quarter mile away—were the humming of flies and the zoom of a bumblebee weaving in and out of some coarse hollyhocks that struggled above the grass. A red-winged blackbird had followed us, complaining sharply, all the way across, and now he settled on a cattail, jerking his wings to let his mate know he had done his job.

"He had a garden there," Barbara said. "I remember this!"

The door was gone, off its hinges, nowhere to be seen, but still it seemed an invasion to enter the house. The three bare rooms seemed to echo even our wet, soft-soled footsteps. No furniture, not even a cupboard or a box. Two holes like eyes showed where the sink had been, and a funnel of greasy dirt suggested the stove. No other plumbing. There was an electrical outlet, but whatever wires had once brought in power from the outside were gone. The dusty floor was pockmarked by rain. Barbara found a pamphlet on the efficacy of prayer for the dead and a pair of red and green shotgun shells. We wondered whether hunters had come over to use the house in winter or whether the old man had waited here in the cold with his shotgun, reading his pamphlet, for any rabbits who would come back to the island across the ice.

It was muggy in the house. The sun was hot outside, but the sluggish breeze felt cool against my skin where I had been sweating. Near the hollyhocks Barbara knelt by a low, sandy mound where green double-leafed shoots poked through the dirt.

"You see? Here's where he planted him some watermelon."

The shoots were too small to have been planted deliberately, I thought. "Maybe he tossed his garbage here. Or somebody ate a melon here."

"You don't believe in my childhood vacation spot?"

I knelt on the other side of the watermelon mound like an archaeologist at a dig. "Of course I believe in it. Why not? In fact— why don't we eat our lunch here?"

She looked pleased but skeptical. "You really want to?"

"Why not?"

"I thought you wanted to see the movie."

"You said it was gloomy, didn't you? Anyway, we could see it anytime."

"But it was—you know, all planned and everything."

"So was finding your childhood vacation spot. It must have been predestined, right?"

She looked at me over her glasses, and I remembered she had said her father could find "a theological argument for anything." Suddenly she grinned, her head cocked to the side and one arm stretched toward me, curved palm downward: a lady. I pulled her up and we went back to the boat to get our lunch.

"We're probably too late for the afternoon showing," I said, in case she needed further reasons. "So why not make it a picnic?"

We poled and tugged our way back to the embankment, beached the boat, and climbed over to the car to get the lunch. It was hot work. Whenever we passed a stretch of open water I could see the frantic fluttering shadow of the red-winged blackbird making dives at the shadow of my head. His sharp, angry yips were as hard to ignore as the barking of a watchdog.

On the way back Barbara carried the lunch and I lifted her into the boat, admiring the taut lightness of her body. As I poled back through the reeds she shouted in delight at the muskrat arrowing away from us under the thick brown water, and at the fish she imagined she saw, and at a turtle sunning himself on an old tire that she said must once have been a part of the bait-seller's dock. "He was an old man," she said, "white-headed and bent over and mumbly. He was kind of scary at first, but he wouldn't hurt a flea. He gave me a soda one time and wouldn't take anything for it. Ah! Get away, you bird!"

When we had explored enough we landed again and had lunch in the shade of the house, kneeling on the ground with the lunch bag between us. The breeze moved softly in and out of the open windows behind us. Barbara tore the bag down the sides and spread it like a cloth.

"Say grace," she said.

"Lord, this is good," I said. But she made me feel flippant and foolish. As we knelt on the ground she took my hands from my knees so that my pulse beat into her palm, my fingers around her forearms, hers around my wrists, and prayed herself in a loud, clear voice: "Lord, bless the soul and the memory of this good old man."

"Amen," I said. She had lifted her face upward as she prayed, her eyes not closed behind the horn-rimmed glasses but opened wide toward something beyond the roof of the old man's house, and at the last second I raised my eyes too. I could still feel the soft slipping of her fingers from my wrists.

Afterward we took the chicken bones to the "garden" behind the hollyhocks and buried them there, and then lay in the sun on our sides on the watermelon mound while we ate the pears she had brought. I asked her if she had ever been baptized with the Holy Spirit.

"How do you mean? Speaking in tongues, all like that?"

"Well, yes. Or whatever else happens."

"Why would you want to know about that? You had to learn all those languages, didn't you? French? German? Hebrew, Greek, Latin?"

"Not Hebrew," I said. "That's first-year seminary. Besides, I never learned them, really. Just enough to puzzle things out."

"But those are the real tongues, aren't they? Why do it, you know, unintelligibly when you already know how to do it—"

"But it's not the same thing at all. Is it? Just tell me whether you ever spoke in tongues, yes or no."

"Why?"

"I'm just curious, that's all."

"Sure," she said. She was chewing on her pear. "Sure I did. It happened a lot when I was twelve, thirteen. You never did?"

"No," I said.

"Your people don't believe in it?"

"No."

I remembered a sermon Boom had preached on the Holy Spirit. We had sung a hymn—Boom daringly had it mimeographed; officially the True Reformed sang only Psalms—which afterward seemed to me a litany of refusal. I ask no dream, we had sung, no prophet ecstasy, no angel visitant, no opening skies. . . .

"I can understand that," she said. "It can be weird." She made a fluttering, fish-like movement with her free hand, her eyes rolling briefly behind her glasses. "People do weird things—they go to excess, like with everything else." She laughed self-consciously. "There was this one congregation that started ripping their clothes off—the minister had to beat their heads to make them stop! My daddy told me about that. You see spit flying around, you see people jumping up and down like epileptics or maniacs, and it can scare you. People go to excess with it."

I had heard of this gift of the Holy Spirit from the author of the book of Acts, who spoke of it respectfully and with knowledge, and from ministers and teachers, who spoke of it slightingly but without, as far as I could tell, any experience. I felt the frustration of a preadolescent hearing discussions of sex.

"But what does it feel like? Didn't it feel"—I could think of no stronger word—"good?"

Her laughter was deep and quiet. "Sure it feels good! It feels warm, and you feel light, and you feel like you're lifting up, up. . . . But you know it's not really that important. It's only so the congregation can see it, you know, so they know you've been converted. It doesn't do you any good personally. Only your conversion does that."

"Your conversion?"

"Your new life. When you start over again, doing right." She looked at me. "You been Spirit-baptized like that, haven't you?"

"Yes," I said. I was thinking of the playground.

"Well, then, you know what I mean. That's the only Spirit-baptism that does you any good. The other—the tongue-speaking, all that— is just so the congregation will know."

"But doesn't the Apostle Paul—" I could hear my speech taking on an old-country accent, as if I were myself speaking in tongues, spitting out *p*'s, *b*'s, and *t*'s like a wrathful elder rising in congregational meeting to dispute the substitution of individual modernistic thimblefuls for the traditional (if germ-laden) common cup in Communion: *And what does the Apostle Paul have to say about this?!* I couldn't help it; I wanted to know.

"Doesn't the Apostle Paul say just the opposite? He says the gift of tongues is for your*self*, but doesn't do the *others* any good."

"Don't tell me about what the Apostle Paul says." She spoke with a kind of grumbling truculence that reminded me of Frankie or Willie. "You let the Apostle Paul tell you about his own church. I'm telling you about mine."

She was the first Christian I had ever heard contradict the Apostle Paul. She did it with such ease, and it was so fresh and beautiful an example of the appeal from the frozen Word to one's own vision and experience, that I laughed aloud, and after a moment she laughed with me. I leaned across the watermelon mound and kissed her. After a second's surprise, she kissed me too. It was not eager or passionate as much as quiet, expectant, waiting; my body was stirred by her nearness and my mind busy with its *what next?* and *why?* and *how?*

But I dampened them both, for I felt I was drawing the Spirit from her, slowly, slowly, and it was something that could not be rushed.

After a while her hand slipped from my arm and I no longer felt, beneath her sunwarmed shirt, her heartbeat ticktocking the seconds. We turned from each other and lay on our backs, feet pointed in opposite directions, and watched the clouds cover and uncover the sun. The humidity was lifting into clouds, and it was getting to be a fine day; it came to me slowly that it was afternoon, it was Saturday, the longshoremen working in the grain elevators and ships whose masts rose above the buzzing expressway were being paid overtime. . . .

"Why did you move away from home?"

Her voice from behind me sounded as if she were chewing the stem of a weed. I pulled one from its socket, the kind we called foxtail, and chewed the white tip.

"Don't you believe I wanted to be closer to my work?"

"I know you like to work." I could feel her laugh through the dirt on which we both leaned. "No other reason?"

"Maybe I wanted to get away from my parents for a while. Or the town. Didn't you ever—"

I was going to ask whether she had ever felt that way but remembered that one of her parents was dead. When I turned to look at her her hands were behind her head, her red shirt glowing against the skin of her neck. I could not imagine the yoke of her father's church lying as heavily as Orangetown's.

"You went away to school," I said. "West coast. Next year to the east."

She laughed shortly. "Makes no difference. Same choices. Marriage. Career. Whatever."

"But what are you really looking for?" I took a guess. "Fame?"

"Not really." From the stubbornness in her voice I suspected that she took it as an accusation, one she had heard before. "Just to do something, be somebody, that will make a difference. Do something worthwhile with my time on earth. Singing. Dancing. Whatever."

I thought of her mother, whose time had run out so early. Perhaps that explained the tempo of the heartbeat I had felt under my arm. It was her summer to choose a direction, to give herself to one thing and do something worthwhile before it was too late. Whereas for me it was a summer of breaking away. I lay on my back again, my own heart beating slowly against the dirt of the mound. We could write

134

letters next year. I would write letters to Barbara, and she to me, while I was away at school deciding what to do and waiting for the Spirit to move.

"What's the matter with the town? Too small?"

"Too heavy," I said, pleased with the expression.

"I wouldn't mind seeing your church sometime."

I almost laughed, picturing the white astonished faces. Orangetown seemed far away. "That would be doing something worthwhile, all right."

"It can't be too bad," she said. "It produced you." I waited for her laugh and finally felt it through the dirt. "Hah."

What would I do, she asked me. Would I teach, or what? Probably teach, I said.

"But I'll tell you what I'd really like to do. I'd like to live on an island, like this."

"Oh, yeah. Live on watermelon?"

"I'd row into town for stuff. Staples."

"Would you work?"

"Sure. Every day."

"At what?"

"I'd be a distributor." I watched the white birds circling the masts in the harbor, wondering whether they were gulls or pigeons. I had seen them too rarely to be sure, but I thought by the slimness of their wings and the way they hovered in the air that they must be gulls, the same that flew over the big lake, over all the big lakes and the oceans.

Barbara was silent.

"I'll have my ships bring in goods from all over the world. I'll store it in my grain elevators. Tea. Cracker Jack. Volleyballs. All the necessities. And then I'll distribute."

No response.

"You ask me how? How would I distribute the goods?" Still no reaction. "According to justice, that's how. That's what a distributor does."

When I turned around, finally tired of waiting, she was gone.

"Hey! Barbara!"

"Find me," I heard her call. Her voice, echoing strangely, seemed to come from somewhere in the deserted house. I got up and went through the empty door. The room was quiet, empty. The breeze stirred dust over small round marbles—rabbit droppings—on the dusty floor. I heard a movement and went for a door I hadn't noticed before: a closet? I tugged it open, was startled by chips of dried paint falling at my feet and the clang of empty hangers on a hook. The sound of knocking from the front, her high laughter. Had she gone through the window? She was gone when I reached it. Rushing out through the door again I met her at the corner. "Found you," I said, grasping her hand before she could get away; she sank to the ground, laughing, though her eyes seemed wide with fear.

I pulled her to her feet and held her, surprised at how easily our bodies fit, her cheek against my shoulder, her springy curls under my chin. My pulse beat loud in my ears.

"Barbara! What's the matter?"

"We've got to stop this," she said.

"What do you mean?"

"I've got to get home. He's waiting on me—my father—he thinks we're in Chicago."

"But that's not what you meant."

"How do you know what I mean?"

She looked at me with such pain in her face that I leaned forward and kissed her lips, closing my eyes, and my blood shook me this time against my will.

She turned her face into my shoulder and I held her, holding her head with its curls tight under my chin, afraid to kiss her again. We stood that way, the breeze coming to us now from the Sherwin-Williams plant, hearing the traffic buzz around us until she moved in my arms and I let her go. She went to the spot where we had eaten our lunch and picked up the torn bag, the napkins, the waxed paper.

"I really ought to go."

We made our way back silently, the blackbird with his flame-touched wings driving us out ahead of him, and this time his smaller, darker mate left the nest as well to cheep with faked pathos around our bow. We beached the boat as we had found it. Then we drove silently back to Calumet, the remnants of our lunch between us on the seat. Driving past Orangetown on the expressway, then up Hoover Street, it was as if we really had been to a movie, the town like gritty daylight after coming out of the dark. I'm going to have to decide some things, I thought. Something will really have to be decided. I had seen the sun on Barbara's skin all day, and lifting her into the boat I had admired the lightness of her body, but now for the first time while I saw her sitting, staring at her own lap, her hands between her knees, I thought to myself that she was beautiful.

"Good-bye, Adrian," she said when we got to her house. I got out to open the door for her but she was too quick. I walked with her up the steps to her porch. I was glad, this time, that there was no sign of her father. She was still looking downward, her glasses slipping down the bridge of her nose.

"I guess I'll see you tomorrow?" I said.

"Tomorrow is Sunday," she said, and opened her front door.

"Oh. Right. I'll see you on Monday?"

She nodded to me, and the door closed. I went back to the car and drove to my room at the Y with the empty paper bag.

CHAPTER NINE

BARBARA'S HOUSE

I first tasted the joys of illicit worship when I was thirteen, on a Sunday visit with my Aunt Pandaria to her Michigan Reformed congregation. There I saw a minister wearing a robe instead of a black swallow-tailed coat. There I heard music performed by a choir—also in robes—instead of just sung by the congregation. (The first step backward into papistry, according to my grandfather: taking music out of the mouths of the people.) There I sang man-made hymns instead of just Psalms out of the Bible, and I learned the hyphenated rhetoric favored by compromisers everywhere: Aunt Pandaria's songbook was called a *psalter-hymnal*.

In my senior year at college I drove to Dubuque and Cedar Rapids and visited some of the American churches there, beginning with the Baptists, as my initial plan was alphabetical. I found among the Baptists a friendliness that was missing in my Hebron and Orangetown congregations, and I suppose it was for that reason that I finally gave them up. Their cross-nave calls of greeting, before the services began, and their pew-spanning, aisle-bridging handshakes made me feel I was in a baseball stadium. So did the spirited singing, led by a man I thought of as The Cheerleader. Another gentleman made announcements about "today's attendance" (up over last year's at this date, 367 to 342; Sunday School up 111 to 94) that reminded me of Pat Piper at Wrigley Field. I found it impossible to maintain a proper air of sobriety and gloom. The congregation was so large that it held two services, one at ten and the other at eleven, and after making both ends of the doubleheader one Sunday, to be sure my decision was not arbitrary or accidental, I decided that I was not a Baptist.

My Lutheran period lasted a bit longer. I felt I was a Lutheran from the moment I opened the blue-and-gold hymnal and found in the Collect for the Day this repeated sentence,

Then shall the minister say or sing . . .

followed by a staff and several bars of music!—a clear admission, it seemed to me, that poetry and music did more than creeds to justify God's ways to man. It was consistent, too, with the split chancel, by which was indicated that neither the sermon (delivered from right of center) nor the Scriptures themselves (left of center) could be regarded as any more than a suburb of the city of truth, which must lie beyond or in between.

The Lutherans whom I met during the post-service dash for the parking lot seemed less pluralist than their Collect and less open than their chancel, though the pastor, a bluff, dour baritone, allowed that he was closer in spirit to Hebron, in some respects, than to "certain Lutherans of Missouri." I became an apostate Lutheran, finally, because of an ingrained literalness of my own which made me see that the truth which lay between Scripture and Preacher was in fact a crucifix, a larger-than-life graven image of a dying Christ never to be resurrected or even buried but forever crucified before the congregation's eyes, Sunday after Sunday. I didn't think I could get used to it.

Among the Episcopalians, whom I next favored with my spiritual custom (perhaps in search of the *via media*, though warned by fellow pre-sems that there was no such thing as a *via dolorosa media*), the crucifix was a stylized wire mobile; but like the Lutherans they never approached it save with offering in hand, nor even passed it by, going from one side of the chancel to the other, without the kind of brief obeisance that gave priest or altar boy, to my eyes, the look of someone nodding to an acquaintance while crossing a busy street, or of an uneasy conscience making its way past a police station.

At this point I realized that I had become spiritually what my mother called a finicky or picky eater. I was approaching each service of worship as though I were an editor of *Consumer Reports*. The fault was not in the variety of congregational cuisine I had sampled, but in myself, that I could find no proper nourishment. It was January, the beginning of the spring semester, and I decided to give up my quest for the perfect worship experience and wait instead, with an open mind and heart, for the truth to come, if it would, to me. I would follow wherever it led. I promised myself that the next time I visited a house of prayer I would do so as a pilgrim and not as a tourist or connoisseur.

It was in the spirit of pilgrimage, seven months later, that I attended the Methodist Holiness service on the Sunday after my first date with Barbara.

From the outside the church seemed a square, but inside it was a diamond. Entering at one corner you saw in the other, facing you, the platform, pulpit, and Bible, with three ranks of curved pews radiating outward. Behind the pulpit was the arrangement of three chairs familiar to me since boyhood, and behind these the golden organ pipes like a row of sharpened pencils, also familiar—though today no one was playing the organ. Below the platform and to the left a great yellow-robed black woman sat crooning and meditating over the upright piano she played, now leaning forward until the white collar of her robe almost touched the music rack, now backward with her eyes closed, her fingers still sliding softly over the keys. Early-arriving worshippers were clustered up front near the piano, not in the rear as they would have been back home, observing the latecomers at their leisure; some swayed from side to side, their hands clapping softly with the softness of the music, like the hands of children at the playground.

The same bald, smiling usher I had seen the week before led me, at my request, to the last pew on the left. I was the only non-Negro in the congregation except for three women in their late forties or early fifties, all of them thin, with stiff gray hair, who sat near one another below the platform to the right, the oldest and thinnest a row ahead of the other two. She wore metal-rimmed glasses and had a pinched, worried face. They all wore dark, short-sleeved dresses, and when they raised their hands—as they each did abruptly every now and then, as if hanging clothes on a line above their heads—the loose skin on their arms looked strangely, almost shamefully, white. I had seen them when I came in and for that reason pointed the usher to the left. Near them in the front I saw Barbara, serene and cool in a white suit, wearing no hat over the curls that laureled her face. She was smiling, her face looking upward toward the organ pipes. Whenever I glanced her way during the service she was smiling. Like the crooning of the yellow-robed pianist, whose music never died away

141

completely except during the sermon, when she took a seat in the front pew, her smile was a continuo of the service.

The men of the congregation mostly wore coats, but here and there I caught the gleam of a white shirt like my own. I had brought a tie and jacket along in the car, but the day was so warm I left them there. One of the white shirts belonged to Lee Roy. I suspected him from the breadth of his shoulders and the truculent set of his neck and confirmed him when he turned to check the clock above the rear door, his smooth cheek perspiring. I didn't think he had seen me. Frankie had, I knew; two rows ahead, he smiled shyly and then kept taking backward peeks, holding up one pink palm to wave—I nodded back, unsure of etiquette, though it seemed we were more formal than the Baptists—and finally making faces at me, until his mother, whose shoulders in dotted swiss under a straw hat seemed too large for Frankie's mother, struck him upside the head, as he might have put it, with the accordion-pleated bulletin that was her fan. Some of the other women waved large, scallop-shaped fans of khaki paper with advertising on them.

I also spotted Verella, lovely in pink and white and a broad-brimmed hat with ribbons falling like long hair down her back, clap-ping hands near the front, and Wesley, swaying from side to side in an aisle seat where one elbow and knee had breathing room, and I saw enough smaller children from the playground to fear an epidemic of turning heads; then there was a kind of silence that began in the back near the door, the piano softening down to a few tinkling fan-fares, and the Reverend Robinson entered.

He came from the rear down the left-hand aisle, carrying a black Bible, head down as if meditating. I felt the air move from his passing and might have touched him as he went by, a liturgical effect I would have approved, had I thought of it that way—his coming from out of the congregation to preach to us instead of simply materializing out of some side door near the front; but my analytical side was dulled, my senses open to what I was about to receive. He was tall, erect, square-faced like his daughter but unsmiling and severe in swallow-tailed coat and high white collar. His expression came mostly from his eyes. As he sat with legs crossed on the right hand of the central chair, his tails flipped out to the sides, his eyes seemed to linger on each individual in the congregation, widening briefly to take that person in, his nostril wings widening too with the effort of absorption, and then pass like a searchlight to another face.

His voice, when he spoke, was deeper and older than Barbara's—he was perhaps fifty, short white spirals descending from his close-cropped head into his sideburns—and although it had her resonance it was more measured, direct, and monotonous. It had the intensity of a focused stream of water or beam of light. It was his eyes and his voice, expecially during the sermon, that I remembered later above everything else except for the testimonials at the end. There was a good deal of singing, some from the pamphlet-sized *Hymns of Holiness* (published in Calumet) that I found in the pew, and some of it from memory. All the music was more rhythmic than harmonic, so that I wished I were closer to the leadership of Barbara's voice. There was the passing of the plate (a ritual more easily understood than music, in my church-shopping experience); there were announcements and prayers; a sister, as she was called, led some of the singing, and a brother read from Scripture; but Robinson was the real focus of our attention from the moment he sat down on the platform, and when he began the sermon it was clear that the other things were preliminary.

He spoke without notes and without looking at the Bible he carried, though now and then he drew his hand across it like a man drawing warmth from a brick that has lain in the sun. Nor did he look at the pulpit Bible, still open at the place where the brother had read. He did not speak from the pulpit, which was too short for him, but from the whole width of the platform, moving from side to side as he spoke, now toward the yellow-robed pianist and Lee Roy and me, now toward Barbara and the three white women, whose shouts and amens were louder than those of the rest. I recall his sermon with the aid of punctuation and paragraphing that in life were supplied by his movements, his pauses, and his eyes. It was as if thought flowed through his whole body—or rather, our body, for our responses were part of his moving, as if together we were one organism, he the mouth that spoke and we the heart overflowing into speech.

"In the book of the Acts of the Apostles," he began, "we read that the Holy Ghost came with a sound as of the rushing of a mighty wind.

"And with an appearance that was like cloven tongues of fire.

"Another place in the book of Acts we read that the house was shaken where the Apostles were assembled together. Shaken where they were assembled together; and they were filled with the Holy Ghost, and spake the Word of God with boldness.

"The wind of the Spirit. The fire of the Spirit. The shaking of the Spirit. Amen."

Amen! the congregation answered, so loud and joyful a noise that I was shaken in my seat.

"In the book of the Acts of the Apostles we read that the Holy Ghost spake by the Lord's servant, David the King. And we read that the Holy Ghost spake by the Lord's prophet, Isaiah. And we read that the Holy Ghost spake by the prophet of the Lord called Joel. In the last days the Lord God will pour out his Spirit upon all flesh, upon all flesh. And your sons and your daughters will prophesy, and your young men will see visions, and your old men will dream dreams.

"The gift of the Holy Spirit, amen."

Amen!

"The Apostles were Jews, and they were filled with the Holy Spirit, and they began to speak in tongues as the Spirit gave them utterance, amen.

"The servants of Cornelius were Gentiles, and the soldier of Cornelius was a Gentile, and Simon the tanner who lived in a house by the sea was a Gentile, amen.

"And the Holy Ghost fell upon all of them, Acts ten forty-four, all of them that heard the word of the Apostle, and they were speaking in tongues and praising and glorifying God. Amen."

Amen!

"The power of the Holy Spirit, amen, the gift of the Holy Spirit, amen, the blessing of the Holy Spirit, amen.

"Say amen to the gift and the power and the blessing. Say amen to the demands and commands.

"The Spirit drove Jesus our Lord into the wilderness, Mark one verse twelve, and Jesus brought forth our salvation, praise the Lord.

"The Holy Spirit commanded Philip to preach to the Ethiopian, praise be upon his name, in the desert of Gaza, and Africa was won, praise the Lord.

"The power and the blessing and the gifts of the Spirit, praise God. The demands and commands of the Spirit. Praise God."

Praise God!

"The Holy Spirit is given, Acts five thirty-five, to them that obey the Lord God.

144

"The demands and commands of the Spirit, praise God. The obedience of the Holy Spirit, praise God.

"Grieve not the Spirit. Tempt not the Spirit. Lie not to the Spirit. Sin not against the Spirit. It is the power of the wind, it is the shaking of the earthquake, it is the burning of the tongues of fire. Ananias lied to the Spirit and Ananias fell down dead. Sapphira tempted the Spirit and Sapphira lay down and died. Elymas the sorcerer grieved the Spirit of God and the Apostle cast a mist and a darkness around him and bade him walk in darkness for a spell. Whatsoever a man sows, that shall he also reap. Amen.

"Elymas grieved the Spirit and he was blinded. But thy commands are a light to my feet, Psalm one hundred nineteen.

"Ananias lied to the Spirit and he died. But I will walk at liberty, says the Psalmist, for I seek thy commandments.

"Sapphira tempted the Spirit and she lay down beside her husband and she died. But I will never forget thy commandments, Psalm one-nineteen, for with them thou has quickened me.

"The gift and the power and the blessing, amen. The demands and commands of the Spirit, amen. The obedience of the Spirit and the fruits of the Spirit, amen.

"Say amen to the demands and commands, say amen to the fruits.

"The disciples were filled with joy in the Spirit and they taught the Church. Thy commandments are the rejoicing of my heart, amen.

"Barnabas was filled with goodness and the Spirit and he served the community round about. Thou art good and doest good, teach me thy commandments. Amen.

"The seven deacons were filled with wisdom and the Spirit, and they kept the family of God. Thy commandments are wiser than my enemies, I understand more than all my teachers.

"The fruits of the obedience of the Spirit, Galatians five twenty-two. Love and joy and peace, the disciples in the Church. Goodness and patience and kindness, Barnabas in the community. Gentleness and trust and self-control, the wisdom of the seven in the family. Praise the Lord. Praise the Lord. Amen."

Amen!

The sounds of praise and amen rose in my throat too, but stayed there, self-conscious. I remembered that I was a visitor, and I noticed that Barbara's responses had to be read in her smile and moving lips, unlike those of the white women near her, whose voices could be heard above the others and sometimes came out on their own, protesting, I thought, too much. And there was something in the Reverend Robinson that acted to suppress the emotion he evoked—in his searching eye and in his voice, which was intense and controlled as if holding great power in reserve, and understatedly emphatic, now and then breaking into a monotone chant that reminded me of the Lutheran minister's *Glo-ry-be-to-the-fa-ther* or even the Jack Benny conductor who used to announce *Train leaving on track nine for An-aheim, A-zu-sa, and Cu-ca-mon-ga*, so neutrally incantatory was its rhythm.

"Jacob had the Spirit. Saw the angels of the Lord ascending and descending into heaven, saw the heavenly ladder of God, the gift of the Holy Spirit." *Amen.*

"Wrestled all night with the angel of the Lord: the power of the Holy Spirit!" *Amen.*

"Lord God changed his name, called his name Israel, said I will make of you a great blessing, the blessing of the Holy Spirit." *Amen.*

"Hear the demands and commands of the Spirit, amen. Lord said to Jacob, Lord said to Rachel, serve me in your family, amen. Lord said to Jacob and Rachel, I want to make you a great nation, amen. Lord said to Jacob and Rachel, raise your son Joseph, raise him up in wisdom and the power of the Spirit, raise him up to save the land of Egypt from famine, and starvation, and want.

"Raise him up in holiness: the demands and commands of the Spirit, the obedience of the Spirit, amen!

"Sister Amanda is here every Wednesday night, she'll tutor your child in reading. Any child, any child, any age, she'll make him to be a great blessing. Is that right, sister Amanda?

"Think Jacob will say, think Rachel will say, Lord, I never know where my Joseph is on Wednesday night? Think Jacob will say, think Rachel will say, Lord, I can't keep my Dinah home on Wednesday night? And they the children of God, and they with the gift and the blessing and the power of the Holy Ghost?

"Grieve not the Spirit. Tempt not the Spirit. Lie not to the Spirit of God.

"Elijah had the Spirit. Brought down the fire from heaven, amen, burned up the offering, burned up the altar under the offering, burned up the trench around the altar, amen, the gift of the Holy Spirit.

146

"Elijah brought the rain from heaven—the blessing of the Holy Spirit, amen!

"Killed all the prophets of Baal, ran down to Jerusalem in front of King Ahab's horses: the power and might of the Spirit, amen.

"Lord said to Elijah, I am not in the roaring fire."

Yes, Lord.

"Lord said to Elijah, I am not in the wind and the rain."

No, Lord.

"Lord said to Elijah, I am not in the shaking of the earthquake and the storm."

No, sir.

"Lord said, I am in the still small voice. Lord said, I want you to serve me in the community. Lord said, King Ahab has taken a good man's property, Second Book of Kings, the vineyard of Naboth. Lord said, Queen Jezebel has taken a good man's life, the life of Naboth, Second Book of Kings.

"Lord said, I want you to go to Ahab. Lord said, Elijah, I want you to go to Jezebel.

"The demands and commands of the Spirit, amen.

"Brother J. R. Emery is running the Neighborhood Watch. You see King Ahab stealing a good man's property? Stealing a good man's car? Raising up the hood, stealing the battery out of his car? You see Queen Jezebel walking around at night, walking around, stealing a good man's life? You afraid to look out your window at night?

"Think Elijah will say to the Lord, Lord, I don't go looking for trouble? Lord, let trouble come looking for me? And him with the Holy Spirit, with the gift and the blessing and the power of the Holy Spirit?

"Lie not to the Spirit of God! Grieve not the Spirit of God! Tempt not the Spirit of God!

"Peter had the Holy Spirit. . . ."

By now something of the sermon's method had worked its way into my consciousness. I was not surprised that the Holy Spirit who inspired Peter's speech at Pentecost—which should have been the climax of the sermon, I thought, for this congregation—and who rescued Peter from prison, and gave him the vision of the salvation of the Gentiles, and empowered him to raise Sister Tabitha back to life, had in mind all along that we should sign up with Sister Marietta Townsend, right after the service, to help teach Sunday School in the fall. I was not surprised, but I was disappointed. When at last the Reverend Robinson came down from the platform for his peroration—tall enough to be seen over the heads of the standing congregation, the drops of sweat on his forehead shining under the low lamps hanging from the ceiling—and raised his hands above his head, asking us to do the same, and I stood with the others, I had heard shouts of joy but had seen no one obviously seized by the power of the Holy Ghost, had heard no one speaking the unearthly language of God.

"We lift up our hands to heaven," Robinson said, his voice now assuming more of the chant and song. "Lift up our hands in prayer. Lift up our hands to shout. Lift up our hands to praise. The Lord fills our hands with goodness! With mercy! With power!"

After the rhythmic amens there was a long pause, as if we were waiting for God's goodness, and I wondered, with my hands upraised, where to look—at the ceiling or at Frankie's mother's straw hat ahead of me—and had the impulse that sometimes struck me in moments of crowd-excitement at a ball game, to check my wallet, before remembering that I was in the last row.

"The Lord fills our hands with blessing, our cup runneth over," and Robinson held up his fingers one by one as if he were counting.

"Little finger leads the way: one God only. Ring finger tells us, guard the senses against false worship. Middle finger, tallest of all, keep our language pure. First finger points the way, regular church attendance. Thumb with its power to grasp and to hold, honor the family, hold to the family. Left thumb, guard my life and my neighbor's. First finger, keep the family pure. Middle finger, guard my property and my brother's. Ring finger, keep my reputation and my brother's. Little finger, keep us from coveting and from those who covet against us.

"Left hand of good works, right hand of piety, the power and the gift of God."

It was only when he gave his benediction—"Oh how love I thy law, it is my meditation all the day"—and I sat down with the others, lowering my ten fingers to my lap, that I realized we had been given the same commandments that were read out weekly in the services of the Reverend Boom in Orangetown.

What followed the sermon, however, was something I had never heard before. The pianist, her eyes closed, played louder, her head

148

now thrown back and now bent over the keys as she crooned, and gradually from the congregation the sounds of prayer and testimony mingled, for the congregation responded "Amen!" during the middle of what I took to be prayers and lifted their heads, sometimes their hands, during testimonials. Robinson from below the platform acted as chairman, recognizing those who stood. "Sister Simson": and a brown, bent old lady with lips working furiously back and forth over her gums as if feeling for absent teeth told how she had been healed and gave thanks for her healing—I could not hear, though I strained to do so, from what she had been healed. "Brother Pendergast": a short, stocky man, his dark suit showing a darker path of sweat down the middle of his back, began praying in a high, thin, excited voice, the prayer rising and falling in pitch and exciting me as well as the speaker since, although uttered almost without consonants, it still had the sound of a meaning, as the loud "Preach it, amen" from the white-headed man on my right confirmed.

Then suddenly the oldest of the three women behind Barbara stood up, or rather seemed jerked to her feet, her arms flailing as if to keep her head above water, her head nodding and jerking as if she were falling in and out of sleep, but faster, like some of the farmers in Boom's congregation who were overcome by the heat of the building after a week of outdoor air—or so my father liked to excuse them—and without waiting for recognition (though Robinson recognized her after the fact), indeed running right into the middle of Brother Pendergast's prayer, delivered not what I expected, a shout or a shriek, but something softer than her strident responses during the sermon, something throaty and almost sensuous which she repeated and repeated. I felt my breath sucked out of me. In rays of light from the window above her I saw tears slide slowly from her closed eyes under her glasses toward her open mouth, where her lips appeared to be dancing. Her head meanwhile kept falling and jerking as if she had been seized by some large hand that gripped her from the neck down. The syllables she repeated were familiar yet strange, and when Robinson from the front of the congregation hissed, "Interpret! Interpret!" above the dying of her renewed utterance, I found myself on my feet—my sensation that of being on a diving board, not having realized before climbing the ladder how far below me everyone would look, and catching in the lower line of my vision first Frankie, and then Frankie's mother, turning around. What I heard first as gibberish, *sa-na-ke-a-no-lo-go*, and then as something like *an-árchy analógous*, had suddenly penetrated as Greek, New Testament Greek, the opening of the gospel of St. John over which I had labored months ago in my class at Hebron, where the significance of lexical and syntactical detail for the interpretation of the text was everywhere emphasized: Ἐν ἀρχῇ ἦν ὁ λόγος, *In the beginning was the Word.*

Before I could speak or be recognized—I am not sure I would have waited for recognition, since the words that seemed to have appeared of their own accord wanted utterance—a thin young man in a white shirt, seated near Wesley, had stood and been pointed to and was saying in a loud, clear voice, "She say 'Great is my faithfulness toward you.'" And then the whole congregation was standing and the Reverend Robinson pronounced a blessing and walked past me again to the front door, the pianist still playing her rhythmic low chords and a high, tinkling decorative right-hand melody, and the service was over; people began filing out.

I left by a side door, where there was only the bald, high-domed usher to shake my hand. "We are very glad to have had you in our midst." I walked back to my car full of wonder. We are too often together, someone is supposed to have said; being by ourselves is coming to our senses. I walked back to my car alone and yet full of wonder, half believing that I had had a revelation, half in doubt as to what it could mean. For one second I had been part of the body, ready to contribute, to be spoken through; then the Spirit had passed me by—or rather, Barbara's father had cut me off. I had been, I thought, more full of the Spirit, more ready, more inspired, than the thin young man with his conventional sentence, his face clearly wrinkled with thought and effort while he spoke. It seemed to me that the Reverend Robinson had been needlessly strict, stricter even than the Apostle Paul, First Book of Corinthians; he, after all, would have allowed two or even three charismatics to speak.

The last week of July was Nature Week. When I first read its title in the Handbook I pictured it as a pleasant oasis coming after a prosaic stretch of superhighway devoted to Crafts, Games, and Hobbies. Now I hoped it would be a repetition of Doll Buggy Week. Lying awake on that hot Sunday night, watching the traffic-light's three-colored pattern repeat itself on my ceiling, I imagined Barbara and myself putting out tables and benches in the shade and setting up the sprinkler for the younger children. We would spend the "dead" hours trading anecdotes about high school days, when she was the rising star of Washington Park High, first Negro on the Student Council, famous for acting, singing, and dancing in the school plays, and I was one of the group of not-living-up-to-potential males at Orangetown TRCH only a dozen miles away and unaware of her existence, as she was of mine. Or about her childhood in those earlier Indiana towns, Gary and Indianapolis, where her father had preached, where she and her cousins had mockingly sung "Ameezing Grace" against the bigger denominations, while I was in First Church's basement learning *red and yellow black and white, all are precious in his sight* under the tutelage of quavery-voiced little old ladies, the real religious business of the day having gone on upstairs an hour and a half earlier when Boom's predecessor, a now-forgotten dominie my father called The Snifter, had preached on the dangers of being unequally yoked with unbelievers or otherwise conformed to the present state of this world.

Barbara would be wearing the red scoop-backed blouse that revealed, when she stooped to tie a child's shoe, the interesting beige hollow between her shoulder blades, just the width of my hand—a sight which moved me conflictingly with tenderness and temptation, plus a kind of awe that a body so light could convey such softness and solidity, even amplitude, finding space over its tiny bones for the layer of baby fat that, as I understood it, was Nature's way of protecting the female body and the babies it was meant to carry, at the same time appealing to the male's urge to touch, hold, and cherish, an urge that would in time, if Nature had her way, produce the baby to be carried. How mysterious and beautiful were Nature's ways!

As we sat talking and laughing together on the grass or at the grass-green tables we would have the children color pictures of real and imaginary flowers. They would cut and sandpaper wooden silhouettes of the pets they had or used to have, or wished to have. They would run to the thermometer on the equipment shed and record the day's temperature hour by hour, and cut out paper resemblances of the cumulus, cumulonimbus, and other clouds that I would remember or make up on the spot, or of the oak and maple leaves above us, or of the robins, starlings, and sparrows on the grass. Hour after hour would go by, and we would tell the children about the tropisms that drew moths and insects to the light bulbs over the john doors, and how the spiders made their webs there and laid their eggs over the dead bodies of wasps, and they would bring caterpillars and cocoons to show us, and catch fireflies in jars, and we would point out Venus glowing in the west as the sun went down and the moon rose, no longer full, above the elms lining Hoover Street. It would be Doll Buggy Week all over again but without the parade or the crepe paper or the Cracker Jack to worry about.

From the Handbook's opening words on the subject, which I read over my cold-cereal breakfast at the cafeteria on Monday morning, I gathered that Nature Week was like that at one time long ago but now was different. "Nature Week is not a time when everyone does what is right in his own eyes. It is a time of achievement and recreational learning, like all the other weeks on the playground." It turned out to be more demanding than the other weeks in the variety of organization and paperwork required. We were to plan a Boys' Nature Hike on Wednesday and a Girls' Nature Hike on Thursday. Interesting, I thought, that boys and girls should be separated on their hikes through Nature. Hikes were to be considered "structured walks," and we leaders would have to submit a statement of plans, purposes, and routes indicating what our structure was, along with a copy of a legal-release form for every hiker accompanying us. There would be no drinks in glass containers. Lunches would be in paper sacks clearly labeled. We would also label rocks, leaves, flowers, and insects (that is, in our notebooks), since the hikes were to be integrated with the Science Fair and Pet Show (Cat, Dog, Rodent, Other) which were to climax the week on Friday.

When I got to the playground Barbara was seated at a table in the shadow of the equipment shed. She was deep in her Handbook and her plans and barely answered my greeting. She wore, I saw, her red scoop-backed blouse and blue pedal-pushers. I made my first-hour tour—opening the johns, watering the sandbox, chalking the ball diamond, pounding in horseshoe stakes—and came back to talk to her just before her lunch break.

"I saw you at church yesterday," I said.

She looked up from the Handbook as if just now remembering. "Why didn't you stay?"

"You mean afterward? I don't know. I was moved by the service, I guess."

"Ahh!" She broke off the laugh. "Really?"

"Sure. I was thinking about it the whole day."

"What about all the, you know, emotionalism? You didn't mind?"

I shook my head. "I didn't think there was all that much."

"Yeah? What did you think of my father?"

"He looks a lot like you," I said, "Older, and more, well, stern, but. . . ."

"No, really. What did you think of the sermon?"

"He was really good. Maybe a genius."

"You're kidding me."

"No I'm not. I was really impressed."

"Would you like to meet him sometime?"

"Meet him?"

"He's said he would like to talk to you."

"Well, sure, I would like to talk to him."

"I always tell him he's got too much talent for this little place." She stuffed the mimeographed sheets on which she had been working into the Handbook and stood up, the gathered papers held protectively against her chest, the Handbook a dog-eared 8½-by-11-inch patch of yellow against the red. "Maybe when his book is finished," she said.

"His book? What book is that?"

She cocked her head to one side and grinned, both bare arms around the Handbook like a schoolgirl going off to class. "Ah, you-all can talk about it when you meet him. Anyway, Adrian, I'm glad you came yesterday. Sometime I should see your church. You know?"

"Ah," I said.

"Now that you've told me so much about it."

"Well, yes. Maybe you should."

"Make things even, *n'est-ce pas?*"

She walked off hugging the Handbook in both arms, her scoop-backed blouse rising and falling above the hollow between her shoulder blades, and I tried to concentrate on my plans for staff meeting that evening.

Seeing her father. Taking her to my church. Taking her, since although I had gone alone to hers I could not simply give her directions and point her to the south. For a moment the reality of Orangetown hit me, Orangetown with its For Sale signs and concern for property values. When she had mentioned the idea earlier I hadn't thought she could be serious. Now what made my stomach tighten more than the thought of seeing her father, more even than the thought of her "seeing" my church, was the thought that Barbara had ideas of her own as to what we could do together, what we should be or become—ideas quite different, perhaps, from mine. At the same time I was glad we had at least this minimum off-playground connection to think about; I could see, as I made out my schedule, that we were going to be apart while at work.

In the afternoon she recruited hikers from among the girls at the sandbox and swings while I worked with the boys on the softball diamond, and the sight of her across the playground, so close and yet separate, the sun glowing on her deep-red blouse, made me ache with a kind of physical memory, as the body is said to ache for an amputated limb. That evening we closed early, because of staff meeting, and when we were alone after pulling the ping-pong table inside the shed I drew her to me and kissed her—on the cheek, for she turned suddenly aside.

"Ah, you *tickle*."

Her voice was almost a whisper, her body stiff. I followed her glance through the open door to the tilt-a-whirl ten yards away, where a child sat revolving in a slow, canted circle, his feet trailing in the dust. As the tilt-a-whirl came around his eyes flashed across the sunlit doorway and the darker space inside where we stood. It was Willie. I had thought the playground was deserted. Once, I remembered, when Willie heard Barbara say the word "damn," or rather when he had caused her to say it, he whooped and shouted his joy across the playground. Oo-wee, now she done it! She knows *all* them words! Now he concentrated on the dust sliding beneath his feet, as if he were meditating on centripetal and centrifugal forces. When I came outside into the lowering sun he hopped off and trotted away before I could speak. "I know, I know," he said. "Park's fitten to close."

I came to staff meeting that night newly shaved and wearing clean clothes. I worked diligently to digest Nikkles' mimeographed handouts and incorporate them into our plans for the week. It was one of Nikkles' blue-thumb nights, as Barbara called them, and the handouts were plentiful. I reminded her that he had not yet fulfilled her promise of asking us to know the children's words for the elimination of bodily wastes.

"He gave us that footnote last year."

She pointed to the release-form's bottom line. *Other things the Hike Leader should know?*

When the meeting was over, Sammy as usual stood on the steps leading up from City Hall's basement into the warm, muggy night and buttonholed each of the other thirty-one, unwilling to begin the week without a party; but he got no takers. "Come *on*, you guys! What's the *matter* with everybody?" The others, like us, seemed burdened by thoughts of Nature Week, or by the heat, or by our ten-hour days, or by the season itself, now moving into the seventh of its ten weeks. As Barbara and I drove south out of the City lot, all four windows open in my Chevy, we saw Sammy getting into his convertible alone.

"Ah, poor old Sammy. . . ."

She did not seem in a party mood herself, with the Handbook and the night's double stack of half-page release-forms laid primly on her lap, her folded hands a paperweight on top. I stopped in front of her father's house, the porch light flickering at us through its fluttering mantle of moths, and instead of trying to kiss her I found myself asking whether she would still like to see the Bergman film with me, this coming Saturday night.

"Of course," she said.

Although she softened it—"We never did get to that film, did we!"—it was almost as if last Saturday and Sunday had never happened, or were parenthetical in some larger, incomplete paragraph. I walked her up under the porch lamp, brushing moths out of the air between us as we said good-night, and going back downtown I had the feeling, though I drove on city streets, that we were locked in place like cars on a busy expressway, limited access, next exit miles away.

On Tuesday she told me, her curly head appealingly to one side, that her father would like to talk with me after we got back from the movie.

"On Saturday night? But it'll be late—"

"But it's okay, isn't it? I told him it would be all right!"

I shrugged. "Won't he be working on his sermon?"

"Ahh! My daddy? On Saturday night? Where you been, Adrian, he's got to have that ready by Wednesday!"

She laughed, but it seemed to me she was as nervous as I about the meeting. For both of us it seemed a kind of test that had to be passed, one that we wanted to do well on—even though, as sometimes happened with other tests I had taken, I wasn't exactly sure of the reason why.

During Nature Week Frankie complained that the big kids were picking on him, by which he meant, as nearly as I could tell, that a ten-year-old girl had raced him to his favorite swing on Monday, and had beaten him there. He would sidle up behind me to slip his hand into mine when I went to swab out the johns or chalk the foul-lines or do any of the chores that in previous weeks he would have raced ahead to do by himself, and I found his hand nestled warmly in mine so often that I developed a habit of shying, like a fly-stung horse, whenever I sensed a child behind me. It was as if he was trying to live up to the nickname his ten-year-old rival coined when she saw him running to me: Park Teacher's Pet. When I was seated at a hand-craft table he would stand as close to my elbow as possible, staring at my face. After shaving twice on Monday I had developed a com-bination sunburn and skin rash, or perhaps it was something from the cafeteria food; at any rate I shaved rarely during the rest of Nature Week, and Frankie would say after staring puzzledly at me and tapping my shoulder to get my attention, as if *I* were the one who was ab-stracted, "You need a washing, Aryan." During the hike on Wednes-day I twice miscounted my charges, coming up one short and throwing myself into a panic, once when Frankie had gone back to retrieve the white shirt he had doffed while climbing a tree, so as not to soil it—he had hung it on a wind-whipped bush near a mud puddle, and his dismayed cry told me where he was—and the second time when he stuck so close to my hip pocket, as I turned and counted the others, that he was invisible until I stumbled over him.

Willie had chosen not to go on the hike. "It too hot to go a-walking. Ain't no law says I got to go on no hike."

Since Monday evening I had felt subtly at a disadvantage with him. I quoted from the Handbook, but without much spirit. "It's supposed to be a group project," I said.

"Man, I ain't no group with all them little tads! I got my scientific experiment to practice on. You let them do all the walking."

"You can practice on Thursday," I said. His experiment was called "A Flame Needs Oxygen," and I didn't care to have him practicing it in my absence. "Look, Rufus and Teddy are going. They're just as old as you."

"Ain't near as chubby fat, though," I heard Rufus say, but Willie didn't rise to the bait.

"If I don't want to go," he said, "who's going to stop me?"

No one, apparently. I was too listless to push; Frankie stared glumly at my whiskers, his hand ready to seize mine as soon as I lowered it from the table across which I had been gesturing; and when Sonny of the honey-colored skin and sunny disposition, who had been rotated to Junior Leadership status for the week, suggested that no-body wanted Willie anyway, he was not contradicted. I let Willie stay behind.

According to the rules you needed seven or more for a hike, and on Wednesday I had seven. I led my minimal group to a golf course a mile and a half southwest, the Calumet Country Club, where there was plenty of Nature to be labeled and recorded in the wooded fringe separating the fairways from Twenty-fifth Street. There were also plenty of lost golf balls, which unlike butterflies and dried weeds were worth real money when you found them, and did not have to be labeled. Up at the picnic table outside the clubhouse, where we had our lunch, I smiled wanly at spiffy foursomes of deep-tanned house-wives and surgeons in white, spiked shoes who had to wait while my charges monopolized the ball-cleaning machine, a slotted wooden racket with which you shoved the balls two at a time back and forth between brushes fixed in a cylinder of sudsy water. Surely its potential as a percussion and rhythm instrument had never been fully realized before—or was it the sexual implication of the apparatus, embarrass-ingly obvious to me as my busy black-skinned boys whooped and giggled and elbowed one another, making pumping motions with their hands, that so enchanted one crinkly-eyed, grandmotherly golfer that against my wishes she positively encouraged the performance?

"No, no, young man, you just let them go ahead. I've nothing to do all afternoon. My, what a passion for cleanliness! Such energy! Makes me feel young again!"

No doubt in our own way we were part of the ecology of the golf course. The boys drove a brisk three-cornered trade, golf balls for quarters and quarters for soda, as they called it, glowering at jingling pockets in checked slacks, whisking the coins with almost arrogant haste out of leather-wrapped palms, and recycling them without delay through the pop cooler just inside the door of the clubhouse. "Hey, lady, lookah here, this here one be a Sportflite, now"—and then whoosh! through the weak-springed screen door to the big red cooler whose series of clicks, grunts, and gurgles as it delivered the goods was more fun to imitate than the call of any bird. "Slip it in, man, now tickle her upside the ruby-duby"—and then to antiphonal cheers from seven thirsty throats: click, grunt, gurgle, plunk, happiness! Six throats, rather, for Frankie stood outside all the while, fanning his muddy shirt through the air, no doubt feeling as Abe Lincoln said he felt upon occasion—like a bear at a wedding: uninvited, unwanted, and not dressed for it. In the morning I had been ashamed of my small group of followers, but now the sextet around the pop cooler seemed more than enough for a minimal group, and as I watched the thin-lipped clubhouse boy watching us, I was glad that Willie had not come along.

I lost my first equipment that week. Despite Nikkles' orientation-week jokes about the Hoover Street practice of "losing" home runs into the hands of an accomplice stationed outside the left-field fence among the lilacs, I was still using the same two softballs I had been issued in the beginning—the only boys' leader, to my knowledge, who could made such a claim, whereas Red Buchler, for one, had already gone through five. My evening ballplayers were as conscientious about retrieving home-run balls as they were about trying to hit them. But during Nature Week I had to requisition two replacements, one for a towering blast by Jake, the Henry Aaron of Hoover, who skied the battered horsehide way over the bushes and into the elms, as we could tell by the squawking flock of blackbirds in its wake; it ended up bouncing through a shower of dried twigs into Hoover Street, and from there thumped and bumped its way north under the gearbox of an astonished fresh-fish van, never to be seen again, while the whole playground let out its collective breath in a cheer, even the little girls singing around the sandbox with Barbara.

That was Tuesday. The second lost lilacer came Wednesday night, after my return from the hike, off the bat of Lee Roy. During his three-week absence Lee Roy's leg seemed to have healed nicely, along with whatever ego-wounds Barbara had left him with. He played center field stolidly and undemonstratively, except for his theatrical posture of crucifixion against the fence while Jake's blast rained birds and branches above him, and he attempted no words with Barbara. To me, serving as umpire behind home plate, he was not so shy. His four-base blow into the bushes came as the climax of a lecture he delivered to me (professional-baseball fashion: never look at the ump while you chew him out) during the interludes while three near-miss foul balls were chased down the alley and retrieved among the trash cans there.

"What you should have done"—spitting a white glob and picking it off in the air with a one-handed swing of the bat—"what you should have done a long time ago, actually, you should have instituted the two-foul rule. Way it is now—"

He measured the next lob arcing in from the pitcher and sent it screaming foul among the black-and-white no-parking posts along the alley.

"See what I mean?" Still not looking at me. Spitting a second shot into the dust and addressing it where it lay as if it were a golf ball on a tee. "Way it is now, a batter can keep trying and trying. Any decent athlete can hit one over the fence sooner or later. Then you've lost your equipment, which is equipment paid for by the City. Softballs cost money."

"We haven't lost a single one except for yesterday," I said, and he turned to me, the white "Indiana" squared away across his chest and his downturned sailor hat cocked confidentially.

"These plumbers don't care, they're only out for a good time." Then louder again, into the darkening infield where the pitcher was ready: "Nope, you're the one who has to take the responsibility. You should have instituted the two-fouls-and-you're-out. Should have done it right away. But, since you *ain't*—"

His fourth try, aimed as deliberately at me as the bad grammar, bounced off the top of the fence and then fell among the bushes, where he helped search for it with as much interest as the rest of us, or even more, since the post-homer search was always felt by the slugger himself as a kind of curtain call; but he made it perfectly clear that without having instituted the two-foul rule we had no moral right to find a lost ball, no matter how it turned out in fact.

The next night, using one of the new softballs I had made a special stop at City Hall for, I decided to call for the equipment a bit earlier. Darkness came a half-hour earlier now. I was surprised to meet resistance. The ball had to circle the infield before coming to me. One last time, around the horn, gang! And then the outfield, for outfielders deserved one last throw too, and the bright white new piece of equipment, which cost the City money, of course, went back and forth while the sky darkened, all under a cover of good-humored playfulness. "Just one more throw to left, Adrian, watch this!" And from the gloaming eighty yards away, "Hey, Park Teacher, line drive all the way to right field, man!"—and the ball would be momentarily lost and scuffed among the confusion of swings and slides in the right-field corner. I began to wonder what I would do if they refused, really refused, to give up the ball. Take down names—of which I knew few, the big boys being notably migratory in their habits? Call the police, or threaten to? Until at last Lee Roy under his pith helmet, a parody of authority, announced, "Come on, now fellas, let's give the man the ball. He's the leader." To my relief and chagrin he was obeyed. "Oh, yeah, man, we don't want to make you no trouble, no way!"

Earlier that day, in the morning before leaving on her own hike, which was a sensible walk with fourteen followers, notebooks in hand, past the front-yard flowers of the neighborhood, Barbara told me how Willie had spent his time during my hike the day before. In the equipment shed, alone. Using the carbon paper which was meant to trace coping-saw patterns on wood. Using it instead to trace characters out of the comic strips, but tracing them without their clothes.

"Clever Willie," I said. It irked me that she seemed to make Willie my responsibility even when I was gone. If she wanted the rule against children in the equipment shed enforced, why didn't she enforce it?

"Like—you know, Daisy Mae?"

"Well," I said. "I guess gentlemen prefer blondes."

"Yeah. What I mean is, I told him you would talk to him."

"Me? You told him I would talk to him? About what?"

"I'm sorry," she said, backing off toward the sidewalk where her girls waited with their notebooks and labeled lunches. "I just didn't know how to handle it. I'm sorry." She gave me a quick, barely apologetic smile and was off on her hike.

From her reaction I guessed that Willie must have committed something graver than the administrative trespass of hiding in the equipment shed or the venial sin of tracing Daisy Mae's beauty in the flesh. Had he said something nasty? "No sweat, Barbara, them carbon papers *spose* to be for boys' handcraft." A ten-year-old's nastiness, even Willie's, had always been something she could laugh off, or laugh him out of. Was it something more personal then, something about what he had seen in the shed on Monday evening, or had imagined he had seen, or had been told by others that he must have seen? Was that why I was being called in on this case?

When Willie arrived I reminded him that he, like all the children, should never be in the equipment shed alone. "You were a Junior Leader. I thought you would know that."

He was feisty. "You can't prove nothing on me, man. I ain't done nothing wrong."

"Maybe not. But this is just a rule we have to—"

"Man, that rule don't make any sense!"

"I'm not explaining it to you, Willie. I'm just telling you what it is. The rule is you don't go in there alone. Is that clear?"

"You tell me what I done wrong, it be clear."

I let that stand, hoping he would trade compliance for having had the last word. While I tried to interest his peers in pressing a few last-minute rocks, earthworms, and insects into service as "exhibits" for the Fair, he sat nearby on one of the swings looking bug-eyed at some folded sheets of paper in his hand. Hearing him chortle, the younger boys at my table would glance quickly at me and then, giggling, at each other. 'Look at that, now," we could hear him say. "Mm, hmm!" I made it my policy to ignore him, something easier to think than do, since he was a master of the bug-eyed look and the secret yet highly audible chortle. All day he nagged at my consciousness like a broken swing, like a piece of equipment that was neither in use nor properly out of use and would therefore, according to Nikkles' playground wisdom, bring me nothing but trouble.

On Friday Barbara rushed me the news that when she got there at nine she found the door already open.

"Open? But I know I locked it last night. It was just after I put the new softball in."

"The only thing missing is the carbon paper," she said.

She was right. The cabinet and equipment boxes were locked, but the carbon paper, which had been left lying out on the box of wood scraps, was missing.

"Driven by artistic fervor. . . ."

She didn't laugh. "We'd better change the locks," she said.

"Again? Twice in one summer? How does that look!"

It was the first break-in since opening day. I had forgotten that day until now, though I had Willie's darts in the cabinet to remind me. It had been a good while since Barbara had let Verella, or anyone else, use her keys, but I had relaxed my own principles enough that when I remembered that Frankie had offered, a week or two ago, to use my keys to open the johns for me, I could not remember whether I had let him. I didn't *think* I had. There was also the possibility that Willie, during one of his helpful spells, had picked my key ring and run down to the Lock-Stop booth at the supermarket, where for a quarter you could get duplicates made. Or perhaps he had a master key?

When I asked Frankie about the shed's being open that morning he shook his head, looking frightened and keeping mum. Willie arrived in the afternoon, just in time for the Fair. As I watched him bluster through his experiment with jar and candle—he did it well, but his voice had a belligerent edge—it struck me I could no longer pretend, as I had been pretending, that my playground ran itself.

"What you looking at me for, man? You can't prove nothing on me."

"I wasn't looking at you, Willie. Maybe you have a guilty conscience about something."

"Don't talk to me about no guilty conscious. I ain't no more guilty conscious than you."

We closed early that day because of a rainstorm that thundered up out of the northwest and with its first winds wiped out both the Fair and the evening's softball for which I had been steeling myself. I sent Barbara racing the drops for home while I switched the padlocks on the shed door and the boys' equipment boxes as I had done back on opening day, giving the door a final tug to make sure. As I drove off to the library with my wiper blades flashing, I found myself repeating for the first time that summer the national prayer of thanksgiving, Thank God it's Friday.

For the Bergman film Barbara wore the white linen suit I had seen in church and, I noticed, no horn-rimmed glasses. After Friday's rain a Canadian wind had swept the heat and humidity of Nature Week away, and with it Chicago's smog, and she could wear her contact lenses. To my own Sunday outfit I added a coat and tie, and I felt ready for the confrontations with Bergman and, afterward, Robinson. It felt good to be dressed up. The wind was a cool sixty degrees, and on the car radio the baseball play-by-play was punctuated with speculations about the first football of the season, next week's College All-Star game.

After we had complimented each other on how nice we looked, Barbara's first words had to do with the week that had passed.

"You been by the playground lately to see if it's still there?"

"Since yesterday," I said, "I haven't wanted to go back."

When she spoke again I thought she sounded defensive. "He's just testing you. He's just waiting for you to *do* something."

"What am I supposed to do? Sleep overnight in the shed?"

"We could change the locks," she said, and though she had changed the "you" to "we" I was still irritated.

"I hate to do that. The first time I could charge up to last year, but this time—" I stopped, not wanting to say, This time it will look like *my* fault.

"Ah, Nikkles won't care! He kind of likes to deal with a, you know. . . . As long as it's minor."

"Crisis. Emergency. Foul-up. Mess."

"Yeah. I'm sorry, Adrian. It's probably my fault."

"No, it's mine. I shouldn't have been so quick to change them the first time."

"I know I've been too careless with my keys," she said. "I've been trying to do better."

"I should have tried harder to get his confidence. Instead I reacted legalistically."

After a moment she said suddenly, "That Willie! He must have got my keys from Verella one time and run down to the hardware store. He can talk his way past anybody."

"Maybe. But if he wants to get in bad enough he'll get in no matter how many locks you put on." She was silent, and I added, "I always thought you knew how to handle him."

"Not me. He can always talk around me if he keeps at it. He needs somebody to lay down the law to him."

We were on Doty Avenue going past Calumet Harbor. Somewhere on our left under clouds glowing with reflected city light was the bait-seller's shack. Neither of us had mentioned it, and I realized then that no matter what the Department hierarchy thought about one leader's dating another there would never have to be a rule against it. After spending five or six hours a day in each other's company, five days a week, week in and week out, in this parody of marriage

163

in which you spent all your days but none of your nights together and still had to argue and squabble about the care of children, hundreds and hundreds of children that were not even your own, any sensible pair of human beings would prefer—would *demand*—that they spend their free hours with someone else. (As my grandmother once put it, wistfully, during the first months of my grandfather's retirement: "He never *comes* home any more. He always *is* home.")

"Why don't we stop talking about it," I said. "After all, this is our night off."

"Right. Let's just enjoy the movie."

She settled back in her side of the seat. When we had driven in silence a while she said, "I hear it's a gloomy one, though."

I remembered: Bergman's Nordic gloom. "Is that what your father wants to talk to me about afterward? The movie's view of Original Sin, Original Guilt, all that?"

She sat up straight again. "Don't worry about that now—let's just enjoy the movie!"

"I'll have to tell him I don't believe in any of that."

"Don't be nervous about it, he just wants to talk to you, that's all."

"The whole idea is just a product of those long northern winters."

"Look at you, holding the wheel so tight—you look like you do believe in it!"

I tried to relax my shoulders and prove I was not susceptible to Nordic gloom, but my smile felt like a grimace.

"It's still summer, isn't it. Maybe I shouldn't have worn the tie." I loosened my collar, picturing as I did so my father stripping his off on a Sunday morning.

"You don't want to do that!" she said. "You look good with a tie!"

"Is that why you wanted to visit my church sometime? Check out the original museum of Original Sin?"

She sat back in the seat again, arms folded, and for a long time said nothing, the lights of Stony Island Avenue and then Jackson Park and the Outer Drive outlining her hair with its springy waves and the delicate rising of her neck. "You know it isn't that," I heard her say. And after a moment: "You came to mine, didn't you?"

When I took my eyes off the road to look at her I saw thin gold circlets the size of a child's ring piercing her ears and I wanted to speak softly to her, to stop and look at the lake and hold her, but the evening seemed to have been programmed a different way.

"Well, maybe I wanted to see a Pentecostal church."

"Well, maybe I want to see a. . . ."

I let her pause. "Reformed," I said.

"Yeah, well, whatever. Ah, Adrian, we don't have to go if you don't want to—"

"I didn't say that. I do want to."

"I don't want to go unless you want me to."

"I do want you to. We'll do it."

"Okay, then."

"Okay," I said, and I felt relieved on one count, at least—that if her father wanted to ask whether I had guts enough to appear with his daughter in my own home territory, as well as in his, I would have an answer.

The movie, when we got to it, was as gloomy as Barbara had predicted, or so it seemed to me—so gloomy in its view of life that I was pleased to echo her admission that she didn't understand it. It seemed to speak well of us that we did not.

I did admit to myself that what we had seen reflected my current experience. From the entire evening I saved only one glowing moment: before entering the theatre I held her and kissed her on a Chicago sidewalk, and she responded, her slender fingers around my neck, our two bodies coming together so easily that it seemed wrong for them to part. Opening my eyes, I saw in the faces of Chicagoans how we appeared to the world. A middle-aged man in white topcoat steered his wife quickly by as if we were two drunks passed out on the sidewalk, instinctively putting his bulk between her and us until the danger was past and he could walk on the curbside again, as politeness required. In her backward glance over fur collar was something else—perhaps shock; perhaps a romantic hope; perhaps disgust. She was not indifferent. The younger couples tried to be. Waiting in the lobby for their tickets, most of them white, some black, they gave us one quick back-and-forth, then another, then tunneled their eyes firmly forward, minding their own business come hell or high water.

Afterward, at the parking garage, we stood next to a stolid, blocky, frog-faced fellow who stared at Barbara so long and so lewdly, it seemed to me—hat over his eyes and hands in raincoat pockets as if trying out for the mob—that I wondered if he was waiting for me to

make him a pimp's offer. Was that his inference from the mere fact
of our appearing in public wearing two different colors of skin? Was
it? Or was he looking for a punch in the big fat nose? As I braced
myself to ask one of these questions his car was brought down—a
long, sleek, stylish one—and he drove away. When my Chevy appeared and the attendant, a black man of the same fiftyish age, gave
us the same kind of lingering look, I pressed into his two-toned hand
a bigger tip than I had imagined giving him, hoping perhaps to shame
him into better thoughts.

At a stoplight we waited one lane over from a squad car, and I
tried not to notice that we were being watched. I remembered a
morning in Calumet when I was stopped by a black patrolman on my
way to work. I had run a yellow light. I was due for a ticket until he
found out that I, too, worked for the City. "Oh, you all right," he said
then, and gave me back my license. "We never be too tough on
anybody working for the City." His sense of brotherhood among City
workers seemed almost acceptable as a substitute for impersonal justice; aside from saving me some money it allowed me to think that
a white cop might have let Barbara off on similar grounds. But what
if the two of us were driving together? If the police didn't happen to
know that we worked for "the City"? I pictured our prone bodies in
a Chicago alley, perhaps after I had made the mistake of punching
Froggy the Mobster in the nose, being sacrificed to the interracial
peace of Chicago's integrated force. "You know these folks, Eric?"
"Naw, Willie. They don't seem to belong to the white community.
You?" "No way, man, they for sure don't belong to the black community, either." "Guess we're not responsible, then." "Nope, guess
not."

While fantasizing I pictured myself in Orangetown explaining to
the elders and deacons (for the Church, if pressed, would have to
take us in, would it not?—unless it could think of a good reason not
to) that Barbara's career as a dancer and singer or, say, a leader in
rhythmic recreation did entail some necessary work on the Sabbath,
but I was sure that when I had explained these texts from the Apostle
Paul they would see the subject in a different light. Or, with Barbara,
facing the smiling usher, who would be smiling no longer, and explaining that in our view of spiritual gifts it was not absolutely mandatory for one to experience the rapture of glossolalia before being

acceptable to the Divine Power, especially if said person had a modest knowledge of several tongues anyway, though excluding Hebrew.

Under a rising half-moon we passed Calumet Harbor again, but neither of us mentioned the bait-seller's house; it seemed beside the point. I imagined that our dirt road, if we could have found it, would bear a sign saying NO TRESPASSING: RAILROAD PROPERTY. I asked her instead whether she had dated much while at UCLA. It seemed odd that we had discussed only our distant, never our recent pasts.

"What about you?" she said. "Did you date much at . . . your school?"

"Hebron," I said.

"Well, did you?"

"I asked you first."

"I know you didn't, you were too busy learning all that Hebrew and Greek and—"

"Not Hebrew, didn't I explain that? If your father wants to talk Hebrew with somebody, he'd better look elsewhere."

She laughed as if I had been joking. After I waited she said, "It's a big school, Adrian. What do you think?"

"Well, did you ever date any, any. . . ."

"Any blue-eyes—that what you mean? Ahh, turn on the light, let me look at you blushing! You think I'm a racially prejudiced person? You think you're the only one?"

I did feel my face grow warm. I had wanted to think I was special to her, but not because of color.

"I just wondered if I'm the first one to visit your father."

She did not laugh at that. After a moment she looked at me. "Of all the men I dated you're the only one who knows Greek and Latin and—"

"And Hebrew. Right." I wasn't sure whether the chance to set this particular record in her life made me feel better or worse. "But you don't mean he wants to sit around conjugating Greek verbs."

I felt her fingers slip quickly across my wrist. "Don't be nervous, Adrian, he won't bite you."

"What about this book you said he was writing?"

"What do you mean, what about it?"

"I mean what's it about? Blue-eyed playground leaders, or what?"

"Well, it's—you know, it's about dispensations in history, that kind of thing. Whatever."

"Look, I don't know anything about dispensationalism and all that stuff! I was only pre-seminary and I dropped out of that!"

She was silent for so long that I thought perhaps she was crying. Most of the girls I had dated for any length of time—Barbara was right, they were not many—had allowed me to see tears once or twice. A sad letter from home, a bad grade, a weepy movie, even joy. It was an acceptable feminine idiom. As a man was allowed to smash fist into palm, when frustrated, or to swear, a woman was allowed to cry, and it occurred to me that perhaps I had been acting in a frustrating way. But although I spent more hours with Barbara, on the playground and off, than with any other woman except the one I married, I never saw her cry except once, and that came later. Instead she came charging out of an emotional tight spot on the force of her laughter, or else retreated into a kind of cold and formal dignity, or, more rarely, into limp fatigue. There was also a kind of resignation that I had heard earlier in the evening—a motherly voice, perhaps, since I felt I had been acting childishly.

"Ah, well. If you don't want to see my daddy tonight it's no life-and-death matter."

"No, no," I said. "Of course I'll talk to him. I've been looking forward to it."

The Reverend Robinson had a firm two-handed handshake that seemed to draw me toward him and at the same time, through a certain stiffness in the elbow, hold me at arm's length. Perhaps he was far-sighted. He was taller than I was by a couple of inches and kept his head backwardly tilted so that his eyes took aim at me past dark, lean cheeks and the tip of his nose—a long nose, unlike his daughter's short one. He was no taller than my father, but he was trim and erect in a high-buttoned vest, and as he hung my coat in the closet facing the stairway, bending forward a little to do so, I had the foreboding experienced when walking into a half-court game of basketball and having to look up at my opponent.

Barbara, my coach, had introduced me ("Daddy, this is Adrian; Adrian, my father") and disappeared, presumably into the kitchen.

"Please be seated," Robinson said.

The living room and the dining room, visible through a square archway, were framed in dark wood, and the furniture was dark and heavy. Robinson sat upright in a leather chair, his eyes seeming to squint in the lamplight which fell across his left shoulder and brought out the white in his hair. On the sofa opposite him I felt somewhat exposed; there were low pillows about but nothing to lean into. I apologized for keeping him up late on a Saturday night.

"Don't trouble yourself about that," he said. I read his mood as genial, though unlike his daughter he smiled without showing his teeth. When he smiled his eyes and nostril wings widened and made me feel, even more than I had when sitting in his congregation, that I was being fully taken in. His eyes were warm and black, darker than his face. "I don't often have the opportunity to visit with young divinity students. In the past I've been fortunate enough to attend some summer institutes in the ministry, but my present congregation is not large enough or wealthy enough for me to ask them, in all conscience, to make such a sacrifice. That gives me reason to be pleased to see you tonight. Barbara"—his voice without shifting from the modified pulpit one in which he addressed me resonated clearly into the other rooms—"Please bring us some wine. You are not a teetotaler?"

"No, sir," I said. "But I should say that I'm not a divinity student. I graduated with a degree in humanities—"

"Oh?"

He sat straighter, his forehead wrinkling as his dark eyes focused on me again. Behind him and on his right, on the upright piano and in the shelves of the glassed-in bookcase, were framed photographs, some of them clipped from magazines or newspapers, of black men in ministerial robes or high, old-fashioned collars who seemed to stare downward at the camera as if severely conscious of superiority. None of them smiled—a fact indicating only that the pictures pre-dated the toothy forties and fifties; still, I would have been happier had some of them smiled. The one woman pictured, her face round and full in an oval frame, I took to be Barbara's mother. She was not smiling either.

"But I understood that you were, at least until recently, a part of the pre-seminary program? At Hebron College? In Iowa?"

"Well, yes," I said. "Until recently."

Through the archway we heard Barbara's laughter. "Don't let him fool you, Daddy, he's the preacher of the playground!"

Robinson's face relaxed in a brief smile. "As to your deciding

169

temporarily against the ministry," he said, "I would not attribute too much importance to that. I wrestled with the problem myself when I was your age. It took me a full year before I saw what it was that the Lord wanted me to do."

I nodded, not wanting to risk more.

"Some of my own communion have referred to this change of heart of mine as my conversion. That may well be. But who is to say whether it was my conversion that brought me to see the light or the training given me by my father and mother? 'Train up a child in the way he should go, and when he is old he shall not depart from it.' Proverbs twenty-two verse six."

He paused and I nodded again.

"That is a truth that your communion emphasizes—witness your attention to separate schools—and I admire them for it. I admire them for it. We Pentecostals often make too much of the conversion experience as opposed to the parent's clear duty to bring up a child in the way he should go. We must not forget that the Holy Ghost works in both. Your communion's doctrines of the election and the perseverance of the saints are a good corrective for us here. For what are the *means* of the Lord's electing and preserving the saints but parents who bring up a child in the way he should go?"

He paused as one waiting to observe the effect of a compliment. The doctrines he had mentioned, familiar as the back of my hand in the context of Orangetown and Hebron, asserted a radical concept of predestination. When you're in, you're in; when you're out, you're out. In the months of decision making before changing my major, when I still believed in the ultimate importance of ideology, I had resented them as fostering rigidity and intolerance.

"Perhaps so," I said. Robinson leaned forward.

"I once had the pleasure of discussing these matters with Willem Bronkema. A True Reformed theologian with whom you may be familiar. A fine gentleman who had just recently come from the Netherlands, I believe—"

"Bronkema?" I said. "You've met Bronkema?"

His eyes and nostril-wings widened with pleasure at my astonishment—though it was not so much his having met the Frisian scholar that astonished me but that Bronkema must have been a creature of flesh and blood rather than of ink, as I had always supposed. I knew his legend: like St. Paul he had grown up as a member of the antagonistic official religious body, the State Church of the Netherlands, actually taking orders in it before becoming converted—in his case by a young cousin of the pioneering Dominie Van Horne, whom he later married—and writing the definitive doctrinal formulation of the church he had joined. Still, one read Bronkema; one did not meet him. I had heard my teachers refer to him from time to time as if he had been a real person, but he became authentic for me only now, when I heard him vouched for by this American Pentecostal preacher.

"A delightful man. Somewhat hard to understand, at times, because of his accent. We were both foreigners to Iowa, in a manner of speaking. Perhaps that was why we got along so well while I was there. Ah, thank you very much. Won't you have some with us?"

Barbara had entered with three glasses of wine on a silver tray. She had removed her jacket and her shoes. She wore a sleeveless navy blouse and, over her white linen skirt, a flowered apron. She bent to serve us, first me and then her father, her arms burnished in the lamplight, and I caught my breath, she was so completely a picture of the young True Reformed wife at home of a Sunday evening— except that this was Saturday after the movie, and her bare arms were brown. She sat in a wicker-bottomed rocker that I imagined to have been her mother's, her sheer stockings slipping fricatively past one another as she crossed her legs, her toes curling girlishly over one another on the rug. I saw her give me a slow wink and a grin across the rim of her wineglass.

"Willem Bronkema was still hale and hearty, even though he was, I believe, at that time in his late seventies. That was the Hebron Institute of Old Testament Hermeneutics, the summer of"—he glanced at Barbara, who smiled back, startled—"yes, the summer of 'thirty-seven, two years after Barbara's mother died. The very depths of the Depression. I shall never forget it. Bronkema and I discussed the doctrines of the election and perseverance of the saints, and I may say he influenced the course of my life."

His voice, in the silence, echoed impressively over phrases like the death of my child's mother, the depths of the Depression, the course of my life. I tried to let my face register approval of Robinson and Bronkema, though not the doctrines they had discussed.

"I wasn't aware that you were so familiar with Hebron College," I said. "Most people aren't." Barbara must have given him my history and then forgotten the details herself, as we give money to a bank.

He looked pleased. "I've recently renewed my interest in your communion because of a current project. Perhaps Barbara has told you about it?"

Without daring to look at her directly I saw in the corner of my eye Barbara's toes clenching and unclenching. "I'm not really sure," I said.

"Ah. Well. Let me fill you in. I am interested in the foundation of communities. In the spiritual forces that bind together any community or communion worthy of the name. Beliefs. Experiences and memories. Common rites. In that regard I'd like to try you out on a theory of mine concerning your own communion. If I may."

In what I took as an attempt to lighten the mood, Barbara said, "Are you ready for this, Adrian?"

"I'd be interested to hear it," I said.

Robinson set down his wineglass. "Your Reformed doctrine is arranged under five heads, is it not?" He held up one long-fingered hand as he had during the Sunday service. "Named acronymically for the national flower of the Netherlands?"

"Tulip." The sound of a ticking clock, the sound and smell of coffee percolating, my own sense of wrapped-up cleanliness and of sitting tense and rigid while apparently at ease—all this made me feel I was undergoing house visitation back in Orangetown. "Total Depravity," I said. My mouth was dry. "Unconditional Election. Limited Atonement, Irresistible Grace, Perseverance of the Saints."

"Ahh! Go to the head of the class, man!"

"Existentially," Robinson said, "I understand by the first of these three nothing more or less than total submission to the will of God. Nothing more or less than the starting place for any community. One finds them implicit, for example, in the thought of Mohammed. I mean in the very earliest suras, those almost certainly stemming from Mecca. Interestingly, 'Islam' is in fact to be translated thus, as 'total submission.' "

"I wasn't aware of that," I said.

"No time for your Arabic?" Barbara said. "Shame!"

Her nervousness was having its effect on me, and I half wished for Robinson to declare that if there were any further outbursts he would clear the courtroom.

"There are other analogies, of course. For example, in what the Marxist must declare his allegiance to. Total depravity of the bourgeois mind. Unconditional election of the working classes, and of certain intellecturals. Atonement limited to the elect group. Irresistible movement of the forces of history. And, very definitely—though not on an individualist basis—perseverance of the saints."

I seized a moment while Barbara was sipping her wine. "Those are interesting analogies. But isn't what they have in common, basically, just a certain kind of—"

"Fatalism?" he said, though I meant fanaticism. "This objection is often raised. But of course this so-called fatalism is in its effect entirely the opposite. In fact it stimulates great effort and activity. For the total submission of the first three heads of doctrine is followed by the utter confidence of the last two. The starting place, again, for any great effort, and certainly for the building of a community. Witness the *jihad,* the holy war, of one community. The revolutionizing activity of another. The migration, I may say, of your own communion. And of mine, or my father's and grandfather's. I told Willem Bronkema"—now he smiled fully, showing his teeth for the first time— "that the real acronym must be far more universal than the word 'tulip.' Far more international. No, no, I told him, the real acronym for any nation-forging set of doctrines is in fact the word 'pulpit.' The same five letters, you see, with the addition of an extra *p.* For Pentecostalism, of course. To account for the *power* of these movements. The only missing ingredient."

He was still smiling, as was Barbara. I nodded appreciatively, though my head whirled with objections.

"Bronkema I must say enjoyed that. I can picture him even now. What a hearty laugh he had, even as an old man! It's unfortunate he didn't live to revise his book. I think he might have used my notion."

I tried to enjoy the image of a younger Reverend Robinson long-striding across Hebron's campus in the summer of 'thirty-seven—he would have been in his mid-thirties, perhaps already graying after his wife's sudden death, but now recovering by means of liberal doses of True Reformed doctrine—with a short, portly, elderly Frisian trotting along like a dachshund at his side and gesticulating like one of those comic referees who accompany the Harlem Globetrotters. How interesting, that of all the ministers present at the Summer Institute for Old Testament Hermeneutics—and the stiff-headed generation of the True Reformed ministry would have been well represented—Bronkema chose to spend his coffee breaks (as I imagined it) with this lanky black Pentecostal! Obviously this was not a story which Robinson could fully enjoy with his usual acquaintance. He was enjoying it now, and Barbara was enjoying his enjoyment, the two of them laughing aloud, Robinson, his eyes shining, making what sounded like a deep-voiced interrupted hum. He even imitated Bronkema's accent: "Willem Bronkema told me: no doubt we will have to put that *p* of yours in *de mittle* of the *pulpit!*"

"Ahh!" Barbara laughed, watching him. "Ah, hah-hah!"

And yet. Were they not making the Holy Spirit—whose work, as I understood it, was the breaking down of all walls of separation between peoples—into a mere engine for what, according to Robinson's own analogies, was the champion set of wall-building doctrines in the world?

When I spoke up my voice sounded high and thin. "But isn't that an impossible kind of mixture? Doesn't Pentecostalism contradict all the others? What about other analogies—for example, what about the Reformed churches of, say—"

"Of South Africa?" He leaned forward again so that his eyes seemed to focus beyond me. "I speak of formal analogies, of course. I do not speak of content. The head of the serpent is analogous to the head of a dove, but we do not value them equally. Nevertheless: you mention the Reformed of South Africa. We can learn a great deal from them. A great deal. An unusual opportunity, to see the birth of a tribe within historical time. A great opportunity. Like the Mormons. The Pilgrims. My own people's trek northward to the industrial centers. Some sort of warfare seems to be necessary. Need it be warfare against flesh and blood, I often wonder, or may it be warfare against principalities and powers? At least the latter. And with it a great trek or migration, or, failing that, a symbolic march. St. Paul's missionary journeys. The Crusades. Islamic *hajj*, or pilgrimage, substituting for the holy wars of old. The Long March. And so on. The experience of being led forward, physically led, existentially guided by God, so that doctrines, rites, and laws gain a community-bonding force which can never be shaken—"

"I'll tell you what 'tulip' ought to stand for," I said. I was interrupting, but it seemed to me I had been listening a long time. "It ought to stand for tolerance and understanding and love. All those things which the South Africans, among others, have no room for in their system."

174

In the silence that followed, Barbara stood up. "Ah, smell that coffee! Why don't we go to the dining room?"

She held her hand toward me and I stood up to follow her. Robinson accompanied me, his hand gripping my bicep, his long fingers embarrassingly close to completing the circle.

"We must not forget that love is a condition existing between separate, existentially distinct beings. Mm? Love presupposes a separation. It is part of the spirit of the present age to deny that."

His grip on my arm and his voice resounding in my ear as we headed to the dining room reminded me forcibly of my own separate existence. As he spoke he punctuated by squeezing. "There can be no love without separate existence. Love your neighbor—as you love yourself. Mm? Separate existence implies pain. My father understood that, though his understanding of Pentecostalism differs from mine, when he separated from the CME's. How it grieves my soul that they now consider changing their first initial to mean 'Christian' instead of 'Colored'! Are they heeding the Holy Ghost? Or merely the spirit of the age? Of course there is pain, but without the pain of separate existence there can be no love. Those who repudiate the pain of separate existence preclude the possibility of love! They wish to dissolve themselves—within the mother's womb. But one cannot go back to the womb. One can redeem the pain of birth, after all, only by the nobility of one's own life."

The dining table was round, with a square red tablecloth pointing to the four chairs like a compass. Robinson and I sat at opposite poles. Barbara brought us coffee and then sat between us. With the cup steaming below my face I realized I was perspiring. The hollows which Robinson's fingers seemed to have left on my arm, under the shirt, were slowly filling with moisture. While pouring my coffee Barbara had given me a signal by nudging my shoulder with hers, which I took to mean that I should converse defensively for the remaining rounds of the bout and avoid her father's knockout punch. I tried to do this by staring at my cup, letting the warm vapors penetrate my sinuses, and now and then nodding acquiescence. Robinson spoke about the function of so-called "legalism"—he pronounced it with renunciatory quotation marks—in preserving community integrity. The dietary restrictions of the Adventists. The prescribed prayers of Mohammedanism. The meatless Fridays of Catholics. When he began praising the strict Sabbatarianism of "my people," however, I could not resist pointing out that had he been my pastor in Orangetown we could not be sitting up so late on a Saturday night, nor could I admit to having attended a movie.

Under the table the small of Barbara's shoeless foot was polishing the toe of my loafer. Her father sat back in his high-backed wooden chair, still lean and loose-jointed in his fifties, his arms folded across his dark, old-fashioned vest. His black eyes stared at me across his slanted cheekbones.

"Your people deserve a great deal of credit. I speak of their century-old resistance to the dominant spirit of the age. Their insistence that all of life, not just a part, should be subordinated to religious ideals."

"Well, yes, but the other side of that—"

"Adrian's invited me to his church sometime," Barbara said, interrupting. Above the ticking of the clock from the living room I heard my own throat swallowing coffee.

"That's right," I said. "Probably in the evening, sometime."

Robinson nodded. "I am aware that you visited mine."

"Yes. I enjoyed the service very much."

When he spoke again he did not look directly at me but rather to the side. "I would make an observation about your relationship with my daughter. I would observe that the Northerner, particularly one who has forgotten his own heritage, will often look to the South to discover or rediscover his own soul. Do you see what I mean?"

"I'm not sure that I do."

He put both elbows on the table and looked at me across folded hands. "Are you aware of drunkenness as a problem among your local churches in Illinois?"

"Drunkenness? Why, no." The wine, I remembered, was heavy, gold, and sweet. I had drained the glass because I thought it was the courteous thing to do.

"One of your pastors, the Reverend Bing, I believe—"

"Boom?"

"Yes, thank you. The Reverend Boom admitted as much to me several years ago at an Area ministerial conference. The purchase of the liquor has to be made elsewhere, of course—for example, here in Calumet—since you've been successful in keeping your towns ostensibly dry. Unfortunately for you, the new marketing centers may change that."

176

"I really wasn't aware of anything like that, sir."

"Let me explain it to you." He leaned across the table, one long finger pointing at me. "On the one hand, you have no need of tee-totalism or any dietary prohibition, even though these are among the very strongest of community-bonding forces. Your Sabbatarianism and other prohibitions serve that function, along with the separate school systems, and so on, and I must say serve it admirably. On the other hand, with your people's over-emphasis on the first person of the Holy Trinity, almost to the exclusion of the others, perhaps, you deprive yourself of the cultivation of the emotions which Pentecostalism achieves."

Barbara's foot was pressuring mine and I said nothing.

"Lacking that, you see, you have a positive need for drunkenness. Or some other emotional safety valve. If it didn't exist, one might say, you would have to invent it. Therefore I would wager that it is one sin never mentioned in your pulpits. Now. When such a person, a person from such a community, visits a congregation such as mine, which typically allows a much greater emphasis on the third person of the Trinity, he is all too apt to imagine license instead of liberty. A particularly dangerous misapprehension when one considers that no one in fact is so excessively emotional, so slovenly, one may say, as the decadent Puritan. Whereas my effort has always been—"

"Daddy!" Barbara said. "Adrian is strictly square!"

I did not know how to respond. Barbara's foot was massaging my toe, my instep, and my ankle as if she were trying at that moment to illustrate the wantonness of those who have suffered from a strict bringing-up.

Robinson leaned back again, the better to focus on me. "Very well. If by 'square' one means 'honorable.'"

"Much too honorable, Daddy!"

"Very well." He smiled and stood up, holding out his hand. I rose and took it.

"I hope you don't mind my speaking openly of these matters?"

"No, sir," I said. "The wine you served was very good."

He smiled briefly. "I did not wish you to be under any illusion about the kind of people my daughter represents."

"Yes, sir."

He raised his right arm then and lifted his face upward to intone the Trinitarian blessing. "May the love of God the Father. . . ."

I dropped my eyes, then wondered whether I should be looking up. Barbara, I saw, had lowered her head, above palms pressed together at her breast.

"And the communion of the Holy Ghost abide with you now and always. Amen."

"Amen," Barbara repeated, and I, a little after, "Amen."

"I have enjoyed talking with you."

In swift reversion to the secular mode Robinson led me to the front closet and handed me my coat. "I judge that you are in good time," he said, "to be home before midnight."

I could not tell whether he was joking. I asked the one question I had planned as part of my preparation for the visit: what was he preaching on tomorrow?

"The power of the Holy Ghost," he said. He said good-night then and went up the carpeted stairs. A door closed behind him, and I heard his feet on the wooden floor above.

Barbara went out to the porch with me, turning out the porch light as she did so, and we stood together in the cool air. Shadows flickered across us from the lamp swinging on its cable above the corner at Sixteenth Street. She put her arms around me under my jacket and held me, her stockinged toes resting on my loafers.

"Thanks for everything. You were wonderful."

Her kiss was eager and enthusiastic, and if not passionate in the usual sense of the word it was passionate with relief and gratitude, like the kiss given a race-car driver after a grueling 500-mile run, or a battered fighter who has survived fifteen rounds with the champ. I was perspiring as if I had done both these things; I shivered when her arms pressed my shirt to my skin.

She waved once, when I got to my car, her white smile showing briefly in the silver and gray of the porch, and went inside. I was as tired and empty as I had ever been. I had no thoughts at all while driving home except that tomorrow I could sleep late, very late, past nine-thirty and eleven o'clock both. But later that night, waking out of a sound sleep well into the hours of Sunday's Sabbath, I had another thought. I remembered that no matter what happened in the future, there was one thing that could never be taken away from me. Of all Barbara's blue-eyed boyfriends, probably of all her boyfriends taken together, I was the only one who had come through a visit with her father.

CHAPTER TEN

FIRST TRUE REFORMED

THE playground season, like the liturgical year of the Church, had its own inner logic, and during Lantern Week we could feel it winding down toward a conclusion. It began, after Get-Acquainted Week, with the city-wide celebration of Olympic Day; it moved us next to the local neighborhoods and their Doll Buggy Parades; and its long central section involved us as individuals in the pursuit of excellence in Crafts, Hobbies, and games. Now, after the "group projects" of Nature Week, it was spinning us outward again. The Lantern Parade was a neighborhood affair, like the parade of buggies and trikes for Independence Day. After that would come the city-wide Talent Show and Playground Circus which would be celebrated, like Olympic Day, at Island Park; and after a three-day Cleanup Week—truncated, like Get-Acquainted Week at the beginning—we would be released again to the wider worlds of area, state, and nation.

The shiny elm leaves of June were drier and crisper now, the grass and weeds had grown rank, and instead of nesting birds we heard the songs of cicada and grasshopper. In the muggy afternoon, flies clung to the bare, sweating skin and stung as though the coming of winter were our fault. The evening of the parade, when we would mount lighted candles in tagboard and crepe-paper lanterns and carry them through the neighborhood of Hoover Street, would be dim and dusky, five weeks closer to autumn than the mellow, yellow sunsets of the Fourth. Olympic Day was held under the trees at Island Park, but the Circus would occur in the band shell, as if to signal a general movement indoors. After Cleanup Week we would come quickly to the nine months of early darkness, cold weather, and school. I suppose it was the twilight feeling built into Lantern Week that put all of us into the mood—sometimes gentle and melancholy, sometimes defensive—of people saying good-bye.

Frankie said good-bye on Monday afternoon, walking away from a meeting of the grade-school boys I had called to plan our part in the parade. In the morning he had brought me a note from his mother (signed "Eulalia Bumpus" and, below that, "Mrs. Franklin Garwood Bumpus") saying that Frankie had never been so happy as when he was my Junior Leader, and asking whether he had been "in any way remiss in the performing of his job." On the back of the recipe-sized note card she had used I explained that the Junior-Leader badges were rotated from week to week and that Frankie had worn his badge proudly, had done an excellent job, and would do so again, I was sure, if he had another turn. He had this note in his pocket when, after tugging in vain at my shirt-sleeve for several minutes, he broke away from our planning circle and headed for home, his wide, skinny shoulders slumped under the white shirt he left unbuttoned so the playground dust would soil his taut belly instead of something his mother had to wash and iron.

There was a new lock on the equipment shed that morning. I had called Nikkles on Sunday afternoon and told him about the suspected break-in. Barbara was half right, at least, about my making the call: Nikkles, listening to the Sox game on a radio or television I could hear when he answered—somebody had just stolen a base—was as bored on the weekend as an old warrior in peacetime, and seemed to welcome our carbon-paper crisis.

"For crying outside," he said, "send the kid over to the main office, we're up to our navels in carbon paper! What does he do, polish his shoes with the stuff?"

I took the question of what he did with it as rhetorical and explained that we knew, because of an argument we had had with him about carbon paper, that this was the same boy who had gotten in on opening day. "I never got him to tell me how he did it," I apologized, "so with this second break-in I thought I'd better give you a call."

"Change the locks," Nikkles said. He seemed all business now. "You can't worry about getting them to tell how they did it. First of all, it's a waste of time, and second of all, it's the wrong psychology. Makes them think they're complex. The thing to do is change the locks. At least that way they know you care about the equipment. It's like these so-called fences they put up around the paths at Island

180

Park. Just a three-by-three slab of redwood stuck in a couple of posts less than a foot above the ground. A kid could step right over it, right? But at least they know somebody cares.

"Okay, we know if they really want to get in they'll prize your padlock off with a crowbar. Places like Marquette or LaSalle with the real old buildings, they'll go through the roof or the floor. Over at West Side one time a kid bent up the flange with a screwdriver and took out three screws and he was in like Flynn. All he wanted was some horseshoes. Maybe your kid's got a master key—it's not impossible. Some of these bozos can jimmy a padlock with a paper clip or a hairpin faster than you can say Jackie Robinson. All we're really doing is letting him know we care. I'll tell you this: if we really cared we'd have lights on these sheds all night long."

I imagined Willie jimmying open Hoover Street's lock at night, and as my imaginary spotlight caught him in the act I saw the vulnerability under his belligerence. He was scared. He was moral; he resisted criticism fiercely because he believed in right and wrong. Three sheets of carbon paper was not a theft—it was a statement, a protest! If he had nailed ninety-five theses to the door, would we ask for a nail-proof door?

I had to stop myself from repeating Harmon's legendary line about not believing the kids would do anything like that.

"Of course," Nikkles said, "the cops don't come around often enough. They're too busy checking the shopping centers. What they don't realize is, this kid starts out swiping softballs or horseshoes—"

"Actually only a couple of sheets of carbon paper."

"—and the next thing you know he's knocking over a gas station or liquor store. They slap him into Boys' Correction, and after a couple of years he comes out a professional. Next stop—Stateville or Terre Haute. That's the way a playground system becomes a breeding ground for crime. Cheap locks, cheap buildings, no cops, no lights, no security. I'll get on it right away, and thanks for the call."

It was not the sight of the new lock that sent Frankie home in tears, however, nor the new flange that folded back sturdily over its own screw. I pointed these out to no one but Willie, and he seemed so unmoved, so innocently and happily concentrated on his plans for making a monstrous Chinese-type lantern, a dragon with smoke coming out of its mouth—as if to ask why I was making a big deal of this when he, as injured party, was willing to call the case closed—that when I had the boys gathered in a circle on the grass I made a speech about trust. In order to work together, I said, we had to trust each other. As a playground we had a good record. We had lost very little equipment. We had won on Olympic Day. We had had a good Doll Buggy Parade. We had had some good times during Crafts, Hobbies and Games Weeks—even Nature Week. But now that trust was broken. Somebody, we didn't know who, had broken into the shed. Because there had been this breach of trust I would not be able to appoint any Junior Leaders this week. I could not trust anyone near the equipment shed. Or my keys. I would have to keep the Junior-Leader badges in my pocket.

It was at this point that Frankie left, and I realized that in aiming at Willie's vanity, hoping he would see the chance for double acclaim—first for the daring of the burglary and second for the altruism of confession—I had hit Frankie's conscience instead.

"He say he quitting," Sonny translated from his place in the grassy circle. I understood Frankie's hoarse, departing sobs well enough, but Sonny wanted to make sure. If we were ever to get on with the craftsmanship, the showmanship, and the playing with fire that was Lantern Week, someone would have to break the moral impasse I had created, and he was glad Frankie was doing it. "He say he ain't never coming back. He say he ain't telling on nobody. He say he don't want to be your Junior Leader."

Willie, his nostrils and lower lip flaring, was saying that you didn't need Junior Leaders to make lanterns, all you needed was the *stuff*. I had the feeling that my next line was to ask in a Nazi accent whether anyone else wanted to try any funny business.

Barbara had been pleased at the changing of the locks, rushing the news to me that morning, and my new key, as soon as I arrived. When she asked me what had happened to Frankie, I told her that as a result of our new get-tough policy I had lost both my Junior-Leader candidates, the good one turning in his resignation and the bad one staying on to subvert—just wait!—all our plans for the week.

It was a cheap attempt to fix the blame, and I probably deserved the answer I got.

"Ah, man!" she said, and she reminded me of the careless, carefree Barbara who had disturbed and intrigued me back in June: "I could have told you never to take my advice!"

182

Our theme for Lantern Week—we had to have a theme, Nikkles reminded us, not just a bunch of lanterns; and the theme, if possible, should be appropriate to the local playground, such as, for example, Industry and Agriculture for West Side, Canoes and Indians for Marquette, Famous Poets for Whitman (located between an airport and a freight warehouse, Whitman chose Transportation)—our theme was The Jungle. Once we had chosen it, the children worked amiably and soberly on their lanterns, cutting out designs in tagboard, pasting in the tissue paper that was to provide the effect of stained glass, nailing together the lath framework on which each lantern would be carried through the gloaming of Hoover Street like a Pope through the streets of Rome—or, more exactly, since there were two children per lantern, like a patient borne upon a stretcher, all but one of his candles out.

It was not, after all, a bad week. There was none of the frenzy and euphoria surrounding Olympic Day, and there was little of the sustained serenity of the Fourth and other days of July, but after Frankie's departure and the disintegration of Nature Week I would have settled for much less. Before issuing the softball equipment to Jake on Tuesday evening I told him about the two-foul rule. That is, in Lee Roy's terms, I "instituted" it, managing to suggest that my boss was miffed that our second lost ball, the one off Lee Roy's bat, had occurred after several fouled-off attempts. In fact, Nikkles was so pleased that we had lost only two balls this far into the season that he hadn't even asked how it happened; but the suggestion took root, because Lee Roy, as if out of guilt or fear, did not appear for evening softball. Perhaps with fall approaching and his leg healed he was training harder; perhaps, as I guessed, he simply felt he had punished me enough.

I was glad to institute the two-foul rule in his absence. I compromised by allowing games to continue until closing, but with no new inning to start after I blew my whistle at seven forty-five, and Jake made sure I got the equipment on time. He was blocky and muscular, his large, full-lipped face solid, as if set in stone; when he smiled his grin spread slowly and stayed long. He was a good friend of skinny Wesley's and, at fifteen, one of our steadiest customers among the older boys. I knew I could count on him. He enjoyed his home-run hitting too much to let anything jeopardize it. Strangely, there were no home runs hit that week, although whenever Jake stepped to the plate the playground silenced in anticipation, as if he were a televised golfer about to sink a putt—even the little children (those who were still there in the evening) looking up from their lanterns to watch. We did lose a softball—my third and last—on a high, backward pop-up that spun into the weeds and stacks of old boards near the valve works and lost itself there; but I didn't replace it. This late in the season I figured we could get along with one.

The theme of The Jungle was a compromise I suggested late on Monday afternoon when we had been stuck for half an hour on "Flowers," which was the girls' final choice, and "Animals," which was the boys'. I had hesitated at first, remembering my queasy moments during the filmed African safari we had been taken on earlier in the season; these were the years when ethnic identification marks were taken off public documents, when the story about the little black boy who dressed in colorful clothes and turned tigers into butter for his pancakes was re-issued as "Little Brave Sambo," and when, on a personal level, I was embarrassed at having to spell my surname. But "The Forest" would hardly do, being too narrowly green and brown in its chromatic range, and "Paradise" offered too much scope to Willie's predilection for the nude human figure. The Jungle was at first tolerated as a compromise, but won more and more enthusiasm as the week went on and it was felt how every flower and animal (including birds, now) had been given a new dimension.

Even Willie, though he held out for his notion of monsters in chinoiserie as long as he could, finally went along with the idea. He insisted, however, on working alone rather than in a pair like the others—which I finally allowed him to do on the grounds that we had an odd number of participants. In reality I had been looking for ways to keep him isolated. He made a kind of cave for himself to work in, under the ping-pong table, and hid the progress of his lantern each night under an elaborate mask made of blank scraps of tagboard. He rolled his eyes at me whenever I went by, warning me that I would have to wait for the big unveiling on Friday night. "You going to like this one. This is right on *the subject*. Mm, *hmm!*" I had no idea as to what his design might be, but I forebore peeking as I stacked the lanterns inside each night. Willie was apt to be hanging around, staying late and watching jealously, and it seemed to me that a tacit understanding had grown up between us, to the effect that if I offered him this last bit of trust he would not disappoint me. At any rate, it was a bridge I could wait to cross until I came to it, on Friday night.

The bridge I was more preoccupied about crossing was my Sunday-night date with Barbara. The delicate negotiations for this event had opened Monday morning when, on my way to breakfast, I found two letters waiting for me at the Y's front desk. One was from my father, and the other, which he had forwarded, was from Elizabeth. I took them both to the cafeteria with me, and after breakfast stopped at a phone booth before going to work and called home.

It had been three weeks since my previous call, but my mother's surprise at hearing from me was, I thought, a bit overplayed. After the preliminaries, including some reminders from me about my schedule, to account for my calling at this time of the morning, I told her I would like to come home on the second Sunday in August.

I could hear her putting down the telephone to get to the calendar on the wall. VANDEN VAARTEN CONSTRUCTION, with one big *V* doing double duty, above the barefoot boy fishing in the pond in front of the red barn. In his letter, under the same single-V logo, my father had written: *Did you hear that Barnema sold his house and three acres to a Darky? Could even be one of the NEGROES (Cora is looking over my shoulder) from up where you work. They say he will move in in September. We hear that Harvey's put up the money, to scare the other two farmers into selling. They call that Blackbusting.*

"Blockbusting," my mother had written in the margin.

My father noted that Elizabeth must not have heard from me, since she didn't have my address, and he pointed out that he was forwarding her letter promptly and unopened. He asked when I thought I would be moving my books and other things out of the basement—"so in case we ever sell the place the new owners won't have to charge you storage." And he said that he and Johnny Van Dyken would be looking at some property in Wisconsin. "We will be gone next weekend and will take the boat. Haven't used it yet this summer."

His mention of the boat, and of what seemed to be a kind of vacation, struck me as out of key with the bad news preceding it. Yet the timing of his planned vacation was such a piece of good fortune, so gracious and unexpected a gift—aside from the fact that the onus seemed to be on the supermarket now, and not on Barnema or the buyer of his house—that I did not care to inquire too closely.

185

"Why so late?" my mother asked, coming back to the phone. "That's two more weeks!"

"Elizabeth says she's coming home then," I said, "and Dad's letter says he'll be away this coming weekend."

"Oh, well, if *Elizabeth* is going to be home. . . . Now I know who to thank for the honor of your presence!"

"I guess so," I said. My tongue felt thick with the effort to deceive. If I took Barbara to the evening service this coming weekend, neither my father nor Elizabeth would be there, and with the favor of Providence my mother might skip church as well. I knew her girlish teasing about Elizabeth implied her relief that I was not intending to bring her gray hairs in sorrow to the grave.

"What did you think of Gerrit's news?" she said.

"Well . . . I thought he seemed in pretty good spirits. Considering everything."

"That's all you know," she said flatly. "You don't see him every day the way I do."

"No," I admitted. "Well, there's a lot to talk about, but maybe I'd better wait until I see you."

"You can come home this week too, you know. I'll be alone with just the boys since Gerrit is going off with Johnny."

"I don't think I can make that," I said. "I'd better hang up now, I don't want to be late for work. I'll see you a week from Sunday."

I had spent the day before in my room reading a book on the religions of Africa and had discovered an interesting saying of Mohammed, to whom Barbara's father had compared my spiritual forbears. "War is cunning," Mohammed had said. The Prophet had had twelve or thirteen wives, and I consoled myself that he, at least, would understand how cunning might apply in affairs of love as well as war.

I would have been less consoled had I known that my father considered himself at war, and was exercising cunning of his own.

I made the date with Barbara on Monday night, on the way home from staff meeting. Why yes, she said judiciously, Sunday night would be good. Once it was arranged we spoke no more about it, though we had time, on those Lantern-Week afternoons while the children worked on their orchids and lianas and monkeys and tawny lions, to sit together on a bench leaned backward against the sunwarmed shed and to talk, as we had talked in those July weeks before Nature Week and its hikes. Mostly, it seemed, we talked about the future and the past. The name of her Eastern school began appearing in her speech. Because she was a recital student and on a scholarship she had to get back to school early—she would have to miss Cleanup Week. Remembering the comments about "pull" that I had heard in the Recreation office back in May, I asked whether Harmon often gave permission to miss part of the season.

"If you've got a good reason, he doesn't mind. Like one year a girl took off two weeks early to get married. Last year Buchler had to leave early—football practice, I think."

"Well, *one* of those is a good reason," I said, and it pleased me to hear her laugh and to know we were both laughing at Red.

One afternoon when I came back from lunch—I was taking my hour lunch-break again, driving to a nearby A & W to read about Mohammed and Nashville over my burger and brew—she was straddling a bench with her wallet spread out in front of her, studying it the way the children at the tables were studying their lantern designs.

"Look here at this old thing! I'd better renew it before going to New York, *n'est-ce pas?*"

She meant her driver's license. I took out my own wallet, and she agreed with me that I would have to notify my draft board of my new Tennessee address. I asked her about some of the photographs she had. There was a dim, worn photo of her mother, round-faced and thin, though obviously pregnant, carrying a grinning, fat-cheeked girl with her hair done up in many ribbons; she was reaching for the camera and trying to squirm out of her mother's arms. "That's me," she said. There were pictures of "old" boyfriends, as she called them, though I thought the pictures looked recent. One was a graduation photo that reminded my of my own. The face was black, but the skinny collar and dark, narrow tie were the same, as was the short haircut and the attempt—deliberate on my part, as I remembered— not to smile but to face the camera and the future with what came out as a kind of quizzical confidence. "He was, you know, *okay* and everything—I mean a nice boy and all that. Kind of shy and quiet and unassuming." I flipped over the plastic sheath. On the other side was a wallet-sized glossy of a basketball player in defensive posture, wearing a mock-ferocious look. "Sports was his big interest," Barbara said, flipping this one over. Next was a thin-faced white boy, pale, with dark, deep-set eyes. Curly dark hair, no tie, hands in corduroy jacket pockets. Somehow he looked arrogant, and it pleased me to note that the neckline of his T-shirt sagged a little above the open collar.

"What was his big interest?" I said.

"Ah! You really want to know?"

"Well, not if you don't want to tell me."

She thought a moment. "For one thing," she said, "he wanted me to marry him."

It was hard to know what I felt then, I was so conscious of what I was trying *not* to feel—insultingly startled, insultingly congratulatory, vulnerably jealous. I think I felt a certain relief, among other things, as if by asking he had somehow reduced a moral pressure on me.

"I guess you turned him down?" I said finally.

"Ah, you genius! You think I'd spend my honeymoon on the playground?"

Her laugh was so loud that twelve-year-old Twyla Taylor, at the table in the shade near the sandbox, looked up suddenly, then smiled benignly—it's only Barbara having her adult kind of fun—and went back to the polychromatic parrot she was creating.

"What was his"—I wanted to know about politics, religion, wealth (somehow, maybe through envy, I saw him as wealthy), regional accent, but asked instead—"his major?"

"He was in Art." She made a brief, incomplete two-handed gesture as if she had meant to put quotation marks around something. His standing as an artist? Or him in general?

"How come you didn't—how come things didn't work out?"

"I could just tell," she said.

"Tell what?"

"I could just tell, that's all. I knew he didn't have the stamina for it."

"Ah," I said. "Yes."

She asked me then to show her some of my own pictures, and I told her I had none, but she refused to believe me.

"Not even one? How about that girl you got the letter from? That one? Ah, look at him blush!"

I had taken Elizabeth's letter along with me on Monday and she had seen me take a look at it. She seemed pleased with her detective work.

"I knew it wouldn't be a boyfriend writing you in a border of yellow flowers. Also, why would your Momma's letter be in your pocket?"

The summer has gone by so quickly! Elizabeth's letter began. There was a description of how she enjoyed her work at the "San," and its lovely dune-and-pines lakeside setting, and of the wonderful family she stayed with—a medical family, for they had a son who was interning in Grand Rapids, in whose old room she happened to be staying, and who came home "now and then" on weekends. *His mother spoils him outrageously, but he's the only child and he* is *very nice, so perhaps it's forgivable.* In her last paragraph she said she was coming home the second week in August—the paragraph I had been checking and re-checking. *You'll be leaving soon after that, won't you? For the South? Perhaps we can get together for a "fond farewell." Are you still looking forward to it as much as you did last May?*

"We've known each other a long time," I said. "Our parents are friends."

"Ah, childhood sweethearts? Mm-hmm, now the plot thickens."

"Well, not—not exactly."

"And not one picture? When I showed you three?"

I found one, finally, in the sweaty leather pouch along with my social security card and my old Hebron library I.D. It was a snapshot Elizabeth had sent me three springs ago, taken of her on the beach during her senior class's outing. It made me nervous to see Barbara looking at it. Elizabeth had worn no makeup, as usual, and without the glow that her skin had in real life she looked pale. Her one-piece suit emphasized the purposeful straightforwardness of her stance— toes gripping the sand, arms unselfconsciously at her sides, her shoulders sturdy. Above it her neck appealingly tilted to one side and her pale face, with its wispy, shy smile, seemed to belong to a different person.

"She's beautiful," Barbara said. I had thought of her as a hummingbird hovering to peer for a moment (through horn-rimmed glasses which she pushed back up on her nose, spoiling the image) at some sort of hardy plant—a sunflower, perhaps—before darting away. I was moved by the compliment.

"Her big interest is being a nurse," I said.

I gave her my graduation picture, that week. I wanted to see where she would put me—whether cheek by jowl with Mr. Nice Guy, Mr. Sport, or Mr. Proposal, or maybe by myself—but she tucked the picture into a shirt pocket instead. She let me take some snapshots of her, most of them alongside Willie or Verella or one of our other customers wielding a single-edged razor blade against tagboard, but I did get one of her alone in front of the equipment shed facing the afternoon sun. "Barbara!" I called, in the time-honored method of achieving a "candid" shot, and she instantly assumed a jazz-dance posture, her eyes wide above the sliding glasses, her seat perkily cocked, and her long thin arms at startling, stylized angles.

"Ol' Barbara," said skinny, fourteen-year-old Wesley, making his hourglass gesture.

"I'll tell your momma you been talking so bad," she laughed at him, and while I rewound my film they went around the corner of the shed to play some ping-pong.

We both knew, I think, although we never mentioned it, that our Sunday evening visit to my boyhood church would be our last date. Like a couple who had finished their dance too early, we would stay together for decorum's sake until the music stopped. But there were moments when I wondered why the love I was sure had existed between us had not taken deeper root, been stronger, more permanent. These moments came usually at the end of the day, when I was driving "home" in my car. How much of our time together had been spent in the car! Remembering her foot caressing mine under her dining room table, her "much too honorable" joke to her father—was it a joke?—I wondered whether in fact I had been too distantly respectful, whether I should have trusted the Spirit, our spirit, to lead us through a more direct and intimate commitment to the green pastures of a higher, nobler kind of love. One with more *stamina*. Perhaps that was all it would have taken, all it would still take, to bring us to something more sacred than a walletful of souvenirs.

There were moments of longing when I remembered our momentary caresses, which occurred always, it seemed, when we were on the verge of going somewhere else. Perhaps that was the secret of the legendary love among the early Christians, to have believed that they were on the verge of a new age when everyone would be going somewhere else. Maybe one could give one's self more unreservedly under those circumstances. I could not imagine Orangetown's evening service as providing such a context. What I feared instead was an ending that would make it impossible for us to think of one another afterward without pain, and so I tried, as the weekend approached, not to think of it at all.

On Friday night our playground bore its luminous tiger, lion, jaguar, panda—for we made no distinctions among jungles, ours was *the* jungle—its verdant snakes and scarlet birds and shimmering double-winged insects through the dusk of the neighborhood streets. Thirty-two lanterns in all. Barbara marched at the head of the parade, keeping the pace slow, and I stayed behind, lighting the candles one by one. As I bent over the lanterns, scorching the hairs on my wrist and coaxing the stubborn wicks into flame, I became aware of a murmuring among the lantern-bearers who were waiting, and looked up to see that Frankie had come back. He was carrying one end of the lantern on which Willie had worked secretly all week, his white shirt gleaming in the diffused candlelight.

"I'm glad to see you, Frankie." He would not meet my eyes, staring steadily downward between his two laths—unlike his partner, who pranced like a horse between the shafts. "Are you ready for this?" Willie kept saying. "Are you ready for this?" So that when I lit the candle inside his tagboard box the five or six sets of lantern-bearers who were left crowded around to see. "Are you ready for this?" He slipped off the tagboard screens he had scotch-taped to the sides, and I could make out that it was a comic-strip caricature of some sort: an orange fire, a large brown pot, and a missionary, I suppose—his white crepe-paper face slashed with a strip of baby blue for eyes, and topped with a bit of yellow for hair.

"Ah, Willie, what make you so *bad*!" Barbara said, coming back from the head of the line, and hearing her laugh the children all laughed with her.

"I told you you have to approve of this. We in the jungle, man!"

We put them at the end of the parade, and they bore the boiling missionary on their two shoulders like natives bearing a sahib out to hunt, the highest lantern in our show, higher even than the vertical giraffe, and from the watchers on their dark porches came shouts of laughter and applause. It made a good ending. As I escorted it and the others up and down Hoover and Sixteenth and the other streets, I was more aware of the pallor of my forearms than I had been since the Friday-night travelogs early in the season. I regretted that Willie's lantern would, most likely, be the snapshot of me that would remain stamped in the mind's eye of all who had seen it. And yet Frankie's reappearance was a good omen. By the time the parade was over I got him to admit that he was glad he had come back.

On Saturday I woke up late—it was hard to shake the habits established by my odd hours—and drove past the playground and then further south on State Line and west on Ridge Street past the First True Reformed Church; then south a block and west again on 192nd past the Grove and Harvey's Supermarket and the three farms next to it, Barnema's with its "Sold" sign on the front lawn where his children used to park after church on Sundays; and then across the railroad track to my parents' new house. The church's parking lot was empty, the supermarket's was full, but tomorrow it would be the other way around. Like a lecturer visiting the empty hall before his speech, I wanted to get a feel for what was coming.

My mother was glad to see me. She had been wondering all morning how she was going to get her shopping done. Gerrit had taken Gordon and Paul off to work with him, both her chauffeur and her bicyclist, and she had been standing in the kitchen for five minutes, she said, putting her apron on and off, wondering whether she should go on with her baking and cleaning and hope they would remember the groceries and get home soon, or whether she should walk all the way up to the old IGA. She hated to push one of those rickety carts across the tracks but there was no telling whether Gerrit would get home before the store closed.

"But I thought you said he was going to be gone for the weekend!"

I remembered seeing the boat still nose-down on its trailer in the driveway, and my sudden panic as I pictured myself tomorrow night introducing my friend the blockbuster to my father the bigot in the narthex of First True Reformed must have registered with my mother as irritation.

"Isn't that just like him? To change his plans without telling me a thing about it? All of a sudden this morning he says they're too busy to go today, they're leaving tomorrow night instead, and then out the door he goes, rushes right out before I can say a word about getting the groceries."

"Did you say he was going tomorrow night? Sunday?"

She looked at me blankly for a moment, her round, deep-blue irises slowly closing in on the dark dots of her pupils as she faced the light from the window, and I could see her eyes focusing backward, inwardly, on the replay of what I had just said.

"All I know is he said before church." Then she turned on me. "Are you setting yourself up in judgment against your father? For missing one single evening service? I've heard of the pot calling the kettle black, but—"

"I'm sorry," I said. "I didn't mean it that way. I was just—curious."

"Oh, yes," she grumbled. "You're curious, all right. You and Gerrit both. Curiouser and curiouser. First he wants to know if you're not coming home for sure until next week, then *you* show up and want to know why *he* isn't going until tomorrow night. Am I supposed to be social secretary around here, for goodness' sake? If you want to be your father's keeper so badly why don't you just ask him yourself?"

"No need for that," I said. "I'll take your word for it."

I took her to Groen's IGA that afternoon, and then afterward to Harvey's Supermarket. She explained that they were buying all their groceries at the IGA now, avoiding the supermarket on principle, but that she liked to go to Harvey's to pick up a few of their specials— if she bought only the loss-leaders, she thought, there was no harm done to the principle. From the full carts of other shoppers—most of them, to be sure, from out of town—it appeared to me that Harvey's was not being badly hurt. I pushed her cart for her and packed her single sack into my car with the others from Groen's and drove her and the groceries home. After the buzz and glamour of the supermarket, Barnema's house on its low cement-block foundation looked old and empty and sad, its tarpaper brick a shabby pretense, its curtainless windows vacant as the sockets of a skull, the welcome mat gone from its front porch.

When we got home I went to the garage and found the old coalshovel from the other house and used it to spread dirt over the front yard, pulling out all the weeds that had grown up in the pile and gone to seed during the summer, and raking it smooth. I got a good start on the backyard as well, and at five o'clock went down to the basement to shower off the sweat and dirt. I could hear my mother upstairs crooning "He shall lead his flock like a shepherd" as she did the ironing. She had seemed almost regretful that I hadn't brought home any of my washing for her to do.

After showering I drove up Ridge Street to Grandma's house to pick up our weekly allowance of home-baked raisin bread, Grandma's regular gift, though after all these years my mother continued to regard it as a reprimand. At least once a month, perhaps in the very act of slicing the loaf, she would grumble, "With three bakeries in town she thinks I should spend my whole day over the stove." Grandpa, recently retired, came out from the den where he had been training himself to watch baseball games on television as the doctor advised him to do, since he had no other hobbies except visiting the sick. (Grandma could not see what good his visits did, since "he never *says* anything.") "Hi, hi, hi!" Grandpa said now, using his Christmas voice and shaking my hand, he was so glad to see me; and Grandma, as she slipped the warm, towel-covered loaf into my arms (quarterback to fullback in the belly-series, I thought), called me "Stranger" and flirtingly complained how "dead" it was around town without me, as if I were one of her long-lost beaux.

I brought home the bread just as the Saturday-night six o'clock siren went off at the volunteer fire department under the water tower, to mark the beginning of the Sabbath and close up all the shops and start the bath water running in a thousand Orangetown homes, and I allowed myself to be talked into staying for supper. I told stories about the Lantern Parade and pleased Paul by trying and failing—he had grown so much—to press him to the ceiling with one arm. Afterward I excused myself, explaining that I was in a hurry, and, yes, there *was* a church near the Y that I had found to my liking, one that was basically Methodist but not, after all, too far from our own in spirit.

My father did not try to persuade me to stay for Sunday, nor did I ask him why he was leaving town then. All through supper he had been unusually quiet. As we said good-bye I wished him good luck on the trip with Johnny Van Dyken the next day.

"Thanks," he said, and he rose from the table to accompany me to the front door. They would be gone for two or three days, "mainly business," as I understood it, but in the doorway he shook my hand as earnestly as if one of us, he or I, were going on a longer journey. In his white socks, stained yellow by the well-oiled boots resting on the back stoop, he was still inches taller than I, yet there was something I felt as pathetic in his sun-reddened nose and chin, his eyes blinking behind his glasses, the day-old stubble of beard showing a good deal of white. I could feel the bumpy knuckle on the third finger that he had sawed off at the tip long ago, when I was a baby. He had walked three blocks to Johnny Van Dyken's house, holding in place with his other hand the bloody fingertip picked up out of the sawdust, and he had held it that way in Johnny's car, with Johnny's handkerchief wrapped around it, as Johnny drove him with the horn blaring through all the red lights of downtown Calumet up to the emergency room at St. Ann's Hospital; and when the doctor put the needle in his hand, he fainted. The wrinkled khaki work clothes and middle-aged belly, the sleeves rolled over upper arms surprisingly white and skinny, the cuffs above the white work-socks—all made him look comically military, a tired and overage doughboy.

I had been ready for sarcasm about my summer work and had met only mildness. It disturbed me that I could not feel free to tell him what I would be doing tomorrow night. After supper he had read not Psalm 121, "I will lift up mine eyes unto the hills," which he usually read when someone was traveling, but Psalm 144. *Man is like to vanity, his days are as a shadow. . . . Rid me from the hand of strange children, whose mouth speaketh vanity, and their right hand is a right hand of falsehood, that our sons may be as plants grown up in their youth, that our daughters may be as cornerstones, that there be no complaining in our streets.*

We shook hands and said good-bye, and as I drove away I thought I had gotten perhaps too full a taste of what it was like to be in Orangetown again.

On Sunday evening Barbara wore a red dress I had not seen before, a red dress with low back and neck and a fine gold chain above the hollow between her collarbones. With our windows open in the twilight I caught glimpses of her in black and red, as the shadows of the houses we passed flickered in and out of the car, and I remembered our trip to her childhood vacation spot in July and thought she looked like a blaze of the Spirit's flame. It was a red that gave off color; when she lifted her shoulder to shrug and smile, as she did when I told her she was looking good, it glowed across the skin of her neck and lower jaw, as dandelions did when the playground children held them under my chin to see if I liked butter.

"Do you really think so?" she said, and she looked more helpless and vulnerable than I had seen her before. "This is an expensive dress, I've never worn it."

I took her hand, telling her she did indeed look very good—and then held it a moment, finding that I needed comfort and reassurance as much as she. I had no hope, as she apparently did, of anything good coming of this venture; my hope was to avoid disaster. In this frame of mind, which grew stronger as we approached my hometown, Barbara appeared less as a tongue of Pentecost's fire, more and more as the "strange woman" against whom I had been warned in many a suppertime reading from the book of Proverbs—that book of the Bible which was valued chiefly, my father would remind us with a glance at me, while my adolescent face struggled to hide the lust within, because it was so *practical*.

I was wearing my navy blue suit in order to feel Puritanical and invisible. We parked in the First Church lot just before seven-thirty, and seeing the last light disappear in the west behind low clouds I felt like the speaker in Langston Hughes's poem who is glad for the friendly cover of darkness, "black (in my case, navy) like me."

My timing was perfect. Leon de Leeuw, known to my mother as "the late Leon de Leeuw" because he was the one we most counted on to arrive even later than the Gerrit Vanden Vaartens, was just slipping into the front door behind his sandy-haired wife and freckled children. Barbara, on high heels, clung to my arm as we negotiated the rough stones of the parking lot. (The question of paving it had been debated in the all-male Consistory since last spring; none of them, as my mother pointed out, wore high heels.) At the side door I paused. De Leeuw, a short, stocky man with a fiery bush of hair, had once charged down these very steps to the basement room where the Consistory held its pre-worship meeting, to challenge them with a legal and moral problem: a visiting Volkswagen had parked in "his" place, a tight spot right in front of the church on Ridge Street near a certain telephone pole, well marked with blue paint from his Chevy, where he had parked for twenty years. Although he was always late, by Orangetown standards, he could strongarm his coupe into this difficult but convenient slot avoided by all the early-comers and still slip in under the wire. (My father's method, by contrast, was to let his short-legged wife and children off at the door, speed to the very end of the lot, and then race back with five-foot farmboy strides. It occurred to me now that this was strange: the early-arriving manager and employees at the supermarket always parked in the farthest corners of their lot, giving up places near the door to the later-arriving customers; at the church it was the opposite—first come, first served.)

196

On the day of de Leeuw's revolt, services were held up for a good five minutes as the congregation heard argument rumbling from below as from the underworld, and then the racing of de Leeuw's motor in the street, where he must have been double-parked, as he departed, he and his household, not to be seen until a week later when the visitor was gone (it must have been a stranger; no Dutchman in those days would have driven a German car) and his place was empty again.

Tonight he had gone straight to worship. I led Barbara upstairs to the empty narthex as the congregation stood up with a mighty creaking of benches for the introit, exactly the moment I wanted. We could slip down the side aisle behind a screen of standing adults busy arranging children and Psalters and the phlegm in their throats for the first song.

"Adrian! Man, am I glad to see you! Listen, we need a third baseman for the tournament—we go up against Grace True Reformed in the first round."

It was Neil Vroom, captain of the ball team and also of the ushers. He carried rolled-up bulletins in his left hand and advanced on me with his right hand outstretched, a high school chum who now ran the Vroom Ford Agency with his father. His hairline had receded, since I had last seen him, and his unbuttoned sportcoat flapped around his new girth like a vest. Something in my face stopped him, or perhaps it was the two fingers I held up quickly, as one might do at a restaurant, before he could seize them in his first-baseman's grip. His eyes, looking past me, halted at Barbara's red dress. For a moment I thought he would try to intercept her and point her northward toward the Baptist districts of Calumet and Gary and East Chicago— no trouble at all, ma'am, I've directed many a lost Catholic and Lutheran before you—or else to our facilities (down the basement and to your left) before getting her on the road again to Joliet or Chicago Heights. Already some faces in the last row had turned to see what the noise was all about, and I remembered a service the summer before when a visiting minister, the Reverend Bart Slinger from the West Side TR Church, had taken offense at Vroom's rumbling bass antiphony; after reading the opening Scripture, "The Lord is in His holy temple, let all the earth keep silence," he had added, "This means the ushers along with the rest"—after which incident Vroom's uncle and aunt, long-time members at West Side, had left the Reverend Slinger's fellowship to join ours, giving as their reason the fact that a minister who felt free to add to the Scriptures would soon be subtracting.

"Two near the back." My urgency, and perhaps also his wish to stay on my good side before the tournament, made him turn in his tracks and lead us down the side aisle, between the full pews and the comfortingly indifferent stone wall, to a spot just under the balcony's shadow. I could see drops of perspiration on his blond forehead as he handed Barbara a bulletin, nodding forcefully, as we do to the speaker of a foreign language, to encourage her to take it. As he passed me going back to his station he whispered something that sounded like "So that's what you do at college!" though I couldn't be sure.

Then we were alone in the space that two people make together in a pew on Sunday evening, and we could lose our self-consciousness in the noise of a hundred grainy-backed Psalters zipping over the edges of the pew-racks. Barbara still wore the taut, eager-to-please, lips-only smile she had had since we entered the church, her slim dark neck affirmatively tilted as if to express all the faith she decently could without doing anything loud or emotional—which I took to be her idea of being good in church, as Orangetown would define it. I smiled at her to let her know that, for the moment, we were safe.

In my imagination I had tried to explain to Barbara the importance of the clock on the wall above my grandparents' favorite pew, where they now sat with Aunt Gertrude (Grandpa Arie's head soberly upright, Grandma's moving subtly from side to side, Aunt Gert's pietistically bowed); and the three big chairs behind the pulpit, only one of which was ever occupied; and the wonderful stained-glass circle or eye, like a grapefruit with blue and red segments, that you saw above the balcony when you stood where the minister stands; and the oak communion table that on non-Communion Sundays served as a place to rest the gold collection plates, first empty and later mounded with green tribute, so that "This Do in Remembrance of Me," which was carved into the front of the table, referred six times a year to God's sacrifice for us and fifty-two Sundays to our sacrifices to God—and also the fact that there were two collections (so that Barbara wouldn't be embarrassed at being caught short), the first for tithes and the second for offerings and benevolences, including the church's schools. Also the territorial habits of the True Reformed male when sitting in the seat next to the aisle: the rule was that early arrivals claimed the aisle seats and latecomers scuttled sideways past them; since my family was habitually among the latter group I knew intimately the bony masculine and plump feminine knees of some of Orangetown's first families by their pressure against my hams and calves. I had hoped to be spared having to explain certain ceremonies—Communion, for example—for which Barbara would have to apply in advance to the Consistory and be examined by them, and during which we would read from a form which specified more than thirty kinds of sinners who were prohibited from the Lord's table, followed by the statement that we who partook did not do so to proclaim that we were without sin.

But now, in the pew under the warm lamps glowing off Barbara's red dress and gold earrings and necklace, I felt the church not as a set of architectural or liturgical or doctrinal forms but as a mighty organ of interpenetrating histories, glances, judgments, legends, auras, opinions, gripes, of mingled breaths and handshakes and gossip, a stew of prejudices and prayers that the Reverend Boom brought to boil twice a week with his refiner's fire—in other words it was the people, I was now aware, that most needed explaining.

My own family I had remembered: Grandfather Arie would head to the front exit for a Consistory meeting after the service, leaving me only the females of the species, Grandmother and Aunt Gert, to contend with. I had spotted my mother and her two remaining sons up near the front, as usual; balancing this was the fact that nowhere had I seen—and had I been Catholic I would have crossed myself— Elizabeth's mother. But there were others.

At the other end of our pew sat "the three V's," as they were known: Thea Voorhands, Adrina Vedder, and Audrey Veen, all of them tall, large-boned women in their late forties or early fifties, the two on the outside widows and Adrina, who sat in the middle, unmarried. One night about a year ago they had gone to the Consistory at its midweek meeting, claiming that although as women they knew they had no right to vote for or serve on the Consistory (only male heads of families could do that), still they had the right to *visit* the meeting. There was a struggle involving the interpretation of certain pages in the True Reformed Church Polity—pages which Thea Voorhands, widow of the late principal of the grade school, had looked up—after which the three women simply sat down in three empty seats in the Consistory room, daring the men, as it were, to remove them if they wished. What gumption! my mother always said when the incident was retold.

My father thought it must have been the other two who put Adrina up to it. Everyone liked Adrina. It was said she never married because she had never found a man she could look up to—at first in jest, since Adrina stood six feet tall in flat heels, but later as a tribute. She was a kind of Protestant nun who worked by day in a nursing home in Calumet and at night showed up unannounced, like an angel, wherever there had been a funeral or a new baby or a long illness, and began at once scrubbing floors and washing clothes or, if there was nothing else to be done, baking bread, as I remembered her having done in the old house when Paul was born.

It must have been Adrina's presence that kept some of the hot-headed consistorymen from sending the chairs of these visitors flying over the well-waxed floor into outer darkness with one kick from a size-twelve brogan. Thea was as sharp-tongued as her late husband, Nick Voorhands, who was known as a spanking principal and had reduced some of these very men to tears, either as fathers or as pupils, when he had them in his office; and Audrey Veen, who sat now in the middle-aisle seat wearing an expensive suit not bought locally, was felt to give herself airs after selling Dirk Veen's farm for real estate. As it was they sat there for fifteen minutes while the Consistory (including my grandfather, whose only comment later was that it had been a "bad business") refused to begin any discussion and sat in silence, except for sighs and the cracking of knuckles, until Boom finally convinced the visitors they had made their point, and they left.

Next to them, and nearest to Barbara, sat Bessie Loon—small, dark-eyed, thin, with a large purse and thick-lensed glasses. Her husband, Rink, was a confirmed "oncer" whose standing offer of a hundred dollars to any preacher or elder who could prove to him out of the Bible that Christ or David or any other hero ever attended an evening service had for many years found no takers. As we sat down after the first song Bessie removed a spiral-bound notebook from her purse; she wrote critiques and, sometimes, appreciations of every sermon, night and morning, critiques which masked her liberalism under a more-militant-than-thou conservatism, and which she posted to poor Boom on Monday mornings. ("Dear Pastor Boom: Were you aware that a woman of the Negro race, she too is a child of God, I am sure you agree, was listening to your sermon on Lord's Day Thirty-

Three last night, the nature of true repentance? What an opportunity for expounding Reformed truth!") It struck me now that these four women were the liberal wing of our church, and that this was why my good friend Neil had found the other side of their pew open and ready for us.

Why did so many in my congregation wear glasses? Three of the four next to us wore them, the horn-rimmed kind with metal rims—only Adrina Vedder's eyes were as naked as God made them—and lenses and spectacles flashed light everywhere in the church, most notably from the pulpit, where Boom with sweeping motions pulled his off to look at the congregation and thrust them back into his fringe of white hair to look at the Word. Was it the well-known love of the Dutchman for ground glass, an inheritance from the days of van Leeuwenhoek? A sign of the True Reformed longing for truth? An emblem of the helplessness of the natural man? Or a mark of middle-class status—poor enough to have to keep our noses to the grindstone, we were yet able to afford the optometrist who enabled us to do so?— two optometrists, in fact: Simon Winkel of the Oak Grove TRC, and Gysbert Hooker of ours.

Farm families like the Rits Klompens, who could be heard kicking the balcony parapet above us in their favorite seats, did not wear glasses; nor did Bastiaan De Boer and his rawboned sons, who came late and sat in the front by choice so they could stretch their legs when they fell asleep, as they regularly did on cold winter days, their ruddy faces glowing in the overheated air and their blond heads jerking downward and downward like the hands of a schoolroom clock until they jerked awake and verticalized. But De Boer's wife, daughter of Groen the grocer, wore glasses; so did Cornelius Sinke, the dentist, as did Karel Van Druggen the physician and Harry Boon the surgeon, who lived in a fifty-thousand-dollar house on the west side (one that my father had helped build) and drove all the way to Chicago to work.

Politically, these three headed the church's hygienic wing, having led the fight during the early days of Boom's tenure against the common cup in Communion. Thanks to them we now celebrated the Lord's Supper with individualized germ-free thimblefuls passed through the congregation in silver trays—all but Harold Steenkop, another farmer, who still claimed his right to be called to the front with his family and sip sequentially with them from the big silver chalice as they had done in the old days. Steenkop at fifty-five had a thick, black, bushy head of hair noticeably absent from the bald surgeon, the fringe-topped dentist, and the white-headed physician, and while the doctor's kids were famous for their sniffles and their peaked appearance (my grandmother encouraged Mrs. Van Druggen to give them a spring tonic), Steenkop's four had the bodies of gymnasts and were never absent from school except during April and May, to help with cutting asparagus.

Ahead of us sat Casey Baal and his son Calvin, whom Casey had kept out of high school on the basis of fairness to the older boys, who had never had a chance to go; and next to Calvin sat his beautiful wife Melissa, who even then wore long brown hair to below her shoulders. Melissa, daughter of Klaas Bangsma the body-shop man, had been worshipped by every boy in school, and no doubt by many of the teachers. She was high-school valedictorian two years before I graduated, and a week after giving her speech, in a splendid act of divine mercy and justice married Calvin Baal. A row beyond sat Enno Meekma, the high school chemistry teacher, who every year sent an envelope to the school fund-raising committee pledging $500 PAID IN FULL, explaining that if he were to teach at Thorndale Consolidated instead of devoting his talents to the Kingdom, $500 more is what he would be making.

Beyond Meekma I could see Marinus Sluis cupping his good ear forward; he had served in the merchant marine in his youth, some forty years ago, and now was ready to retire from the Ford plant over in Harvey. He had come to Orangetown during the war from one of the Great Lakes cities, and as a boy I was always intrigued by the left side of his head, where there was just a hole and a miniature lobe instead of an ear. He steadfastly refused any contribution to foreign missions, and I attributed this to his rage at whatever heathen Turk or Chinee or Hindoo had sent his ear to Davy Jones's locker, much as Captain Ahab would have refused to support ecologists trying to save the sperm whale. Later I learned that his missing ear had been taken by a falling metal hawser somewhere east of Duluth, and that his stand on missions was that what was good enough for the Apostle Paul, who paid his way by making tents, was good enough for our contemporaries.

Up front at the organ sat Wanda Oopsma, visible to us from the side as a large round body under a round face and a pair of round-rimmed glasses swaying in tempo adagio (her other tempo being largo) over the keys, carefully, carefully, so as not to miss a note. Mrs. Oopsma was the old organist. The new organist was Sheila Starr Spaan, whose black eyes and bright earrings flashed as she fluttered red-polished fingers across the keys. When Menno Spaan, of the clothing store, first brought her down from Michigan some five years ago, her playing caused a sensation, and only recently had the Consistory settled the dust by arranging the alternate-Sunday regime we now followed: one Sunday adagio, the next allegro. Though the snappy Sheila Spaan was nearer my own age, I was glad we had Wanda Oopsma tonight; one could sing in harmony when she played, if one had breath enough, whereas Mrs. Spaan's creative arrangements often masked harmony and melody as well, even melodies which some of us, like my grandfather, had sung for fifty years. It was a bad business, my grandfather said, the first step toward taking the Psalms out of the mouths of the congregation and giving them to a choir; and that night, as I sang with Barbara, I agreed.

There were others whose presences I felt, though I could not see them. There was Anna Kroon, who had been my father's sixth-grade teacher and before that my grandfather's, whose strong contralto we could hear on the Lord's Prayer, the Creed, and the Law, finishing up a syllable behind everyone else with perfect enunciation, still teaching us though she had been retired for fifteen years. Sometimes when my mother corrected my father's grammer (shorter than *me*, taller than *him* was a cross he gave her to bear every day of their married life), he would complain that she was "tougher than Anna Kroon." An empty space under the window four rows ahead marked the unseen presence of Siebert Kool the undertaker, who always had to sit by the window, winter or summer. From somewhere behind us I could hear the sighs of Mrs. Swart the baker's wife as she shifted from one overweight thigh to the other, and the sniffles of the Slifstras, eight pale-faced children who ran a fresh-egg route with their balding, pale-faced father, Wim, and their mother—"Poor Jennie," as my grandmother always called her. Whenever I had a cold Grandma would hand me a tissue and say, "Oh, oh, oh, you make me feel like poor Jenny Slifstra." Poor Jennie's family had allergies and always seemed to sit downwind from the widow Rozenboom or Winnie Witvoet, white-haired ladies whose perfumes, powders, and colognes were the most powerfully allergenic substances known to cosmetic science. Somewhere near us the lucky tribe of Grandma Misselijk were breathing out fumes of peppermint and anise, and Ollie Romp's family were chewing their gum, two sticks per person per sermon, and crushing the crinkly wrappers; and if I closed my eyes I could picture the families whose surnames, along with the Romps', I always enjoyed hearing read aloud at school because I thought them even funnier than my own: the Rumps, Putts, Potts, Punts, Hootens, Kootens, and Eeks.

With my eyes closed I remembered names associated with tragedy: Nellie and Gysbert Rippema, whose three children were at the state school for the deaf, and Pastor Boom himself, whose sermons were said to have taken on their melancholy tinge when his wife died of cancer and both parents were killed in a car crash in a single year. And Arlo Doorn, who was elected to the office of elder at only twenty-six after his wife died of a hemorrhage during the birth of their first child. All the Consistory, in fact, were men singled out by unusual prosperity or pain in their lives, these being the two ways the Lord marked the men of his own heart, as he had marked King David by both. The male head of a family who had been dignified in either way could expect election sooner or later. The one exception was Myron Scheerenga, the left-handed barber whose touch as he parted and combed my hair always thrilled me, for it was the touch of a man who in 1935, when fresh out of his father's onion fields, had been offered a contract to pitch for the Philadelphia Athletics—which he turned down because it required him to pitch on Sundays; so that ever after, instead of brushing Gehrig and DiMaggio away from the plate he brushed the hairy necks of his customers and whisked away their aprons with his strong left arm while the Sox and Cubs played on the radio above the Brylcreem—a pain-filled figure to me but perhaps not to himself or others, for he had never been elected to the Consistory as either elder or deacon.

I wanted to tell Barbara about all of them, I found, and, strangely, since they were people I had spent four years trying to forget, I wanted her to like them.

The text for Pastor Boom's sermon on true repentance was Matthew's story of the woman who anointed Christ's head with precious ointment, and the disciples' criticism of her wastefulness, and Christ's defense of her act as a good work. Boom at sixty-five was tall and thick-shouldered, his voice still at the volume that made our expensive public-address system superfluous except for visiting pastors of a newer, more effete generation. No sermon of his, even in his late or melancholy phase, was complete without its thunder, and tonight he pictured us as heirs of the ungenerous disciples who measured out our love in dribbled installments; I could easily imagine cynical voices after the service saying that Boom was angling for a precious gift of his own at his retirement a few years off. But mostly the sermon held up Matthew's unnamed woman as a moral model, she who had taken her life's savings and without haggling over price had spent it in one sweet outpouring. It was she, Boom said, and not the disciples, who had experienced God's love and thus could be Godlike herself—and during this section the congregation was utterly still (you could hear a pin drop, Grandma would say), a sure sign that it was moved. I was surprised at Boom's flirting with the Higher Criticism (certain scholars, he said, without condemning them, associated this woman in Matthew with the "sinner" in Luke who anointed Christ's feet instead of his head), and at his quoting, with approval, the American modernist Emerson: "See how the masses of men and women worry themselves into nameless graves, while here and there a great soul forgets herself into eternity." Surely he would be called on the carpet for this.

But how we sang, that Sunday evening, Barbara and I! Barbara was a soloist, a soon-to-be professional heading for her Eastern school in two weeks, but she could blend with lesser singers as angels in the Bible could condescend to human speech. That night our voices blended as they had before on the playground and in my car, but more fervently, I thought, her UCLA-trained twentieth-century Afro-American and Methodist Holiness soprano condescending richly to Psalms 33 and 68 from the *Koraalboek* of the sixteenth century, and to 103, "Good is the Lord and Full of Kind Compassion," a tune known to Barbara as "Danny Boy," and to Haydn's Austrian Hymn, the basis of "Deutschland Über Alles," which I had learned during the war as Psalm 98, singing in my boy's soprano "He alone will judge the nations" with my mother on alto and my father on bass to either side.

Barbara was good, but I was on my home ground now—I had used the Psalter five times a week in school and twice on Sundays, in a religion where song was the emotional outlet (along with collection-taking) and music (including hymns for the youth groups, as a special treat, and school choirs and oratorio societies) the only art.

My earliest memories of churchgoing, or of anything, were a forest of adult legs and a many-colored river of sound. So we harmonized, soprano and bass, backed by an eager choir of hundreds and Wanda Oopsma's long-drawn organ chords.

From that Sunday I date my theology of Paradise. Perhaps the image of the heavenly choir is not to be taken literally; nevertheless, it disturbs me to see churchgoers staring dumbly at a hymnal. What do they expect to see in heaven? What I expect is a four-part score lined out into eternity, to be sung forever in my great Choirmaster's eye. If music is the most ideal of the arts, made out of vibrations in thin air, so that writing one's name in water were a gross act by comparison, surely the music of a choir is also the most physical, even sexual. I don't mean the sublimated Christmastime eroticism around parlor pianos where married matrons and fathers of families let their voices twine and mingle and caress, singing hopefully, "All we like sheep have gone astray"—although even here, who knows? may be something of Paradise. I mean that the four-part choir depends on elementary facts of the flesh: on tongue, teeth, belly, larynx, and lung, on differences deliberately exploited between female and male. Boys in Shakespeare's day played Juliet, women play Hamlet in ours, but no soprano will sing that the people who walked in darkness have seen a great light, no bass tell the daughters of Jerusalem to rejoice. Yet what art speaks so eloquently of the equality of the sexes? Bach and Handel need us all, the high and low and middle ranges alike. Isn't heaven the place where we are needed for exactly what we are? Golden streets leave me cold, and I wouldn't care much for a heavenly fish-fry, still less for a gradual weaning away from things of earth or slowly-consummated marriage with rocks and trees. Give me soprano and alto, tenor and bass, plus all the other parts that an infinite Composer can devise, forever and ever, hallelujah.

My boyhood dreams of interracial harmony in which I made double plays with Jackie Robinson and took perfect pegs from Hank Aaron in left field were fulfilled that night when Barbara and I held the same Psalter and sang a new song to Jehovah, and while it lasted the fact was better than dreams.

But even with Wanda Oopsma at the organ the singing could not last long. After the benediction, the postlude, the communal sigh of a hundred Psalters slipping back into the rack, came the everyday scuffles and shuffles of getting out of church. "You have a lovely

voice," Mrs. Loon said across the space between us; she stared hard
at Barbara through thick lenses, and I imagined her spirit going out
to Boom in the morning mail: "She was black, but her voice was
comely—was that not all the more reason to communicate the basics
of Reformed truth without all the frills from Emerson et cetera?" I
nodded to her, accepting the compliment for Barbara, and then to
old Casey Baal as I moved swiftly to the aisle to block his passage.
My aim was to get to the safety of the car before being spotted by
the two women whose hair I could be made to rue having brought
in sorrow to the grave. They would hear of it later, of course, but
would have had time to ponder the information in the silence of their
own hearts before confronting me—or, worse, Barbara—with their
first, naked reaction. Barbara showed signs of wanting to linger, however; warmed by Bessie Loon's compliment, she had begun a happy
chatter about how the organ was so nice and the hymns (as she called
them) so interesting to sing until Bessie said they were interesting to
sing because they were God's Word. After that she moved into the
aisle ahead of me and we filed out as the postlude played, Barbara's
red dress catching the light like an apple, a circus balloon, dropped
suddenly among the somber tones of the church.

We had been noticed by Pastor Boom. Deserting his station at
the central doors for a moment, he moved to intercept us at the side,
wiping his forehead with one handkerchiefed hand and with the other
swinging his glasses off and then on again as we approached. "And
who is *this* lovely young lady?" The lenses of departing worshipers,
halted now in their exit, flashed light from before and behind us. If
there was a note of suspicion in Boom's voice—the rhythm of the
question was exactly as if he had said, "And what are *you* doing
here?"—it was no doubt meant for me, whom he would have remembered as a catechism student who enjoyed posing questions but not
necessarily in order to get an answer.

I introduced Barbara as the daughter of the Reverend John C.
Robinson of Calumet, passing her off, thus, as a visiting church dig-
nitary, and sidled into the narthex, leaving Pastor Boom to dispatch
this information to my mother and grandmother—now converging
on him from either side of the church—as best he could.

The narthex was a slender transitional space at the head of three
stairways leading divergently into the summer night. Married men
and women went down the broad front steps to the streetside patio

where they could light cigarettes (the men, that is), and where there was room for the smaller children to dodge in and out among the legs of their parents. Down the eastside steps went high school girls and older unmarried women, to cluster as closely as cottons and crinolines would allow, as if in imitation of the parsonage's beds of peonies, tulips, mums, or at this season, roses, which they overlooked; and down the westside steps to the parking lot exit, where they could stand and compare notes on cars and drivers and maybe fling a stone or two, went young unmarried males. What a distance between east and west! When I first asked to take Elizabeth home after church, during the summer of my driver's license, I had crossed it not by the narthex passage but by the subterranean one through the basement.

Thus a difficulty for the courting couple (as my grandmother defined our fourth tribal estate) who did not simply meet at church but had arrived there together: which stair to descend? To exit at the front argued seriousness of marital purpose, and would do so now in front of my parents' friends—through the oak doors massively swinging I saw Jake the milkman and Lamberts the electrician lighting up together—whereas either of the side doors exposed us to a gauntlet of the unmarried. On the east I glimpsed part of Elizabeth's constellation (Wilma, Dorothy, Katherine)—not to be thought of; on the west were last summer's softball buddies (Pete, Fritz, Clary, Klaas), some of whom, no doubt tipped off by my friend Neil Vroom, had already hailed me in order to get my reaction, which was a stern nod and wave of the hand. These might shortly include Gordon and Paul, unless they had gone directly from one of the chancel exits to the car.

In this trilemma, or rather quadrilemma—for behind us I heard my grandmother exclaiming to one of her Scrabble partners: "Oh, oh, oh, how tasty it was, and everything so spotless *clean*!"—I turned momentarily back to the nave and met my mother, cool and quiet and meditative in her dark blue suit and white pillbox hat, probably turning in her mind Matthew's unnamed woman and the deed which had become her memorial, and my choice was made.

"Hello," I said, in order to get her attention. And in order to alert Barbara, who was nodding and smiling pleasantly in the direction of Boom's coattails, having no one else to talk to: "Hello, Mother," my voice as hollow and heavy as if we were at a funeral.

She looked up and brought me into focus out of the mists of first-century Jerusalem and the house of Simon the leper. "Oh. Hello."

And then, her eyes narrowing at the disruption I had brought into her chronology, "But this is only. . . . I thought you were coming home *next* weekend."

Only then, I think, did the red dress and colorful face and earrings next to me come into focus as well, as part of the picture I was asking her to view. "Hello?" I heard her say softly, involuntarily.

"Mother, this is Barbara. Barbara, this is my—"

"Ahh!" Barbara said, her released voice rushing out gladly, and so loud that for a moment other voices, even Boom's, seemed to be stilled. "So you're Adrian's mother!"

She had leaned forward, unused to greeting adults who were shorter than she, her right hand moving forward too (in a white glove, I noticed suddenly), and there was a moment of physical awkwardness, so unusual for Barbara that I moved as if to catch her, when my mother instinctively drew back. It was an instinctive movement based on shyness and her slowness at taking things in; friends who knew her well confessed to having thought her "stuck-up" at first meeting. But in the context of that evening her infinitesimal shrinking movement, and Barbara's quick half-step of recovery, and my own aborted gesture of aid, which I translated as authentically as I could to a finger-combing of my brush cut, left us all looking at the space separating us as if it contained an indecent object.

Into this space came my grandmother, unashamed, unafraid, "as bold as brass and looking just like she owned the place"—which was the description she would later apply to Barbara and repeat many times in my hearing. She loomed large in her dotted swiss, carrying a black purse across one forearm like a football and giving that athletic impression also because of the bent-forward attitude in which she walked—a posture she may have learned from someone with arthritis in the hip or a difficulty in hearing, but which she kept, I was convinced, for the same reason a fullback did: because it enlarged her personal space. Behind her Aunt Gertrude tagged like a trailer behind a car, her broad, freckled face bobbing now to the right, now to the left of her mother but never entering our circle because Grandma, with instinctive pivoting motions, kept her out the way a good center in basketball keeps his man blocked off the boards.

"Hello there, Stranger!" This was addressed to me, to make clear her primary claims to my attention; then, turning to Barbara, but with a nod rather than a look in her direction: "And who is this you have with you?"

There was something arch and girlish in her tone and, as always, she played the *naif* very well. As when she saw her first football game on Grandfather's new television: "Oh, oh, oh, look how they put their heads together. They're *scheming*. And only one ball? No wonder they're upset!" Or to the milkman: "Yes, they tell you it's fresh, but do you believe them? How do you *know* it's fresh? You shouldn't let people walk all over you!"—as if *he* were the one she was worried about. I heard the challenge behind the girlishness and knew who it was she suspected of walking over whom.

"This is Barbara, Grandma. She works with me on the playground. Her father is a minister. The Reverend John C. Robinson."

"I'm so happy—" Barbara began, this time softly; but my grandmother, caring not for Barbara on her right or Cora on her left, nor for Aunt Gert bobbing from side to side behind, was carrying on this conversation with me.

"A preacher! You say he's a preacher?"

"Yes, he is." I looked at Barbara, who was nodding and smiling helpfully, but Grandma didn't follow my look.

"But does he preach the Gospel? That's the question!"

"Yes, of course," I said. "And the Acts of the Apostles too."

"Of *course*? How do you know *of course*? You can't tell a book by its cover, can you? You can't tell a suit is all wool just because the sign says all wool—isn't that right, Cora?" She turned toward my mother so that now she blocked both Barbara and Aunt Gertrude from the action. My mother—wide-eyed, her cheeks pale, taking us all in slowly—seemed to be readying her forces for something, but not for this particular question, to which she nodded absent-mindedly.

"There, you see? Cora knows! You have to snip off a thread, that's what you have to do, and burn it with a match and see how it smells. That's how you know it's all wool. You can't just let people walk over you!"

"He happens to have met Bronkema personally," I said. "You know, the theologian?"

"Oh yes, Bronkema this and Bronkema that." She spoke with such surprising readiness—I had counted on this as a red herring—and with such bitterness that it occurred to me that my mother must have thrown Bronkema up to her in some discussion, perhaps predating my birth, and never been forgiven for it. "Anybody can read Bronkema, but Bronkema isn't the same as the Bible. Is he? Is he? You bring your father along once"—she suddenly turned to Barbara, surprising even herself, I think, by the ease with which she could speak to her person to person, at the same time blocking off my mother—"you just bring your father here and let him hear the true Word once."

"Ahh!" Barbara said, as at a delightful joke. "Ah, hah-hah! I'm sure he would enjoy that!"

"A preacher!" Grandma said, her eyes slipping to Barbara's dress. "Is he with the Salvation Army?"

"No, ma'am. He's Methodist."

"Methodist!"

"Yes, ma'am. Methodist Holiness."

"*Och heden*, what a name—are you sure? What won't they think of next! Arie—that's my husband—always wants to give to the Salvation Army, but I tell him to give to our own people. Then you know where it's going. But he says no, give to the Salvation Army— he has such a good heart, that man! He lets people walk all over him!"

"Oh, yes!" Barbara said, and I saw no trace of irony in her face. "Some people will do that every time!"

"What about your mother? What does she think of you traipsing all the way down here?"

"Grandma," I said, "Barbara lost her mother."

"Lost her mother!"

For a moment I thought she would repeat Lady Bracknell in Oscar Wilde's play and accuse Barbara of carelessness. *If she kept things where they belonged, a place for everything and everything in its place, how could she lose something as large and important as a mother?* At this point Aunt Gertrude, finding an opening between her own mother and this orphan in our midst, suddenly asked, " Do you speak in tongues?"— her broad face and hasty surreptitiousness giving her the air of a Soviet citizen asking a visitor about cultural freedom in the West.

"Do I—no, well, Adrian, he's the one that studied all the languages. I am a student of music and the dance."

I was sure that she had let this particular cat out of the bag inadvertently. It was a new motif and one that threatened a change of key and dynamics just when I had hoped to end on the sympathetic minor chord of the loss of a mother. The lines from the True Reformed baptismal formula that I had wanted to spare Barbara from hearing came back to me now: *when we leave this life, which is nothing but a constant death. . . .*

In the silence created by that last sound, *dance*, my mother spoke words for which I will always thank her and which she herself will never forget, though she has suppressed those earlier words about gray hairs in sorrow to the grave. "Would you two like to come over"—here her voice faltered and she looked away from me to the floor, and then to Barbara—"would you like to come over for some tea and—something?" It was the last word that I remember best, suggesting as it did all those *somethings*, down to the third and fourth generations, that we might have been coming over for, and that she must have been revolving in her mind before she spoke. It was a lovely question, as lovely in its way as the anointing we had just heard preached about, though memorable also to my mother as marking one of her infrequent triumphs over her mother-in-law. "So then I just asked her to come over for tea," she would retell the story later, "just like that—and you should have seen the look on Gerrit's mother's face! Talk about shock—she looked as if she had just swallowed a good dose of castor oil!"

"Ah, thanks very much," I said, "but we'd better not stay. We have Circus Week coming up and everything, the last full week. . . . But thanks anyway."

"It's been very nice meeting all of you," Barbara said, nodding quickly three times, and then we were off down the nearest stairs, those to the parking lot, where the way opened miraculously before us, Neil Vroom and my other contemporaries having gone around to the front to smoke, perhaps, or driven away to find girls of their own, and we were out in the friendly darkness.

Behind us I heard my grandmother saying, ". . . just as bold as brass, she looked like she thought she owned the place," and Aunt Gertrude, "Remember, Ma, you can dance before Baal or you can dance before the Lord," and from Grandma again, "What can you expect from a child without a mother?"

I heard nothing from my mother, who must have been, I thought, still standing in the narthex pondering what it was that she, and I, had done.

212

"And now where are we going?" Barbara asked.

Though I remembered feeling weary after my visit to her father, she seemed still excited, triumphant, her fingers warm and nervous in my hand as we half walked, half ran across the parking lot to my car, like children getting out of school. Somehow I had made no plans for after the service, perhaps thinking that afterward we would simply go back, if we could, to our "normal" life on the playground, or perhaps, in my anxiety about the service, thinking that time itself would end there. Now I too felt I didn't want the evening to end just yet.

"Would you like to see the town?" I said. "Now that you're here?"

"The town?" she said. "Well—okay."

There was a reluctance in her voice that I took to mean she was hoping for graduation, not another exam. Was she wishing we had accepted my mother's invitation? I had answered instinctively, and now I wondered what my answer betrayed—whether, in fact, my mother had reversed the scenario I had imagined earlier, showing up my liberal principles by taking them seriously.

"Just to give you an idea of where I grew up," I said.

We drove through the downtown area, where everything was dark, and into the residential neighborhood of West Ridge. "See that water tower over there?"

"What water tower? Everything's dark."

"Over there. Behind the fruit stand."

"You mean the shed with potted plants out front?"

"Right. That's Zuidema's Produce. See the dark shape above it? With the red airplane light? That's the water tower. The big building underneath it is the firehouse. The little one next to it is the library."

"Mm-*hmm*," she said.

I drove past the library, and since there didn't seem much to say about it headed west again, to Chicago Street and beyond.

"There's Dommer's Diner."

She sat up straight and looked out. "A diner? That might be nice"—though I thought she might wonder how much I knew about diners in the way that a non-white person would. I didn't know what the reaction of a typical Dommer's crowd would be were we to walk in, but I could guess we would not pass unnoticed. "Is it out of business?" she said, looking from one side to the other of the dark street.

"Just closed," I said. "For Sunday. As your father said, we're strict Sabbatarians." The "we" felt awkward, but less so than the alternative, which was "these people."

"The whole town?"

"Pretty near all of it."

After a moment she said, "And what about your father?"

"My father? Yes, I'm sorry you didn't get to—"

It was so bald a lie that I could not complete it. Still less could I say what I thought—that my grandmother was biased on the personal, family, religious, and national levels, but with my father it was a matter of business first, then all the others. I could imagine writing her about it, perhaps, from Nashville in the fall—no, years after that. *I'm glad you found my father so friendly and charming. That's the way he usually is, unless real estate is involved. It may surprise you to know that there was a time when I actually felt afraid to introduce you. . . .*

"I know," Barbara said. "You told me he had to be gone. But wouldn't that be"—she paused so delicately that I felt she, too, wanted to preserve something intact from our visit tonight—"wouldn't that be against his principles, then, to be gone on a Sunday? If he's as strict as you say?"

I laughed, then, suddenly remembering our many arguments on the subject and my father saying solemnly *No system is perfect* and *You've got to draw the line somewhere.* "I'd say his principles are pretty flexible," I said. To her, nervous as she probably was about the theological debriefing she would get from her father, my laugh must have seemed strange and harsh; perhaps she thought I was keeping something from her.

It was in fact about that time, as I later pieced things together, that my father and Johnny Van Dyken were finishing a last hand or two of Rook, and a last can or two of beer, and preparing to leave the Van Dykens' old barn, south of town, where they had been staying—hiding, if you will—since nightfall. It was the same old barn where the youth of their generation had gathered (once Johnny's parents had left the farm) on Halloween nights to lean against the stacks of onion-set crates and smoke their cigarettes and plan whose outhouses would be toppled this year, and which ones burned; and where the youth of my generation brought hampers full of frozen tomatoes or rotten eggs to decide which unpopular teachers' houses would be "peppered." When the town was dark enough to suit their purpose, and free enough of traffic, they would roll silently up to Barnema's house in Johnny's car, still pulling my father's trailer and gas can, and do what they would think of as necessary work—because the line had to be drawn somewhere against the godless chain store and its dupes.

Thank God no one was in the house—a statement I would hear later, and use myself, after the event. My father and Johnny Van Dyken thanked God before the event that no one was in the house—particularly no one who could be used in "blockbusting" by the absentee ownership of the supermarket, people who had no interest in the town whatever except to gobble up all the land they possibly could, and in the process turn my father's imaginary Semaphore Estates into a shopping-center parking lot, and his real, expensive new house into a white elephant. They intended to keep no one in the house if they could. If in the process they had to stoop to what was illegal—well, no system is perfect.

Perhaps it occurred to them that at other times it had been illegal to help a runaway slave to freedom, or to throw British tea into the harbor and put the blame on the Indians, or for Jesus' disciples to pull ears of grain out of a field on the Sabbath, or for David to seize Jerusalem and call it "his" city, or, for that matter, for the Israelites to have left Egypt and entered Canaan in the first place. These are the kinds of thoughts that occur to other decent men who want, for one reason or another, to break a law—many of them men who, as my father would remind me later, "got off scot-free." Perhaps it occurred to them that if everything were done according to *legality*, very little in history would get done. I do know that my father later told me he had *prayed about it*. My first reaction—of course—was that this added blasphemy to his other sins. Later I would remember the strange things that all men pray for, the South for slavery, the North for Sherman, and—finally—I remembered my own cowardly prayer of that very night, that my father would be absent from church.

But at that moment in the car with Barbara I only knew that we both wanted to keep the evening as it had been so far, stressful yet not disastrous, and with moments of disturbing joy; and for that reason, the less said about my father the better.

West of Chicago Street I pointed out to Barbara the Westside True Reformed Church, where the janitor was closing up, and, across from it, my old high school. Beyond the church was the grade school, and beyond that the cemetery where my grandfather's father lay under a headstone in Dutch and English. Going east again, I pointed out the old sugar-beet loader near the tracks—for no reason I could think of except that I used to find a spilled beet there now and then, and slice it with a jackknife and chew the juice out of the slice. Then I drove down 182nd, past the house where I used to live.

"Where's the new house?" she said. "The one you said your father just built?"

I nodded toward the darkness to the south. "I guess I don't really consider that my house," I said. "I never really lived there."

On Ridge again we drove by my grandmother's house, where Grandfather, having settled the parking lot and other Consistory business for the time being, would be putting the car in the garage and heading inside for post-service coffee and the ten o'clock news. Tonight my grandmother's news would overshadow the networks', I thought. I could imagine Grandpa shaking his head and saying, probably, nothing at all. Apart from the onion-set business he had gained his reputation for wisdom by knowing how to keep his counsel. Don't tell everything you know, was one of his proverbs. Still less everything you think. His silence would impress this on my grandmother. Time will tell, he might say, if she persisted. And at last, to let her know she should drop the subject, Man proposes, God disposes. That was always the last word. Rebuked, she would suffer in silence and take her troubles to the Lord, who would not shut her up. Why me, Lord? Why him, my first grandchild? What will his poor father think? I would go to the top of her prayer list, and perhaps Cora too, so that we would both repent; I could not imagine her praying for Barbara.

"It's a big place," Barbara said as we went by. Of all the places I had pointed out, she looked at my grandmother's house, I thought, with the most interest.

I turned south on Calumet Road and went past Bok's Grove and, beyond it, the dark supermarket, then across the tracks into the country. A new forest preserve had been opened there, an oak-and-bramble woods skirting a marshy area that extended east across the state line, and I thought we could sit there for a while and talk. There seemed a lot to talk about still. There was one other car in the parking lot when I turned in, its windows open and lights out.

"Well?" I said. "What did you think of it?"

During the service and afterward she had seemed to me to glow and glitter with suppressed excitement. Now, after our trip through town, she seemed subdued.

"Think of what?" she said.

"Well, you know. The evening. The service. All the people."

"Oh, yes, all the people!" she said with an irony I decided not to explore. After a moment she became explicit. "I thought your mother was nice," she said.

"Really? You did?"

She nodded, her arms folded. "I was disappointed we didn't go with her. She asked us, didn't she? It might have been nice."

I wondered again why I had said no. Was I afraid of her spilling the beans about the colored buyer of Barnema's house and my father's habit of saying "nigger" and admiring Jamaicans for knowing their place, and then asking Barbara politely if she would mind very much not marrying her son because it would bring her hairs in sorrow to the grave? Or was I afraid she would merely give us tea and conversation? *You say your father actually met Bronkema? Oh, wait till I tell Gerrit! And you're a singer and your mother was too, how wonderful! Oh, how I've longed through the years to have a daughter, nothing but men in the house, especially a daughter who could sing! Come here, Barbara—may I call you Barbara?—to the piano, it hasn't been used in years. . . .*

Barbara, after all, had thought about the matter, she had been proposed to; but for me it was all new, a future I had no way of forseeing, one that I might not have the stamina for and wasn't ready for.

"Maybe it wouldn't have been so nice," I said finally. "I'm still sweating from seeing your father."

She was silent, looking out at the shaggy shadows of the oaks. "You don't want it to go any further, do you."

"Neither of us wants it to go any further," I said.

"Oh?"

"Well, do you? After tonight?" She was silent. "In a few weeks I'm leaving, after next week you're leaving, nothing is settled for us. How can we go any further? We could maybe write to each other. . . ."

"But not meet your mother," she said.

"But you did meet her! Okay, look, we can go back now if you really want to." I reached for the key.

After a long moment—my heart thumping strongly—she put her hand on my arm and sighed.

217

"Maybe you're right. I guess I don't really want to go. Maybe I just wanted you to ask me."

I put my arm around her and held her head against my shoulder. It was the first time we had sat together in that comforting, domestic kind of closeness. Before, we had only touched in order to play, or to kiss, saying good-bye.

"There wouldn't have been much to talk about," she said. "Not like you and my father talking about theology."

"Theology?" I said, glad of the red herring. It occurred to me that music might do more for the two females than theology had for the males. "Theology? I thought the purpose of the whole thing was for him to give me as many zingers as he could about our—whatever he said it was."

"Re-la-tion-ship," she said, imitating his pulpit tone.

"Anyway, she never likes unexpected company. She asked us, but I'm sure she didn't have the house ready. Not the way she would want it. My grandma always has the house ready, but—"

"But she never would have asked us."

"So you noticed."

I felt her head nod, almost a shudder, beneath my chin. "I'm perceptive that way," she said—with just the right touch of humor, but my laugh was brief as I thought of how many more chances she had had to be perceptive than I.

I wanted to say that it was probably just the shock of meeting us for the first time, that Grandma had grown up with certain idioms, that she was basically good-hearted and probably over the course of years would come around; but then I didn't know whether any of it was true, and it all seemed beside the point.

"What did you think of them on the whole?"

"Of them? The people at church?"

"Who else?"

"Well, it was a very nice service, I thought."

"Nice?"

"Well, you know. Sort of dignified and—you know. Stolid."

"Stolid? You mean as in the familiar stereotype, stolid and phlegmatic?"

She pulled away and looked at me to see whether I was joking. I didn't know whether I was or not.

"Ahh!"—a nervous, questioning laugh. "I said dignified, didn't I?

218

You have to admit some of the hymns were kind of slow-moving—"

"Psalms, my dear girl. Not hymns. Hymns are man-made."

"Yeah, well. That's what—that's what the lady next to me was saying."

"Bessie Loon," I said.

"Well—maybe I didn't catch your introduction."

"Look, I'm sorry, I was nervous—"

"Anyway," she said, interrupting, "weren't they a little? Slow-moving?"

I shrugged, feeling like one of the stiffhead generation myself as I refused to look at her. "There may be more real feeling under the surface than you think. Even though there isn't the obvious display of emotion you find in other places."

She sighed, and leaning forward put a finger on my lips, one hand around my neck.

"Let's not waste our last night quarreling about religion," she said.

I turned to her and kissed her, and we held each other and kissed again. Her eyes were dark and shiny in diffused light from the clouds, her dress a neutral shade of darkness. I pulled her onto my lap and thought only of how close she was. Her words—*our last night*— seemed to give depth to the present. To the accompaniment of sounds I had heard in automobiles since reaching my teens, in parking lots and on back roads in Iowa, Illinois, Indiana, and Michigan, in Sunday-night cars that had traveled to and from church twice or even, in the country, three times (morning worship, afternoon worship, True Reformed Youth in the evening), sounds like the zip of Sunday tie through stiff collar and the rustle of Sunday taffeta and nylon over pressed worsted wool—to the accompaniment of sounds like these we let ourselves love each other with our hands and lips, while outside the open windows crickets sang in the grass.

More cars arrived, headlights bouncing across our mirror. A door slammed. Other cars departed, courteously easing along dim-lit in the dark before hitting the road to roar away under full illumination. Like many others in True Reformed automobiles, like scores and hundreds, perhaps, on that same evening, as Sunday night fell westward from Passaic to Chula Vista, from Miami to Saskatoon, I let myself approach the moment of truth when if you really really loved someone, everything would be all right. If nothing were done but what was legal, what history would ever be written?

No one was so slovenly, Barbara's father had said, as the lapsed Puritan. He had mentioned alcoholism as the secret sin among us. Fornication and adultery were not secret; they were the only sins I had ever heard confessed aloud by individuals in the church (following another liturgy I had hoped to spare Barbara on her visit, the Form for Confession of Public Sin): fornication by a high school girl who stood round-bellied and alone in a front pew, wearing a wide straw hat with pink ribbons, in the springtime of my twelfth year, and adultery a year later by a couple who confessed on the same morning but on opposite sides of the sanctuary, one rising from the pew where she sat with her parents, the other from beside his wife and two daughters.

These public confessions, the last of the forties, were succeeded in the fifties by another form of confession: infants who arrived too early and weddings that came too late. They did so frequently enough that old-timers among us spoke of reinstituting the Frisian custom by which a wedding did not take place until courtship had proved itself in pregnancy.

If I ended the evening with less to confess than my father it was not owing to me. Barbara, however, had been brought up in a different tradition. Was it only that there were fewer automobiles in her congregation? She had been given practice in discerning the spirits, in freeing but at the same time disciplining the emotions, in letting one's self go, yes, but avoiding, as she once put it, going to excess.

"Let's not do this," I heard her say. And, as I let my head sink to the hollow of her neck and insistently murmured her name: "No, no, we don't want to do this!"

She pushed away from me, her rustling dress making sparks along the seat covers. "If we're going to be writing letters let's not be writing about the past, let's end it clean."

With jerky motions she rummaged through her purse for the plastic cylinder where she kept her contact lenses and then, grimacing, her head held painfully first to one side and then the other, fished them out of her eyes and dropped them in, and I felt a mingling of shame and lust, as if watching a private undressing. She turned to me suddenly and struck at me with her slender, sharp fingers, and then plunged her face against my shoulder.

"Oh, how I hate you!" she said.

I held her that way, her warm, damp tears soaking through my shirt, my chin on the springy curls of her hair, faint strains of country music from someone else's car coming through the window. Something not a back street affair. Something something will go on year by year.

"I guess we'd better go back," I said at last.

We drove out slowly, our lights dimmed although there were only a few cars left, and headed north. There was a glow in the sky that flickered across the horizon from Gary to Chicago like a red-tinged northern light—the usual city glare. But with Barbara's last words like a premonition in my ears I may already have picked out the strange orange glow, separate from the rest, that banked off the low clouds to our left. It was the glow of a sunrise or a steel mill, but from the wrong direction, the direction of Barnema's house.

"I didn't mean that." She was wiping her eyes with a handkerchief. "I only hate—I only hate to be crying with my contacts in."

"I'm glad you didn't mean it," I said. We drove slowly north with my arm around her shoulder, her thin arms around my waist.

When we crossed the tracks separating Orangetown from the country I could see, off to our left, smoke rolling up against the sky. When we stopped again at 192nd and I looked past the dark Grove and the supermarket, I must have known—at some level—that my father was involved, although I could not tell for sure whether it was his house or Barnema's, or one of the other farmhouses, that was ablaze. But my mind, as if to resist the truth—or, perhaps, to deal with a dreamworld morality while ignoring the question of what it was I thought I had just been doing—began flooding itself with the kind of absurd, half-mocking stories I had heard as a teenager about the punishment of Sabbath-breakers. The young man whose new car, parked outside a Calumet tavern on a Sunday night, was picked up by a tornado and dropped upside down behind a church. The housewife whose stove, when she was baking a Sunday cake for unexpected company, burst into flames and took the kitchen with it.

When I turned left, Barbara moved from me and sat up straight. Her eyes blinked and widened.

"What is it?"

"A fire."

It was Barnema's house, I saw: for a moment I felt only relief.

221

It was not the house my father had built. I stopped the car. We were
the first ones there except for the Orangetown fire truck, which had
pulled off the road into the yard, its searchlight jabbing erratically up
and down into the smoke. Black and white plumes rolled from the
windows and walls and joined above the roof, and orange flames
flickered in the rear. One of the volunteers, whose hat must somehow
have fallen off, led a group trying to reach the house with a hose. The
old tarpaper brick would go fast, I thought. And might not my father
consider that to be in his best interest? But luckily he was out of
town with a reputable friend. Suddenly, like a marshmallow toasted
too long, the house threw out flames from the roof and lower windows, and the firemen with the hose, two with hats and one without,
fell back. I stepped out of the car and felt the heat of the blaze on
my skin.

"Is it anybody you know?"

"Not really," I said—but by then I had seen something that confirmed, sickeningly, the racing of my heart. Across the ditch, just
beyond the shadow of the homemade sign that once said PICK YOUR
OWN BERRIES and now said SOLD, I found something overturned
in the long grass and picked it up. It was a five-gallon gas can with a
flex-necked nozzle, like the one I had seen in the garage that summer,
which my father had bought for the boat, but empty.

"Stand back!" one of the volunteers shouted, and suddenly, with
a sound like a cracking of tree branches in a high wind, the roof of
Barnema's house sagged, orange and black sparks coiling upward.
Through the scrubby trees lining the railroad tracks I saw that the
yard light at my parents' house was lit, and the bedroom windows
where, perhaps, my mother and brothers would be watching. I took
the gas can to the rear of my car and, feeling out of breath, put it
into the trunk and locked the lid, and went back to sit next to Barbara.

"It looks dangerous," she said. "Take me home, please. If it's no
one you know."

I turned around carefully in the narrow road and we drove away,
pulling into the supermarket parking lot to let a hook-and-ladder
truck go by, its siren blaring.

The street into Calumet was quiet, the street lights flicking quietly
in and out, in and out, across Barbara's red dress. In the silence as I
drove I thought wildly and angrily of Barbara's father, as if to release
against him my energy born of panic. *Are you satisfied now? Didn't I*

222

warn you this might happen? These questions helped still, for a moment, the many others to which I had no answer: why I had put the
gas can into my car; why I had taken Barbara to Orangetown in the
first place; why, in this life, which was nothing but a constant death,
so much of what we wanted, and so much of what we did, caused
pain.

"You like to look at fires?" Barbara said.

"Not really. It's just something that doesn't happen every day."

"You pick up a hubcap or something?"

"Just some junk," I said. "People are always littering along that
road."

Her house was dark but the porch light was on. I knew she felt
I was acting strange, holding something back. She was being stiff and
formal and correct, and my throat ached to say some word. She got
out of the car without waiting for me to open the door, and I walked
beside her up the steps. When we reached the front door I took her
hand.

"Barbara, I wish—"

That was all I could think to say. She squeezed my hand, then,
almost like a handshake, and gave me a smile, no teeth showing.
Perhaps, like me, she wanted to weep or to embrace, but was afraid
to go through all that again.

"Only one week left on the playground, hmm?" she said at last.
Her head was cocked in the politely affirmative tilt I had seen at
church. I tried hard to remember some saving grace from the evening.

"Thanks for going with me tonight," I said. "Thanks for singing
with me. I really enjoyed that—I'll remember it."

"Thank you for taking me," she said. After a moment she let
herself in and said, from behind the screen door, "Good night."

"Good night, Barbara." I added, feeling not enough had been said,
"Say good-bye to your father for me." As I spoke I imagined his voice
answering the question I had put to him earlier: *But of course that is
not what I meant. That is not what I meant at all.*

"And you," she said. "Please say good-bye to your mother. From
me."

As I drove back to the YMCA I thought I could smell gasoline
fumes from the can that rattled in the trunk as I crossed Calumet's
brick streets and railroad tracks, and I whispered soundlessly and
repeatedly, Lord please forgive us, Lord please forgive me, help—a

223

prayer that eased my mind as I repeated it, though I could not have explained who it was that I included in "us," or precisely what sin I needed forgiven, or what form help might take.

The streets were empty, but sometime during the hours after midnight, perhaps not long after I had parked my car and gone to my room, my father drove the same streets going south, still pulling the boat on its trailer. He was going home to Orangetown from St. Ann's Hospital, where he had brought Elizabeth's father to the emergency room, his body covered with burns.

CHAPTER ELEVEN

CIRCUS WEEK

THAT was our good-bye, Barbara's and mine—the Sunday when Boom preached on Catechism Lord's Day Thirty-Three and I found my father's gas can in front of Barnema's house. During the next week when we saw each other it was with a kind of tentativeness, as if we were meeting again for the first time, or when we were too busy to say good-bye. There was a lot to do, that week. And after that week—though it seems strange to say it, since I've thought of her so often—we never saw each other again.

Afterward, it was five years before I stayed long enough, on a vacation trip back home, to drive up to Calumet and see what once had been the Reverend Robinson's church. I was married, then; Elizabeth was in the car with me, and our new daughter, Barbara, sat between us in her infant-seat. As I stopped at the corner of Sixteenth and Pine, my heart beating a little faster, just as it had when I drove by five years earlier, I could see that the church had gained a fresh coat of paint and a Spanish-speaking congregation, the words "Iglesia" and "Cristiana" and then some other modifiers following each other in large letters across the door. Within five years after that, the playground had become an off-ramp and Hoover Street a throughway, although the church, with its paint job badly faded, remained in the old spot. It was sometime after that, when our Barbara had entered upon her love of horses, and her sister Linda her love of the dance, that Elizabeth caught a glimpse of Barbara Robinson one day—though she said she couldn't be entirely sure of the name—on a television show. It was the kind of game show in which celebrities answer quiz-questions along with non-celebrities. Remembering her joyous way of amplifying the joy of children on the playground, I knew she must have been a success at this game, and I followed the TV listings for some weeks after that, hoping to see her; but she did not reappear.

Once, though, I saw her picture. I was paging through an *Ebony* magazine article on the Reconstruction period and suddenly came upon her face, in half-page black and white, as part of an advertisement for a hair-care product. Her broad, bright smile was exactly as it had been in the first pictures I had seen of her—one in the Calumet newspaper and the other, taken while she was singing the national anthem at the Playground Circus, in Harmon's office. But her face seemed to me somewhat drawn or strained, perhaps because her hair, which I remembered in short, springy curls, now fell in a nearly straight line to the shoulders. From the brief text I gathered she was an actress and a singer and that her name was still Robinson—though of course she might have married and retained the name. She might even, perhaps, have married another Robinson. It's a common name.

Among my regrets concerning that summer I do not include that fact that she did not marry me. We were too much involved in changes in our own lives, I think, for that to have worked; we were too much enamored, for a while, with the places from which the other had come, too little concerned about the direction in which she, or he, was going. When nowadays people speak of the "Spirit" and how it "moves," it strikes me that a moving force is fully known only afterward, when the movement has calmed. Surely the Spirit—many spirits—moved among us that summer. Barbara and I were like horses in a pasture who raise their heads suddenly, at the scent of a storm passing in the distance, and run together to the end of the field, then separate and begin browsing again. The Spirit moves and we feel the wind of its passing, but only afterward, from the height of a weather balloon or satellite or something higher still, can anything like a path be traced.

But I do, often, regret the way of our parting. I've wished that it could have been different, that we could have resumed our "separate existence," as Barbara's father called it, after singing the last Psalm that Sunday night, or after hearing my mother's invitation, or even, perhaps, after accepting it. There should have been the kind of ceremonious parting mentioned in the book of Acts: *And they all wept, and fell upon Paul's neck and kissed him, sorrowing that they should see his face no more.*

Sometimes, having imagined Barbara and my mother singing, or

226

her father and my mother discussing Bronkema, or my Aunt Gert hearing her father's views of the gift of tongues, I go further and imagine that in some other realm of possibility they have done so, or are doing so now. I've wished that my father and grandmother and Barbara's father—but here my wishes grow thin and sparse, not so much, I think, from failure of imagination as from my own reluctance to forgive, my fear that I not be forgiven. I suppose forgiveness, like these wishes and dreams, is the positive side of regret.

The biblical letters remind us of another way of gaining something from a loss. A letter, communicating across distance, denies the separation that it recognizes. So, too, a confession: looking back in regret, we may win a change of heart. Looking back on the summer of my graduation, I see it as a somber painting full of hands, my own among them, groping toward one another and missing, or striking painfully in the dark. I look back in regret; out of regret come wishes, dreams, forgiveness, these letters, this confession.

During the rest of that Sunday night and Monday morning, my thoughts were all of my father. Lying awake, unable to sleep, I invented what stories I could to fit or explain or excuse the facts. Barnema might have left some old paint-rags lying in a corner. Perhaps "faulty wiring" was the culprit. My father could have emptied the gas can into the motor, and as he drove away it could have fallen from the boat and bounced across the ditch into the grass, unbeknownst to him. Someone else could have dropped a gas can there. Didn't all gas cans look alike? Someone else could have lit the fire, for that matter—some outside element with no interest in the matter except a generalized bigotry and hooliganism. Or someone else in Orangetown, unknown to my father or Elizabeth's father.

On the other hand, there was the oddity of my father's leaving on a Sunday night, before church. There was his portentous goodbye of the night before. The fact that he and Johnny Van Dyken were interested in the sale of Barnema's property.

Each time I made the circle it seemed clearer that my father had inadvertently confessed to me what he had done. But what should I do with the confession? As I pictured him and Johnny pulling into some North-Woods cabin for a few hours of shut-eye before the morning's fishing and land exploration, I had a moment of grim, vengeful pleasure in thinking of doing my public duty by going to the

227

police. It would have to be the County Sheriff; Orangetown's two or three part-time cops, the terror of teenage drivers and illegal parkers, would not know what to do with evidence of arson, especially when it involved their mayor. But the County would be happy to deal with the Republican stronghold on its southern border.

On the other hand, he was my father. Should I not give him every chance to make his own confession—as I had tried to give Willie, for example—before taking the harsh moral line?

But now I was in Willie's position. The evidence was in my car; I was an accomplice.

Toward morning I fell asleep, and when I woke the sun was high and the day already warm. I was sweating on top of the covers, my hands gripping the cool metal frame, and I remembered I had forgotten about the fire itself. There should have been little danger to my family. They were awake; there was no wind to speak of except a light westerly; a good fifty yards and a double track and a rock roadbed separated them from the fire, and the firemen were already there. And yet—if the punishment for Sabbath-breaking was a burned kitchen, what would it be for arson?

As soon as I was dressed I called home. It was comforting to hear that the line was still in operation, but although I let the telephone ring ten times, I got no answer.

Barbara and I had agreed, the week before, that I would plan a boys' act for the Circus, she a girls', and then in the afternoon we would plan an act together. When I arrived at ten o'clock she was sitting with her girls near the sandbox, and without speaking to her— without interrupting, I put it to myself, but I was afraid to speak—I carried my benches and table over to the swings on the other side of the playground. I sat almost alone for an hour; now and then one of my boys came up to stare with me for awhile at my clipboard. On the top I had written: "Boys. Circus. Singing?" That was the act we had spoken of long ago—at the beach, on the Fourth—for boys and girls together. Singing the two-part song about the man who died after courting his girlfriend on the mountain without a hat. I needed something else for boys alone, then; but I could not think past that one word. As she left for lunch at eleven Barbara waved to me and smiled, I thought; I waved back but did not go to her.

During the next half-hour I added the words "Willie. Frankie.

Sonny." Those three, plus some others whose names I was too dis-pirited to write down, were playing piggy-work-up on the diamond. Getting their brains in shape, Willie said, for all the hard work of planning that was coming up. He said it several times, looking at me for a reaction; but I let them play, glad that someone was exercising some kind of leadership in my absence.

At noon I left for my car and almost bumped into Barbara as she came around the corner of the equipment shed. "Oh—hello!" she said, and her smile became taut and small as I hurried past her.

"I'm in a hurry, I've got to make a phone call, I'll see you later—"

I drove to the Y as quickly as I could, and in the lobby placed another call home. With the telephone ringing, the senseless clatter of ping-pong balls as background, I tried to imagine what Barbara would make of my behavior and could picture only her sick, wan face.

"Thank God you called," my mother said, "I didn't know how on earth I was going to get hold of you!" She sounded so much at her wits' end that I thought Gordon or Paul must have picked up some other evidence—a pack of my father's Chesterfields, perhaps—lying near Barnema's charred foundations. Or that the vengeful God of my imagination had sent an east wind roaring across the tracks after all, burning everything but the telephone at which she sat.

She had been lying awake last night, she said, "after seeing you at church." She paused, thinking perhaps that I had called in reference to this, but I did not interrupt. Then there was a fire next door, she said, a "three-alarm fire at Barnema's"—thank God no one was in the house. Then, just as she was finally getting to sleep, sometime around three in the morning, Gerrit came in with the news that Johnny Van Dyken was in the hospital. Badly burned, she said. Ginny Van Dyken could hardly talk—Gerrit had seen her in the hospital—but was going to try to call Elizabeth and tell her to come home right away. She was afraid that if her father died Elizabeth would not have a chance to hear his last words. . . .

The news struck me a double blow. There seemed no doubt about what had been done—by Elizabeth's father, my father, and now me—and Elizabeth's father was paying the price. I had been thinking of my family, of Barbara, of everyone but Elizabeth, and it was her father who was dying. I did not believe literally that I had anything to do with his death, and yet, perhaps knowing in general the power of rage to act beyond our will, I felt accused. I could hear nothing but the pulse-beat in my ear and, from some flickering corner of the brain, the memory of a Handbook rule: *The play-leader is not a physician. In an emergency first contact the parents. . . .* It seemed baking hot in the lobby and I put down the receiver, thinking I might pass out. When I picked it up again my mother was saying that she and Gerrit had not slept at all but had sent the boys to work and spent the morning at the hospital, where Johnny was still listed in critical condition.

There was a pause, then, and although I had no heart for it I asked the question I thought she was waiting for. "How did it happen?" I said. With the answer came a new weight on my chest, the suspicion that she answered too promptly, that she had guessed something and was trying not to let me know.

It appeared that they did not get away to Wisconsin on Sunday evening as they had planned. Trouble developed with the outboard motor again—the carburetor, she said—and they had gone to the Van Dykens' old barn to fix it. During this time Johnny must have spilled a lot of gasoline on his clothes and later lit it by accident while lighting a cigarette.

Through the screen of her imagery, which involved singed hair and the smell of roasting human flesh—like "burning meat in the oven," Gerrit had told her—I gathered that my father had gotten the fire out with his jacket and had driven Johnny to the hospital, despite suffering some severe burns himself. As she talked, it somehow became clearer and clearer to me that my decision about what to do with the gas can had already been made; having done A, I would now go on to do B, and C, and D. . . .

I could hear her sob, her throat catching on her words. "Why we ever had to have a boat in the first place I'll never understand, and if I warned him once about smoking I warned him a thousand times."

About the "other fire" she said only that the house had burned quickly, right to the ground, and that it was a mercy no one was inside. Thank God no one was hurt, she said again. And then: "Oh, Adrian, think of Ginny and Elizabeth!"

I wanted to be with her for the comfort we could have given each other. At the same time I was glad I didn't have to look into her face, or let her see mine.

When I got back to the playground Barbara had moved her table into the shade of the equipment shed, and she was laughing and gesturing with her girls around her as they planned a show for stilt-walkers. She looked up as I approached and they all hushed, looking up with her. She was wearing her patriotic outfit from the week of the Fourth—red shirt, blue dungarees, white socks; and remembering that week it pained me again to see her so uncharacteristically defenseless and wary, a stunned bird who can't fly—like the warbler, back in June, that had flown against a window in the valve works and crouched at our feet for some minutes, its throat working silently like a bullfrog's, before suddenly whirring away.

They were all so silent as I approached that I found myself saying an awkward "hello," apologizing, in effect, for my presence there.

"Yes?" Barbara said softly. She sat up straight on the bench as if expecting bad news, her dark, bare arms braced on the table, two fingers tapping. The girls at the table with her—Verella and Twyla, Sugar, Elvirah, Bettye Lou, girls who had known me all summer—seemed to stare deliberately away from me, as if I were here to complete the familiar trio of male sins (seduction, impregnation, desertion) and they had already judged and found me guilty. They need not have known anything. My face ached, and I must have looked as guilty as I felt.

Standing awkwardly—no one had moved to make room for me—I asked Barbara whether she remembered the girl whose picture I had showed her. Her eyes dropped for a second, and then she sat up straighter still, her smile flashing, her hands parodying Gallic gestures.

"Oh, but of course! You showed me one picture, I showed you three—how could I forget?"

I found myself shifting from foot to foot, hugging my bare elbows protectively across my chest, then rubbing my face, like a man hiding something that wants to escape. "Well," I said, "her family are friends of my family, they're friends of my parents—"

"Oh, yes, yes, childhood sweethearts, didn't I tell you?"

Some of the older girls, Verella and Bettye Lou, looked at me curiously. I didn't know how to respond.

"The thing is," I said finally, "her father is in the hospital." With this brief toehold in their sympathy I scrambled on. "It was an emergency thing, it all happened very fast, and now he's—" I was going to give the name of the hospital, but then, my stomach tightening,

decided I should not. "He's in critical condition. I think I should—
I'd like to try to visit him in the hospital this afternoon. If it's all right
with you."

My desperation, though it had as much to do with a gas can in
the trunk as a sick friend in the hospital, was genuine enough.
Barbara stood up suddenly, as one does at hearing of a neighbor's bad
luck; she put her hands forward as if offering something—help, or a
comforting touch—then spread them in resignation.

"You go ahead," she said softly, using what I thought of as her
motherly voice. I had heard it twice before: when she told Lee Roy
he was too young for her, and then in the car on the way to see her
father, when he told me all about my people, and the Mohammedans
and their holy wars, and how we were alike. "You just go on ahead.
We can do this circus thing without you."

"Thanks," I said. "I'll try to make it to staff meeting tonight. I'm
afraid I didn't get much planning done this morning."

I hated leaving her with the feeling that my sudden reticence must
have imparted, that in her visit she had somehow failed a test; I
wanted to tell her, but could not, that she had done splendidly, better
than I with her father, that it was we—my family and I, my people—
who had failed. It was a relief to hear the conversation beginning
again as I left; they were planning the stilt-walkers' acts. I remembered
the two-part folk song again but decided not to mention it. She could
have taught them both parts, but I didn't want her to do it without
me.

St. Ann's was an old hospital near the center of the city. My two
brothers and I had been born there, and among the three of us we
had gone back for two broken arms and two sets of tonsils. As the
oldest I had been to the hospital often, and over the years I had
become familiar with it and learned, finally, to like it. At first, I had
been put off by what seemed a flagrant display of Catholicism: robes,
candles, bells, statues, incense—all the things I rather vaguely thought
(drawing on my impressions of Reformation Day sermons) had disappeared somewhere about the time of the publication of Calvin's
Institutes and King James's Bible. Then too, it was humiliating to find
that we Orangetowners had no hospital of our own; for all the su-

periority of our faith, we had to drive to Calumet, when ill or injured, and use one provided by the Catholics.

Now, as I drove across town to St. Ann's from the playground, I remembered Barbara's father reminding me that we had no liquor store, either; and, in my mood of nervous introspection, I wondered whether the two things went together—whether, while regarding suffering as the chastening of God, we preferred to have the sufferer out of the way while he was being chastened, out of the way with drunkards and prostitutes, like children sent to their room for punishment. St. Ann's did make much of suffering—even, one might say, flaunted it; beyond the sick and dying themselves, seen under sheets being wheeled here and there as in any hospital, there were ghastly crucifixes everywhere one looked, and pictures of Christ sweating blood and wearing thorns. There was a statue of Jesus with an enlarged purple heart worn across his breast—as a boy during the war I thought of it as a medal won for bravery while suffering—and another of St. George with his foot and swordpoint on the head of a dragon, a surprisingly small dragon when one considered all the pain within these walls.

The Catholics also, when compared to us, seemed to flaunt their sins. There were many priests to be seen in St. Ann's, black-garbed like our ministers, like Boom, but with white collars, and I learned in an early visit that one of their duties was to *hear confession*. I believe that was my first acquaintance with the term. At home we prayed for the forgiveness of our many sins, but generally left it up to God to find out how many there were. When I was eight, visiting the hospital after the birth of my brother Paul, I got to hear a confession myself, made by the Polish woman who shared the room with my mother. I was intensely interested, even though, owing to the sheet which the priest quickly pulled between the two beds, I could hear only the number of the sins—I something four times, I something something seven times—and not the sins themselves. From one of the ladies in Sunday school I had recently learned about counting my blessings and naming them one by one, an exercise that was relatively pleasant. But imagine counting your sins!

As I looked for a place in the hospital parking lot, I was aware that my motives were mixed and confused; it did not seem possible to disentangle one sin from another, or even from a good deed.

233

Since my last visit, years before, the hospital had added an emergency wing and several new floors, and now it seemed a labyrinth of halls that curved into dead ends and elevators that rose five flights on one side of the building and eight flights on the other. I was waiting for one that went up to the intensive care unit on the sixth floor, and when it arrived, with a ring of its soft, old-fashioned bell, Pastor Boom stepped out. Though the hospital was warm in midafternoon he wore the dark business suit he used for midweek calls, and seeing him there I felt my heart beat suddenly in my throat. I had no idea what he knew or could guess about why I was here—whether he remembered that Elizabeth and I had been considered a courting couple, or whether he thought last night's visit with Barbara had canceled that out. But, as we squeezed together to let a dark-robed nun and white-collared priest filter by, a nun and priest who might have been hearing a last confession, administering a last sacrament, I had the sudden fear or hope—I hardly knew which—that Pastor Boom might have been hearing a last confession himself. And that I might make a confession, of sorts, by giving the gas can to him. Wouldn't it be better on his conscience than on mine?

"Pastor Boom?" I said, and it took him a moment to recognize me. His eyes, deep-set without his glasses, seemed to stare at me.

"Have you seen Mr. Van Dyken, sir?" I said, and then added, "Elizabeth's father?"

"I have tried to see him," he said. He seemed to me to emphasize the verb, as though there were those who would accuse him of not trying. "No one can see him except the immediate family. Mrs. Van Dyken has been with him, but he is unconscious. He cannot speak. They tell me he is very bad."

His voice, always resonant, seemed to me to echo rather publicly the words "cannot speak" and "very bad." After a moment I asked, "Did you happen to see my father there?"

"He was in the waiting room," Pastor Boom said, nodding as if confirming this fact to himself. "I didn't speak with him. He seemed to be taking a nap. He must have had an exhausting night. You've heard about it?"

"Yes," I said. "I talked to my mother this morning."

He nodded, and then after a moment nodded again and said "Good day." I had the feeling as he passed me on his way outside that he wanted to take his glasses from his pocket and give me a closer look—and then a second feeling, that he hadn't done so because for him, as for me, there were things he didn't want to know.

When the elevator came down again my father was on it, alone. Nerving myself as I was to discover to him, for the second time in my life, one of his own crimes—I remembered how once, long before, I had come across him listening to a ball game on Sunday—I was shocked by the sudden sight of him. He wore a fresh set of tan work-clothes and had recently shaved, but he looked worn out. His eyebrows were gone, I realized after looking at him a minute; there was a jelly-like substance smeared above his eyes. Part of his forelock stood up short and frizzed, as if he had tried to give himself a brushcut with a hot iron before thinking better of it.

When he saw me, his face worked with emotion, and before I could speak he had stepped out and pulled me to his chest in an embrace. I remember thinking of a phrase my grandmother used to indicate a hearty welcoming, "a real bear hug"; like an animal he pulled me to him with his forearms—I remembered, then, that his hands were burned—and I felt his wrist patting me on the back. I couldn't remember his having embraced me before, as an adult, although sometimes when I was a boy, after one of our painful "heart-to-heart talks" in the basement concerning a sin of mine—talking back to my mother, fighting with my brother—and the punishment that inevitably followed, using a board that I would get to pick out myself from the scrap pile under the workbench, he would put his arm around my shoulders as we went back up the stairs: a heavier weight to bear going up than the thought of punishment had been on the way down. It made me feel strange to be embraced by him now, and to think that last night I had held Barbara in my arms while he had been burning a Negro's house.

"You've heard about Johnny?" he said, stepping back at last and looking at me. When I nodded, he suddenly turned away, and with his handkerchief carefully wiped the corners of his eyes and then blew his nose. It seemed that in a crisis my quiet mother resorted to words and my talkative father to physical displays of emotion. The last time I had seen his face this white and shocked was on the day of a great snowstorm eight or ten years earlier, when we had driven and shoveled our way through drifted roads to the South Shore station, trying to get to the funeral of my mother's brother in Michigan. As we hurried into the crowded terminal, heavy with the smell of wet wool and echoing with confused sounds, he heard himself being paged over the loudspeakers—I couldn't remember why—and he looked as if it were the voice of Death itself calling.

I told him I had heard the details from my mother on the telephone. I did not mention my visit to the church. If my mother had not wanted to add that extra straw of crisis to the load he carried—and I guessed she had not—why should I?

"A good thing you happened to call," he said, and though he sounded suspicious about my happening to call at that particular moment, I did not contradict him. For a moment I felt sorry for his anxiety, knowing that he must have wondered what rumors were already on the wing, and how far they had flown.

I walked him to the parking lot, and as we went outside through the glass doors into the sunshine he found his voice. "Look at my hair in front," he said, pointing to it with his right hand. His hand was thickly bandaged. "Look at my eyebrows. Look at my hand." His left hand, too, was raw to the touch, he said, the hair singed off halfway to the elbow. "I can still drive, though. I drove him to the hospital. I got the fire out with my jacket. I rolled him on the ground. It was awful, I could smell his body burning. Like cooking meat, all the way here."

When we reached the old Dodge in the parking lot I told him to raise his trunk lid and wait for a minute—I had something I wanted to give him. I found my car and drove it down his aisle until my trunk was next to his. He was still standing patiently next to the unopened trunk, like a tall old horse, his face shocked and surprised with no eyebrows. "Give me your trunk key," I said. I tried not to look at him, wanting to feel only my haste to get the job done. After he had fumbled painfully in his pocket, I took the key and opened his trunk. It was crammed as usual with rope, chain, tools, bags of nails. I opened mine then and took out the gas can—light, empty, but smelling of gasoline—and threw it in on top of his building supplies and slammed the lid. But not before the reality of it struck me again. It was red, new, almost unused. The cap on the top was loosened, for air to get in, and the thimble-sized cap for the flex-necked nozzle dangled from its chain as it had when I picked it up. I could picture the two of them in the dark trying to pour through the skinny neck, botching it in their hurry, then getting scared and hurrying still more. Had they been drinking, I wondered, as they waited there in Van Dyken's old barn for the churchgoing traffic to die away and the lights of Orangetown to go out? A couple of six-packs in the old deserted barn where Halloween vengeance was plotted? Did they tell a few bigoted stories as they waited? Did they use the word "nigger"?

"I stopped at the fire at Barnema's house last night," I said. "I happened—I just happened to be driving by. I found our gas can there in the grass."

We were alone on the lot in the late afternoon light falling through the thin, city elms with their curled, drying leaves; besides us there were only three nuns shimmering by in black robes two aisles over. I was trembling with haste, fear, anger—the anger directed partly at myself and my own complicity, the necessity I still felt to deceive. When I turned to give him the key I could not look at him. When I did, finally, his face was working again with emotion—shame and gratitude this time, as well as sorrow—and this time it was I who stepped forward and embraced him, though saying as I did so, *Dad, how could you do it? How could you?*

Nowadays the hug as greeting seems a more common occurrence than it was when I was young, almost as colloquial an idiom as the handshake. Wondering, sometimes, about why it should seem so much more affectionate a gesture than a pat on the back or even a friendly look, I've concluded that an embrace is, as we awkwardly say, "nonjudgmental." A look of any kind, even the distance at which a look is possible, implies seeing and judging; in an embrace we hurry past the judging eyes of the other. I did not want to judge my father any longer—still less, perhaps, did I want to be judged—so I hurried past the point where our gazes met to embrace him and be hugged in return. Nevertheless, a last word of judgment: how could you ever *do* a thing like that?

His left wrist was patting my back. "Just remember Johnny," he said, and with his forearms he squeezed my face into his shoulder. His khaki shirt smelled violently of sweat and the cigarette smoke of the waiting room. "He was only trying to help us," he said. "I was too. That's all we were trying to do. Maybe when you're a parent . . . ," he added—words that did not help me understand.

After a moment I pulled away, though his arms were slow to release me. "Did you tell Mother?" I said quietly, not looking at him.

"No. You didn't—you didn't tell anyone?"

I shook my head. After a moment I said, "We can talk about it later, I guess. I'd better get back to work now."

"Listen," he said. "Don't go yet. I want to tell you this first." He came closer to me, his eyes wet with moisture his hands were too clumsy to wipe away. "I never had time to worry about that gas can," he said, "there were too many other things to worry about. Now here it turns up in your hands. Maybe it's providential you should be the one to find it, maybe it was meant to be—"

"I don't want to hear that," I said, backing away. It seemed to me that, his eyes brimming, he was going to embrace me again. "Please, I don't want to hear any of that! At least let's not make something *pious* out of all this misery!"

He was working at his eyes with the handkerchief again, poking clumsily, left-handed, under his glasses. He seemed mildly surprised at my anger. "God moves in mysterious ways," he began again, and this time I turned my back on him. Then, since I was facing the wrong way, I turned again and walked quickly around my car to the driver's side.

"I just can't take any more pious hypocrisy," I said. I slammed the door. "I've got to get back to work."

"Adrian, listen," he said, following me patiently around the car and talking through the window. "I want you to know this: I prayed about it."

"That's enough!" I shouted, so loud that the three nuns, seated now on the bench outside the hospital's entrance, looked together in our direction. "That's enough! Enough!"

I started the engine and drove away and out into the street, but not before hearing his last words through the window. "You've got to understand this, Adrian: I prayed about it *a lot*."

I got to the playground in time to help Barbara close up early for staff meeting. As we worked together hauling in the heavy equipment I found myself asking her one question after another about her afternoon and how it had gone, and what plans had been made for the three Circus acts—not, I think, from any planned strategy of evasion but out of a generalized feeling of having deserted her. At last I said what had been on my mind since the end of the morning, when I had seen that sick, hurt look on her face.

238

"Barbara—about last night—I just wanted to tell you how great you were."

We had pulled in the ping-pong table and were alone together in the shed as we had been during Nature Week when I kissed her and she pulled away, because my unshaved face tickled and because she saw Willie watching us from the playground outside. She came up to me now and put both hands on my wrists, holding them at my sides. She looked up at me through her glasses—seeing them, I wondered if she had been crying, but saw no other sign of it; her eyes were bright and alert, her body taut, her fingers firm on my skin.

"Adrian?" she said. "How is he?"

For a moment I must have looked puzzled, thinking she referred to my father.

"The father of the girl whose picture you showed me? You know"—she tugged downward at my wrists with, I thought, a strange insistence—"you know, your 'childhood sweetheart'?"

She let me go, then, and although we stood very close and I had wanted to hold her and comfort her, it was as though my arms were tied, a thin, impassable wall between us formed by her words "childhood sweetheart" and "how *is* he?"—and by something else, a kind of determination, in her look.

"It looks pretty bad," I said finally. "He's unconscious, he can't talk. He's still alive, though."

"He's still in a pretty bad way, then?"

"I guess so. Barbara—I hope I didn't say or do anything last night that will—you know, spoil our summer." I was going to say "your summer," thinking of mine as already spoiled, but that seemed cold.

She shook her head, a quick movement of denial. "Anyway, I was the one who suggested we go there in the first place, wasn't I?"

I nodded—as I recalled it, she had been—but afterward it seemed to me that this was not precisely what she wanted. "I just wanted you to know," I said, "that I'm sorry if anything I said—"

"Now you've got enough on your mind to worry about," she said, tugging at my wrists again, "without worrying about last night." She turned suddenly, picked up the thin black sweater hanging over one of the ring-toss boards, and went outside. With the swift, graceful movement I had seen hundreds of times, a flick of the fingers like a caress across the key ring on her hip, she took out her key and undid the padlock.

"I suppose she'll be coming back home, then? You know"—a little of her old pertness here—"your childhood sweetheart, the one whose picture you showed me?"

I followed her outside. Brisk, efficient, she pulled the door shut, hooked and snapped the padlock, tried the lock, slipped the keys back across her blue-denim hip.

"I suppose so," I said. "Her mother was going to call her—that was my understanding—and ask her to come home."

"What was it, Adrian—a heart attack?" She turned to me, sweater over arm, black on brown, purse in hand, ready for her walk home to supper. I felt protective, without knowing exactly who it was I was trying to protect, and I could not bring myself to speak of fire or burns.

"He was in a bad accident," I said, finally.

"I don't blame you for not wanting to talk about it," she said. With a brief, sympathetic touch of my arm she left me, calling over her shoulder as she turned the corner of the shed that she would see me tonight, she hoped, at City Hall.

I went to the staff meeting that night but felt jumpy, nervous, and exhausted. I asked Nikkles before the meeting began for permission to be excused early, as I was waiting for an important phone call from the hospital, regarding a friend of my family. It was the first time since June that Barbara and I were at opposite ends of the table. She was at the far end with Jeannie, Schultz, and others—she had taken the bus in, I supposed, and would probably ride home with them, as she had done all last summer and the early weeks of this one, before we had started riding together. I sat with the latecomers, up at the "head" of the table, nearest to Nikkles' raspy voice.

I remembered how during the first weeks Nikkles, making one of his jokes, warned us that we would be judged by our suntans, meaning that play-leaders should be out in the sun *leading*, not sitting in the shade and shooting the breeze; and Barbara immediately rubbed forearms with me and announced, with her attention-getting laugh, "Look here who's laziest!" While our two arms still lay side by side in my minds eye, like sunburned wheat and plowed earth (or, perhaps, as my father might have put it more prosaically, like walnut and pine), she nudged me to make up for the laughter, a sharp elbow and soft shoulder simultaneously in my side. "Don't blush, man, you know it isn't true!" It was in fact during the time when I was working more

240

doggedly than she. It pained me somewhat now to hear her bright laugh from the other end of the table.

At my end there was unusual decorum tonight, a kind of silent sympathy for me, based probably on the fact that Sammy had heard my question to Nikkles and passed it on, one person at a time, to all those around him. After each new party was informed he would turn back to me and say he hoped it wasn't as serious as it sounded. When I had to leave, finally, halfway through the meeting, there were murmurs of encouragement from around me—Red Buchler, I remember, offered to bring some after-meeting pizza and beer to the hospital, if I wanted, and Sammy said, "I hope this doesn't keep you from coming to the *Circus*, Adrian"—and in the silence after that, before Nikkles began to speak again, I heard Barbara's loud whisper to Jeannie: "It's his girlfriend's father. They called his girlfriend to come home, they think he's dying."

My mother called me early Tuesday morning with the news that Johnny Van Dyken had died during the night. Somehow this seemed to clarify things for me. When I called Mr. Harmon to tell him what had happened, I found myself speaking of the death of my girlfriend's father. At Harmon's suggestion I took both Tuesday and Wednesday off from work. On Tuesday I settled my accounts with the YMCA and moved all my things back to my parents' house, and on Wednesday I attended the funeral.

In later years I remember asking a ministerial acquaintance what he could find to say at the funeral of someone who died in suspicious or embarrassing circumstances; he shrugged and said, "Clichés." Perhaps he is correct; still, one could choose a kinder term. As I think of Johnny Van Dyken's funeral I remember Pastor Boom (or the Reverend Boom, as he was called in the *Area Times* obituary) emphasizing some important human and biblical truths. I remember that we sang Psalm 49 ("Dust to Dust the Mortal Dies") and the Londonderry version of Psalm 103 that I had sung with Barbara three days before. As for man, his days are grass, but the mercy of the Lord is from everlasting to everlasting. My father, too emotional to sing, stood clumsily blowing his nose with his left hand. Instead of Barbara's soprano on my right there was my mother's alto, and I caught glimpses of Elizabeth singing up in the front row of pews, her skin not pale above the black dress but rather glowing and intense. Her face was

241

tanned from the summer. Beside her mother's stooped, weeping help-lessness she looked sturdy and young, one of the daughters who are cornerstones in the Psalm my father had read on Saturday night.

For those who did not know what I and my father did, there was only, besides gossip and rumor, the closed casket in the front of the church, surrounded by banks of flowers from the many church and civic organizations to which the mayor had contributed—including a wreath from the Area Development Committee and another from Harvey's Supermarket—and three separate notices in the paper. From the column-long obituary we learned that John Van Dyken had been a director of the Orangetown Savings and Loan and was listed in *Who's Who*, had attended Hebron College as a pre-seminary student from 1925-27 but had not graduated, and had served his church as deacon during the 1930's, as elder during the 1940's, and as president of the True Reformed Youth from 1922-25. On the same page, under the heading "Sirens," was a notice about a fire of unknown origin at an unoccupied residence on 192nd Street, and another story, head-lined "Orangetown Mayor Dies," in which the cause of death was given as an accident involving gasoline for an outboard motor. The County Deputy Coroner was quoted as saying foul play was not sus-pected. If there were other speculations I was kept from hearing them, probably, by the fact of my father's friendship with Johnny, and perhaps by the thought that whatever it was that had happened, they had both suffered enough.

After the funeral I went to Elizabeth's house, a narrow, old-fash-ioned home in the neighborhood of the house where I had grown up. She met me on the brick-pillared front porch, and as we embraced and wept together, her head on my shoulder, I heard the voices of her Michigan and Wisconsin relatives coming through the open win-dows. "You remember Uncle Buddy, with the scars up and down both arms? He lit a cigarette once when he was fixing his Model T." "It seems like the good ones go first, where you take these murderers and like that, they get out of jail after a year or two for good conduct or something and they live to a ripe old age." "Or take these drunks driving along at night, half the time with no insurance—how often do they get killed? Ninety times out of a hundred it's the other guy."

It seemed strange that, hearing these voices, and seeing what I had seen and knowing what I knew, I could still feel that Johnny Van Dyken, and my father too, were basically good men—flawed, clumsy, mistaken, *sinners* in a more obvious way than most of us, but somehow good men, perhaps even men "after God's own heart," as it had been said about David the King. And then it seemed more strange that, feeling this way, I could wonder as I did whether I would ever find it in me to forgive them for what they had done, for what they had attempted, for what they had made us all go through.

I saw Elizabeth several times during the next week while she stayed with her mother. After she went back to work, the week after that, I drove up to see her on Friday night, and spent Saturday with her on the beach near the sanitorium before driving back with her to spend Sunday at home. That was after the last week—Cleanup Week— on the playground, and just before I left for Nashville and the University. During my first year at school we wrote to each other often, and I came back to see her on Thanksgiving and Christmas, and in the spring we were married.

It was during those Christmas holidays, as we were talking of our parents' friendship and, somehow, began touching on the fact that close friendships may encourage less noble tendencies as well as noble ones, that I mentioned to her what I had found in the grass near Barnema's house. She wept, of course, but she wept easily then at any mention of her father's name. She had already guessed at what my finding of the gas can confirmed, and she had been looking for a way to broach the subject to me. My father was still alive to be injured, and it was for him, and for me, that she had hesitated. Girls tend to idolize their fathers, she said, and find it hard to face the fact that they are less than perfect. In that way she was luckier than most; the immediate shock was greater, but perhaps less harmful in the long run. She said she wished she had made it clearer to her father before he died that she loved him not as a perfect being but as the actual human father he was. Like me, she often reproached herself with the thought that we might have done something, if only by staying more concerned about our families, that might have made a difference; she took comfort in the belief that God, being God and not man, could be more merciful than we were toward the sinner, though stricter toward the sin.

It was a relief for both of us to be able to talk about these things, but it was especially so for me. Elizabeth by this time had had several talks with her mother. But I assumed I had an agreement with my father, a tacit understanding reached when I had given him the gas can, not to discuss these things with anyone else; and as for my father himself, we had one extended conversation on the subject of the night when Johnny Van Dyken died, and that one was the last.

It was the evening after the funeral. We were standing in the backyard, looking eastward across the tracks to where the charred cement-block foundations of Barnema's old house stood like a piece on a chessboard, waiting for the next move, and my father was smoking a cigarette. His right hand was still bandaged, but he had gotten himself a cigarette lighter which he handled as easily as if he had been left-handed all his life. Somehow I had forgotten, by then, that I had an unconfessed secret of my own; perhaps I had already written my father off as a moral force. I should have suspected from his silence during and after the service that there was something he wanted to say to me; but when I stepped out of the gloomy house to get some air, and he followed me out, pack in hand, weed in mouth, I was mainly conscious of what I wanted to say to him. Probably it was the cigarette that caused the last measure of self-righteousness to rise inside me—as if, after all that had happened, he could set fire to tobacco again and resume his life just as it was before! Yes, he said, when I asked him, he *was* sorry—for Johnny and Johnny's family. And to some extent for himself. Also for the stupidity and ineptness of the deed, since the supermarket people would no doubt get the land anyway; no one would now lend him the money for it after what had happened; at best he had managed to delay the sale of the two intervening properties. But it was only a matter of time. He would have to go on living in the new house, expensive as it was, for the foreseeable future, and turn the adjoining lots into apartments, since who but apartment dwellers would want to live next to a shopping center?

Self-pity was not what I wanted from him, and in my silence he must have felt disapproval. I did disapprove of burning someone's property, whether that person happened to be there at the time or not; but there was a more personal element in my desire to see him humble himself. I was aware that I had to go back to the playground the next day. He had given me something to be ashamed of before Barbara and the others, something I had to hide. He had made me look bad.

"I guess I must be a pretty bad guy," he said finally, without looking at me. "It's a crime, isn't it? Arson?"

"Yes," I said.

He took a last, sad puff, like a convict about to face the firing squad, and threw the cigarette stub into the pile of black dirt I hadn't finished spreading the Saturday before.

"Maybe I am," he said. "I guess I must be."

The mound of dirt, reminding me of my largest contribution to the family this summer, my *only* contribution, and of my refusing his offer of partnership, on this same spot two months earlier, kept me from audible agreement. He went on talking as if to himself.

"It's easy to go too far in defending your investments," he said. "You know what I mean? Especially once you get your priorities wrong. Take me: seems like I had my whole life tied up in that place." He looked at the house and then across the tracks at the low blue mists stretching across Barnema's yard to the onion fields beyond. "After you went away," he said, "I used to spend a lot of time planning street names for the subdivision. Cora Street down the middle. Adrian Street, Gordon Street, Paul Street coming off of that. Maybe even grandchildren. I used to lie awake nights thinking about it. Naming the streets after my kids. To their lands they give their name, in the hope of lasting fame, just like the Bible says."

He looked at the backs of his two hands—one bandaged white, the other showing the pink of scar tissue—like a surprised child who has just had them slapped.

After a moment I said I didn't think that was *necessarily* such a bad priority, and he turned toward me eagerly.

"No, not in *itself*," he said. "But meanwhile where were the real kids, the ones I was naming the streets after in my head? I couldn't even have answered the question! All I knew was, Gordy was out with the car someplace, and you, I thought, were someplace in Calumet. See what I mean? Wrong priorities!"

"Well, don't blame yourself for *every*thing," I said. "We're not kids, we're adults"—though I wasn't sure I wanted Gordy in this category. "You're not supposed to have to keep track of—"

"Don't get me wrong, Adrian," he said. "By 'kids' I mean 'family.' I know you're an adult; you've taught me a lot already. In fact I owe this whole train of thought to you. Remember that time you called us up and told us you were reading the Bible all day? I never paid any attention, I must have just figured you were bragging or something, until later—until I brought Johnny to the hospital. I'm sitting there in the waiting room and I see this Gideon Bible. 'Adrian's read this from cover to cover,' I think. 'And how long since I've tried that?' "

"It was just part of the New Testament—"

"Sure, sure," he said, waving this off as modesty, "but I never even *tried*. So I started in. I was reading almost all Monday morning. High time to get your priorities straight, wouldn't you say, with your best friend dying in the hospital? Because of you? You know, I didn't even make it through Genesis, but it suddenly dawned on me what the whole book was about. The whole story. It's all about a family and a piece of property, isn't that right? The two biggest things in the Bible, a family and a piece of land!"

It sounded true as he said it; I wondered if the aura that the playground had worn for me came from its evocation of these two older-than-biblical themes. But the train of thought my father said I had started for him seemed to be getting up steam, and I had no idea where it was headed.

"That's possible," I said.

"Adrian, it never dawned on me before, but I was practically reading about my own life! All that scheming over a piece of property, sometimes lying, sometimes cheating, sometimes violence, even—"

"Wait a minute," I said. I imagined the voice of my instructor in Greek warning us against departing from a strict construction of the text. "You can't compare someone like Abraham to someone who— well, to someone in the present. That was before the coming of the Law. It was like the wild West."

"Don't worry, Adrian," he said, "it didn't make me feel any better. It made me feel worse. Maybe that's why I didn't read any farther than I did. Because what I noticed"—he looked at me and I nodded, though not sure of his drift—"what I noticed was, the land always had to come second, the family first. You see? Seems like they got away with a lot in defense of their property—*except* if they neglected the family. Like Lot and Abraham. What's the difference if you get the best land, I'm thinking, if you let your family go to hell. Isn't that the point?"

I couldn't disagree. In the many sermons we had heard on the case of Lot vs. Abraham, it was public schools vs. religious schools; it was harvesting on Sunday—or, later, golfing—vs. worship; it was

246

once on Sundays vs. twice. His interpretation seemed as close to the text as any.

"It's a funny thing," he said, "but my dad always told us it was the New York Dutchmen who were like Lot—you know, Roosevelt and them—and us in the Midwest, Van Horne's bunch, we were like Abraham. And here I was acting like Lot! I mean Abraham would give up the property for the sake of his family, if he had to. He would even sacrifice his son to God, if he had to. Those were his priorities. Whereas Lot went for the property first, and when push comes to shove he's ready to sacrifice *his* children—to a bunch of strangers! Wasn't I doing the same thing? The result is he gets burned, he loses children, property, God's blessing—"

"Wait a minute!" I said. I didn't mind his being Lot, if that's what he wanted to confess—though I thought of myself rather as Isaac, about to be sacrificed on the altar of the True Reformed ministry until Providence intervened with the picture of Barbara and the play-ground—but his apparent sympathy for my plight sounded too much like Sammy's and Debbie's and Red's early concern about whether I could handle the job at Hoover Street. "All you did was let me live at the YMCA," I said. "Is that supposed to be Sodom and Gomorrah? As for the playground, we never approached the kind of violence there that you had right here"—I waved toward Barnema's, my heart thumping with anger and at my own daring—"in your own backyard."

"Okay," he said, holding up his hands defensively. "Okay, okay! That was my wrong priority, don't you see? Property first? Let's leave you out of it for a minute—let's take Gordy for an example. That's another thing I wasn't paying attention to in my own family; Cora finally nagged me enough so I said something to him about it. Wrong priorities! He was going off with one girl after another, *every Sunday night*, to that new forest preserve they put in south of town. Did you know about that?"

I shook my head, startled; I was beginning to lose my sense of this as a conversation about a biblical text.

"Only reason Cora knew was, some old biddy at church finally put her wise. Old lady Willing. Widow Willing, lives on that last place out of town. 'I see your boy Gordon is quite a nature lover,' she tells Cora. 'Oh, yes, I see him going by and stopping at that new forest preserve every weekend. Sometimes three nights in a row,' she says, the old hen. You remember her, don't you, Adrian? Married to Fred

Willing—Fred of Bill? He was hit by lightning on his tractor just about the time you went to school?"

My mouth felt suddenly dry. "I don't know anything about that forest preserve," I said, "but—"

"I didn't either," my father said. "At first. Then I remembered some of the guys at Dommer's calling it the Passion Pits. They say you go there on a Monday morning and you'll find enough rubber laying around so you could patch up thirty inner tubes, if you wanted to. I hadn't been paying any attention, don't you see? This was the week before Johnny and I were going to be making our big move." He shook his head. "Wrong priorities.

"So I check the car on Monday morning, and sure enough it's got that kind of orange, barky dust from the forest preserve parking lot all over it. So we had a heart-to-heart talk. 'So help me, Gordy,' I told him, 'if you get some girl in trouble over this you're going to do the right thing by her, you know that, don't you?' That was on that Saturday when you came home and spread this dirt over the lawn for us. Probably the last thing I said to Gordy on that weekend, so at least I did one thing right.

"By the way, I don't know if I ever thanked you for helping us out with the lawn like that. I don't think we would ever have gotten to it by ourselves."

"That's okay," I said. My voice sounded hoarse. "Dad—did you ever think that Gordy might have gone there, you know, just to talk? I mean, there's nothing else to do on Sunday nights, is there?"

He nodded. "That's just what your mother said. 'Kids got nothing to do after church but go off and get themselves in trouble,' she said. And you know what she said then? She says, 'From now on I'm inviting them here after church. That way they can have coffee or something, or tea or something, with us. Then maybe they'll realize courtship is a serious business,' she says. She's right, you know? Otherwise the poor kids are in the soup before they even know what hit them. In fact, that same Sunday night, when I was out doing what I thought was so right, and so important, she had Gordy bring his girlfriend over here. They set up that old ping-pong table in the basement."

My face had grown warm, as if it were trying to match from inside the pink scars on my father's hand. "But at some point," I said finally, "you just have to trust them to—to do what's right."

"That's right," he said. "But then if they *don't*, you see what I mean, you still have to face up to it. I mean they're still your flesh and blood, not so? Fact is, Adrian, this whole thing first hit home to me just last night. Tuesday."

"Last night?" I said. I remembered moving all my things back into the basement, then waiting for a long time to get a call through to Elizabeth at the Van Dykens', where the line was busy, busy . . . .

"That's when your mother told me," he said. "While you were on the phone with Elizabeth. She told me where you were on Sunday night."

He was lighting another cigarette now, his hand trembling, this time, like that of a lawyer trying to build a case for a guilty client. For a moment I could not think what my mother must have told him.

"I was in church on Sunday night," I said, somewhat ingenuously. "I suppose she told you I was with Barbara?—my partner? I was going to tell you about that—" This had little of the ring of truth, since what I meant was, *I didn't know how I could avoid telling you eventually.* "Good grief," I said, "doesn't she know Barbara's father is a minister? What could be wrong with that? Doesn't she have a right in our church just as much as I do in hers?"

His face wore the same meek, scared look I had seen at the hospital, as if he were waiting for someone, an expert, to disclose exactly how much trouble he was in—as if it were I, now, rather than Johnny Van Dyken, who was on the operating table in intensive care.

"I wonder is she sitting at home now asking herself the same question," he said. "Don't I belong in his church with him? Shouldn't I be at the funeral of his father's best friend? Don't I belong with him if he's in any kind of trouble?' "

"What are you talking about!" I said, though hearing the shock in my voice I had an inkling, all the same, of what it might be. "Do you think we're en*gaged* or something?"

"Are you?" he said. At my vigorous denials—a series of of-course-not's, how-on-earth's, whatever-gave-you-that-idea's—he looked not relived but rather puzzled.

"That's your side of the picture," he said. "What about hers?"

"Hers? Look, I never gave her any rings, I never asked her to marry me, I never . . . I didn't think I was ready for that! Do you think I should have?"

Looking at his worried eyes behind the paint-flecked glasses, I realized that he knew I had taken Barbara to the forest preserve; that he knew, even, through some masculine intuition, how I had let the level of my caring will sink lower than that of desire, letting hands, lips, and body sing love and marriage as long as they would until Barbara stopped them; that he was going to say *Yes, you should have.* Stranger still than hugging him in the parking lot after embracing Barbara: I would be defending myself now, to him, for not being engaged to her.

He worked awkwardly at the cigarette with his left hand. "Well," he said, "you just told me you went to her church? And then you took her to yours?"

"But that was just a *visit*—"

"Right, that's what *we* say," he said, nodding at me. "But what do *they* think about it? Her father is a minister, isn't he? Wouldn't he take an interest in what his child was doing on Sunday night, especially if he's the only parent she's got, like Cora tells me?—unless he's got his priorities mixed up, like *your* old man. Or was this a secret from him too?"

"Dad, he knows all about it!"—though even as I spoke I hoped that he didn't know quite all. "Barbara told him where we were going. I heard her tell him myself."

He took this in for a moment, throwing away the cigarette and lowering his forehead against his fist as if trying, literally, to pound something into his thick skull. "You say you've met him? Her father? At his house?"

I nodded. "Just once. It was after we—" I stopped, but I needn't have.

"I guess you maybe must have gone out with her once or twice, too, in the meantime?"

I nodded, tight-lipped—I did not mean to count the number of times we had "gone out"—and he struck his forehead again.

"Okay," he said. He held out four fingers which he struck, one by one, with his bandaged fist. "How does this add up to you, if you're the girl?—or say her pa, who is a minister, remember. One, you take her out a couple times; two, you go to her church, then you take her to yours; three, you visit her father, then she visits your mother—or anyway, Cora tells me she asked you to come over, though I guess you didn't actually come to the house, did you. And then—"

I waited for the fourth finger to come down, like a brick, but he had thought of something else.

"Remember, now, this is a colored family we're talking about. We're asking how serious is this to *them*. What kind of minister is he, would you say—I mean, is he old-fashioned? Cora tells me he hob-nobs with the bigwigs, he even knows one of these Frisian philoso-phers she's always talking about—"

"What are you getting at?" I said. "He's a Pentecostal minister, he wears a dark suit, he's a good preacher; sure, he's kind of stern, but—"

"In the old days," my father said, "there was something they called breach of promise, or tampering with affections—something like that. In my dad's time they would even have people horsewhipped for it. I don't know how far this minister goes back, but . . . . Is he from the South, do you know?"

"For Pete's sake, Dad, this is the twentieth century!"

"Okay," he said, mildly, "I'll grant you that. Anyway, it's a special deal for anybody to go to a strange church, one that they haven't been raised in. Once when I was selling pickles I invited a customer to come with me. He was Episcopalian, where they stand up and sit down all the time and even kneel down, right on the floor. I thought our worship would be like falling off a log for him. You know that he was completely flustered? He had never even *seen* a Psalter before, much less tried to sing out of one. Besides, I'd forgotten about half of our people didn't speak English yet.

"So how special is it going to be for this girl that you invited? I mean, like you say, you can't compare apostolic times to the present day. This is the twentieth century. In Bible times, sure I guess the Ethiopian could walk into any church anywhere any time he felt like it. But in the present day even the colored ballplayers, *big* leaguers, can't go just anywhere—even Joe *Louis* doesn't get invited just anywhere—"

"But that's because of people like *you*!" I said. "That's because of your bigotry!"

He nodded—patiently, as if this was one of the things he admitted to, but only the beginning. "So maybe you did it to teach us all a good lesson," he said. "Was that it?"

I looked down at the lawn sprinkled with new lumps of black dirt; I could not honestly say that it was, not entirely.

251

"But what did *she* think?" he asked then. "Was that the reason she came along?"

I shook my head. Even if it meant a horsewhipping for breach of promise, I hoped her feeling had been more personal than that. "I don't know what she thought," I said finally.

"I could have used the lesson about that time," he said. "I should have been there. Sure, it's one thing to take somebody's property away. You tell yourself you've got a better right to it than he has. You tell yourself you've been waiting longer, you *deserve* it more. You tell yourself you don't hate him, just what he's doing to the land. What he's doing to your plans. You tell yourself nobody will get hurt; you tell yourself the insurance will pay for it. That's if you don't know the guy in person, just like you don't know the insurance company. You figure you'll never see him.

"But what if he's a guy sitting right there in church—or maybe his daughter? Because now we're talking about somebody's *family*, you see what I mean? Here's somebody who knows you, Adrian. Somebody whose house you've sat in. Somebody I'll have to go and face in person, maybe, and explain where my kid is, and how he can be reached—"

"Wait a minute!" I said. What I thought was a confession of his sin was turning, again, into a confession of mine. "What makes you think you would have to do a thing like that?"

"Well, for a paternity suit, maybe, in case his daughter—"

"Paternity suit!" My laughter seemed not to convince him. "Where do you get this stuff? I never even touched her!"

He nodded, looking at the ground. "Adrian, I saw that orange dust from the forest preserve on your car. I saw it Monday at the hospital. I just finished talking to Gordy about it—I couldn't miss it. Are you telling me you didn't take her to the forest preserve after church was out instead of going to our house with her like Cora asked you to?"

"I was going to tell you that," I said, and, at this second instance of full disclosure after discovery, the blood rushed to my face. "There was nothing to be ashamed of. All we did was talk." I added, for emphasis: "I swear it."

He sighed and put his hands, one scarred, one bandaged, on my shoulders. "That's good to hear," he said. "Sometimes you can go too far, just when you think you're in the right." The weight of his hands

252

felt heavy, as if with his warm breath on my face I was being made literally a co-conspirator. "Only one thing," he said. "I'm still worried about how it looks."

"How it looks! What do I care how it looks! Anyway, you're a fine one to be caring about how things *look*, aren't you?"

I had shrugged away from his grasp; he turned his head, meek-faced, patiently nodding as if this was what he expected and deserved. "All I'm saying is," he said, "we've got to see how the other party is thinking of this, don't we? For example, what would people think if Elizabeth . . . what would you think if Elizabeth, what would Elizabeth's *father* think—"

His lips began to tremble, and he looked away. I was preparing to say his analogy wasn't relevant, that Barbara's father could not feel about anything in the way that Elizabeth's apparently could—but it was not kindness, or respect for the dead, that stopped my thoughts. I remembered the Reverend Robinson's forceful hand on my arm, his insistence that my intentions be not only "square" but "honorable," his intimation, insulting but relevant, that my fervor about the "spirit" of Barbara's people might be a cloak for disrespect, might be little more than the urge to escape the clear commandments of mine— nothing more than *hot pants*, in short, as I could hear the men at Dommer's saying, or the widow Willing thinking—and I could think of nothing to say.

"Maybe when you see them on the playground all the time you get the impression that they don't take these things seriously," my father said. "Just like me when I used to see them fishing in Calumet Harbor, where there aren't any fish. But it's like your mother says: they take the family seriously, though. Like when Joe Louis beat up on Max Schmeling in their second fight; he was *serious* about it. And that wasn't even anything real personal between them, it was just some remarks that *other* people made.

"Adrian"—his hands on my shoulders again—"I wouldn't let this get around too much. There might be some people in this girl's church—hotheads, maybe—who would think their minister's daughter was, you know, compromised. I mean even if you just did it to teach us a lesson. Even if you never even touched her."

It was his air of protective confidentiality, now, the implication that I had as much to hide as he, that made me pull away. I looked at him angrily. "Are you trying to equate what you did," I said, "with what *I* did?" It was humiliating, preposterous. His crime only against property, mine against people! "Is that what you're trying to say?"

Surprised, he shrugged his shoulders. "What would be the point of that? What you did is what I did too, isn't it? Don't I have to face it either way? So what's the difference?"

It was something I didn't want to hear. I turned away and began to walk down the driveway, past the back door, out toward the street, the railroad track—anywhere.

"There is a big difference," I called over my shoulder, though at the moment the only difference I could think of was in his burned hands. "So just keep out of it. Let me handle my sins by myself."

"Ah, don't be a stiffhead," he called after me. "You must be just like your old man, can't you take any criticism?" And, as I kept on walking, he came after me once more and called from the top of the driveway's slope: "Anyway, don't forget what I told you. When you think you're in the right, that's when you can go too far. See what I mean?"

Those were our last words on the subject, our last "discussion"; but as time went on I had the feeling that we were carrying on our conversation in indirect ways. During the next few years, while Elizabeth worked in the hospital in Nashville and I continued my schooling there, not far from where the Southern Christian Leadership Conference was beginning its efforts in the South, on behalf of black people and civil rights, we became the kind of supporters of the cause—that is, by mail and money—who were known in those days as "white people of good will." Our letters home often found ways to make mention of this fact. And during those same years, and afterward as we moved from job to job over the next decade and a half, my parents in their correspondence would often make reports on the activities of William Holland, Sr., the black man who had tried to buy Barnema's house.

It appeared that Holland was a carpenter and handyman who wanted to move out of the East Chicago area in order to find better schools for his children. Eventually he bought one of the two farmhouses next to Barnema's and had it moved to a vacant lot near the sugar-beet loader, north and west of my parents' land—though whether the money came from his own funds, or the defrauded insurance company, or the supermarket people, or possibly some other source, was never made clear to me. My father, then on the school fund-raising committee, helped him get his children into the Orangetown True Reformed Christian Grade School and, later, the high school.

Holland's oldest son was a star forward on the basketball team that in the early seventies won the state small-school championship. My father sent us clippings of the progress of Will Holland, Jr., as if he were the boy's godfather. I remember one in particular in which an opposing coach was quoted as follows: "The only way to beat Will Holland, Jr., and the Orangetown Crusaders is to get a forfeit. Play the game on Sunday." He also, I learned, worked with Will Senior on several of the apartments he built surrounding the new house—Holland was by this time a member of CLOSE (the True Reformed anti-AFL-CIO local labor union), though he retained membership with his family in a Baptist church somewhere in Calumet. I'm sure that all these references were his attempt at having the last word in our discussion as to who in fact was holier-than-thou—just as my references to SNCC and CORE and the SCLC were my attempts to do the same. The bulk of correspondence (excluding newspaper clippings) was my mother's, however; and her enthusiastic seconding of my father's interest in the Hollands made me think he must have shared his secret, finally, with her.

As far as I know he never shared it with anyone else. Despite his work on behalf of the schools, despite my two brothers' successes—Gordon as a teacher in a True Reformed high school in Iowa, Paul as a young preacher in California—and despite his good standing in the community, he was never elected to his church's Consistory, either as elder or deacon. This was frequently lamented by my grandmother. Whenever I came home for a holiday I would hear her say it, though not in my father's presence. Never made elder or deacon—what could the male, voting members of the congregation be thinking of? I heard her mention it at the time of my grandfather's funeral to Pastor Boom, who had come down from his Michigan retirement home to pay his last respects. Arie's one disappointment in life, she told him—this was in her living room, when only I and our former pastor happened to be present—was that Gerrit, his oldest son, was never elected to the Consistory. What was the matter with these people that they couldn't see a good man right in front of their nose?

Pastor Boom, whose broad shoulders and white hair were both thinner by then, looked startled for a moment, and it occurred to me

255

that the question represented unfinished business for us both. The pastor, a year or two from retirement, had not wanted to find out more than he could conveniently know. Elizabeth and I had retired in our own way, by living always in towns where there were no True Reformed churches and no one who knew our families. He put his hand on her shoulder then and said, "Oh, but Susanna, you know there was that matter of the fire, on the night when the mayor, your grandson's father-in-law"—and he glanced briefly at me—"died. He never cleared that up, don't you see?" After that, I never heard my grandmother mention the subject again.

I spent my last two days with Barbara, Thursday and Friday of Circus Week, helping her ready the stilt-walkers' acts. I held out for a while for the two-part song we had once talked of doing, but as Barbara pointed out—humorously and crisply—we had only two days left, and moreover Hoover Street was not known for its great numbers of Scotsmen. So I pitched in on the stilt-walkers' acts.

Somehow things fell into place. We worked together as well as we had ever done, Barbara handling costumes, dialog, and "choreography" while I occupied the boys in scavenging lumber, building the stilts, and steadying novice walkers. I remember the girls' wearing colorful crepe-paper skirts, to hide the stilts; and Willie, with great élan, stuffing a basketball through a hoop; and a skit in which a whole family, from a "toddler" (played by Frankie in a bonnet) to a grandma (played by chubby Elvirah), had to walk on stilts to stay dry, because a "Hoover Street plumber" (Willie again) couldn't stop a leak in their faucet.

After being away for three days I noticed a difference, a new kind of adultness, in the playground. Frankie, for one, had a new name. "Call me Frank," he insisted; perhaps it was in reaction to his stint in the bonnet. A number of children came up to me to say they were sorry about the funeral I had to go to. Some of them referred to "the death in your family." One of the older girls—Verella, who seemed to be passing serenely from girlhood to adulthood with no adolescent trauma—spoke easily of my girlfriend's father; another, Bettye Lou, said she was sorry my "girlfriend died" and then, realizing her mistake, reverted to teenage type by collapsing in giggles.

I was glad to see from Willie's skit that the term "plumber," introduced by Lee Roy during our pre-Olympic practices, had lost its sting and become an honorific, like "Yankee" to the colonists. Lee Roy himself, it appeared, had dropped by to help with the skit on Tuesday afternoon, and then on Wednesday evening brought a load of scavenged Park-Department lumber for the stilts.

As for Barbara—she seemed content with our regime of hard work and plain talk, never warming our conversation above businesslike friendliness. She spoke directly, now, of my "girlfriend." How was my girlfriend taking it, did she get back home all right? Her firmness about my status as Elizabeth's boyfriend left me with two unpleasant thoughts: I had never been more to her than that, or, if I had, it had been only to take advantage of her, to "tamper," in my father's phrase, with her affections.

Finally I gave up thinking and concentrated on the Circus.

We had a good two days, Barbara's seamstresses and actresses laughing and singing as they worked, my sawyers and hammerers flashing their rhythms in the sun, pounding them out in metal and wood—her side of the playground providing color, movement, life; ours the solid structural underpinning. At Friday's dress rehearsal we put it all together, and seeing the playground children "rising to new heights"—Barbara's pun, made happy and true by her laugh—I thought we had the perfect blend of discipline and verve, we had the triumph of Olympic Day but without all the stress and strain, perhaps because in art there are no losers; if it's done right there are only winners.

Afterward, during the rush of cleaning up, the pell-mell of last, shouted instructions to our performers, and directions to Island Park—no nonsense this time about name-tags—Barbara gave me a present. She stopped me as we met in the equipment-shed door, she on the way out with sweater and purse, I going in with a last can of nails, and handed me something—a small, square box, the size of the ones our thumbtacks came in, but wrapped in white paper.

"What is it?" I said, stupidly. I remembered then that I would not see much of her that night. She herself was part of the Circus.

Looking at me over the tops of her slid-down glasses, she did a bit of her comic schoolmarm role, wagging her finger at me, and then tapped me lightly on the chest. "You'll see when you open it," she said. "Just something to remember me by"—and then she was gone, around the corner and through the last clusters of children who tugged at her attention as she walked.

I opened it when I got to my car and found a set of cuff links, musical cuff links, one shaped like a bass, the other a treble clef.

My mother had supper saved for me when I got home, but I didn't have time to eat it; I had stopped on the way to get Barbara a card. *May the road rise up to meet you,* it said, *may the wind be always at your back. . . .* The others had eaten. My father was with my brothers in the driveway in front of the garage, tuning up the outboard motor which he had offered for sale, along with boat, trailer, "and equipment," in this week's *Area Times.* "Now he wants me to find him a shirt with French cuffs!" my mother complained to him when he stepped in the door behind me. I heard him pulling off his boots and heading downstairs to the refrigerator for a beer. "In August! First it was movies, then parties and dances, now it's a circus. With French cuffs. In August."

"Let him go, Cora." His voice came rumbling up to us from below, punctuated with the pop of an opening can. "He's old enough to know what he's doing. I hope."

I mystified her further by immediately rolling up the sleeves of the shirt, when she found it for me, keeping the cuff links in my pocket. When I got back to the car I found that my father had nailed the corner of a red bandanna, presumably using his left hand, to the end of the longest of the stilts sticking out of my passenger-side window.

Our performers were good, that night, but the star of the Circus, as she had been the year before, was Barbara. When she walked out to the center of the Island Park band shell, wearing her white linen suit, the audience, rememering her from last year, and from her high school days when she had sung the anthem at football games, was already applauding. Harmon, acting the part of a scholarly, dignified master of ceremonies, introduced her, as if she already belonged to the wider world, as "Calumet's own" Barbara Robinson. When she finished singing "America the Beautiful"—our liberty confirmed in law, our brotherhood from sea to sea—her arms were outstretched and her head thrown back as I had seen her in the picture in Harmon's office, and flashbulbs flared on all sides from among the green benches in front of the band shell. The audience stood and applauded until, having waved good-bye and walked off, she came back and led us all in singing "God Bless America."

I was in the rear of the crowd when she sang, standing with some other play-leaders under the oaks and rough-barked hickories among the people in their folding lawn-chairs who had arrived too late for the benches. Barbara herself had arrived late, in her white suit and high heels, and I had not seen her except at a distance. My sleeves were still rolled up—once at the park I realized I didn't want to explain the cuff links to Sammy and Jeannie and Debbie and Red, who stood near me in cotton dresses and T-shirts—and the good-bye card, damp after my exertions among the stilt-walkers, was still in my rear trouser-pocket. Now or never, I thought, and began working my way through the standing, singing crowd toward the stage. *God bless America*, they sang, parents standing up stiffly with a thumb-sucking youngster over one shoulder; a grandpa with a cane; a straight-backed black lady with a shawl, whom I thought I had seen at Barbara's church; a pale-faced young couple, who must have worked inside all summer, handing a baby back and forth. . . .

Running into two of Hoover Street's children I had to solve an argument about whether or not they got to keep the stilts after the show, and if so, to whom they belonged, and when I got moving again she was halfway through the song. *From the mountains . . . to the prairies. . . .* I headed toward the outside, deciding to circle the remaining singers rather than go through them. True to the first newspaper clipping I had seen of Barbara, in which she found that *all* children loved to sing, everyone was singing—everyone but me—and with spirit enough to be annoyed by interruption. *To the oceans . . . white with foam. . . .* I was struggling through the outskirts of the singers now, among families sitting on blankets, their children in strollers or buggies, and at last I gave it up, thirty yards short of the stage, and stopped, joining the others in the repetition of the last line: *My home, sweet, home.*

Before the notes died, the stage of the band shell was crowded with well-wishers, not only Barbara's black friends from high school and, perhaps, college—aside from the Wright brothers, Julius and Teddy, whom I had seen from time to time on the playground, I didn't recognize any of them—but also Harmon and Nikkles and Mrs. Nikkerson and others with gray in their hair, including, I was told at the playground during the next week, her high school principal and an official from the valve works, which had sponsored her scholarship. I watched the handshakes and smiles, and some more flashbulbs popping, and then went back up the hill to collect the remaining stilts and put them in my car again. It seemed to me that she belonged to all of them, and that as between the two of us, our good-byes had already been said.

My good-bye to the playground came a few days later, during Cleanup Week. On Monday and Tuesday the children and I cleaned out the cabinets and equipment boxes, and on Tuesday night we held a last watermelon party, followed by a hot-dog and marshmallow roast over a bonfire of handcraft scraps. It pleased me that Lee Roy came to this last after-supper event; possibly he had come to play ball, but by the time we had cleared away the rinds and started the fire it was deep dusk, the red of his Indiana sweatshirt almost indistinguishable from the blue of his jeans. "Ol' Fleet the Plumber!" Willie greeted him; he addressed the boys as Sonny the Plumber, Frank the Plumber, even Brother the Plumber.

He sat between me and Frankie—or Frank—on the bench, meditatively turning a stick with a marshmallow on it, as white as his own down-turned sailor hat, over the coals. There were about fifteen of us left now, after the cleaning up, the watermelon, and the hot dogs, to enjoy the last orange embers. Everyone seemed in that quiet mood that comes with staring into a fire during the last moments of twilight. Across from us on their bench Verella and Twyla, who had been taking Barbara's place as song-leader, began the two-part Scots folk song I had been trying to teach them. They did a creditable job; even Lee Roy, who hadn't heard this before, joined in, and I realized with a last pang of competitiveness that he had a deep, clear voice to go with his barrel chest. At last only Willie wasn't singing; he preferred to scamper about waving a blazing stick and creating excitement or trouble, if he could, by bellowing out his own song,

Going down to the river, gonna jump overboard and drown,
Because the one I love has left this town,

holding his hand over his heart, dying with lovesick eyes, and addressing this pantomime toward Lee Roy and me.

It seemed he meant it for both of us: two of Barbara's exes, as it were. I had seen Lee Roy at the Circus the night before, dressed much as I was—a white shirt with rolled-up sleeves—taking his sailor hat off as Barbara began to sing. Or perhaps he meant it for all of us, a last good-bye to Barbara, the summer, the playground and the season. As satire it didn't take—even the older girls had had enough speculation now about Barbara and her boyfriends and her career—but as lament, or mock-lament, it did. Bathos, Barbara had called it. Finally we all joined Willie and sang it with him, a rousing, raucous, bathetic chorus as the fire died.

"You know," Lee Roy said to me after the children had called good night and gone home, and we had doused the fire and taken the benches back inside, "you guys didn't do too bad a job here."

We stood outside the locked shed and he looked across the empty park, shadowy under dim streetlights and cloud-darkened moon, with an affection that surprised me until I realized he had grown up here; until he'd won the track scholarship to Indiana, this had been his home.

"Maybe you'll want the job next year," I said. "It doesn't pay like the Park Department, but I think—I know the kids respect you."

"You're right," he said. "The pay isn't the same." In the dark I could see only the outline of his face, and the round, smooth cheeks looked like a grown-up version of Willie's—hardened, somewhere between adolescence and now, in a permanently serious shape. At that moment he smiled.

"Who am I trying to kid," he said. "Sure I'll want the job. Barbara's going away from home, she's going to be a big *star*, you know, but she'll be surprised someday when she looks back. This is where it was all the time."

Moonlight words, I thought later, driving home; campfire words. But also some of the athlete's premature wisdom, won by seeing his best skills decay even as his contemporaries begin to find what theirs are.

On the last morning it was raining, just as it had been on opening day back in June, though this rain was less a storm than a kind of gray drizzle distilled out of the mugginess of the August air. On that wet Wednesday Frankie was the only one who came. He arrived shortly after I did, carrying his white shirt rolled up inside out to protect it from the drizzle, which sat in little droplets on his shiny skin and in the coils of his hair. He hung up his shirt and we worked together in the humid shed, taking inventory of everything in the boys' and girls' equipment boxes and the cabinets as well as the jumble of outside items I had packed in the night before. Around noon, when the green pickup truck from the Recreation Department arrived to collect our equipment, we had the boxes inventoried, packed, and locked, and the ping-pong table and its sawhorses, the tables and benches, the bulletin board, ringer board, and beanbag board stacked neatly near the door, ready to go.

"Hey, you plumbers!" said the driver of the truck, hopping out. It was Lee Roy, his sailor hat and navy sweatshirt appropriately nautical in the rain.

"How's the leg?" I said. He looked nimble enough as he unbolted the tailgate and swung aboard.

"Okay. Little stiff in this lousy weather."

Seeing us struggle with the ping-pong table he jumped down again and took a hand. "The City is paying me Park Department rates by the hour," he said, giving me a wink, "so it's no skin off my nose if we take all day. But what the heck. No sense letting you guys herniate yourselves. Right, kid? I didn't catch your name." He bent down to Frankie, cupping his ear.

"Frank the Plumber," Frankie said in his throaty voice. After the deadening clerical routine through which I had been putting him, he looked now as if he were just waking up.

"Incorrect," Lee Roy said. "You know what your name is, just for today? Frank the Yank. Jump on up there, Frank the Yank, and shove this little old crate in the corner. Way to go. Anybody ever tell you to wear a sweatshirt in the rain, Frank? You want your muscles to get stiff like this old man?"

Frankie shook his head, and Lee Roy flicked some droplets out of his hair for him, a quick finger-whisk across the top.

"You're right, Frank the Yank. Listen: tell your momma Fleet the Plumber told her to get her boy a sweatshirt. Tell her Fleet the Plumber says stop putting you in white shirts all the time. Hear?"

Frankie nodded.

"Where's your buddy, Big Willie—still in the sack?"

"I just came by myself," Frankie said.

"Good show, Frank! Attaboy! You tell Big Willie to get himself out of the sack next summer and come on down here. We'll get him in shape, you and me. Okay?"

"Okay," Frankie said.

We worked on until the shed was empty, the truck loaded, and as Lee Roy shut and bolted the tailgate, Frankie, who was inside buttoning up his shirt, suddenly looked out at us. "Hey," he said, his face lighting up. "Is *he*—" He looked from me to Lee Roy. "*You* fitten to be Park Teacher next year?"

Lee Roy spat a cottonball out toward the sandbox and gave his sailor hat a two-handed adjustment. "It's tough work, Frank," he said, "but somebody's got to do it."

Frankie took this in. Then he came out and stood with us on the cement stoop, turning his shirt collar up against the rain.

"You going to carry me home in your truck?" he said. "So I don't get wet?"

"Sorry, kid. Not in the rule book. Not cricket. This truck is Rec Department property."

"I guess this is it," I said. My keys, whistle, and lanyard were locked inside the boys' box. I took a last look inside, found the shed clean and empty, then closed the door and fastened the lock.

I said good-bye to Frankie and shook hands with Lee Roy. He finished the handshake with a salute.

"So long," he said. "We'll try to keep the place intact for you next year."

When he went to the front of the truck Frankie was waiting for him in the drizzle. "What do you think this is, Frank the Yank, a fricking Noah's ark? Look, don't tell anyone and don't say I never did anything for you." He hoisted Frankie up, not hands under armpits, as I had hoisted him over the fence after opening day, but by an elbow and the seat of his pants, and slid him over to the passenger side. "I'll carry you to the backstop," he said. "After that you can hoof it."

I remembered the rule against touching the children but figured Lee Roy would find out all about it and know what to do. "So long," I said, raising my hand to them both. Lee Roy started the engine, and as I headed for my car around the corner I heard the truck with him and Frankie in it creak slowly away across the wet grass.

THE END